⸺◄DIMENSIONS►⸺

STORIES OF THE PAST, PRESENT, AND FUTURE

by

CHARLES NUETZEL

The Borgo Press
An Imprint of Wildside Press

MMVII

Dedicated, with all my love
to my wife:

Brigitte Marianne Nuetzel

FIRST EDITION

⊶CONTENTS⊷

NEW DIMENSIONS

—‹INTRODUCTION›—

The following collection of stories is a result of a number of publishing ventures.

My book *Images of Tomorrow* was released by Powell Sci-Fi way back in the late 1960s; it contained most of my previously published sci-fi, including the short novel, *The Ersatz*, in a somewhat different version than is now being offered separately in book form by *Wildside Press* (this volume also includes an original story, *The Talisman*).

In *Dimensions* I'm adding tales that take place in the *Past*, *Present*, and *Future*, along with a number of never before published sci-fi stories for the section titled *New Dimensions*.

A casual glance at the titles in all these "dimensions" reveals that my main interest as a writer was in the SF world! But there is a number of other stories which are being offered up here as a cross-section of my writing career—and which is also reflected in the longer works being reprinted by *Wildside Pr*ess.

I started writing shortly after the pulp craze in the science-fiction world had died down. My agent directed me to what was, at that time, the new "pulp" field: the girlie magazines. Well, the top of that line was *Playboy*, of course, which tended to ignore my literary talents. But I managed to survive to publish more than four million words in print over the following years. A small number of those words appearing in these magazines. (*Fluff*, also being released simultaneously by *Wildside*, is a collection of some thirty such "treasures"—as a light-hearted illustration of how things were way-back-when in that "pulp field"!) I soon learned, in my second year of writing, that I felt far more comfortable in longer lengths, and did most of my writing thereafter in short novel form.

Much of my early experiences in writing and publishing are fairly well covered in the interviews on my website, Hal-dolen.com. In my Egomania page are the following comments concerning my career:

> *I was lucky enough not only in selling my work to publishers, but also ending up packaging books for some of them, and finally becoming a "publisher" much like those who had bought my first novels. From there it was a simple leap to editing not only a sci-fi anthology, but a line of sci-fi books for Powell Publications. Throughout these active professional years I had the chance to design covers and do graphic layouts for pocket books & magazines.*

My father, Albert Augustus Nuetzel, was a professional commercial artist all his life, and he ended up selling a number of covers to sci-fi magazines such as *Amazing Stories, Fantastic Stories, Fantasy & Science Fiction, Famous Monsters of Filmland*, plus a number of pocket book covers. We became a team, selling art and manuscripts to publishers, and finally being able to make our own deals and package books and series. I've reused his art on much of the work offered by the present publisher.

Hopefully, something here prove both amusing and entertaining to the reader and fan.

—CHARLES NUETZEL
THOUSAND OAKS, CALIFORNIA
August 2006

PART ONE
PAST DIMENSIONS

DIMENSIONS, BY CHARLES NUETZEL

*This is one of the few westerns I ever wrote. I offer it up as
nothing but an example of a...*

⊸PLAGUE OF THE PAST⊷

Kerk Claymore nervously rolled another cigarette and lit
it, clamping his lips around the tiny cylinder. His gray eyes
snapped to the window, taking in the mud covered street below.

What was keeping Karen? he wondered anxiously. It
was twenty minutes since he'd sent the Mex kid with the
note.

He tried to relax, stepping over to the lumpy cot in the
corner of the dark room. His large hand picked up the holster
where the Colt .45 was snugly resting. For a moment his
eyes examined the wooden handle. It was polished, unmarred, new looking; it didn't reveal the fact that it had
killed two men in honest dueling: it gave no hint of this
short, bloody life.

Kerk's fingers pulled the weapon free of the leather and
fondly tested the action.

This was his ticket to revenge; oiled, practiced, in perfect condition for this long awaited day. The town owed him
a lot, and the highest debt he'd only learned fully about this
afternoon. There was revenge for Karen, too.

And the one man responsible for this was Bart Hanson.

Anger spurted uncontrollably through him. His hand
shook as thought of the tall thick set, highly mannered, self-
styled "Baron" ripped bare memory of the past.

The man who had stolen his girl by force and run Kerk
out of town three years before.

Well, things had changed since then. Kerk had merely
been a hot-tempered kid. Now he was a coldly calculating
man who had seen enough killings and enough brutality to
have made him a sure match for Bart Hanson.

But first he had to see how things were set up in town,

before making any blind moves. He had waited this long, a little longer wouldn't matter. That had been his mistake before. He'd rushed into town, looking for Bart Hanson with only blind, foolish courage, when he'd learned what had happened between the "Baron" and Karen Smith. Hanson had taken the young girl up to his hotel room, forcing her into intimate relations with him. Most of the people had whispered rape amongst themselves, but to the gunman's face had remained silent. Maybe if Karen's father had been alive—but the old Captain had died a few months before. There had only been Kerk, and he had tried to fight for Karen's honor. Everybody feared Bart Hanson, a professional killer and gunman who had come to Bittercreek and taken over. That blunder of moving without thought and plan had almost cost Kerk his life. But it took more than courage. Right wasn't always the winner. But the winner was always right!

It had taken him weeks to realize this truth. That night Bart and his men had beaten all the fight from his youthful body and sent him out of town on the first train with the warning never to return again. When the terror had numbed away a slow building determination for revenge had settled in its place. But this time he had decided to prepare for the moment when he could take the life of. Bart Hanson. He had gotten a job as a ranch hand in a town miles from Bittercreek and bought a Colt .45 and holster, practiced every moment he could until his hand was merely an extension of brain, until he could think about grabbing his gun and it came alive in hand. It had taken time and there had been moments when one argument or another had brought him too close to death at the gun of another man so that he'd practiced again. Months before, he'd been ready but a cattle war had stopped him. Now he was at last here, waiting for the woman he had been in love with as a boy.

Kerk jerked around, looking at the dark wooden door as footsteps sounded outside the hall.

It could be Bart's men—if the mighty Baron knew he'd returned.

It had been a risk to even let Karen know about his arrival—but a necessary one.

10

The footsteps hesitated. There was a light knock.

"Come in," he offered, jerking the gun toward the door.

It opened and a tall blonde stood there in the gaudy red and black dress of a dance hall girl. Her face was painted in cheap bold strokes. For a moment he didn't recognize her.

"Kerk!" she cried, stepping forward, slamming the door behind her and rushing into his arms.

"You shouldn't be here!" she sobbed. But the soft caress of her lips told him that regardless of the dangers, she was happy to see him.

It was the kind of kiss that the Karen Smith he'd known three years before would have never given a man. The kind of kiss which only an experienced saloon girl gave to her customers, after hours. It was silky velvet, moist and trembling. Her lips opened wide to his, in brazen invitation. He responded, bodily crushing her to him.

The full breasts were like supple cushions pressing on his chest, bringing the passion like rippling lava through his veins.

For only a moment longer the kiss lingered and then Karen stepped away, staring at him. Her eyes were a confusion of happiness and fear.

"When did you arrive? How'd you slip into town without—"

"Last night, late," he told her briefly. "I got this room, and, this afternoon, sent the note for you—I wanted to see how things were set up before making any moves."

"You shouldn't have come back!" she exploded emotionally. "Bart would kill you if he knew you were here."

"You knew I'd return!"

"You don't understand—things are much tighter than before—you don't know what he's like!" Karen warned.

"I've gotten a little tougher myself," he assured Karen. His eyes ran the full length of her body. The dress opened at the front, showing the fullness of the breasts, barely hiding the rose of her nipples. It was cheap, but exciting. "You've matured. Filled out!"

He forced a smile. She had changed a lot; maybe too much! Karen had become the kind of woman he'd found in many saloons—been to bed with scores of times; the kind

11

that men talked about in coarse voices, in crude terms. A woman completely opposite from the one he had left behind at the mercy of Bart Hanson.

"You've changed, too. Bigger than I remember," she observed without humor. Her eyes went to the ratty cot, pausing at the gun belt, then moved to the .45 still clutched in his strong hand. "I see you carry one of those!"

He carefully put the weapon down on the cot, smiling. "I know how to use it, too."

"Don't Kerk!" She returned her gaze to his face. "You tried to go up against Bart before—this time he won't just run you out of town. You'll be killed."

"I don't think so!" Heated threat had hardened his voice.

Karen dropped her eyes, swallowed and then turned away. "Too many changes," she choked out in a small voice. "Too much to go back to where we were!"

When she looked up again, tears were beginning to form in her wide eyes.

"Kerk—it's too late!" she told him in a trembling voice. But the words were more questioning, pleading.

He stepped forward. He looked into those wide blue eyes and saw that the girl revealed in them was still the same one he had known. A girl of dreams, of love, of summer scents and cool winter breezes. A little more mature, hardened by life in the small western settlement which catered to the rough cowboys, conmen, professional gamblers, and misfits who had run from themselves and their lives in the eastern civilization.

He raised her head so the full red lips were tilted a fraction from his, then smothered himself in their soft warmth. The long building desperation and hunger burst free after three endless years of waiting and wanting.

Her tongue surged deep into his mouth like a hot flame. Her body tensed firmly against his.

Kerk felt the breath caught like a captured ball of fire inside his chest. The hammering of his heart burst the blood through his veins like molten lava, bathing every nerve with its one desire; and the passion became overwhelming, overpowering every other thought.

Now words weren't necessary. Years before there might

12

have been long, awkwardly embarrassed conversation, with flushing faces and shame. Now there was simple acceptance of what would follow; what they had waited for all their lives.

He moved the gun and holster to the floor and they slid down onto the cot.

Karen helped him remove her clothing, and caress by caress she stripped aside the last of his. They gently slid together, for the first time feeling the raw warmth of each other.

He wanted to wait. He wanted to take in the softness of her, without moving, without allowing the passion to overwhelm him. But the years of waiting, the nights of dreaming of her, the lonely times on the trail or in a hotel room, with the vision of her lovely form vivid before his eyes, welled up through him and moved his hands anxiously along her body, across her thighs, into the supple swells of her velvet breasts.

She trembled and writhed. A moan broke from her lips. He felt the clawing of her hands as they moved down his back, her body tightening against his.

Kerk's lips slid down the cream of her throat, caressed the fullness of her breasts. And with every caress and every kiss, she moaned, writhed, trembled, until a wildness surmounted them, lacing their bodies tightly together, feeding their desperate hunger, and finally satisfying their needs as the last throbbing movement of their forms burst ecstasy through every nerve and cell of them, leaving a purity of complete exhaustion.

It was a long time before either of them moved. Then he stood and went to his clothes, got out a pouch of tobacco, rolled a cigarette and lighted it. Taking a deep drag, he let his eyes move to the woman, run along the full, voluptuous form which had given so much pleasure, so much wonderful perfection.

All the other women who had given themselves to him had lacked one final ingredient which made such acts more than two bodies joining in animal passion. They had lacked the one quality of love which he had shared with Karen in the merging of their bodies. They had a history together which couldn't be simply wiped away.

13

It was that last thought, that one awareness, which made the decision for him. Regardless of what Karen had become, he wanted her; wanted her even more than revenge for the injustice which had been pounded into his youthful body when Bart Hanson's buddies had beaten him senseless and shoved him on the train.

The woman stirred and rose up on one elbow. She looked into his eyes and half smiled. It was a sad expression.

"You're coming with me, Karen," he told her. "We'll leave this town. We'll get out of here and build a life on our own."

Sadness broke away her smile. She lowered her eyes. A soft moan of defeat sounded from her parted moist lips.

"What's wrong?" he demanded, moving to the side of the cot and turning her head toward his. "You don't want to stay? You can't want to stay!"

"It's not that easy!" she managed to breath out, hardly loud enough for him to hear.

"What're you talking about? All we gotta do is leave! Find another town. Go to California! There's a new world being built out there!"

"You don't understand, Kerk!" She swallowed, dropped her eyes. "I—I have a son."

The shock of those words numbed him. He sat there, dazed, unable to think clearly, unable to quite understand the full defeat of what she had told him.

Then he stood, stepping to the window and looking out into the street.

"We'll take him with us, then!" Kerk suddenly decided, whipping around to face Karen.

"It's Bart's son!" she announced in a fully defeated voice. "You see—too many things have happened—too many to go back to where we were." She stood, magnificent in her nudity, but defeat in the expression on her crumbling face.

"You see—there's nothing here for you, Kerk. Nothing at all!"

She gathered up her clothes and began to get dressed.

He watched in silence, trying to adjust to this final shock, trying to find some way around it, some way to es-

14

cape it.

Hate and anger were slow to return, slow to wrap up inside him like a snake, tightening throughout his body and mind. When it finally came into full knotted existence, Karen was dressed, looking blankly at him.

"We can't leave it like this!" Kerk exclaimed, rushing toward Karen.

"We have no choice!" she stated in a dead voice. Her eyes were expressionless. "I can't leave without Jimmy—"

"We'll take him with us—go get the boy and—"

"It's no use, Kerk!" she cried, desperately. "Bart would follow me to the ends of the earth if I took Jimmy!"

"I'd kill him if he came after us."

"He's surrounded with gunmen. You couldn't get near him here in town and you wouldn't have a chance if they came after us. They'd string you up so fast."

She dropped her eyes and then shrugged her shoulders. "It's useless!"

Karen turned away again, stepping toward the door. "It's no use, Kerk! Get out of town before it's too late!"

She opened the door and closed it behind her.

Kerk stood there, staring helplessly for a long time, not knowing what to do.

Suddenly all the fight had left him; all the feelings of power and sureness that this time he had might, as well as right, on his side.

Kerk dressed and then sat down on the cot, folding his hands over his face in complete defeat.

He didn't hear the footsteps coming down the hall, and wasn't aware when they stopped in front of his door. Not until the door swung violently open did he become alive to what was happening.

His eyes jerked up to see the doorway crowded with tall, hard-faced men. He leaped for the gun on the floor next to the bed.

"I wouldn't do that!" a tight, cultured voice ordered. Kerk recognized it immediately.

Bart Hanson, the self-styled "Baron" of Bittercreek was standing in the doorway, clothed in an expensive black suit, his right hand holding a silver plated Colt, which was pointed at the middle of Kerk's chest.

Cold ice formed along his spine as he gazed into those dark taunting eyes. He slowly stood, facing the man he'd come to kill.

"I see you came armed to the teeth, Bart!" Kerk spit out.

"I see you came back! That was a bad mistake, ranch boy. You should have stayed out—now I'll have to see you don't make the same mistake twice!" The voice had changed from soft coolness to hard contempt. The gun never wavered one moment from Kerk's chest.

"You might be a powerful man in this territory," Kerk pointed out in an unshaken voice, "but you can't get away with murder!"

Bart Hanson smiled, his thin, hard lips spreading across the white of his teeth. "You were always a fool! I thought maybe the years might have taught you something."

"Don't try a bluff! You don't dare murder an unarmed man!"

"Who said anything about murder?" Hanson murmured smoothly, between smiling lips. His left hand opened the front of his coat, revealing the shiny tin star which announced the office of Sheriff. "You came to kill an officer of the law. I'll merely take steps to see that's not done. Put you in jail and you'll be killed trying to escape. It's not very original—but nonetheless effective!"

"You know that won't hold up—where's your witnesses?" Kerk demanded, knowing the uselessness of his bluff, but refusing to give in.

"There's Karen. I'm sure she'll make a good witness!" Hanson explained in a victorious voice. "You didn't think you could come back after three years and pick things up where you'd left them, did you?" He paused and then laughed. "You should be shot for being stupid!"

"Karen wouldn't back you up against me!"

"She'd do exactly as I told her! Your mistake is you believe she'd still care enough about you to turn against her *real* friends!" Then his attitude changed. The humor faded and his eyes set, narrowing.

"Enough talk!" Hanson motioned to his men. "Take him to jail and lock him up!"

16

Three men stepped forward, guns still in their holsters, as if by this act they were showing their complete contempt for Kerk.

One brief flicker of tension and he relaxed and let the men shove him out of the hotel room and down the hall.

Kerk had sat for hours in the small cell. The cot was even harder than the one in the hotel room, but he hardly noticed. The walls which made up three of the barriers to freedom were solid three feet thick adobe. The iron bars which blocked the final side of his cell were modern and strong.

There was no means of escaping from this jail and anybody in his right mind would know that. When they came to kill him, it would be pure murder and everyone in town would know it. But they wouldn't care. Fear could do that to nice, honest people.

But these weren't the thoughts which were plaguing his mind. Instead of escape, or even trying to figure some way to wreak his hopeless revenge against Hanson, he was thinking about Karen and those intimate moments they had shared with each other a few hours before.

How long he was there in the cell he didn't know. But finally a deputy sheriff came to the bars and looked tauntingly at him. His cruel lips grinned over crooked teeth.

"What you want?" Kerk demanded, a sudden, desperate plan suggesting itself to him at the sight of the almost sadistic expression on the man's face.

"Watching a dead man!" the deputy taunted, leeringly.

"You can go to hell!" Kerk cried, springing from the cot and extending his hands toward the man's throat.

The deputy jerked back, out of reach. He pulled a set of keys from his gun-belt, holding them just beyond reach. "This what you want, ranch boy?"

"You goddamn bastard!" Kerk screamed, as if overtaken by insanity. "You dirty coward! You come in this cell and I'll bash your brains in with my bare hands."

The man grinned, his eyes laughing. "That's an idea!" he snarled, his face suddenly hard.

"You do that! I'll bash your damn grinning face to a pulp." Desperately Kerk flung out every dirty insult he could think of to antagonize the man into barging into the cell. He

17

cursed the deputy's manhood, insulted his birthright. It was a dangerous gamble he was taking, for the other was armed and he would be almost helpless—but there wasn't anything to lose. He might be dead in a few hours anyway.

As the string of insults bombarded the deputy, the man's face turned slowly red and then drained to white.

Kerk continued his vile outburst, waving his arms insanely, as if out of his mind and helpless in his emotions.

The deputy's face slowly creased into a snarl and a low moan sounded from his curled lips as he jerked forward, unlocking the cell and pulling the gun from his holster.

"You asked for it!" the man cried, leveling the gun at Kerk's stomach. "You asked for it!"

He leaped forward, with such speed that Kerk didn't have time to fend off the first blow which sent the barrel of the gun deep into the pit of his stomach.

Kerk doubled over, agonized, his lungs choking, his head spinning. The impact of a fist crushed into his face, jarring him backwards against the stucco wall, gushing blood from his broken nose.

Dazzled by a blinding flash of stars whirling before his eyes, Kerk swung blindly outwards with his huge arms, hoping to fend off any new blow, hoping that his fist would smash damagingly at the other's face or body.

His efforts slashed through empty air. Then he felt another staggering pain rip through his groin as something bone hard rammed upwards.

Blackness folded around him. The only thing that kept sanity and consciousness was the demanding scream of his mind that ordered him to fight back, to somehow gain the advantage.

A pointed boot kicked into his side and then as it kicked a second time, Kerk managed to grab hold of it through the red blaze of pain. His body buckled around the leg, his hands gripping with all the strength left in him, and he was rewarded by a yell of surprise as the sound of a body slamming to the floor gave him his first chance. Kerk followed that dark shadowy form, hammering his fists into its body. He felt the crunch of ribs giving under the impact of his blows. Then he aimed toward the contorted face and felt the man's

18

nose break inward, bursting a volcanic flow of sticky red.

The deputy was silent, unmoving. Kerk collapsed on top of the man, groaning in a flood of nausea which emptied his guts, agony ripping through the nerves and cells of his muscles and flesh.

You gotta get up! Get away—you gotta get away! his mind screamed at him.

Get up! Get up!

Slowly he forced his muscles to tighten, respond to the desperate need to escape while he still could. Kerk inched his body upwards on quivering arms. His eyes squeezed against the hurt the effort cost him.

Finally he stood, looking down at the unconscious deputy.

A moment passed and then he moved from the cell, locking it shut and stepped down the short hallway, and into the empty outer office.

It was only a matter of moments to spot his gun-belt on a wall peg, take it down, strap it around his waist, tie the holster to his leg and search out the rifle rack. He saw a sawed-off shotgun which served his purpose perfectly.

Three minutes later he was stepping outside the jail house, carrying the shotgun in his left hand, his right posed over his holstered .45.

Kerk walked down the wide, mud street, toward the town's main saloon. Karen worked there, but what was more important, chances were that he'd find Bart Hanson or at least discover where the man was.

The saloon was smoke filled, crowded with men and dance-hall girls who surrounded the gaming tables and bar. At first nobody noticed the tall, hard-faced man who jerked in through the swinging double doors and flattened his back against the wall.

Kerk's face was bruised and blood smeared, set like granite, his dark gray eyes flashing around the room. The shotgun in his left hand was pointing forward, swinging slowly from left to right, poised ready. His right hand went to the holstered .45 and whipped it out in a blurred motion.

Several people noticed him and turned.

Kerk pointed his six-shooter toward the ceiling and

squeezed the trigger, his thumb jerking over the hammer and snapping it back, ready for immediate use.

Slow silence whispered over the room and eyes turned.

"Where's Bart Hanson?" he yelled when the complete silence faced him.

A murmur answered back. "Bart Hanson—self-made Sheriff—I called you a coward—raper of women, murderer!" he yelled.

A barman spoke up: "He ain't here!"

Kerk's eyes flashed toward the heavy man. "Where is he?"

"At the hotel! A private party!" the man answered in a tense voice.

Kerk slipped toward the door, edging slowly out.

"Anybody steps out this door, I'll blow his head off!" he warned.

Nobody moved and he turned and started hurriedly down the street. There wasn't any sound from behind him.

Kerk broke into a run and rushed to the small hotel which was at the next corner. Stepped into the small lobby.

The hotel desk-clerk looked up, a puzzled frown creasing his thin face.

"Where's Hanson?"

The man gaped at him wide-eyed.

"What room is he in?" Kerk demanded, pointing the shotgun at the helpless clerk.

"Upstairs, down the hall," was the trembling answer. "205!"

Kerk didn't break stride as he turned and rushed up the steps and then slowly moved down the hallway toward Room 205. He paused only a second before the last door and then kicked it violently open, and leaped in, the shotgun extending before him in steady hands.

The scene that met his startled gaze was two figures throbbing naked on the bed. Bart Hanson was smothering himself in the large breasts of the writhing and moaning woman. It took him longer to recognize who it was with the man.

Karen.

The realization that she was enjoying what the man was

20

doing made Kerk cold inside.

The two figures suddenly froze, aware of his presence.

Kerk felt anger well like fire in his throat and it was only with control that his finger kept from squeezing the shotgun into murderous action.

Instead, he leaped forward, ripping the man's shoulder cruelly around, throwing him bodily from the bed and onto the floor.

Hanson growled, starting spring to his feet.

"Hold!" Kerk fired tightly at him.

Bart Hanson froze, staring at Kerk with slow terror squeezing his blood-drained features.

"How'd you get out?" he choked a dazed voice.

"Shut up!" Kerk turned his eyes to Karen, a mixture of emotions killing everything in him. All the feelings which had built inside his mind and body for this woman had been dashed to meaningless nothing at the sight of her writhing hungrily under the body of Bart Hanson. That vision had squeezed dry all feeling in him. He looked into Karen's eyes and tried to understand how a woman could be like her. She must have known he was in jail; she must have realized that Hanson was going to kill him. Yet she was in this room, letting the damned bastard make love to her—and enjoying it.

"Kill him!" Karen hissed viciously making no move to hide her nudity. The large swell of her breasts, with their cherry rose centers, were heaving with wracking emotion.

"Kill him—while you can!" she screamed in such a violently coarse voice that Kerk suddenly realized how utterly useless it really was for him to pick up where he had been three years before. Too many changes. Too much had happened to Karen. What he had seen in her eyes earlier that day had been his own wishful projection. She had changed.

The sound of movement brought Kerk's attention back to the man.

Hanson had sprung to his feet and his lashed out wildly for the shotgun.

Kerk was surprised by the sudden attack. Hanson had more courage than he'd given the man credit for.

Strong hands wrapped around the shotgun's barrel, twisting, pulling with insane strength.

21

The weapon was suddenly wrenched from Kerk's hands.
The other man leaped back, raising the gun's barrel.

There wasn't time to think. One instant and his chest would be burst open, instantly flooding out his life.

Kerk's right hand flew toward the holstered .45. All the months of practice, the careful training of nerves and muscles to respond instantly and instinctively to his mental command, went into this one attempt to escape the sure death facing him.

He felt his fingers gripping on the holstered gun, wrapping around the handle, as his arm yanked upwards.

The shotgun was level with his chest and a triumphant laugh of victory burst from Hanson's lips as his finger began to squeeze the weapon into life.

Kerk's own hand made that practiced movement which was a fast squeezing as it moved the .45 upwards, pointing at the center of Hanson's chest

It seemed as if the explosion of the two guns broke the tense silence of the room at the same time.

Everything froze. Then Kerk's body jerked around. Fire seared through him, but he couldn't locate the pain

He twisted around. His gun leveled automatically at Hanson.

Then he slumped backwards against the wall; the .45 slipped from his fingers and clattered to the floor.

Hanson was standing stone still, his hands clutching the shotgun pointed at Kerk's chest. His face was contorted in agonized struggle. His mouth hung open. A red smear was slowly forming on his chest. Then like a toppling statue be slowly started falling forward, gaining momentum until he smashed face downwards to the floor.

There was a long silence. Neither Karen nor Kerk moved. Then he was aware of heavy breathing and the pain in his left side.

Kerk turned his eyes toward Karen.

The woman's beautiful features were struggling, frowning, as if unable to completely understand what had happened. Then slowly her lips formed words. "Hanson—said—you were in—jail!"

He didn't say anything because the pain waved through

him at that moment.

"Kerk—I love you!" she cried, toward him. "Take me way—take me out of this town."

Kerk just shook his head slowly from side to side. "You were right, Karen—too many changes. It's too late to go back to what we were before...I'm sorry."

His eyes took in the shape of her wonderful naked body once more. The proud breasts, high, supported by their own firmness. The narrowed waist and the flaring hips which blended down to such beautiful thighs. But there were many women like her where he would be going. Exactly like her. With their own tragic stories of why they had become what they were. But the fact was they were tramps—prostitutes— not because they couldn't do anything else, but because they liked their work. Karen wasn't the marrying type. It had already taken him too long to realize that.

He stooped down and picked up his .45, holstering it. Then turning, slowly walked out of the room.

Men were rushing down the hall. They jerked to a halt at sight of him. One made a threatening movement for his gun.'

"Hanson's dead!" Kerk announced, his gun suddenly gripped in his right hand. "Your meal ticket is in there!"

The men looked at one another, and then suddenly relaxed.

Kerk walked past then unharmed.

As he stepped out into the street, Kerk headed toward the stables at the edge of town, where he had left his horse the night before.

He'd been all wrong to think it was possible to go back. Well she had freedom from the terror of Bart Hanson. He had given her that much! For himself, it would be California. There was a new land out there , a new world being built—a world with a future for a, man willing to work hard.

He walked down the street, his step taking an awkward springing action as he moved toward the edge of town and the stables

He was leaving his childhood and the childhood memories of the past right here where they belonged.

For Kerk Claymore there was only the future ahead, a future unmarred by the plague from the past.

Another western, of which I didn't write very many at the time. This one tells about...

—·THE STAND-OFF·—

It was a moment before Bill Martin recognized the savage cry over the noise of the stage coach. Reflex action brought his hand to the .44 strapped at his side. Years living in the west told him all that was necessary to know. What had started as a return to the West with his new bride was about to become a nightmarish hell. To him this was a natural move back to where he'd been born. Even if California was slightly west of New Mexico. At least it was not Boston!

His eyes darted to the young woman sitting beside him.

Helen hadn't wanted to come out West with him, and now for the first time he thought maybe it had been a mistake. She had wanted to settle in the town of her birth, raise a family near her father and mother and sisters. Yet, even with that longing desire, she had come with him, because she loved him and because she felt it was the duty of a woman to follow her man, wherever he might take her. To Helen that was almost a Biblical demand. And now, because of that, and his own foolish stubbornness, they might be doomed even before they reached their distant destination. And what was that? A dream, a magnet promising riches, maybe even gold in California. And he was following his dream. Blindly. Foolishly. Stupidly.

"What is it?" she asked, frightened, looking at the gun in his hand. "What's wrong?"

Brent Henderson, sitting opposite them, the only other occupant of the coach, answered the question with one word: "Apaches."

The coach jerked, the sound of a whip snapped overhead, and suddenly they were charging across the desert floor.

"Oh God—God help us!" Helen screamed, her face

white.

Bill wanted to take her into his arms and say all the things they hadn't had time to say. But that was impossible, now. So many things to say, so many which had seemed special and important but saved for the future when they were together in their own, freshly build home. Out West. Into a world of hope and new adventure, and the chance of making it big, somewhere, somehow. Follow your dream, was his motto. Foolish, stupid, childish dream. Yet a part of all that he had been raised to believe. He was a part of the frontier life; but not like his father who was struggled in a small western town to make it as a store keeper, then as a farmer. All those failures had killed the old man. No, John had better dreams. And they had enveloped this wonderful woman who had promised to share his life, wherever he might take her.

And now what?

A bullet smashed into the coach's side and he quickly learned out the open window.

There were at least a dozen bareback Apaches, speeding after the stage, almost enveloped by the collective dust which was whirling around their horses' hooves.

A bullet whipped through the air inches from his head, smashing into the door.

Ramming his gun through the window he returned the fire.

He heard Henderson firing from the other side of the coach. An Apache leaped backwards from his horse, smashing under the hooves of the one behind him.

Bill fired again, missing.

Helen screamed, and he turned to look at her.

She was curled up on the floor, her hands clutching at her drawn, pale face.

"Helen—don't!" he yelled, slapping her face. "Snap out of it!"

Emotion flared in her eyes and then she slumped back in a faint.

That's better, he thought, returning his attention to the pursuing Indians. He emptied the gun at them, only hitting one Apache. In the middle of reloading he heard a cry from the driver's seat. His eyes snapped to Henderson. The neatly

25

dressed gambler shook his head.

"Smithie," was his only comment before firing again.

The coach suddenly lurched to one side, tilting, and then slamming down on four wheels. Bill looked out the side door window, trying to see if anybody was controlling the horses. It was impossible to tell from his angle.

The coach smashed over a boulder, toppled for a moment and then righted itself.

"Better check!" Henderson spat out.

Bill was just opening the door so that he could climb out and up the side of the coach, when the world suddenly spun around his head.

Instinctive action caused him to leap from the coach, rolling with his fall.

Dazed, choking in dust, he managed to spring to his feet, the .44 already in steady hands. The Apaches were racing toward him and he fired point-blank, seeing one man fall from his horse. He fired again, hitting another.

The Indians veered off, racing several hundred yards away.

Sure, you bastards—you don't have to do anything but wait! he cursed.

Turning, Bill rushed for the stage, which had been dragged half a dozen yards by its momentum.

Opening the door, he dragged Helen's unconscious form free of the coach, placing her on the opposite side from the Apaches.

In a moment he discovered that Helen had only suffered a few bruises.

"We don't have much chance," Henderson's voice said from behind him.

Bill looked up. "We can't just stand here and die."

"How many are there?"

"I don't know. I dropped a few. Maybe two, three, four. There were less than I'd thought at first."

"It'll be dark soon," the gambler said, brushing some of the dust from his dark suit.

"So they'll wait till morning—if we can hold them off," Bill sighed, defeated.

A wild yell drew their attention away from conversation.

In the next minutes Bill emptied his .44, reloaded and emptied it again, as the Apaches circled the upturned coach. It seemed like a nightmare from which he couldn't escape. But as the sun drifted down below the horizon the Indians turned and disappeared into the desert.

Helen had revived, but cowered close to the coach, saying nothing. When the Indians had withdrawn, Bill heard a soft sobbing coming from her.

Turning, he went to her side.

"Take it easy," he whispered. "We might get out of this yet."

"How?" Henderson's biting question interrupted.

"One of us has got to try to reach Bitter Creek. It can't be far. The Apaches won't attack at night—so we have a little time."

Henderson's lean features were thoughtful, his dark eyes narrowed. "I guess one of us might give it a try."

"I'll stay with my wife," Bill stated.

Henderson nodded. Taking a small bottle from inside his jacket, he opened it, swallowed, and then tossed it to Bill. "Keep the whiskey."

Then, without another word, the man turned, dropped to the ground and crawled his way into the desert.

Bill watched until he'd disappeared, wondering if he would ever see the man again. Chances were that if the Apaches didn't kill him he'd simply disappear into the night. From the gambler's point of view they were doomed; why should he risk his life trying to save theirs? And again, maybe the man was ethical and willing to risk anything to save his fellow man. That was the Christian way. But was a gambler touched by such ethical thoughts? There was a code in the West, but certainly that didn't mean people were fools.

Bill pushed such thoughts away. The war had turned him bitter; he'd seen too many horrors to be sure of any one man's honor. But there had been nothing to do other than let Henderson leave.

The Apaches were out there somewhere. The night blanketed their movements, hiding their locations, but they were there, silent and waiting for dawn.

Bill tightened his grip on the .44, wiping the sweat from

his forehead. He didn't look at the woman huddled beside him, he didn't have the nerve.

"Bill," Helen's voice whispered, "don't you think they might have gone away?"

Oh, how he wished they would, he thought bitterly.

"No," was his only reply.

"What do they want?" she cried, her voice edging once more on hysteria.

"Who knows? The Apaches are at war with us—all of us. To them this is their land; we're the invaders. That's all that matters."

The truth was one thing he couldn't tell her; the last thing he would ever let her find out. If they took her alive it would be to face a living hell. This was one thing he couldn't let happen. He had only twelve bullets left, eleven for the Indians, in case Henderson didn't return with help soon enough, and the last one for Helen.

Nausea clutched his stomach.

Why hadn't he listened to the reasoned pleas she had made in Boston? There was security working for her father. Nothing grand or even with much future other than being with her, having a family, living in the safe embrace of civilization. Why'd he been such a damned stubborn fool about going back out West, and to California? Following a dream? But wasn't life meaningful only if one had a dream to follow and then followed it to the end of its trail. No matter how short. Better to die fighting for what is important than to die on false hopes. The South had lost the war; and the world of dreams and come tumbling down about that society, that culture. Life might have been simple and boring in the East, but it would have been life. Now death waited out there on the plain—the end of everything; the end of glorious dreams of striking it rich in California—the end of happiness with the only person he had ever loved.

"I'm scared," Helen sobbed clutching at his arm.

"Henderson will be back by morning—the Indians won't attack till dawn. There's nothing to worry about," he lied. It was true, except for the minor fact that Henderson might not return. If he got through safely the man might just disappear. Nobody would know the difference.

"I shouldn't have brought you out here, Helen—for what it's worth...I'd give my life to change it." He laughed inwardly, because he would probably be giving his life away without a chance of saving Helen's. But he couldn't tell her that. "In any case—when we get out of this—we'll go back East." That was the least he could give her.

Helen's surprised cry cut into the night.

Bill clamped a hand over her full lips. "Not so loud."

"You really mean it?" she whispered, looking lovingly into his eyes.

"I mean it," Bill announced, hiding the defeat in his voice. The future, either way, was grim. Life in the East working in a stuffy bank, for Helen's old man, or death.

He stared down into her face, taking in the soft, delicate lines which sang happiness brightly up into his. Her high cheekbones framed lovely wide blue eyes; the full softness of her lips pouted slightly, as if ready for kissing.

Bill slowly, helplessly, moved his mouth to hers, feeling the velvet warmth press eagerly to meet the kiss.

It was some moments before either of them spoke.

"You really sure you want to go back East?" she breathed softly in his ear, clutching tightly to him.

He wanted to tell her it wouldn't make any difference what he was sure of, but instead found himself saying: "That has nothing to do with it. I can't take the chance of endangering your life—I didn't realize until now..."

Bill hated himself for the lie, but it was the kindest thing he could do. At least her last hours would be happy ones.

"Oh, I'm so glad," she sighed, kissing him.

She's so childlike, he thought, tightening her against him. *Even now she can't imagine how close death is.*

Bill found himself burying his lips into the white silk of her throat, his hands searching out the large swells of her breasts. Passion moved through him, passion which he hadn't even begun to express to her, probably would never be given the chance to do so again. And suddenly that's all that seemed important.

They slipped down onto the dusty earth, locked together, their lips blended in the deep warmth of one another. The madness of their situation made the passion even more in-

29

sane. Yet in the fact of death what human being could possibly not want to die only after one last ecstatic moment in the arms of the person they loved.

His hand moved along her dress, then slowly he slipped the skirt upwards, caressing her legs, the firm flesh of her thighs.

Helen moaned, trembling under his touch. Her body went rigid and then she clawed, frantically urging him onwards, pleading with the movements of her hips against his. And suddenly they were clutching, trembling, clawing at one another. Her dress slipped away and he soothed her body with his, bringing it up through the passionate fire which finally locked them together in the final burst of ecstasy.

Later, Bill returned to his silent watch as Helen lay, half asleep, relaxed in the gentle aftermath of their love.

Maybe it wouldn't be so bad to live the soft Eastern life that Helen had begged him to. Maybe it wouldn't eat the guts away from him.

He argued with himself for a long time, as if it made a difference, as if they really had a chance to survive.

But, in the end, Bill realized that Boston held nothing except safety for Helen—a safety which was as useless as if it were on the moon, instead of a little over two thousand miles away. It simply hadn't held his dream, foolish as that might be. Every man must decide what is meaningful and best of himself, and to hell with what others thought. Dying with his nose to the grindstone was not a promising dream That's what would have been offered in Boston. Secure, maybe. But locked into a daily routine without any real future beyond more of the same thing day in and day out. No hope; no room for growth. Not the kind he wanted. At least his dream was filled with hope for a better, richer future. So he had convinced himself.

Bill was feeling terrible pangs of self-hate. Anything would have been better than what faced him in the next hours. Maybe it would be less cruel to simply put a bullet into Helen's lovely head, ending the anguish of waiting for death. Then a second bullet into his own head, before the Apache's came for what they wanted. A white woman was considered quite a prize. He couldn't let them have her.

30

And he couldn't just kill her as long as their will might be hope. Henderson might still return to rescue them. As long as that dim hope existed it was impossible to consider killing his bride—even if it might save her from unimaginable horrors.

Maybe there was hope. Perhaps it wasn't as terrible as he imagined. Maybe he could somehow survive, avoid death. Maybe...was a word of dreams. And now all those dreams which had brought him back to his beloved land out West were shattered. Doomed. And with that any hope of survival.

Still he would not end it until the last moment.

He wondered how many Apaches were out there. There couldn't be many. But enough to make the final moments end as if there were a thousand.

The night slowly slipped away, the stars dimming out in the dawn, announcing the arrival of the sun.

Bill had dozed off several times, but still the hours had been like an endless wake. He looked down at his now sleeping wife, and felt a choked self-hate for what he had brought her. He had lost track of how many times he had checked his .44, counted the remaining bullets. How many times had he tried to understand the blind drive which made the call to California so important to him? He didn't know any more.

But one conviction the early hours had finally brought: if by some freak they got out of this, he would return East—forget dreams of fortunes and the West, where he had spent most of his life. His first duty as a husband was the protection of his wife and future family. How foolish he'd been; what a damned selfish, narrow minded man. He had taken his beloved out of the safety of her home and brought her here to die. For nothing but a foolish young man's dream.

He had learned for the first time the full extent of his love for Helen. He had discovered that she, in the end, meant more to him than anything else in the world.

As the sun crept over the horizon Bill turned his full attention to the surrounding desert. They would be out there somewhere—probably all around.

He waited.

Only the silence of morning answered his alert ears.

The sun moved upwards.

Sweat covered his body.

Then he heard the call of a coyote, where there weren't any.

Bill cocked the .44. His eyes swept the desert, which lay like a naked blanket of sand and rocks. Then something moved to the right.

He turned, fired, and saw dust kick up.

A yell shattered the silence and, suddenly, half naked forms leaped to their feet. His eyes picked out at least four in front of him—maybe there were more to the sides and behind, but he didn't have time to look.

The .44 blazed, darting from target to target. He didn't even wait to see if he hit one before aiming at another.

Helen screamed.

Turning, he pointed the gun, firing at the Apache who was only inches away from him, knife clutched in the dark red hand.

The man crumpled, but his body kept coming, smashing into Bill, and knocking him over.

He struggled free, pushed to his feet, firing at another Indian who was leaping for him.

Then he felt something hit his back, knocking him forward. His face ate into the sand. Desperately he whipped around under the weight of his attacker. Saw a knife plunging down. Rammed his gun into the man's belly and pulled the trigger. The hammer clicked.

A yell broke from his lips as he raised his empty gun into the Apache's plunging arm. With all the strength left in him, Bill strained against the warrior, finally pushing the Apache away. Then he swung the gun down against the man's skull and leaped to his feet in time to meet another redskin.

It was like fighting a maze of arms and legs. Then suddenly this last antagonist fell away at the same time he heard Helen's screaming.

Turning, Bill saw an Apache holding his wife, a knife held to her throat.

A savage snarl broke from the Indian's thin lips as he started backing away.

Bill looked at the .44, still clutched in sweaty hands.

32

Then he thought what would happen to Helen if the Apache got away with her, and he realized that death—quick and brutal—would be better than the fate in store for her.

"Stop where you are," he cried, pointing the empty gun at the savage.

The Apache stared at him, his eyes narrowing, the knife cutting a thin red line in Helen's throat.

"Bill—don't!" she screamed.

Then as he rushed forward, Helen slumped in the Indian's arms.

The Apache looked at the woman and then at Bill. Shoving Helen to the ground he hefted the knife, waiting for the white man's attack.

Bill threw the .44 aside and the Apache grinned, leaping forward.

Bill's hand whipped out for the threatening knife, gripping the Indian's wrist.

The two men strained, sweat making their bodies slippery. Then Bill felt a foot lock behind his leg and suddenly he was failing backwards. The ground slammed at his back and for a moment the air choked out from his mouth. Dazed, weakened by the long hand-to-hand battle, Bill attempted to keep the gleaming blade from cutting the life from him.

The knife's point was only inches from his throat, still descending under the weight and strength of the Apache on top of him.

Then he felt the steel touching his neck, starting to sink in. Every muscle strained—pushing upwards for one final effort to avoid death. He was fighting more for Helen now, than for himself.

The knife slowly moved upwards, hovered and then inched down again.

Bill knew it was only a matter of seconds before his strength would give out. Then he saw a shadowy shape behind the Apache. It was Helen, something held in her hands.

One more second was all he had to hold out. One more second.

His arms were quivering. Then the knife started inching closer and he felt steel biting into his neck.

A blackness was starting to cloud his vision.

33

Then he heard something smash into flesh. For a moment he believed it was the sound of his own death in his ears, of his blood exploding life from him.

The knife bit deeper and then relaxed. A soft moan breathed on Bill's cheek as the Indian relaxed against him.

"Bill—Bill," Helen's voice cried, hysterically.

He struggled free from under the Apache and then stood, bringing the woman's body against his.

For a long time they kissed, tasting each other's mouths in a frantic release of tension.

Then slowly he disengaged himself from Helen and sighed, "I guess we'd better make sure these guys don't—"

Horses' hooves cut him short and he turned toward the sound.

A half score of men rode up to them, reining a few yards away.

Bill noticed Henderson with them. "I see you made it."

"A little late, I'm afraid," the gambler announced ironically.

Bill looked at Helen. "Well, let's get out of here."

His voice was exhausted and dead, but most of the emotion was drained away because of the promise he'd made to his wife the night before when life seemed about to end.

"This land isn't a place for women," he sighed.

Helen looked seriously up into his face. "You don't want to go East, do you?"

"Yes." But the word lacked conviction.

"But I don't."

"What're you talking about?"

"When I saw you almost dead—almost killed—something happened—I can't explain it, Billy, but I realized that if you lived that was all that mattered. It wasn't important where we were—what we did. I just wanted you to live and be happy.

"Maybe I was afraid to grow up and be completely on my own with you. Well—I think that maybe I was born this morning. 'Wither thou goeth—I will follow'."

Regardless of the audience, Bill swept his wife into his arms, kissing the sweet, brave lips which had just given him life again, for the second time in the same day.

34

This story kind of bridges the Past with the Present, for it could have taken place not long ago at...

⊸THE END OF A TOWN⊷

It was even too dark to see shadows. A blackness that covered Thomson so completely that he couldn't see his own actions.

But that was all the better.

If only such a blanket of silence was surrounding him too.

It was impossible to keep all sounds from exploding into being. And every noise seemed like a cannon, or gigantic pieces of grainy paper, brushing together.

He knew he was sweating.

If he was discovered now, he'd shatter into a million pieces.

He had to keep his mind on the job.

The job!

That was a laugh! One hell of a laugh!

Kill Widow Jones and make it look good. Do it right and you get completely off the hook, out of debt. And your boy Johnny will live.

Just get that woman!

That's what Kerby had told him. And he'd do what the man had said. And that would get him off the hook.

And they wouldn't kill Johnny!

All he had to do was...

Shoot Widow Jones.

Black Widow Jones.

That's what he was looking for, needed to find: a black shadow against a blacker bed, against a blacker room. Against a blacker terror in his guts.

He knew something inside him was shaking, and if he didn't keep it under control he'd be shaking all over, unable to stop himself.

35

His bones would rattle together and make horrible sounds. His nerves would rub each other, making a grating noise.

No, he couldn't shake!

He moved his feet forward—very slowly.

Making no sound. Not daring to.

Widow Jones.

A harmless young woman, with a big mouth. An attractive lady, with too shapely a body for a small town teacher.

He didn't have anything against her. Period.

So she talked against the farmers! That's what Kerby had said she did. So she did? So what?

He wasn't the kind of man who would kill her just for that.

In fact, he might have liked her, if he'd gotten the chance.

He hadn't had a woman for years, not since his wife Mary had died. No time for that kind of thing. Raising Johnny since the boy was three was a full time job. Even with the help of Bess and her husband Jim, his housekeeper and cook. But now, his ranch—everything he owned—was being up for grabs; pulled out from under him.

And all he had to do was kill Widow Jones...

Why?

He'd wondered about that, because the reasons given had seemed shallow, mean, maybe even a bit insane.

How come Kerby hadn't had some of his gunmen take care of her. Wouldn't that have been easier.

He tried to reason out all that. But it didn't make sense. And he was under such pressure it was impossible to think straight.

Plus he was a simple man; a man who didn't understand the complex workings of killers; town rulers; would-be barons. They were totally out of his social circle of ranch workers.

He only understood the land, and that a man had to do what was necessary to support his family. And when everything was threatened, he had to do whatever was necessary to survive.

"Look here, Thomson," Kerby had said the day before,

36

"I got this here mortgage on your place...it says pay up or shut up! Simple. No ifs, mights, or maybes. But I'm an understandin' man. I know you have a kid to feed and clothe; and the farmin' business ain't what it use to be so I'm goin' to give you a deal...you do me a favor; I'll do you one!"

"What is it? Anything! Anything to keep my Johnny fixed up like he should be.... Anything to keep my farm...and...anything at all!" He almost broke down into tears then. It was a great relief to suddenly discover he had been pulled out of a deep, never-ending well, and saved from the horror of hitting bottom. He'd do anything to keep his farm.

"I got a job that needs doing, that I can't have the boys involved in..." Kerby said, looking deep into his eyes. "It's important...very important."

"Yes...anything Mr. Kerby...anything at all!"

"Well, you know Mrs. Jones.... Widow Jones the school teacher..."

"Yes...yes. What about her?"

"Well, she's been spoutin' off about certain people, and things...said quite a few nasty things about you...you farmers...And she's against other people...tryin' to get the town against me...and the farmers..."

Shock took over his facial muscles. He hadn't known such things. Hadn't realized. And Johnny had been going to her school, and learning all those lies.

"She's bad for the town...I've done everythin' to stop her. But she won't move...she won't shut up, and she...well, she's got to be stopped. Or your Johnny and every boy and girl...and many others will be turnin' against certain factions...and...well, if you could do this job for me...I'll just tear up the mortgage. I'll just put an end to all your debts in town...is that fair?"

He'd said it was more than fair. Then he was told to kill Widow Jones. Instantly he objected, stunned. That's when Kerby had gotten nasty and made threats, saying he'd kill Johnny. Said that it would be an easy thing to hold him here, while one of the men went and got his boy. But this, cold blooded murder, was sickening it made his stomach icy and his insides painful. He was sweating too much.

It wasn't that he hadn't killed before. But in battle. Or in a fight it was different.

Suddenly an explosion of noise rebounded across the room, hitting all the walls and bouncing back to his ears. He had bumped into a piece of furniture. It felt like a bed post.

He wanted to run.

"What's that? Who's that?" came a high pitched, silky voice. "Who's that?"

There was the sound of movement a few feet in front of him, then the sliding, metallic, clicking noise of a gun being cocked.

He wanted to run.

He couldn't move.

He was so terrified he didn't know what to do.

"Just stay put...I'll pull this trigger the instant I hear a sound...and I warn you...I know how to use this!"

There was more movement, and after a few moments an oil lamp lighted, and the room burst with dim light.

Widow Jones sat on the edge of her four-poster bed, holding a gun, pointed directly toward him.

His eyes bulged in their sockets, more from her lack of clothing than from the danger of the weapon.

She had nothing on.

She didn't seem to realize her exposed condition.

And scared as he was, terrified, he couldn't get his eyes off her beautiful body.

It made him warm all over, excited.

He hadn't seen a woman like this since his wife. And there was no question in his mind that she was more than just attractive. She was beautiful.

Firm breasts, large and well formed. Narrow waist, flat stomach, and full hips and thighs.

Suddenly he didn't want to kill her, regardless. He wanted to make love to her, to take her body and totally escape into its embrace. This was not a woman you killed, but a woman you make love to.

All at once all he could think of was how wonderful it would be to hold her, to touch her, to caress that lovely body, to literally possess it in every way.

Surprised horror covered her features and in one impos-

38

sible-to-follow movement, she had covered herself up with a bed sheet.

The terror returned to him, once her exciting body was hidden.

And this time it was a horrible grinding twist of his insides; sweat poured from him and his hands were shaking.

This was the end of everything!

Widow Jones looked at him carefully, questioning, trying to understand.

"What are you doing here, Mr. Thomson?" she asked, motioning with her gun for him to sit down on the small chair a few feet away from the bed.

He did so. Without hesitation. His legs were weak, his own body exhausted. His mind confused.

"Now, tell me what this is all about!"

Everything had left him. Everything was finished. He was done.

Nothing mattered any more, and he began wondering if he would have been able to kill this woman anyway. He wasn't a killer.

And maybe he wasn't meant *to kill her!*

That one shocked him.

Why, if Kerby had wanted her killed he could have sent one of his men to do the job. But this man must have known something would go wrong! He wasn't a fool. Just, maybe, smart enough to set something up that was far more subtle. What?

And why?

"I...I didn't...I didn't want to—really!" he blurted out. His lips were trembling, and he couldn't look the woman in the eyes.

He was terribly ashamed; and frightened.

"Want to what?" She had put the gun on her lap, and was looking at Thomson with concern. The fright had left her face.

"He sent me to...kill you. I don't know why. But he threatened my boy...he threatened to kill my boy if I didn't kill you...now he'll do it...he'll kill Johnny..."

Thomson put his face in his hands and sobbed. "What'll I do...what'll I do?"

"But why? Why does he want me killed?" she asked, looking at the far wall.

Thomson forced control over his emotions as he looked up at her. "I don't...really know. He said you were talking against the farmers and other people...trying to turn the kids against all of us...I don't know...but I didn't care...my boy...my Johnny...he said he'd kill him...and I was afraid!"

She didn't say anything for a long while. Her eyes only looked at the far wall. Then finally she put aside the gun in her lap, laying it on the bed stand. She stood up, then re-membering her nakedness slid back under the covers.

"I think I know what he's afraid of...he knows I see right through him...He must have heard about the meeting last week...He wants me out of the way. I'm a threat...that's for sure. He's power mad. Got this town under his thumb...and afraid of organized resistance..."

She had been talking as if to herself. But now she turned toward Thomson. "He sent you to kill me...why?"

"I don't know..." he said, shaking his head from side to side. He didn't care either. He was worried about his son.

He'd do anything for that boy.

He had to save him.

He had to...

She was talking out loud again to herself.

But he hardly heard the words. He didn't care about them.

"He must have had some good reason...why not his own men...why not his own men?" She paused for a second, thinking. Then she straightened upright suddenly. "That's it...set up one of the town's men, and after he's done the dirty work...kill him...show the other people of the town how much Kerby was really for me...how much he was for town reform...then with me out of the way...and the town behind him...he could continue his own reforming...tighten his hold on the town...people...little children in the hands of an edu-cated man. That's why they need help! Oh, how they need help..."

"But my boy...my boy Johnny...he'll kill him now...he'll kill him now!" Thomson felt sick inside; he felt horribly sick.

He didn't want his son to die.

Johnny had to live. It was all that still existed of Mary. And that *had* to live.

He must do something—anything!

Suddenly he realized what was to be done. He realized there was nothing else he could do.

Widow Jones wasn't even looking his way; she was still talking out loud to herself.

All he had to do was pull out the gun that Kerby had given him, then his Johnny would be safe and his farm. His Johnny had a right to live.

Thomson pulled out the weapon from his pocket, and pointed it at Widow Jones.

She turned his way just at that moment. Terror filled her eyes.

"What are you doing?" she screamed. "Don't be a fool. That's just what Kerby wants...you kill me and he'll have just the thing—the event—to take control of this town completely. All he needs is to have me out of the way...an educated person, willing to fight him...and the others won't do anything, especially if he hangs my killer...you're just killing yourself...don't be foolish!"

He pulled the trigger, and she jerked backwards against the bed frame, a shocked expression on her face.

"I'm sorry...but my Johnny...it's for my Johnny...I had to...I had to..."

He walked over to the bed, looking down at the still form of Widow Jones. He reached out a hand, and tenderly touched her body. Tears filled his eyes, but he hadn't been able to do anything else.

For Johnny.

Without knowing why, he reached out and touched the soft flesh of her breasts; it was warm, full and exciting. Even in death.

Horrible, disgusting thoughts ran through his mind . .

He had a terrible urge to make love to her.

Her body was wonderfully attractive.

Then he fell across the bed, sobbing...

He didn't know when or how it happened. He didn't know how long he had been lying there but suddenly strong

41

cruel hands pulled him upwards. Hard voices yelled and cursed.

He tried to explain that it was for his boy, his boy Johnny; but no one listened. And in a way he didn't really even care.

His boy would be safe now—Kerby wouldn't kill his Johnny.

There was no wasting of time.

Kerby saw to that.

"Hang the man who killed poor Widow Jones...Kill the terrible creature..." the town ruler demanded.

The town was awake, everybody was up and watching, watching, as their new hero ordered his men to hang the farmer Thomson. They watched, and realized how wrong they had been about Kerby, how wrong Widow Jones had been.

Kerby was a good man; he was looking after the town's good; he was proving it.

Wasn't he hanging the cold blooded killer of that nice, but misinformed school teacher?

Wasn't he?

PART TWO

PRESENT DIMENSIONS

DIMENSIONS, BY CHARLES NUETZEL

Now we reach into the present period, well, at least into the twentieth century. Here's a story about a guy who got himself into a jam with the lovely lady who was...

➝GARDIA'S MISTRESS⊷

Dan stood shivering in the darkness of the doorway, his guts churning like ice against his spine. There was a terrible sickness of cold sweat boiling over his trembling body. The black night around him was the only cover he had from Gardia's men. He could hear the sound of their feet clomping like hammers hitting hard rock, their low voices hissing on the hot night air.

His hand inched into the right pocket of his pants, feeling the small, snub-nosed .38, trying to find courage in its steel form for what he would have to do in the next few minutes.

But you'll find no courage there, he thought angrily. *You're a goddamned blasted coward and fool, Dan Carson!*

But he'd always been a fool for a sexy lady—especially one like Vicky Lopez. Such free spirited women were ideal for one night stands—no complications.

Yet, this woman was something else! He had been fascinated by her the very first moment they met. Almost a school boy crush! Look but don't touch.

Now his mind turned back in time, picturing the beautiful face, oval and delicate, that had tempted him beyond human endurance. She wasn't the kind of woman that a man could easily ignore. And if she decided to capture a man's attention—that was the end.

Dan had come to Benjanda island at Gardia Benjen's request. That had been a calculated mistake. He knew something of the man's reputation: a shady fellow with questionable ties in South America. And, perhaps, not against murder, when necessary. Stories of violence and intrigue swarmed around the man. The authorities would be delighted

45

to capture him in their dragnets, only Gardia had remained way ahead of the law; what he couldn't bend he bought. Plus, few successful men, on either side of the law, had super clean reputations. Nobody was without fault; nobody without a charming, good side. Nobody was pure evil or pure saint. And this was true of Mr. Gardia. Not all of his business activities were below the belt, so to speak. Many of the things he was involved with were legit.

Dan had hoped for the best.

Maybe just some quick money, much needed, to do a small job, nothing illegal.

That's what his friend had implied when setting up the deal for him.

Thus, in his mind, it had been a simple enough business deal, channeled to him by a friendly contact. Maybe edging on the shady, but certainly nothing really down and dirty.

So he convinced himself before meeting the man in person.

Even then, after it was too late, he rationalized that it would not be something totally bad. The borderline between was a shadowy wasteland far broader than the outer, safe, limits. That darkly shaded place was where he had landed! Gardia had Dan clutched in his fat little pudgy fingers!

It was probably the way the man worked with everybody. Once in his clutches it might not be so easy to break away.

How could he have guessed. His friend, Eddy, had claimed there was nothing to worry about: "Just don't ask too many questions…and it'll get you out of your immediate bind."

And he was bound for cash flow. Really desperate. But that was not all that strange. He lived on a shoe-string. Hung by it, literally. His whole life had been a series of desperate moves to manage another day—to somehow survive. The only thing he owned was the boat *Marianne,* named after a woman he'd been in love with but lost through lack of action. That was a number of years back; but he had never forgotten her and how down right cowardice had caused him to back off when another man wanted him out of the way. She and the man had been killed in an auto accident a few months later. She'd been torn between her feelings for both him and the other guy. He backed off when the man threatened to kill him. And ever since been running from that fear and from that nightmare memory of what might have been.

Since then, Dan had lived pretty much on the edge. Without his boat he'd be next to a street bum. The *Marianne* was his means of survival. And without funds he could lose her! Ever since the terrorist threat had complicated matters, his own business had suffered. People weren't going out as much, and what "importing" business that might be offered was simply too dangerous. So when this offer came along he'd decided to bend his own personal, rigid rules and ask no questions about this job—otherwise his boat would be history, and without it he was a bum surviving in the streets.

He was that desperate! He'd been running all his life and now rushing blindly down a side alley into a place which was dark and dangerous. On the surface it all seemed innocent enough. A safe deal. But nothing was ever all that simple, that clean cut. There was always the underbelly.

He was to ship bananas to the mainland, with a little unidentified package that he guessed might be heroin, or worse, for a private party. Dan had never done anything illegal on that level. Most of his "jobs" included minor activities of taking people on Sunday outings. A couple of times in the past he helped to get people into the states who claimed they were in danger for their lives back home; he never knew for certain what happened to them—but had figured that was their business—and the government's. In the last few years, though, since 9/11, he'd avoided any such "human smuggling" as far too dangerous and downright "iffy."

The day he met Vicky Lopez, he was sipping a tall rum drink with Gardia, on the huge patio behind his host's rambling island plantation. At first he hadn't realized, exactly, what he was getting into. Not until a few moments before when the deal was spread out before him. He was angry with himself for having bought into this trap, and frustrated about the fact that it was too late to back out. He was now stuck in a deal which made him somewhat nervous. In fact, very nervous.

Gardia was relaxed in a massive bamboo chair which

was having difficulty containing his bulk. His beady little pig eyes snapped toward the house as the tall woman stepped out and moved toward them.

"Hi there, Vicky baby. Come on over. Meet a friend!" he called in his high, grating voice.

It took just one instant, one glance, and he was hooked, lined, and sunk completely: totally devoted to the pleasure of just staring. Every nerve fired to total alert. There was an overwhelming force to her body and movement that simply focused a man's mind on it—everything else vanished in her presence. She was a dark-haired girl with a creamy, darkly tanned skin. She glided gracefully over to the table and stood behind Gardia, but her eyes were searching Dan's. There was a half haunted expression in her stare, as if she were afraid of something and hoping to find some escape through him.

Dan found himself being suddenly overwhelmed by the raw ravishing beauty of her—the full, large red lips, wide dark brown eyes. But most of all her voluptuous curving fig-ure caught his attention. He simply couldn't get his eyes off the woman. And from the expression on her face it was ob-vious how much she enjoyed being stared at by a man. Even more so, she seemed to enjoy looking at Dan, as if she felt as drawn to him as he was to her. They continued to gaze into one another's eyes as if engaged in an invisible embrace. In a way they were almost touching one another in some magical sub-space. He had never experienced such a thing before in his life. Her gaze floated along his body like a very real ca-ress, firing the nerves to a peak of desire that was startling.

"This is the guy I was telling you about. He'll be staying a few days," Gardia announced, smiling. But there was a hard steely coldness to his voice which boldly revealed that he had noticed the prolonged look the two of them had ex-changed. "You know how I am. Got to get to know a new guy I'm doing business with…so treat him nice."

That last was not inviting anything but formal friendli-ness. Yet it was flavored with a subtle hint that Gardia knew exactly what effect she was having on Dan; and wanted to merely tease him with what could never be.

"Glad to meet you," Vicky greeted formally in a low rich voice. It was almost as if warm finger-tips had run down

48

his spine. "Hope you'll enjoy your stay."

The striking quality of her voice fitted perfectly with her lush figure.

That had been the first casual meeting, but it was enough to fire his attention and a natural hunger for her, a desire which was to develop in the next couple of days into a raging, overwhelming need. Every time she walked into the room it was stunning. And it was impossible to not stare, opening admiring and hungrily devouring the vision of her. A man couldn't look at her without wanting to possess that body, to literally ravish it in a fit of uncontrolled lust.

In the evenings he would sit in the bunk of the *Marianne,* thinking about her, delighting in the wishful dreams his mind conjured up.

He kept wondering what might happen if she were to come to him, slip onto the *Marianne* and make some kind of blatant offer to share a mutually desirable union on his bunk. Hell, he realized, just a hint and he'd be all over the woman, unable to control the animal urges to simply dive in and drown himself within her embrace.

Some women had that effect on some men.

She had it in spades over all of those female vamps, man-traps.

To possess her for only a few hours would be worth a lot to a man. Of course, he realized, any chance of that happening was part of fantasyland. Normal enough; just not real.

Even if she were to throw herself at him, he rationalized, *he was hardly foolish enough to chance crossing Gardia.*

Without a question his host was not the type of good-hearted fellow who shared his woman with all takers. Chance were he would kill any man who might touch her. It was one thing to admire her; that was flattering. Look, but don't touch.

Even thinking such thoughts might be dangerous!

He had to laugh at that last musing. Luckily nobody could read a man's thoughts. And if Gardia could, Dan's life would be cooked as fully as Vicky fired it with such wild fantasy dreams.

They saw each other every day, but nothing more had passed between them except sideward glances and polite conversation. Yet Dan was well aware that she knew how he felt about her. In fact, a woman like this would automatically find men easy to seduce.

In fact, he guessed she must have come out of the streets, into the saloons and finally through a series of circumstances into the arms of Gardia! She was his mistress—his total property. A literal golden prize to show off to the world as to his manly powers. Money. Power. Position. These elements easily over road all consideration of that gross body shape and nasty disposition. Gardia was a nasty package to deal with, if crossed; a delight if pleased and pampered.

No doubt the man could be charming, a delightful, generous host. He even, politely, at one point, offered a girl to keep Dan company—a temptation accepted the first night. And the young lady was certainly pretty, even if a bit plump. She came to him on the *Marianne* shortly after he'd returned to the boat. Without a word she simply took off her blouse and skirt, presenting a totally naked body in the dim moonlight for him to enjoy. She was very casual and direct, coming into his arms, helping him undress. Then they slipped onto his bunk while she began to draw him to the fullness of her body. Right from the start she was all over him, giggling with joyful pleasure and delight as he quickly responded to her kisses. Throughout it all, he mentally held Vicky Lopez in his mind, ravishing her imaginary body. It was over rather fast. Afterwards the woman indicated a willingness to spend the night, but he wasn't interested. He politely thanked her and watched as she dressed and left as casually as she had come.

Gardia, at least, would not be insulted by a turn down of his gift of the woman. The man had an ego; and it was rather polite to at least accept his gifts—not refuse them outright.

The man bought what he wanted and shared some of it; laughed easily and obviously enjoyed the good things in life. Especially his paid for mistress; which he didn't share.

Vicky Lopez was obviously skilled at pampering a man's ego as well as his body. And she was being paid in spaces; a luxury life as the man's personal trophy.

And Dan couldn't keep from imaging what it must be

like to hold her, to caress her, to smother himself against her, to literally feast upon all of that woman's lush body.

So, he spent the next nights alone, imagining, helplessly enveloped in a desire which could never be fulfilled. And during the days when he saw her, his desire deepened to such a hurting level that he would once again find it impossible to avoid the fantasy of holding her in his arms when he was alone on the *Marianne*.

It was not until this last evening that the fantasy began its trip down nightmare lane.

Just before the tropic sun had set against the orange-red horizon, Vicky had approached him directly and privately on his small cargo boat.

A dream coming true in such a starkly startling manner that he could only ride along with the overwhelming power of it. Reason had nothing to do with action. He was on automatic shock from the moment she found him.

Dan was resting in the bunk, trying not to think about the fact that this evening he would be leaving Benjanda island and would probably never see Vicky again. He knew that her vision would continue to plague his thoughts for a very long time. In Hollywood she would have been offered up on the screen as some Goddess of Love to cash in on the male fantasy for such a perfect woman! Well, that was his inner most feelings—overwhelming hunger. He was almost devouring a whiskey and water, in an attempt to avoid the natural hunger she inspired when he heard the soft approach of feet walking along the wooden dock, then clamoring on the boat.

He quickly rose and stepped out onto the deck, thinking that maybe it was one of the native boys or a messenger from Gardia. He hadn't expected to find Vicky standing there.

She was dressed in a flaring red skirt and loose fitting white blouse that did nothing to hide the curving shape beneath them. Her dark hair was flowing gracefully over her half bare shoulders. For a moment she stood there without expression. Then her lips turned up at the corners in a bright friendly smile. But she didn't say anything. The woman didn't need to speak to say everything all at once. She was aware of her powerful effect on men, and confident in her effect on him.

"Well, what can I do for you?" Dan asked, his eyes moving along her figure, pausing at the low neckline of her blouse. Then he was mentally caressing her all over, and hating himself for the school-boy crush. It was so pitifully obvious what he wanted, how much he desired her, how helpless he was in her presence. The words flowed automatically from his lips, yet hid nothing of his harsh desire. He might as well be stammering, stuttering.

She hesitated and then murmured in a soft, frightened voice, "I have to talk to you."

Her eyes dropped slightly. "Could you give me a drink, first?"

That stunned him to a new level of reality. There was something going on beyond a mutual sexual flirtation or even a mere erotic tease. Instantly his mind turned to a new alert level, calculating, wondering, suddenly aware that Vicky would not be on his little floating home for some seductive purpose. Fantasy was one thing, but this was hard reality.

That they were both aware of his blatant interest in her on a sexual level was one thing; but this reality before him was totally different, involving something beyond male/female attraction.

The mood didn't change so much as shifted to a more reality based level. The two elements interlocked, embraced, while totally aware of each other. She knew he wanted her, and there was something she wanted from him.

The implications were stunning and his mind was numbed on one level while working on automatic.

Dan led her to the small cabin and picked up the bottle of whiskey from under the bunk. "You don't mind? No glass."

Vicky shrugged her shoulders, causing the fabric of her blouse to shift. Then she gratefully took the bottle and gulped from it. There was a desperation and nervousness about her actions which suddenly fed into his own confused thoughts.

Maybe there was something serious about to happen, having nothing at all to do with fantasy dreams of possessing this woman. In fact, reality suggested something totally alien to sexual fantasy.

Reality shocked his mind.

They were two strangers and suddenly in an odd situation.

After a moment her eyes turned to Dan. There was a desperate, fearful expression burning in them. "Can you take me off the island? Let me go with you tonight?"

For a moment Dan hadn't been able to grasp the full implication of what she requested. He just sat there, stunned. The idea of being out to sea with Vicky, alone together, where nobody could possibly know what happened was just about too much to think possible. They could relate on any level, and would, perhaps, actually become involved intimately. That idea alone was just down right overwhelming. And not about to take place in his life-time. For sure. Or would it? What kind of game was she playing? Was it some kind of trap? Or was she seriously needing his help?

God, she's beautiful. I'd give an arm and leg and much more to have her just for one night!

That was school boy crap and Dan knew it.

"Why?" he finally managed to ask, his mind slowly coming out of the freeze her words settled over it.

"I have to get away from Gardia. I've tried before—but he stopped me. You don't know what kind of man he is. You're the first person to come here for a long time. Please help me. He's a madman!"

"What makes you think I won't just go to him and tell him all that's just happened?" Dan asked, hiding the choking fear knotting a lump in his throat. "What makes you think I'd—?"

"A woman gets to know something about men— sometimes. I've seen how you look at me."

"Hey, don't start—"

She smiled, a knowing, confident smile, then shrugged: "I'm desperate! And, anyway, I'm beyond the point of being careful. And I know you find me...well, bluntly put: desirable! Most men do. I know that. Sometimes it is nice. Sometimes it is annoying. With you...well, it is quite nice. But anything I'd say along those lines, would sound like a come-on, just to get you to help me. I don't think that's required, or fair. Sure. I know how men are. I know how to turn a man around my fingers, if necessary. But sometimes it is best to be blunt. Honest. And simply play the game out as fair as possible. I won't just play you!"

"You're more than just...well...you're right! Any man would look at you and want you, and that's the danger!" Dan stated simply.

"They do. Believe me. I'm used to it. But I won't play you, Dan. It wouldn't be fair. In fact, that'd be like taking candy from a baby!"

The very generous and honest smile she gave him with those words caused Dan to grin, relax a little. She was quite right about how easy she could make a man crumble in to her arms.

But he knew Gardia's reputation much too well to attempt to get involved with the man's property. And Gardia's mistress was property—much too personal.

Fantasy was one thing; harsh reality another.

"So don't make too much of all that!" he added, trying to keep his eyes away from her body.

It was rumored that Gardia had killed several men in the past—with his bare hands. Cold sweat trickled over Dan's body just at the thought of what could happen if Gardia even knew that Vicky was with him right at that moment.

"He'd kill me!" Dan blurted. "You know that."

Vicky stared blandly at Dan for a moment and then put the bottle to her full lips and swallowed several gulps of raw whiskey.

"Yes. He would! But...please," she pleaded a moment later. "I can't stand it any more. He's a terrible man!"

"How'd you get mixed up with him in the first place?"

"It's a long story; it boils down to this: I was a girl just struggling for survival in a cheap bar, hardly making enough to get along. He came in and spread money wild. When he showed interest, well, I thought that anything would be better than—than what I was doing at the time. So I let him take me to his hotel rooms. I know it's not a nice story to be telling, but a girl will do stupid things. And, quite frankly, he wasn't the first man to want, nor take me.

54

"The end result was that I came to the island with him, not knowing what kind of brute he really was. I found out later. Now—I'm a prisoner!"

Dan felt a gnawing fear grind through him. He couldn't help feeling sorry for this woman, but it wasn't enough to make him do what she was requesting.

"I'm sorry," he said. "I can't help you!"

For a moment Vicky stared blankly at him, then her voice choked out, low and frantic. "I'll do anything you want! Damn it. Anything! Just, please, help me! I know what I'm asking. I'll make it worth it to you!"

She looked down at him as if promising paradise in her arms. That was illusion, yet there was no doubt about the woman's confidence in her ability to please a man in any way he might desire.

There was no need for her to say more. Dan knew he could possess her in exchange for passage to the mainland, and the thought caused a mixture of emotions to whip through him. He was torn between excitement and terror. Most of all, frustrated by the hard business deal being offered. He could have her at a price. But was that what he wanted? Just her body as payment? Was she required to desire him as much as he hungered for her?

All, silly school kid musings.

Vicky knew the danger she might be putting him in, and was offering the biggest payoff she could give: her body. And certainly for longer than just one fantasy-filled night of lustful passion in her arms. Maybe a prolonged arrangement, even an affair. At least longer than a one night session. It would take a bit of time to get back to the states, away from Gardia. And that meant being together with this woman fulfilling every possible fantasy his mind could conceive. And, who knew, maybe lost at sea could be a wonderful way to keep things going day after day. Maybe even find some little known island to escape to, living together, safe from the outside world—safe from Gardia's men who would certainly be searching for them.

His guts tightened and his eyes closed against the heat which throbbed through him at the very thought of what she was offering. It was too tempting. If he hadn't been a damned coward all his life, avoiding physical danger, he would have quickly taken her offer. He closed his eyes even tighter.

Dan felt the movement on the bunk even before he heard the rustling sound. He didn't have to open his eyes to know what Vicky was doing.

The movement continued for a minute and then the bunk was quiet and still.

He sat as if frozen, afraid to open his eyes and look at her, yet at the same time desperately wanting to. Sweat poured freely from under his arms, and he found it impossible to keep his hands from shaking. He didn't know whether it was a result of desire or of fear. Probably both. It was an insane situation; and the woman could hardly be in a well-balanced frame of mine to be offering her body for the price of escape...from an obvious hell. Gardia's mistress was not about to give in easily to his refusal.

This was a moment where he could cross an invisible line, beyond which death certainly threatened to drive him into a deep, watery grave. All for a moment of unlimited passion in the arms of a lovely lady.

This was fantasyland; and he was frightened to bring it into reality.

Yet he driving hunger to simply look at her was throbbing at his whole body. Looking certainly wasn't a sin! Just looking and wanting was a normal act of a normal man.

Finally he couldn't keep his eyes closed any longer. The tension and the sure knowledge that he couldn't sit there forever waiting for her to disappear, caused him to open them.

Facing the reality was better than wishing it away.

Vicky was sitting nearby, wearing only her thin panties. The hard lump in his throat ached and then moved into an even tighter knot as he attempted vainly to swallow it away.

Nervously he wiped the sweat from his forehead with a trembling hand, as his eyes focused on the full, smooth roundness of Vicky's body. Dan had never seen such a magnificent woman, such a beautiful figure. He felt the throb of his temples hammering frantically, sending waves of heat throughout his body like tides of molten lava.

"Anything," she breathed, reaching her arms out to Dan.

Her lips parted; the tip of her tongue moistened their red surface to a silky brightness.

She was so beautiful, a goddess offering herself to a mere mortal human male, who was helpless against her seductive powers. And she knew it.

For a moment Dan thought he might be able to resist her brazen offer. But her fingertips caressed his forearm, urging him into her arms, and his willpower cracked and crumbled.

He found himself sweeping her towards him, crushing her close. Their lips met, warm and moist. Pleasure ripped aside the last edge of fear, leaving raw abandon to take control of his body and thoughts.

Her hands caressed over him like fiery waves, opening such fury that he could not control anything that followed. His own lips discovered her breasts and he literally smothered himself against them, unable to do less than be enveloped by this lovely feast, this soft, yielding warmth that flowed all around him. Her fingers and finally her soft, moist lips searched over him with greedy hunger. She literally played on every nerve, creating a fiery desire so intense that he simply found himself flowing on a rich sea of sensation. He was aware of being enveloped by her in such a manner that it felt as if she had swallowed his whole being within her embrace. It was a wild, yet amazingly prolonged ride of ecstatic pleasure bathing over him again and again, almost reaching a peak, only to be gently soothed back simply to flow again towards a new peak. It was like riding the crest of a magnificent wave, racing towards the sandy beach miles away. She literally drown him within her voluptuous embraces until he was aware of nothing beyond those sensations her body so generously offered.

Time had seemed to stand still as they continued to embrace, locked in one another's arms as true lovers will after having totally satisfied their mutual need. There was something amazingly real about the woman's reaction to him. It seemed as if she had actually cared, enjoyed. He slowly became aware of the fact that her moans and sobs of pleasure had certainly been real. No woman could fake it that well. Or if they could, it didn't matter, for it had sounded as real as her body had been real in those lush moments in shared ecstasy.

Neither of them said anything for a long time. It was Vicky who broke the silence after sitting up and gazing down at him.

"I didn't know it would be like that. I've known a lot of men—" She broke off because her voice had become a raw rasp.

"I don't want you to think I'm...conning you...just believe what we experienced was real..."

He merely nodded, unable to speak at that moment. He was literally overwhelmed. It hardly mattered what she had said; only what she had done so totally to him. If given a chance he would want to rediscover those pleasures. He was totally helpless to her will. No man could turn down such an offer—such a woman.

Then, after a moment's hesitation, she asked: "You'll take me, then?"

Dan didn't have time to think that out. His gut was sick, but he said: "After that, you know damned well I will!"

There was defeated bitterness in his voice which he didn't even attempt to hide. "I'm being a damned fool, but... you're really something!"

She smiled knowingly, said: "And I might be playing you for a fool. I know...but I promised you. I won't play you. We can be together as long as you want. Or you can kick me out! But please, just get me away from here!"

He nodded, realizing what her words truly meant. The woman would do what she promised. The idea of possessing her, even for a week, was maybe worth it. Maybe or maybe not didn't matter; he was unable to even consider changing course—they were beyond that choice.

Maybe nobody could really imagine their own death really taking place; that kind of thing happened to others.

Maybe it simply was a fact that nobody could resist nor avoid their destiny. And, apparently his destiny had been locked the moment he saw this woman. If they could get out of there alive they would be together, for at least a while. By now it was too late to back down. The moment she had come into his arms the future was fused into reality. He could no more escape what must take place in the next hours than he could wash away the delicious memory of what the two of them had just shared.

He decided, saying: "We can leave right away! Before Gardia has a chance to find out—"

"No!" Vicky broke in, heatedly. "I have to get a few things first. I'll be damned if I'll leave without something to show for these rotten eight months! And I'll pay you... good...for your help! Hard cash! All this other stuff...what we just did...is not part of the deal; it is simply what happens between two people who can enjoy one another like that."

He stared at her, actually believing the woman's words. "How long will you be?"

"It'll only take about fifteen minutes—but give me half an hour!" Vicky gathered her clothing and began to dress.

She was gone in a few minutes, leaving him alone to think out the possible results of what they were doing. If Gardia found out, neither of them would leave the island alive.

He was emotionally riding a roller coaster, from ecstatic joy, amazement, at what had happened and what might certainly take place in the days to follow. Failure meant death. Why was any woman worth that kind of price tag? It really didn't matter, now, for events had taken place which made it impossible to back away from the obvious danger that Gardia might very easily crush down upon them. Death would be his simple answer. What kind of death might be another matter. The pleasure might be matched to the pain the man would inflict on him and on his mistress. Gardia was certainly not beyond enjoying revenge to the fullest. A slow, painful death would certainly be prime in the man's mind.

Dan had heard rumors as to what Gardia was able to do to those he wanted to make a lesson of—brutalizing death, slow, lingering torture.

Whimpering death at the hands of a madman.

Such thought tormented his mind, alternating with the total pleasure of the memory of being so completely enveloped in Vicky's arms.

Thirty minutes passed without Vicky returning. Dan had prepared for a quick escape and had been thoughtful enough to arm himself with the little .38 which he kept in his cabin.

It was a weapon he hadn't used once since he'd gotten it, more than a year before. The gun had been merely a psychological boost to his cowardly nerves. He hadn't ever really planned on using it. In fact; he'd always been a little afraid of guns.

The thing that didn't hold with his fears about violence and death was the fact that he'd managed to get in a tough dangerous business, jockeying questionable cargo for questionable people like Gardia. But his love for the sea, and his lazy personality that didn't like to work and desired easy money, had pushed him into his "profession". Up to this point he hadn't been so deeply involved in dangerous cargo. Now it had all caught up with him, as he'd been sure it would someday. But like most people he'd told himself that things like this would never happen, except to other people.

All that was over now.

Dan had become worried about Vicky and decided to return to the bungalow.

Stepping onto the dock and walking across it and into the surrounding trees, he had just found cover when the sound of footsteps brought him to a stop. Only caution had caused him to wait to be sure it was Vicky. Then he heard the rough voices of men.

"...said to bring him back to the bungalow alive. Gardia wants to be doing a personal job on Mr. Carson!"

"Sure, sure. But he don't say nothin' 'bout not messing him up a bit, first!"

"A mere warm up for what he'll enjoy once the boss gets started. Screaming death! Stud-man screwin' Vicky— how stupid can you get?"

There was a thick laugh, then the voices faded out as footsteps clomped onto the wooden dock.

For a moment Dan had stood there, realizing that his world had shattered down over him. It was crushing with such force that all he could do was shake in reaction. His first thought was to run, get the hell out of there. But he couldn't return to the *Marianne* at this point. Those two men were heading in that direction. He would have to kill them. And he had never killed a man in his life. Plus, could he really leave Vicky to her fate?

60

Finally his feet were moving frantically. It wasn't until he came to a stop at the clearing outside of Gardia's huge home that he realized where he had headed.

Ice formed in his spine and slowly worked its way over his whole body. He had come to somehow get Vicky away from Gardia. He realized he had a good chance against one unarmed man. It wouldn't be hard to bluff, because Gardia wouldn't know that he was unsure of his ability to use the gun.

Dan started across the clearing. A shout stopped him.

The two men had started to return to the bungalow the moment they discovered him missing from the *Marianne*. He ran, seeking out a hiding place.

Now he was shivering in the doorway of the back entrance to Gardia's home, afraid to move either into the house or out to face the men searching for him. It would only be a matter of a short time before they would find him. That much he was well aware of. Yet his fear caused Dan to stand there, unmoving, wanting to drag the final moments of his life out for as long as possible.

Suddenly Dan thawed out of his frozen terror, realizing that no matter how long he waited he was going to have to face the terrible climax one time or another in the next few minutes. The longer he waited, the smaller his own chances were of seeing the next day. His best bet was to attack—go into the house and find Vicky and whoever was with her.

Dan tightened his gut and slowly, quietly turned around in the doorway. His hand reached out and gripped the doorknob. It twisted under his grasp.

Carefully he pushed inward, then took several silent steps and swung the door closed. He stood in the back porch listening for the sound of voices.

The bungalow was large, spread out over more than twenty rooms.

Everything was silent for several moments, then he heard Gardia's voice growl in the distance. There was a snapping sound, as of wood breaking or a face being slapped. Dan guessed the latter.

He forced himself to accept that, because the thought of a man like Gardia hitting Vicky burned away some of the fear and replaced it with smoldering anger. He listened harder for a moment, as Gardia's voice became louder.

"...and don't think you get away with it! I'll fix you good!" Another snap, followed by a light moan.

Red vengeful haze spurted over Dan's vision. As it cleared away he found himself rushing into a brightly lighted room.

Vicky was bound tightly to a chair, her face battered and streaked with blood. Dark bruises were beginning to form.

Gardia stood over her like a brute animal, his face distorted with rage. A low moan hissed from his thick lips as he swung his beefy hand toward the woman's terrified face.

"I wouldn't do that if I were you!" Dan warned in a tight voice, finding himself leaping forward. His hand whipped around Gardia's twisting the huge man around. His other hand was balled up around the .38, ramming it violently into that huge mountainous gut.

A terrible sound burst from Gardia's mouth and for a moment he stood there, looking raw hatred into Dan's eyes. Neither of them moved. The sheer anger which had surged through Dan was slipping away as he saw the minor effect his attack had created. This was the first time he had ever really gotten involved in personal violence, and the man he had come after was a murderous mountain of steel muscle.

Gardia's lips twisted thin and his body arched slightly forward.

"You should have killed me!" he growled, stepping toward Dan.

"Freeze!" Dan cried, pointing the .38.

"You won't use that, Danny baby. A man of action in your position would have killed me already!" The grin widened and his beady eyes seemed to gleam savagely as he lunged forward like a charging bull.

Dan swung a fist at Gardia's face. The blow was glancing and had little effect. Frantically he attempted to avoid the other's hammer-like fist. For a moment he thought he had it made, then steel bone and flesh sledged his face.

Dan felt himself being shoved backward. He stumbled over a chair and a second sledge smashed his nose with a sickening sound of gristle and bone breaking. He felt the

62

moist ooze of blood fill the hollow of his nose as a third blow whipped against his stomach.

Red haze blinded Dan as he doubled over. Nausea ripped up from his gut, spitting vomit and blood over his lips, choking the air like a clamping hand had rammed down his throat. Blackness closed sharply around him as another last hammering blow broke down on the back of his neck.

He smashed to the floor and complete dark escape closed in.

The coming out of it was slow pain, for with consciousness was a returning of the terrible fear which had been like ice when he was standing outside the bungalow.

He knew that now he would be killed.

It was that fear which kept him from moving. He lay there, listening, afraid to let the others know he wasn't still unconscious.

Gardia was talking. "…as for the woman, I can take care of her." He laughed, then continued. "But first let's let her see what happens to this hero of hers. And remember, Vicky baby, you were responsible for his death—and the agony he will enjoy in dying. You can live with that!"

"You goddamned son-of-a-bitch bastard!" Vicky cursed, spitting out the words with all the hatred and violence that her voice could generate. "Let him go. It was my fault. I'll stay with you as long as you want—willingly."

Gardia laughed. "You'll stay as long as I want, anyway. And willingly, too, if you don't want to have your face battered every day to make you willing!" He paused and then said in a strangely tight voice: "He was that good, huh?"

"You're damned right, you fat pig!"

There was the sound of a stinging blow slapping across a naked face. Vicky moaned and then let out a cursing string of words in two languages. Gardia's hand slapped out again and again until her voice faded into silence.

"That's better!" he told her.

Dan was fighting with the terror tightening his gut and the anger whipping through his mind. His eyes opened slightly and viewed the room.

There were three other men standing around the chair which Vicky was bound to. They were grinning down at the battered face of the woman.

Then Dan's eyes spotted something black and ugly, small and deadly, within a few inches of his outstretched hand on the floor. It was his .38.

This is your only chance! he thought desperately. *Take it, or die!*

Just as he was moving his fingers toward the weapon, Gardia started to turn in his direction. Frantically he scrambled for the gun. His fingers grasped it at the same instant that the fat giant spotted him.

Dan leaped to his feet and faced the four men, pointing the gun, swinging it back and forth to cover each one.

"He won't use it!" Gardia announced. "Go take him!"

"Don't move, any of you!" Dan ordered, tightening his grip on the .38. "I mean it this time!"

"He talks too much to act!" Gardia leered at him. "Come on, hero baby. Why not pull the trigger? That's your only passage out of here. All you gotta do is squeeze. Kill me and they won't do anything to you. You'll be free—free to take Vicky. You can have the slut! That's what you want, isn't it? To possess her body every night, every moment of every day. All you have to do is kill me!"

Gardia was walking forward slowly, his face split wide with a challenging grin. He was supremely confident that Dan wouldn't fire.

"Come on—what's keeping you! Kill me and you're a free man! And you get the woman as a booby prize!"

The others were following behind their boss, grinning knowingly.

Dan took a step back, unsure of himself. He knew that Gardia was telling the truth. His only chance to save himself was to use the weapon in his hand. They planned to kill him, slowly, painfully. He knew that he didn't have a chance against even Gardia, alone. Even if he did, it would be impossible to take the other men.

"Use it, Dan!" Vicky shouted. "Kill the bastard!"

Dan's eyes flicked in her direction, took in the puffy broken flesh of her face where Gardia's hand had worked it over. His fingers instinctively pointed the gun in the fat man's direction.

"Come on, Danny boy. Come on. Can't you do it?" Gardia snarled. Then a change in the man's expression showed that he had tired suddenly of the little game.

"Come on. Let's get him!" He rushed forward.

Dan wanted to run, but knew that there wasn't any place to run to. This was the moment of final decision. He either killed or was killed. His finger squeezed on the trigger and then froze.

Gardia was reaching out for him with huge thick hands, the fingers curled inward.

The .38 exploded. Red flame spurted out, burning into Gardia's gut. The man's face took on an expression of intense surprise. His eyes widened and rolled up into their sockets, showing only whiteness as a red splotch spread at the center of his stomach. A sputtering sound bubbled from his suddenly pale lips. Dan squeezed the trigger again, feeling a grim satisfaction.

Gardia staggered and then for a moment stood frozen, his hands clamped to his chest where the second bullet had entered. Then slowly he began to lean forward like a huge redwood which is about to fall.

Dan pulled the trigger once more and watched as the man jerked backwards, twisted and then toppled to the floor.

The other three men stood, staring in dumb shock. Their eyes were wide in terror as they looked at the dead form on the floor.

"Get the hell out of here!" Dan cursed, motioning with the gun.

They didn't wait for him to say or do more. All three turned and moved from the room, leaving Dan alone with Vicky.

* * * * * * *

The open sea was like a cool tropic drink to Dan's lungs. The past couple of weeks had been a healing time. Both he and Vicky had needed hospitalization. But now things were better. The police had taken their reports on the death of Gardia Benjen in the hospital with an obvious sense of relief. The man had been a problem; now resolved. Vicky had a

65

nice bundle of cash and jewels which would keep her quite comfortable for some time. Now they were on their way home, and freedom at last.

The events which had taken place on the island had changed his life dramatically, shifting his whole future. He knew that even for a life of ease there was a price which one had to pay sooner or later. His had come soon enough to bring an end to it before it was too late.

Dan placed an arm around Vicky Lopez, pulling her closer to him as he guided the wheel of the *Marianne.*

"I never knew I'd find a man like you," she murmured contentedly, "I mean it. Somebody who really cared enough to…kill for me. Somebody I could really care about."

He remained quiet, but thought: he'd never known what kind of a man he really was, until meeting Vicky Lopez.

His eyes gazed at the thin line of the mainland edging the horizon. In less than an hour he would be in his small room; then he could show her what she had come to mean to him.

A thin smile spread across his lips as he dropped his eyes to look at his woman. She had been worth becoming a man for. And every day he possessed her would be a bonus. If it lasted a day, a week, a month, or years, it would be wonderful! Somehow he figured it would last well beyond his greatest fantasy.

Having lived in Hollywood and actually worked in the "Industry" and even toyed around the fringes of show business before becoming a writer, I did a number of stories and novels dealing with "behind the scenes" look at the town, plus doing a fact book, Hollywood Mysteries *(also available from Wildside Press). But this little story simply told of one lady known as...*

⊸THE WITCH OF HOLLYWOOD⊱

I'd heard a lot about Miss Lois-jean Lee Belle ever since I'd gotten to Hollywood. Behind her back everybody called her the "witch of Hollywood." Beyond that the only thing I knew about her before we met, was that if she took a liking to a person she could open doors to success; she was powerful enough in Hollywood circles to take a "nobody" and turn them into a big name star. Being producer and director and hiring and firing expert for one of the major studios, she had what it took to get their career on the fast track.

Of course the price tag could be pretty much the same as young women had paid on the casting couch throughout the history of Hollywood. In this case, of course, the cushion was turned upside down. Actually nothing new, really; an endless power game popular throughout the business world, even *if* hidden and outright illegal.

The idea of catering to her demand for a quickie on the casting couch literally turned my stomach. Not only wasn't she my type, but, in fact, hardly anybody's type. And she used her power to get favors on demand.

Maybe that was why she called *The Witch of Hollywood!*

I had always liked the tall slinky woman who has to be squeezed into one of those low cut skin tight evening dresses. And that was the kind of woman I was escorting that first night I met Miss Lee Belle at a cocktail party given by one of Hollywood's biggest stars—to remain nameless for obvious reasons.

At that time I was going under my real name, Jack O'Dell. It wasn't very original, like the one which the studios finally picked for me, but it was the one given me by my dear parents, who in their elder innocence believed that farming might be a more substantial way for their son to make a living than going off to Hollywood with the wide eyed hopeful dream of a future in big lights, and large bank accounts—to say nothing about the beautiful women. After all there are a lot of perks, even for a struggling young actor with few legit contacts.

Dora Milton was the name of the girl I was out with that evening. She was one of those starlets the boys around Hollywood call girls. A tall, well-built blonde, with a bright smile and even white teeth. The kind of looks that any man would like to have accompanying him on any date where a beautiful girl is something worth showing off. And the kind who found it necessary to be pleasant to any number of men offering parts. So she surely knew the rules of the game.

This was one of those times when a large party offers chances to score with big time producers. A dozen smaller ones. Name directors. Stars. Extras. Bit players. Starlets displayed their charms and plenty of booze was flowing to liven up the otherwise stilted atmosphere of small names trying to get a chance to say "hello" to big names. And, of course, there were the many nobodies, acting important, so that they could get some struggling starlet in bed for the night.

Me. Well, I had Dora. We had just met, but sparks were instantly alive and flying. We just kinda had lust as first sight. And we both had a hankering to be together all night, later on. That was obvious from the moment our mutual agent, Eddy Landrum, had gathered us up in his car earlier and brought us here.

He was now playing the scene for me.

As it turned out, Lois-jean Lee Belle unexpectedly showed up and she became his instant prime target. She was a woman who must have been old-looking at twenty. At forty-five she looked old enough to be somebody's grandmother, who had enough money to go to the proper hair dressers and dress shops in an effort to make herself seem to be younger than she actually appeared. But all that did little to improve on a basically tired body that never was much to begin with.

But Miss Lee Belle had other traits which outstripped the most beautiful women at the party. She had what most struggling actors, writers, starlets and artists called "null." Which meant that when she said "jump" there were a lot of people willing to do just that and as high as it was necessary to impress her. If she did a thumbs down, that was "null"—a career stall!

At the moment, I was occupied with my delightful Dora and a couple of martinis, in a more quiet corner of a dimly lighted portion of the patio, which stretched out into a long darkness beyond the circle of light coming from the house. This was a neat place to do a little pre-fooling around, those lingering touches, light conversational flirtation and even some rather moist kissing.

Actually, I was more concerned with the girl than I was with the drinks. The cocktail glasses were neatly placed on a small table. My full attention settled basically on pawing Dora as a preamble to what we both figured would be a nice backup—a desired all-night intimacy. The way things were developing it seemed we'd be "heading out" sooner than later. Neither of us were much interested in playing the Career Game that night.

She had just about the silkiest lips I'd ever had the pleasure of caressing with mine. She pressed closer. "Why haven't we met before, my tall, dark, handsome escort?"

Her fingers worked playfully through my hair.

"Well, all I can say is that these casting agents have the most delightful way of arranging dates and getting the right people together. Now don't they?"

She agreed, laughingly, and then kissed me again. It was sheer delight.

In the condition the two of us were in we might not have stayed at the party any longer if my agent, Eddy, hadn't come storming up, just as we began to stand.

"So, *there* you are!" he cried in relief. "I've been trying to find you...all over the place!"

I smiled helplessly, looking into Dora's beautiful blue

69

eyes, and then turned to Eddy. "Okay, what's the pitch?"

"It's taken me all evening to arrange to get Miss Lee Belle interested in talking to you. About the part in...you know *what* movie!"

I felt my heart open wide with excitement. Everything changed. This was what we had been hoping for. But not quite so soon. My real *big* break! One word from her and a contract would be on my agent's desk. On the other hand, a different word from the lady could do real damage to any person's career plans.

"I didn't know that she was here, or I'd have had you come stag," Eddy said, turning toward Dora. "I'm sorry, but he'll be busy. I'll play escort, maybe even hook you up to something!"

"How do you like that? He sets me up with one of the most beautiful, desirable women I've ever met and then he wants to take her away from me!" I cried, half in jest and partly in real disappointed frustration. But, of course, business before pleasure.

"She'll be here when you get back," Eddy assured me.

Dora smiled frozenly at him. But she didn't say anything.

"I'm sorry, Dora," I said, affectionately squeezing her hand.

She returned the embrace. "I know the ropes. Business is business." Her voice was genuinely sad sounding, even though her lips were still smiling.

Giving Eddy the high sign, I pulled Dora off to one side. "Look, this isn't the way I usually like to operate. I know we just met. An all that. And I know—"

"Tonight I was supposed to be window dressing. We both know that."

"Well, yes, damn. But things are moving very fast!"

She stopped me with a finger on my lips. "Just give me your address. Your key; and I'll be waiting."

That's the kind of woman a man likes! Adult. Realistic. No false pride. We had connected and she wanted to keep things going in a very warm, friendly manner, where ever it might take us.

Also, I realized, she was playing both ends against the

middle, and she was the middle! If I might be up for an important part, then it would be good to play me; she didn't know where it might help her career. And that's where us men make out big.

I kissed Dora on the cheek, and Eddy and I left the patio. A moment later we were approaching a small group of people. Eddy whispered in my ear. "Play up to this woman. She can do you a lot of good. If she likes you, *you're in! And like Flynn, if necessary!"*

I mentally jotted that down. From what I knew of Eddy, he was talking about doing anything she wanted. Up to, and including, taking her to bed. And treating her like a Goddess of Love.

That sounded like a nice deal—and at the same time a funny situation. Men had always played the casting couch game with all the lovely young, innocent women who came to town with stars in their eyes. It had always been part of the Hollywood scene. Not much different from any other business—only just a bit more visible. But it could be played the other way around, too. Men might be offered a gay couch to service for rewards unknown. At least this contact was a female casting coucher. But why would some big-time broad be wanting to shack up with a nobody like myself?

Then I saw Miss Lois-jean Lee Belle, and I realized why she was such an easy mark.

Tall. Kinda lumpy. What shape she had in front looked like dried, sagging prunes; and they were readily displayed in the low cut of her black evening dress.

I tried to smile; it was probably the best bit of acting I'd done up to that time.

Eddy managed to push his way through the small crowd which had gathered around Miss Lee Belle, and quickly introduced us.

She gave that long, careful look a woman will give a man about whom she is trying to size up. In this case: was she interested or not. I suddenly felt like a piece of meat in a deli sausage rack. The woman's calculating eyes were gazing right into mine, not anyway near my waistline.

I almost hoped she would turn me down on first sight. In fact, I did my best to make the smile look frozen and forced.

Her eyes paused at my tightly pressed lips, then moved back up to my eyes.

"So you're the young fellow that Eddy here has been burning my ear off about."

I just shrugged.

Eddy, out of sight of Miss Lee Belle, made a few frightening faces at me. I ignored him.

For one glorious moment I actually thought she was going to bring our relationship to a quick close. She opened her thin lips and said, "Okay, darlings, you can all shoo-bye, now. I want to be alone with Mr. O'Dell."

I was stuck. And stunned.

She reached for my arm and pulled it under hers. I could feel the repulsive pressure of her breast as she let my hand slide slightly into it.

"You look like a nice boy," she observed, leading me across the room. "I want to get someplace where we can talk. Get to know one another. Alone. Our host has a private office which I think we can use."

My heart caught in my throat. I felt like I was going to a funeral. Slightly yucky, and somewhat depressed.

"You don't mind if I call you Jack, do you?" she inquired. Maybe it was my imagination, but it seemed as if she pressed closer to me. "You can call me Jean.... Yes, just call me Jean. I think I'd like that."

I might have come from the country, originally, but there wasn't any of the hayseed, wide-eyed innocence about me—not any more. I'd brought the dumb hick to Hollywood along with my childish dreams of quick success. And then I let that creature simply die! It had been a frustrating three years climbing to this level. If I played things right, tonight, I had a chance of making a big leap onto the screen in a prime part that could really get my career into action. I simply had to play her and do whatever she wanted. If I walked out on this connection Eddy would be really pissed. And it was a good chance he'd dump me!

"Well, now, let's get acquainted a bit," she suggested, leading me over to one of the sofas, having already closed the door behind her when we entered the room. I had heard a small click as if a bolt had slipped into place, soft, but so loud it sounded like a crash of doom.

I felt that hot hard knot searching through my insides, trying to find a place to locate itself. Sweat was beginning to soak the shirt under my armpits. I felt light headed and slightly feverish.

Suddenly my mind was screaming, *Is this how it feels to those lovely young girls selling themselves body and soul to old fat men, or shriveled power execs? Cheap, whorish.*

She sat down, placing an arm around the back of the sofa, the spot where she expected me to sit. I sat, trying to swallow the lumpy tightness in my throat.

"Well, Jack, tell me: how long have you been in Hollywood? Eddy said a few things, but I want it from your own lips. A person reveal a lot by the way they talk about themselves."

Her free hand reached out, expecting me to take it. The flesh was a bit hot, but she gently urged me down next to her.

I'd been knocking around for too long a time, now; it wasn't until Eddy took me over that anything at all had happened in the way of getting jobs. A few bit parts, then a small supporting role in a Z-grade movie had followed. This was the next big step he had planned out for me. And though I knew I couldn't really let him down, I wasn't quite sure I'd be able deal with Jean the Mean—as I began thinking of her. Mean, demanding old hag. Of course, so far, she'd been remarkably polite, smooth and hardly seemed to notice my body, which most women always admired. I worked out hard and had a lean frame with the kind of hard muscles that caused one woman to say: "Oh, gosh, you're so hard all over." With the right woman that was cute. Actually rather exciting and erotic.

I was glad that, so far, this Jean of the Bells hadn't demanded, yet, that I start ringing them full trot. But that, certainly was coming; that's why she had brought me to this room; that was the purpose of our meeting here and now. And that's why I was sweating at the very thought of being taken on by her at full tilt.

In the middle of the room a desk was sitting like a huge brown blob. On each side of it was a sofa; large and inviting—if you had the right kind of woman with you. Only the desk lamp was on. The doors slipped shut behind us; then I heard a click and realized that they had been locked.

This was a place to have Dora—not this "witch of Hollywood!"

I felt like a virgin in the presence of an aged nymphomaniac.

The best thing was to make the most of it and simply consider her a challenging acting job.

Her eyes were glassy, her lips half parted and damp looking. Her nose was like a protruding hatchet cutting her face in half.

"Well, I came to Hollywood after the service gave me my freedom. Thought maybe I might be able to get into pictures."

She just nodded at that. "Well you have the looks. And the body. I saw that when you came towards me. You have an animal walk and a way of looking at a women that would send…well, enough of that. Please continue!"

I stared at her, feeling somewhat uncertain. It was run or dive right in.

"Go on—go on!" she encouraged me, after a long pause.

"Well, there's hardly anything else to tell. A few bits in the movies and TV. One supporting part in a rather poor picture."

She nodded again. Her head looked like a bobbing beacon sitting lop-sided on the surface of a choppy sea.

"That's blunt. No BS. Okay." Then she blinked, looked up at the ceiling, thought for a moment, and those think smiled. Those eyes slowly lowered to meet mine: "I like your honesty. From what Eddy said, one would have thought that you'd won the Oscars for the best actor three years in a row. But that's his job. Over sell the client!"

She laughed and her hand reached out and touched my thigh, lay there for a moment, then her fingers patted me and withdrew. She seemed satisfied about something. "You know, Jack, there aren't many honest people in this world nowadays. They say a lot of things that aren't true, just to get ahead. They tell you this and then they tell another person something else. *They* don't know if you should believe them or not. They simply say what is considered the best sell for the moment. It can get somewhat…boring, being able to play out the script from memory. Oh, darling, they'll say, I'm so wonderful, just the greatest and you're what I've been looking for all my life. Ha!"

Her hand returned to my thigh, this time staying there. It felt like some horrid evil thing from a rotting grave. Clammy; almost slimy. An illusion, but real enough. I was trembling, but she'd think that was a pleasure reaction.

I was, of course, over reacting to the situation. After having been fired up to the moon and back by one lovely young woman I was now expected to carry over the flaming torch and place it in the hands of this female power broker. The very idea shivered through me like a wave of revolting horror.

Of course, that was something I could certainly use to my advantage. She'd think it was passion for her that was racing through the muscles of my body.

Her fingers gave my thigh a playful squeeze to silently communicate her own awareness of my apparent response to this intimate connection between us.

"You know, Jack, a woman like myself is in an odd position." Her voice seemed to dip away for a moment. Her eyes lost some of the glassy look. "I'm not what some people think of as…well, pretty." She turned her eyes in my direction. "What *do* you think of me, Jack?"

There was something in her voice that just challenged me to be blunt, honest, lay it out on the line. Sure. Of course. Hardly the fast track to success and fame. I could hardly say, *lady you are a real turn off!*

The question hung there for a long time, as I desperately tried to find an answer to fit it. One that would work! What could I tell her? The truth? Hardly!

Instead, I shrugged my shoulders. "To be honest, I hardly know you."

She smiled at that in a strange way, her lips curling at one corner. "That's funny. I think *I* know *you*."

She was silent for a long moment, and then continued in a much heavier voice. "I guess I know you because I know from actual experience people who are completely different

75

from what you are. You're mostly honest. Maybe *too* honest for your own good. Strong. Tall. Young!" Her eyes gleamed and they looked beadily in my direction. Eager and bright. "You're the type of man I've always wanted. Hell, the kind of man most women would sell their soul for—and of course that's the prime set of charms you may have to offer the public at large. Assuming the machinery strikes up the band and the music from the PR rooms start churning loud trumpets in the name of whatever name you are given to put on the screen. Well…you are a dream. No doubt about that."

The mood had suddenly changed. It was now moving directly toward the one direction I feared most. And it was like some kind of horror flick, badly scripted by a hack writer who simply didn't care.

And that's exactly how she was playing it; cause she didn't have to care.

She leaned close. Her voice throaty. Her lips trembling.

"Take me in your strong arms. Hold me, close. Let me feel you. Caress you. Kiss me!" The last words were a command and the lids of her eyes lowered like heavy sheets of thick metal. She waited there, eager and wanting. Her hands reached searchingly and blindly for my arms. The fingers clutched frantically, pulling me to her.

"Kiss me!" she demanded, again.

Kiss me, you fool! Rang silently in my brain. Right from some cheap Hollywood script!

I tried to think of Dora, who would be waiting in my apartment when I got home. I thought of all the other women, beautiful, desirable, passionate and young. Women who were loveable because they were physically attractive.

I tried to place their image before my eyes, as I lowered my lips onto her thin old leathery ones.

On contact the image of all those beautiful women shattered and my stomach retched.

I *can't do it, Eddy!* my mind screamed in defeat. *I just can't do it!*

I frantically pushed her away, unable to withhold the knot of disgust.

For a shocked moment her eyes remained tightly shut. Then her face slowly turned crimson. Her mouth trembled and then the uneven teeth clamped down hard on her lower lip as her moist eyes opened.

I couldn't help feeling sorry for her. She was just an ugly woman, trying hard to look and be glamorous and desirable to men. A powerful woman who could get men to climb into bed with her, just because they would do *anything* to get that first real, serious break in the movies.

But suddenly I had realized I wasn't that type of person. It was one thing to take a beautiful woman to bed with you; and quite another to attempt to make love to an old hag who not only didn't interest you, but actually affected you in a repulsive way; turned your stomach against you.

It was prostitution on the lowest scale. Just like a street walker, or main street whore selling her shattered body for a quick fix or simply to have a place to sleep for the night. Anybody in a storm.

Yet this was high class prostitution, for high stakes. With many women it would have been possible to willing submit to their desires. Perhaps.

I suddenly didn't know how much I really wanted a career in films—if I wasn't willing to pay any price to get there. If you didn't have obsession blinding you of all moral sensibilities then you might never make it. This was my moment of decision. I'd already told Eddy that the gay couches were out. Now I'd have to claim another limit.

"I'm sorry," I told her, as gently as I was able, "I'm terribly sorry!"

Standing, I fought the defeat down, knowing that I'd just blown my one big chance. From now on it would be either starting all over again, with another agent, if I could get one, or giving up the whole idea of fame and fortune; and my name on the big screen.

But regardless of everything, I couldn't have made love to this pitiful, repulsive creature, if my life had depended on it. Yet I didn't really want to hurt her. There was a real human behind that ugly mask—a pitifully desperate female who used her power to make men service her body like a male prostitute. That would have been the last thing I would have wanted to do. "I'm terribly sorry. I should never have let Eddy…"

"Don't!" she managed to choke out from between clinched lips. "Don't! Just leave me."

For a moment I hesitated then left, went to my car, drove to my apartment and a moment later opened the front door, then closed it behind me. I felt an eager, delightful form fold into my arms. The room was dark, but I could feel the delicate shape of Dora Milton. She sighed contentedly as I lifted her up into my arms.

"I told you I'd be here!" she laughed, throatily.

"How lucky can a guy get?"

"Hey, I'm the so lucky one. You're fab. I mean, a dream!"

A moment later neither of us was saying anything. Instead, we were locked in a wonderful normal embrace.

* * * * * * *

The next morning the phone awakened me.

"Hello?" I asked, sleepily, into the receiver.

"Boy, what the hell did you do?" Eddy Landum's voice drummed into my ears.

"Oh, that!" I felt sickness inside. I'd been able to almost forget, in the sweet embrace of Dora's body.

"Oh, *that!* That's all you can say?"

"Well, to be honest...."

"Yeah, Miss Lee Belle said something about that honesty thing of yours. Swore she'd never met anybody so honest as you are. Brutally, was her key word."

"Well, I couldn't help it...."

"Sure you couldn't. You crazy guy!"

Suddenly I was more awake and aware of the odd quality in his voice.

"You must really be a lover-boy. And all the time she thought you really meant it. What an actor you'll make!"

"What the hell are you talking about?"

"You got the part. Said that you made her realize something that she'd never had the guts to admit before. Whatever *that* means. Said it was because of your simple honesty..."

I wasn't listening any more. For a long time I sat on the edge of the bed, my legs dancing over the end. I was thinking about that poor lady who had had her age and lack of beauty and sexual desirability slapped across her face by a brutal bastard who'd tried to make himself think he was just being honest.

Maybe it was honesty! I didn't know any more. But I could now almost regret that I hadn't made love to her. Right then I could have done the deed to the oldest, ugliest hag in the world.

They say that beauty is skin deep, and in some cases that's true. And ugliness can be merely skin deep, too. And in her case this was totally true!

I'd learned a very real lesson about people because of her. Maybe to some Miss Lois-jean Lee Belle was the "witch" but to me, from then on, she was my personal "Angel of Hollywood."

This little bit was offered the editor and he snapped it up for some reason or other. And there's nothing fishy about that. But it isn't a fishing story, regardless of the fact that it is about...

⤚SHARK BAIT⤙

"You have the damnedest luck," the fat man announced, stepping away from the green covered poker table, his heavy features frozen with a stiff smile.

Greg Cannon laughed, hoping it would sound embarrassed. "Don't play much. Guess you're right."

He gathered in his winnings with huge, flexible hands, counted up to a little over six hundred and stuffed the money into his wallet.

The thin, retired Captain narrowed his eyes at Cannon. "If I didn't know better I might think you pulled something on us, Stranger."

The man's voice revealed his belief that Greg had cheated.

They couldn't prove anything, Greg thought.

"No such luck," he lied, standing. "Thanks for letting me sit in."

"You'll be in town again?" the large Sheriff inquired.

"I'll make it a point," he promised, seeing an easy opportunity of making more money. "Give you guys a chance to win back some of this."

Three pairs of angry eyes followed him out of the room. Greg sighed with relief once the door was closed behind him.

The saloon which fronted for the weekly poker game was filled with customers. There were only a few places left at the bar and Greg made his way to one of them.

After three hours of sweating out a tight, careful game, he needed a drink. It hadn't been easy to cheat, with those three men's eyes hawking every move he made. But the skill of his hands had made it impossible for them to accuse him

80

openly—there wasn't a thing they could do.

Sitting down he ordered a triple shot of whiskey. He was on his third drink when a feminine voice sounded at his side.

"You're the stranger in town, aren't you?" The words were low and throaty.

Greg turned, stared at the attractive dark haired woman that sat down beside him. The green dress hugging the bulges of her figure dipped in the front, giving an attractive view of her jutting breasts. Her smile was a warm invitation.

"I'm the stranger," he admitted with a smile.

A woman. he thought, *would be a good topping to such a rewarding evening.*

His eyes ran over her compact figure. Then he studied her face. She had full, supple lips which pouted in the shape of a subtle kiss in the offering.

"The Big Three are really bugged about your big haul," she told him, with a bright twinkle in her seductive eyes. Amusement revealed even white teeth beyond her warm smile. "About time they got cleaned. They cater to strangers who come through town. Figure they have an edge, working together like they do."

"They cheat?" He was amazed. It had been such an easy take—amateurs at cards never had a chance against is professional skills at the gaming tables.

"No—they play an honest game," she assured him with a wink, "otherwise you wouldn't have won."

"Well, I can thank the bartender for telling me about the game. Though, to be honest, I had a totally different entertainment in mind when I asked about the town's action." His eyes stripped her figure to lend force to the words.

Several moments of silence followed and then the woman asked: "Want to buy me a drink?"

Invitation smoldered in her blue eyes.

"Why not?" he offered, his hand reaching to her thigh, enjoying the soft feel of her flesh under the skirt. She made no effort to move his hand away, and actually leaned a little closer, looking up into his yes in a rather intimately promising manner.

She murmured softly and said: "My name's Joanie."

"Greg." He withdrew his hand after having let his fingers explore her inner thigh. She had gently squirmed under his touch. "How about us getting a bottle and—"

Without missing a beat she was quick to interrupt with: "Good idea! I was hoping you'd get the message."

Baby, he thought, *I sure as hell got it and expect a lot more!*

Women like her were expected to be found in such saloons, in this part of town. And Joanie was making no secret as to what she expected from him as they walked out into the street.

A little later they were in his motel room, drinks poured, laughing intimately at nothing other than the promise of what was soon about to happen. She sat on the bed, her legs crossed, her dress high up, giving him a wonderful view of smooth, firm thighs. He stood over her, a glass of whiskey clutched in his large hands.

"How'd you manage to win?" Joanie asked, in an innocent voice. But her eyes were flowing over him like a hungry tigress in heat.

Greg laughed. "You wouldn't believe me."

"You're a professional? A cheat?" She almost made the words sound seductive, very throaty, and even admiringly intrigued.

He hesitated and then the temptation to brag overcame the urge for caution. "Let's say I helped things along—when necessary."

"You a gambler?" she offered, with a contented smile. "I thought so."

"More or less," Greg admitted, only slightly annoyed by his rash honesty. "But, quite frankly, it didn't take all that much skill to trim their pocketbooks!"

Joan doubled over, laughter bubbling from her red lips. "That's one on *them!*"

After that they were silent for a while. When the drinks were almost finished she asked: "We gonna sit here all night? Or do you have something more…fun and intimate in mind, honey?"

Greg answered by simply reaching for her. Joanie slipped into his arms, her supple body pressed hungrily to his with a contented sigh of wanton pleasure. The soft, yielding lips opened wide, and he felt the dart of her tongue search deep into his mouth. It was a long, exhausting kiss and when she moved away she seemed as overwhelmed as he was feeling.

She stared at him for a few moments and then her hands went around to the back of her dress. It came off in a fluid movement and fell to the floor, around her feet. She hurried the bra off and the large swell of her breasts burst free, thrusting outwards like firm silk, their centers rosy and erect.

She took his hand and led him to the bed. Lying down, she waited while he undressed. Her eyes moved brazenly over the hard muscles of his body. She didn't have to say a word to communicate her obvious approval as he moved to her.

When they slid together, a tremble rippled over her body as if she couldn't wait to be totally taken by him. She clawed to Greg, her breasts welling up tight against him. He had the feeling of being encased in warm velvet. The perfect texture of her flesh responded to his touch as he slipped his hands along the supple curves. His lips buried themselves against hers, their mouths working eagerly together until she urged his head down to the invitation of those warm breasts.

To him it felt like trying to contain a savage tigress. In the last moments he heard frantic moans rack her throat as her body moved like hot silk against him. Then fire blazed ecstasy across his nerves. Greg rolled over, exhausted.

She had been damned good, he thought happily, anxious to reenter her warm embrace.

It wasn't long before she once again was at him, and this time complete exhaustion crumbled all awareness and sleep paralyzed him until late in the morning.

The sun, shining across his eyes, brought Greg awake. A quick search of the room told him Joanie was gone.

He felt disappointed, having hoped to once again enjoy her lustfully demanding body. But, at least, she'd been a wonderful bonus for a hard night's work.

Greg got up, dressed. He pulled out his wallet to count the winnings of from the poker game. That's when he discovered it was empty, except for twenty dollars, and a note.

"The bed was wild," he read, "but the money practical!"

Anger blared red. It didn't occur to him that the night had only cost him twenty-five dollars of his own money. He was still blazing raw when he rushed into the Sheriff's office.

"I've been robbed!" Greg shouted at the huge police officer.

The Sheriff stared at him and then shrugged. "What can I do about it?"

"Find the tramp!"

"Tramp?" the Sheriff looked somewhat stunned. "What're you talking about?"

"The little whore!"

"Come, come. No name calling."

"Okay. She was...well, Joanie something or other."

"That's not much to go on."

"Well, she had dark haired. Pretty as hell. She picked..." His voice faltered, helpless. "Certainly you must know who I'm talking about. This isn't that big a town."

The man shrugged as if to say he couldn't know everybody.

"Come on. This town is small potatoes. You surely know every whore and prostitute and tramp and slut—"

"Name calling won't get you far, mister!" The Sheriff's face was bland, but there was a twinkle of amusement in his eyes.

"Well what are you doing to do about it?" Greg demanded, furious.

"I can't do anything..." The man's huge shoulders shrugged. "You might as well leave town—consider yourself lucky nothing else happened to you."

"Lucky, *hell!*" Greg cried. "You do something or—"

"There's no woman in this town by that description. Must have been a transient. Just like you. A bum, passing through. We get them, too. Even if we are nothing but a hick small town. We don't allow that kind of woman here! We're a moral, upright place. A church going community. We don't have any place for...what you are talking about."

"You gotta be kidding!" Greg sputtered, amazed. The man's attitude was totally contemptible. "Morals, my eye! With illegal gambling...come on, give me a break!"

84

"Believe me. You're getting one!" the Sheriff snapped, standing like a huge walrus behind his desk "You're damned lucky I don't arrest you for immoral practices!"

The man's eyes hardened. "But if you aren't out of town in an hour—I will lock you up and toss out the key!"

Greg stared open-mouthed. For a long time he stood there uncertain what to do. The other man glared at him like a giant considering an annoying bug. Then his right hand waved Greg away. "Get out of here, you no good bum!"

Greg knew when he was beaten. Defeated, he turned way from the man and left.

When he was gone the Sheriff grinned and walked into the back room where a dark-haired woman waited.

"You did a good job, Joanie. Though I wish there had been another way to see justice done."

Joan smiled. "I'm just glad this is Nevada," she laughed. "I took a little extra—from both sides, to pay for my services."

She extended a handful of hills which the Sheriff pocketed.

"I'll see everybody gets his money back." He was thoughtful for a moment, then added with a pleased grin: "That's one card shark that won't come into town again!"

There are all kinds of ways of "getting even" with people one believes have "done 'em wrong," and this nasty little lady is more than anxious to…

⇥DRINK DEEP OF REVENGE⇤

Lois looked seductively at the man who had killed her husband, holding down the bitter hate as she smiled invitingly.

The man's eyes smoldered over her trim, curving figure. For a moment he didn't make a move, only his eyes studied her. From the pinched expression on his chiseled features, it was obvious he was puzzled by the open invitation of her smile. He didn't know her and didn't even realize that Henry Laymont had a wife. That was one of her advantages; the other was the sensual shape of her body. It was the first time in her life that she was proud of the fact she'd been a stripper.

Lois let her eyes flash warmth as she wetted the redness of her lips to a silky shine.

This time he didn't wait. Picking up his drink he stepped down the row of bar stools to the one she was sitting on. His eyes dropped to the curve of her legs where the white skirt was suggestively high.

"Wonder if I could buy you a drink," he offered, sitting down next to her.

Lois nodded, without saying anything. Right then the hate was welled up tight inside her and didn't allow a vocal answer.

"What you drinking?"

"Scotch and soda," she managed in a low voice which sounded sensual and yet very seductive.

The drink was ordered and came before any conversation developed, but his eyes were busy devouring the shape of her, mostly fascinated by the low cut of the neckline that revealed a bulge of thrusting breasts.

"My name's Greg Martin," he introduced.

"Lois," she offered, taking a sip of scotch. Control had hardened her nerves.

There was an awkward silence and then said: "I couldn't help noticing you looking at me."

She smiled, forcefully raising the corners of her full lips. The bitterness knotted tight in her stomach as if a red-hot poker had been rammed there. With an effort she said: "You're a good-looking guy."

That much wasn't a lie. He had clean features, a sharp expression in his gray eyes, a nicely shaped mouth. His body was tall and broad; it looked hard and solid.

Just the kind of a man some women went for.

"I guess there's no reason to kid ourselves," he said in a harsh voice. "I'm not just looking for idle conversation and, from the way you were studying me down, I don't believe you're the type of woman out for just a couple of drinks!"

You bastard! she thought bitterly. *You don't believe in giving a girl much to lean on!* But her approach hadn't been subtle, either. The bar was cheap and the kind of place where pick-ups and prostitutes were catered to. She had been following the man's activities for weeks, had gotten used to his routine and noted that on every Saturday night, his only evening off, he had made it a habit to come here and pick up some woman to take to a hotel.

"I guess you're right," Lois admitted, finishing her drink. "I suppose I am after some real hot fun. I'm crazy to get me a man."

"You don't have to be crazy to want me, babe!" he assured her, a bit too confident.

"Maybe I'm just insane and out to get you alone somewhere to do terrible things to your body."

"Now, baby, that sounds wild."

"Maybe mad?"

"Wonderfully mad."

"You're in for a real surprise, believe me, you are!"

"I sure hope so!" He squeezed her arm in such a way that his fingers just pressed into the side of her breast; and not accidentally, either. The pig!

Like all men, monstrous beasts who wanted nothing but

87

a woman's naked body.

Well, not all men; her husband hadn't been like that. He'd been into other things. And he had treated her right even when she was sometimes acting silly and dumb and simply crazy nuts in her demands for his attention.

All other men were bastards in heat and she knew exactly how to handle them.

The hogs. Sweaty muscles, hairy bodies clawing in the night. Panting, sweaty, freaky animals.

She could twist them all around her little fingers. And tonight she had to put on her best act as the opening to her total revenge against this man she had learned to hate so passionately.

They walked out without another word. As they stepped down the street to his car, he took her arm, asking: "What's a high class broad like you come to that kind of place for?"

"Kicks! What else? Men like you are...a nice change of routine for a woman like me."

"Slumming?" He helped her into the convertible. "You look like you have plenty of money, from the way you're all dolled up."

"Well call me crazy if you wish, or mad, or insane or just loosely passionate for a man any time, any place. You name it and I'll dive right in...with the right man, of course."

"And how do you know I'm that kind of man?"

"Just one look at you, and I knew. Big and broad and so powerful. I bet you could kill a person with your bare hands. You look strong enough to break a man in half, let along a small little woman like little old me."

"You're hot, honey," he laughed in delight, "You'd make any Sampson turn weak in your arms."

"I'll do my best." She murmured seductively, while smiling up at him. Her eyes promised him the answer to all his fantasy dreams of a night of passion with a lustfully needed woman.

Slipping into the seat, behind the wheel, the man started the car, pulling it out into traffic.

"Know of some place you like particularly?"

"What difference does it make? We aren't out to kill the town. Are we?"

88

"I suppose not," he grinned, sounding delighted.

"Well, then take me where we can have a lot of fun, in private. Is that blunt enough for you?"

"Right to the point." He placed a hand on her thigh and patting it intimately.

"Drive. You can do all that later. And a lot more."

"I'll stop someplace and get a bottle," he told her, moving he hand moved back to the steering wheel. "Then we'll go to the Ritz Hotel—okay?"

She let silence be her answer. She didn't know the place, but guessed the name was some kind of ancient joke. People like this man didn't know classy hotels, didn't have the money for that kind of action.

As expected the hotel room was cheap, like the old sign outside which named it. Greg Martin closed the door behind them and then walked to the dresser. Opening the bottle, he raised it to his lips, gulping, then, slamming it against the dresser top, he turned savage eyes toward Lois.

"Okay—what's the pitch?" he snarled, threateningly.

"What you talking about?" Lois demanded, alarmed, her stomach tightening. Near insane terror choked at his throat. What had she done wrong? What could he know? Not the truth. Anything but the truth. That was her edge.

"You've been following me for days! What you after? This isn't any casual pick-up!" He stepped forward and, before she could do anything to protect herself, his large hand clamped brutally around her arm. "Don't try to play coy!"

Without warning his hand slapped across her face in a stinging blow. God, he must know something! How'd he find out? Maybe the same way he had...found out about her husband.

Lois cringed away, horrified, and really scared, now. This was like some nightmare from which she couldn't escape.

"What's with you?" she cried, struggling to get free from his grip. She had to be free of him, just long enough to do what was necessary. For a long moment it was difficult to even focus. The panic was ripping away at her gut so painfully that even visual images seemed to distort into a rage of disjointed colors, shapes, weaving around her head: twisted

89

corridors, men screaming, women clawing at black walls. A nightmare of madness just bubbled up into a churning frenzy of monstrous illusion. The terror grew then faded and then slammed into at her again.

Even memory shifted, shattered, slithered away only to reshape itself. What had she done? What had gone wrong? Everything was crazy, insane, distorted by shattered bits of her memories, life, pictures which had no reality.

Focus. Focus.

Recreated.

She felt lost in a corridor in her brain that wouldn't function for a long moment. Then slowly her mind refocused: this was the man she had determined was totally responsible for her husband's death.

For only a moment had the world seemed illusionary, distant, without logic or past. For a moment she believed she was back in the hospital. But that was months ago, right after her husband had been killed. That's when the world had shattered. Things had changed over the months, years, since then.

Focus, damn you!

"I told you—don't play coy!" His other hand wrapped around her other arm, and his narrowed eyes bored into hers.

"What you take me for? I haven't been a private dick for ten years for nothing. I can spot even a professional shadow—you're not very subtle about it!"

Oh, God, what does he know about me?

She fought the growing emotional crisis as she'd been taught to do so many times in the past. Life had been hard on her since her husband's brutal death. But professionals had helped and given her wonderful mental tricks. Meditations, mantras. She forced them into place: *"Three, Two, One! Zero!"* her mind traced into the magical method she'd learned to us in order to bring back a normal level of control, a normal level of sanity in a world gone unhinged. Nothing had seemed normal after she'd lost the only man who had ever meant anything to her; lost her very world itself.

And it had taken a long time to learn to control the deep, dark pit that always tried to open up under her and suck all sanity away.

This is the man who is responsible for everything horrible that happened to you. Settle down. Control the fury. Don't panic.

Three, Two, One! Zero!

She forced calm, deeply focused sanity in a world gone mad. She had to convince him of her own version of reality, of her truth, not his never ending lies. She had to make him believe her cover story; or everything would turn into total defeat and all the plans melted down in defeat. For the deep dark drink of revenge had to be finished off in one huge swallow or her one and only chance would be lost forever.

Be seductive. Remember all the stripping tricks. Teach this man what a woman will a lovely body, a seducing mind, a determined...passion...yes, convince him, now!

Control yourself!

Three, Two, One! Zero!

Composure slowly settled over Lois and she said: "I just noticed you—and wanted to be sure!"

He blinked at her, taken aback by this statement. "Now what's that supposed to mean?"

"I told you—I like kicks!" She forced a laugh. "I get kicks out of following a guy and finding out about him—before approaching him. I want to know what to expect before I climb into bed with a man. Especially a stranger like you. A big, strong, lovely hunk of a man. The kind of guy that can really make a woman weak all over."

He blinked again, his hand dropped to his side. "What the hell?"

Lois smiled, but her insides were on fire.

"So, I'm a nut! You want what we came up here for—or are you going to keep playing muscle-man with me? Or rather, threatening the wrong kind of muscling. I want you to do me up right, love. If you got what it takes; and you sure look like you have plenty of it!" Her fingers started to edge on her purse. All she needed was a moment—a quick moment to get the gun out.

Greg grinned and then casually reached out, taking the purse from her fingers. "Okay, baby—let's have a party. So you get kicks following a man—I get kicks sharing beds with attractive broads!" He stepped over to the dresser, placing her purse on it, picked up the bottle and returned. "Want a drink first?"

Sweat covered Lois' body and with effort she kept the trembling of her hands under enough control so it wasn't visible as she reached for the bottle. Lifting it to her lips, she gulped several large swallows. The whiskey burned raw down the lining of her throat. Greg Martin took the bottle from her and replaced it on the dresser, turning.

"Well, there's no sense in standing around like dumb jerks," he announced, taking off his jacket and starting to unbutton his shirt.

Sickness surmounted Lois as she slowly started unzipping her dress. She *had* to get to the purse—get the gun. After that she didn't mind what happened to her. Life without her husband wasn't worth living. Only revenge against this monster nightmare that cluttered all reality, all thoughts, awareness. Nothing mattered except getting even!

The man looked greedily at her body which was naked except for a white bra and panties. His eyes fastened on the brimming of her breasts overflowing the tight fit of the bra.

Abruptly Lois saw her chance and then slowly, tauntingly, slipped her hands around her back and started to remove the bra. She made a brazen production out of it, dragging it out in slow,

Lois wiggled her hips as she swung the straps over her arms. Slowly she edged the left cup lower, smiling as sensually as all her stripping experience on stage had taught her.

He followed the movement of the bra as it intimately and suggestively glided downwards. First the creamy white of silken flesh and then the pink suggestion which flared out slightly, revealing a teasing nipple to his view

Lois was carefully moving forward, very carefully edging toward the dresser where her purse lay uselessly.

The movement of her hips attracted his hungry attention for an instant and then she jerked the bra free, giggling lightly.

"What the hell!" he exclaimed, now breathless from her little performance

She rotated her hips, pushing them forward and then giving a little rhythmic jerking motion to them, just like she had learned to do with all the customers who flocked to see her strip before them. What a thrill it was to turn men on, to make them lusting fools hungry to feast on her naked body. Men were such simple creatures, see a woman flaunting herself, exposing secret places, flashing quick images, and they were helplessly tangled in an overwhelming web of passion where they couldn't think any more. Very simple creatures of wanton desires, perverse needs. Stupid, one track minded.

And that was her real power over this creature before her.

She bumped and ground her body before him, slowly slipping the clothing away until he was able to watch her wild display. She knew all the tricks and now used all of them, grinding through a series of movements that were almost magic in their effect over a man.

Beads of sweat formed on his forehead.

"God! What a kook!" he mumbled, his eyes watching the swaying movement of her large well-formed breasts as she swung them from left to right, just as she'd done so many times on the stage.

She knew exactly how to do it, and now was moving faster and faster, arms flung high above her head, hips gyrating, breasts swinging, waving, bouncing in a visual dance before his eyes.

Distraction, she thought. *Keep the distraction going! Men are such fool for a woman's body.*

Lois had edged half way to the dresser and now she paused, noticing, with the trained eye of a professional stripper who has watched countless customers burn their eves raw at her undulating body, that his attention was lapsing. Now she slipped her fingers under the elastic of her panties.

"You crazy or something?" he hissed out, trembling slightly from the sight of what she was doing. "Wild crazy. But what madness!"

"I like kicks!" she said, teasingly, rolling her hips, letting the elastic band lower a fraction. Her voice was husky as she suggested: "Why don't you lie down on the bed—enjoy it—and I'll give you something you won't ever forget!"

The promise of her words seemed to have a hypnotic effect on Greg, because he stepped over to the bed, his eyes

93

still fascinated to the action of her hips. He didn't say a word. Amazement was still keeping his mouth half open.

She ran her tongue along the full surface of her lips, winked at him and then edged the panties downward again while taking several bold steps toward the dresser. She would need several long seconds to grab her purse, to open it and pull the small revolver out, turn and aim.

Thrusting her hips forward, subtly moving them and taking several bold steps towards the dresser, she suddenly felt herself press against the wooden frame.

"Oh!" Lois cried, as if startled, and at the same moment, timed to a split instant, she jerked out of her panties, as if having been scared out of them by the unexpected touch of the dresser.

Greg Martin convulsed in laughter, and Lois jerked around, her hand clasping the purse, opened it at the same time she heard a shout of alarm explode from the man.

"Goddamn!" Footsteps pounded, scurrying.

Anxiously she reached the gun with her fingers, drew it out and turned.

"Freeze!" she sneered, triumph on her face.

Martin stared at her, only three feet away, his face draining white.

"You bitch!" he cried finally.

"Back away—and don't make any sudden moves!" she ordered, tightening her grip on the gun.

"What is this?" he cried, desperately. "I knew there was something in that purse—but...why? *Why?*"

He was pleading.

"Henry Laymont is the reason!" she announced as he moved back around the room.

"What you talking about?"

"You framed him on the hold-up job—you planted evidence in his apartment. You saw to it that he didn't have a chance to defend himself. Walked in with the police, after having made sure he was scared silly—because of the narcotic bit—and armed—you shot him down—legally—sure—from the point of view of the law!

"But you aren't going to get away with it! I've waited for months to set this thing up—now, you're going to die, like my husband did—without a chance!"

Without hesitating, Lois slowly squeezed the trigger, the gun spurting out red flame which tore crimson holes in the man's chest. Then, calmly, without any feelings of regret she called the police and, after telling them what had happened, sat down and waited. When they arrived they didn't bother to handcuff her because there were two attendants who came gently forward.

"Mrs. Laymont," one said in a friendly tone, gently taking the gun from her relaxed fingers, "You don't know how glad we are to see you again. We missed you at the Institution—now why did you have to do this?"

She smiled up at them, happy for the first time, sure in the knowledge that no one would harm her, or hers again. She stood and followed the two men out.

One of them turned to the police investigator, saying: "She's all right now—nothing to worry about. They get violent and imagine things—sometimes the most fantastic things."

Lois kept smiling inwardly—they'd never know the truth, they'd never believe her; they hadn't before when she had told them about the murder and that her husband was innocent because he was with her the night of the robbery. Maybe she'd gotten a little hysterical then—maybe they were right about her having had a nervous breaking down; but they were wrong about Greg Martin. They would take her back to the padded cell and keep her there for a long, long time, and someday would probably release her—but they'd never know she had been quit sane while committing the execution. They would never know that.

Suddenly she was laughing, laughing down the ball between the two attendants—laughing and laughing and laughing because it was all so funny.

But she had already forgotten what was funny—she had forgotten where she was. All she knew was that they would be taking her hack to her husband. He was waiting for her; waiting to take her into his arms.

The two men struggled with the hysterical woman; the woman who had insisted her husband had been murdered. But her husband had killed himself two years before over debts and then discovering his wife had been cheating on him.

Nobody knew the truth about Henry Laymont except Greg Martin and Lois—and neither of them were speaking about it.

This one offers a look at the Vegas scene—well, sorta. It could have taken place in any gambling town, or elsewhere in the present day and age, even in the twenty-first century. Maybe even in a far distant future. But, also, this takes place in the present and closes this section of Dimensions *with a...*

⊣VEGAS LAST LAUGH⊢

I didn't notice the woman because my full attention was centered on the roulette wheel.

It was the sharp, feminine intake of breath just behind my left ear that attracted my attention to her. The sound accompanied a large winning that was placed before me. I turned, surprised at having an audience.

The woman was tall and dressed in white. A low neckline supported gigantic, but beautifully featured pink-cream breasts.

She smiled pleasantly and placed yellow chips on my green stacks. "Hope I don't break your luck," she said casually, sitting beside me.

We watched the wheel slowly turning as the little white ball twisted its course in the opposite direction, speeding around and around like a racing satellite. In the background was the madness of slot-machines, numbers being called out, and conversation generally blending with the trip in the Lounge off to our left; the melody of all Vegas clubs which becomes a soft madness which the mind blanks out.

The wheel-man called one of our numbers and the woman clapped her hands excitedly. When we won again her right hand impulsively gripped my arm, squeezing. After the fourth straight win, she cashed in her chips and turned to me, asking, "Can't I buy you a drink?" Then quickly added, "If you weren't so lucky—I wouldn't have won!"

The bold suggestion of intimacy which flickered in her sky-blue eyes caused me to take only one last glance at the wheel and then say; "I'll buy the drinks!"

97

A flicker of amusement flashed over her face. "Well, thank you."

I wasn't in the least concerned by the fact that Sherry Martin, the girl I was engaged to, would be coming to the hotel the next morning. Still being a single man, I reasoned, there wasn't anything keeping me from one last fling.

As we settled ourselves down in the Lounge, the trio of entertainers announced a break and disappeared, surrounding us with the noisy silence of the Casino.

The woman looked at me from across the two foot expanse of the table and her eyes were anything but subtle. Finally she said, "I hope you don't think I'm..." A shrug finished the statement. "Vegas does things to people—doesn't it?" Her warm smile revealed evenly spaced, white teeth.

Laughing, I patted her hand, "People *are* more friendly here!"

"Never been to a place like this before. Just a small town girl on a spree." The tone of her voice explained the rest quite vividly—maybe *too* vividly. Her eyes examined me, making no attempt to hide their interest. "What's wrong with a little fun, anyway?" she hurriedly inquired, as if trying to convince herself—or *me?*

Suddenly it felt good sitting there with her. It was quite a contrast to Sherry's cold, matter-of-fact personality. I'd be marrying Sherry the next day and if it weren't for her money, she wouldn't have gotten a second look. She's a pinched, bitter woman in her middle thirties who has worked all her life and made her own way. It had taken a first-class conning job to convince her that it wasn't the money I was after. What Sherry couldn't do in physically exciting a man, she balanced out by her checkbook. She was one of the sharpest business women in Los Angeles, if not in the country. She didn't take chances on any investment. My ace was that she loved me—and that accounted for one hell of a lot!

We ordered Martinis and by the time they arrived I'd discovered the woman's name was Joan Temple. When the drinks came we downed them and reordered. By the third Martini a light heady feeling had settled over my brain.

"You know, I like you!" she murmured.

"There was a strong feeling of honesty to her words

98

which was surprising.

"I like you, too," I admitted, "how about an afternoon of it?"

It was some time before we left the Lounge to gamble. In the next hour or so we covered all the tables, winning and losing, but laughing and joking and enjoying ourselves regardless of which way the chips fell. There was a light-hearted excitement about the woman that appealed to me. Maybe it was the drinks, maybe something more subtle, but it was a long time before any thought of what might happen later, entered my mind. We had a snack in the Coffee Shop, and then, while drinking after-lunch cocktails, Joan stared evenly at me, her expression a mixture of emotion, slightly veiled. Finally she said, "You really want to go out to the tables again?"

The meaning was clear. "No—not really."

Minutes later we went to the room which I had rented— at Sherry's expense.

Joan moved to the large double bed, sitting down on it. "Real nice."

"I try to live good," I told her.

I stepped to the bed, sitting down next to her, and made a pointed effort to see down the dip between her creamy breasts.

"My, my, aren't you're the curious one!" Joan laughed throatily. "One thing I like about you is—you're honest!"

Without warning Joan stood and her hands went around to the back of her dress. A quick motion and the white gown slipped to the floor. Joan stood before me in bra and panties. The bra was strapless and cupped her magnificent breasts upwards and out, making them thrusting points of intriguing womanhood.

"Why play games?" she asked, staring down at me, amusement burning her eyes. "You want to make love to me?"

The breath had gushed out of my lungs at the sight of her voluptuous body. She had silken flesh, white and flawless; her waist narrowed and the flat expanse of her stomach was supported by flaring, rounded hips.

She stood there for a moment and then slipped down on

the bed next to me. "Want to take my bra off?" she inquired in a frank questioning

I had seen many women in the past but none quite as wonderfully built as this one, without being a professional prostitute or a dancer. She was formed in curves of silk, supple and firm looking.

My hands reached around her silken body, freeing her of the restraining bra.

She pressed flush against me and her arms wrapped around my neck as she slowly fell backwards onto the bed.

Joan's lips were like sweet nectar against mine and her body was warm. I found myself hungrily seeking out the full thrust of her breasts, the soft cushions of their supple shape. She trembled under my touch. Her own hands were already stripping aside my clothing with a burning hunger.

She moaned as her lips closed around the lobe of my ear.

The texture of her flesh, the nearness of her nakedness as it strained up against me, caused an inner doubt of guilt to form in my mind. I'd conned a lot of things in the past but never a marriage for money. I felt sorry for Sherry. It was only a passing thought, for Joan's body writhed suddenly and all I could think of was kissing the fullness of her red lips, taking in the sweet wine of her mouth, tasting the moist delicacy of her tongue as it raced past my lips. Then I was sliding my kiss downwards to the white cream of her velvet throat which trembled under the caress. The smoothness of her shoulder responded as I moved to the invitation of her breasts.

Emotion, overwhelming, mixed with the fire racing through me.

It was like riding the tail of a flaming rocket, whose fire blazed over us, racing us upwards into the infinity of space. I hardly even knew when it ended. Ecstasy burst through me and the aftermath kept the pleasure lingering. I knew this was more than mere physical joy—it was a spiritual blending of mind and body. I'd never met a woman like her before.

The caressing of her hands on my shoulder soothed away the numbness and I looked up into her eyes.

She was smiling like an angel. "I didn't know it would

be like this," she murmured softly, a hint of sorrow shading her voice.

"Neither did I," was my husky reply.

"You were good—but it was more than that. Something which built from the first moments of conversation. Something which was more than just a casual...casual flirtation." She hesitated, dropping her eyes sadly and then I felt her hands tense "Hold me—hold me again," she murmured, almost pleaded, as she slid her body against mine. "You don't know how lonely a girl like me gets..." She broke off suddenly and her lips were covering mine.

This time it was even more perfect. This time there was some other meaning to the rhythm of our bodies. When it was over I lay exhausted, bathed in a darkness of half-sleep. I was aware of the woman moving from the bed, then awareness slipped away. I dreamed of the months ahead when marriage would bind me to the vast fortunes of Sherry Martin, giving financial freedom to have everything I wanted, except a woman like Joan. But this was what I'd been working for all my life; a soft touch; an easy life without the worries that my childhood had been plagued with in the small tenement house my family had lived in.

Then suddenly the dream shattered as I was startled awake. Bright light blasted my eyes. It was almost as if a sixth sense told me something was wrong.

When I opened my eyes I saw Sherry standing at the foot of the bed, her thin frail body dressed in a mannish business suit. Her eyes burned into mine.

Next to her was Joan, a strange, veiled expression on her face.

"You filthy pig!" Sherry exploded in a nasty sneer. But the expression in her eyes was filled with triumph. "I thought you'd turn out like this!"

"What are you doing here?" I demanded, dazed. I couldn't quite believe the realty of what was taking place.

Sherry didn't answer. Instead her eyes turned to Joan. "How much?"

"Usually a hundred dollars. But—he won a lot of money and I thought maybe..."

"Take it!" Sherry said. "Take it all. It's all yours. You

earned it!"

"Hey, wait a damned minute!" I objected, grasping desperately at this last straw. It didn't hit me then that I wasn't as broken up about the shattering of my dream with Sherry and an easy life as I was numbed by the fact that Joan had turned out to be a call-girl. I was numb, reacting blindly.

"You were gambling with *my* money!" Sherry pointed out icily, "So the winnings are mine, too! She's welcome to it! You're not!"

Joan robbed my pockets and then turned, looking unhappily at me. "Sorry—but business is business!" she stated in a flat voice as she turned to leave. Then added; "I'm *really* sorry, Eddy. You were *damned* good!" She opened the door and walked out.

Sherry burned her eyes at me without saying anything.

"Look, baby—you don't understand."

"Cut it, charm-boy! You didn't take me for a sucker, did you? I've been on to you for a long time—but..." A little doubt of emotion shaded her face, softening it for only a moment. "I'd hoped maybe you'd turn out all right. A woman can't take chances with a man."

"I guess there's nothing else to say, is there?" I asked, vaguely relieved. Any woman who could treat the man she was supposed to be in love with in such a casual, cold-blood way was certainly not a turn-on. The idea of being stuck in her clutches suddenly seemed less attractive then my foolish imagination had believed it would have been. "I can't convince you—"

"No!"

I gathered my clothing and dressed. All my dreams had been blasted to hell but suddenly it didn't matter. What hurt most was that Joan had been conning me. In her arms I'd believed she really had enjoyed herself. It didn't seem possible that a girl so full of gaiety and excitement could have been all acting.

Without another word I walked from the room, slamming the door behind me.

Joan was standing outside in the hallway. She smiled as I stepped out.

"What are you here for?" I snarled. "To gloat?"

102

"No, no, not at all!" she murmured invitingly. "A girl in my profession doesn't always get a chance with a man like you. I didn't dare tell you...the only thing I could do was to...well, try to let you know I really cared—really enjoyed myself." She indicated the money in her hands. "I asked for it so maybe we could spend it together."

I stared at her, finding it hard to believe what had happened.

She laughed and said, "That woman in there's a bitch, one hell on a bitch, isn't she?"

Suddenly I laughed, seeing the humor of it. Maybe Sherry had done me a favor. I didn't know, yet, but there wasn't anything better to do than make the most of it.

Laughing again I took Joan's arm and we walked down the hall together—with Sherry's money. It was going to be fun spending it, more fun this way—with Joan—than anybody else in the world.

DIMENSIONS, BY CHARLES NUETZEL

PART THREE
FUTURE DIMENSIONS

⊷PREFACE⊶

Now we gaze into the distant horizons of our world and other places across the galaxy. These stories make up the main body of this collection, mainly because I happened to especially like social satire and sci-fi. To me there is no better place to make nasty little comments about our lives, than by setting things into a future context.

This is a place, too, where escape fiction *really* escapes from the real world and lets the imagination climb out of the present place in which we all live and discover new horizons, new worlds, across the limitless infinity of our universe.

Not to be too serious about it, I have included some short things of a tongue-in-cheek nature, and even shorter ones that are purely meant to bite one's tongue in a pun for the sake of fun. But some of these tales have their so-called "meaningful" statements, and others are just nasty little slices of possible future nightmares none of us want to experience in real life.

And here begins a journey into the real future, one, in this case, that's somewhat grim. It's a story which has appeared a number of times, and in its present edition it has been brought up to "date," so to speak. Originally written during the "atomic" threat of a "cold war," it has now been re-processed to reflect the present time, when terrorism is the major threat to our modern civilization, and tells of a man with…

⊸A VERY CULTURED TASTE⊷

He sat alone in his room, listening to the exciting, mellow sounds of the recorded reproductions of great jazz moments of a history now gone, a time demolished, from a civilization destroyed.

He was alone and happy.

Now days he had saw few people beyond his servant Tommy. And those admitted into his presence were sad reminders of humanity. There were hardly any survivors since the rotting sickness had finished off most of those who had lived through the first few waves of death.

He laughed; both bitterly and ironically.

It was a worldwide disaster, a plague of hate, that started slowly with explosions here, there, then everywhere.

No country was innocent, none were saved from the violence of hatred that seethed throughout the lands. If you didn't believe the Real Truth, then you were doomed. If you didn't submit to the will of the fanatically dedicated terrorist, left and right, or even middle, then you must die! The world had split into not just two opposing power groups but split again and again. Finally the number of warring, hate-filled small nations, cults, sects, tribes, or mere one-man warriors, were beyond even wild estimates. It was a chain reaction as violent and deadly as an atomic holocaust. But it started in single acts that mounted into hundreds and thousands, Human bombs sacrificing themselves for a few lives were mere

107

sparks that led to bigger weapons of mass destruction. Nobody knew when it actually ended.

Then suddenly it was over!

The cancer of hate had destroyed Mankind, and those it hadn't killed it had driven insane, or changed into savage animals, lusting for each other, fighting and killing for a bite of food, a drink of water.

But not Révis Montrey. Révis was a cultured man, with cultured, well-rounded tastes.

Like this excellent French Chablis, he thought almost savagely, sipping from the small, hand-cut crystal glass gripped in his thin, wrinkled fingers.

He ran a few drops of the liquid around in his mouth and dreamily closed his eyes, as he listened to the mellow, soft sounds of Don Bagley's bass move through the air of the tiny, comfortable room.

His eyes surveyed the furnishings surrounding him. The dark leather chair set between the twelve speakers set inside all four walls, the coffee table sitting beside him, hand-carved by a German craftsman, the *Salvador Dali* original hanging on the wall to his left.

Yes, Révis, a cultured man of taste, had preserved a little portion of a now dead civilization here on the mountainside, all for himself. His art gallery displayed a collection of some of the finest artwork of all time. He had been lucky, far-seeing enough to be aware of the end of a world. It had taken thousands of years for Man to perfect a complicated civilization that religiously ate upon itself like a fanatical cannibal, leaving nothing but the rotting, twisted guts to digest away the rubble.

His lined, narrow face crinkled, the thin wine red lips snarled into a cruel twist of contempt. Anybody with intelligence would have realized the end was near. It was in all the papers, all the magazines, cable TV, and especially on the Internet! So obvious ever since the first atomic bomb was exploded on a Japanese town, and later when the religious wars slowly began to seethe as a result of the Middle Eastern conflicts. And the terrorist movements that followed had become the sparks that fired all out destruction.

But none had believed, none would believe that the danger was real. Or if they believed they were convinced that their Truth would certainly win in the name of their personal god! The fanatics of the world rose up and crushed civilization.

Nobody believed it could happen!

Only Révis Montrey had acted wisely.

Or so he told himself. Of course there were others who had been far-sighted, but all too few had survived very long.

He had prepared years in advance, far before the lines of insanity closed around the civilized head of Man and choked off its life.

He had lived in his mountain "castle" with his servant Tommy many years before the end had come.

Isolated or not, the Internet kept him posted.

Révis had had to take cruel, cutting remarks from the surrounding countrymen who thought him mad. Sure he was mad, like a fox, until the end of the world had proven him a sane man.

That was when everybody had come begging at his door for food and clothing, shelter, and help.

What had they thought he was? There had been only so much room to store food. The fools!

What did they think him—truly mad?

"Oh, no, sir, you are not mad," they had pleaded.

But you thought so before; why not today?

"Please pardon our outrageous actions of then—we did not realize; did not know!"

But you had your fun, your jokes, at my expense.

"But it was harmless. Only a joke. It did not hurt you."

You had your fun, jokes. Now, I'll have mine!

And he had closed his doors upon the savage madmen, who kept on hounding and pounding until hunger forced them to eat upon each other.

It was a good thing he had been careful and kept his food supply for himself and Tommy. Already it was running low. It would have run out a long time before if he had not taken protective measures. There was nothing like a good grilled steak or southern fried chicken—but now they were so scarce.

Yes, the human race had been made up of fools, and had

109

paid the full price!

Others had not prepared.

He had his atomic powered reactor that generated all the electricity he would ever need for the rest of his life. He had a huge, room-size freezer full of food that would last for years—as long as he continued to keep the more priceless meats of civilization for only special moments.

Révis flipped a switch at the side of his chair, and a machine somewhere in the paneling of his huge "castle" fortress clicked off and another one turned on, filling the room with the music and voice of Charles English, another of the great masters.

Yes, he thought, *this was the life, no worries, no struggles...*

He lived the life of a cultured man, even now, when all that had made culture did not exist any more.

A knock sounded at his door.

His insides shook with sudden violent rage, his face darkened, the wrinkles pulling tight.

Tommy knew he was not to be disturbed when he was listening to his music. Tommy knew that the Music Room was off limits when he was enjoying the relaxation of the music mems.

"Master, there is someone knocking at your door!"

"Well, hell, you know what to do—shoot him!"

Servants! The damn fools had to be told every move to make!

"But it is a woman!"

A woman? It had been a long time. Maybe too long!

His face relaxed and he thought dreamily of all the women he had so lustfully possessed through his life. Révis was a passionate man who had known the wondrous pleasures that only a female could dish up to delight a man's basic needs. One could never tire of a lovely feminine delight. He surely would never tire of such delicious treasures.

Ah, women! The gift to man! From young man on, such pleasures had been his to enjoy to the fullest. But being a man of very cultured tastes, he was starkly critical as to who would share his bed. Not every woman survived his harsh judgment! Only the very best won his favor.

110

Of course, today, one couldn't always be that choosy! Most survivors were not your most tasty tidbits—hardly fit for a cultured man's passionate tastes. Those who still clawed out an existence were half-mad, anyway. Who but the most insane could stomach a world gone "coo-coo-nuts"?

There weren't many women left since the rotting sickness had eaten its way into the very bones of all those who had survived the bombs and plagues. Women and children had been first to die. All too few of the women had survived. But when one had come offering themselves to him for the price of a meal, he had picked carefully—turning the others over to his servant, Tommy, whose taste in such matters was more coarse and common. Maybe that was why the two of them got along so well together.

The idea of a woman certainly appealed to Révis in a completely different way than it did to Tommy. Maybe that was good, too.

Now there was a woman wanting to get entrance into their castle fortress.

"Pretty?" Révis called out.

"Yes, Master...thin. Ragged, but pretty," came the voice of Tommy through the door paneling. There was rich thickness caressing every word, revealing the man's obvious hunger for this female treat. The man had little taste and no cultural value, but sometimes he did manage to select winners even in Révis' judgment.

"Okay, let me have a look. Let her in." A female might be just what the doc demanded to satisfy his rather basic cravings, in a cultured way, of course.

Révis waited silently, listening to the music. It seemed to take forever. Then finally a knock sounded once again on his door.

"Master, I've brought the girl."

Révis touched the button on the chair, and the door opened, the room flooded with light. Tommy walked in, leading a shabbily dressed woman into the room. Her hair was filthy, knotted, matted, and tangled. Her face, clothing and skin were covered with grime and dust, smeared thick. She had the haunted look of a wild animal in her eyes as she took in the finely furnished room.

111

Her eyes kept twitching slightly, and hands clutched as they took in her surroundings. Much like a mad animal she was, apparently, sizing things up. But the haunted, blank look in those eyes suggested something else.

What?

Perhaps the mere desperation of a lost child was being revealed. For certainly she was that!

Though hardly the delectable, delicious, desirable, delovely woman of choice! He laughed inwardly at his rewrite of the Cole Porter more skillfully phrased lyric.

Révis' stomach knotted slightly at the smell of her. His nose revolted, his eyes squinted against the sight of that sad body. He controlled the impulse to be crude and cutting about her appearance. Instead his more cultured side revealed itself.

"Hello," he greeted in a pleasant voice, forcing a smile onto his aged lips. "My name is Révis. I'm Master of the house."

"Hello, I'm Betty Wilson." She looked timidly at the Dali paintings then at him, her eyes falling on the empty trousers hanging where his legs should have been. They hovered there momentarily, pulled away and then snapped back.

He smiled more broadly, feeling a strange satisfaction at her embarrassment.

Such emotion was rather charming, in its way, he realized, almost sadistically. Perhaps it might not be too bad to offer her a few moments. A short conversation wouldn't hurt; Tommy offered so little intellectual stimulation. Now and then Révis enjoyed even lowbrow verbal exchanges with a stranger such as this.

Those eyes seemed to be fascinated by his non-existent legs. Why it should bother or interest or faze her was strange, but who knew what drove people in these last days. Perhaps she was truly half-mad; or half-witted; or merely somewhat dulled by hunger.

It really didn't matter to him.

"The rotting sickness," he explained in the soft, patient voice of a father to a daughter. "Just the rotting sickness. Somewhat annoying. But at least the rest of me is quite alive and well, and fully functional!"

At his announcement she shrank suddenly back, fear lighting the shallow fire in her haunted eyes. Her feet stepped towards the door. Her still well-shaped lips trembled as thin hands clawed at her breasts.

Obviously he revolted her.

"What's wrong with you, lady!" Révis inquired in an almost comically controlled, puzzled voice. "You aren't afraid of me, are you?"

Tommy quickly barred her way.

"Let me out! Let me out!" she screamed in sudden, blind terror.

"Calm her!" Révis snapped.

"I don't want nothin'…let me go! Out!"

Her unreasonable terror suggested something more than mere normal dread of the rotting sickness, which in reality couldn't be caught if she'd survived its original impact.

And the woman do doubt realized she would be expected to offer something in return for a meal. Nothing came without a hard price! Not even before hell claimed the world. That body had no doubt been offered up to many men for a shared meal.

Her reaction made little sense; but nothing made sense any more. Each moment offered its own strange and distorted rules. Reason and insanity blended together like a flip-flopping magnet gone berserk. So why should this woman be stable in any way?

"Shut her up!" Révis demanded, a bit annoyed and unwilling to tone down his anger.

Tommy slapped Betty across the face, gripping her right shoulder so that she could not get away from his cruel blows. Time and again his thick, pudgy fingers brutally hammered against her cheeks, until the screaming turned into sobs of pain.

"That's enough!" Révis motioned her over to the center of the room as Tommy released his grip on her arm.

Révis smiled warmly like an oily snake about to strike. "There's nothing to be afraid of, Betty. The sickness was over more than a year ago. It just left me a little scarred in the face and body, and I had to have Tommy here remove my legs at the knees before I rotted all the way up to my

113

heart."

She didn't look too reassured, her eyes were still large fires of fear, but she moved to the center of the room, as ordered.

"Turn around and let me have a better look at you.

She just stood there, frozen in terror, her arms huddled in a heap across her chest.

"Come, come, now, we're not going to bite you!" He made a circular motion with his right arm. *"Turn!"*

She didn't move.

"Oh, Tommy, turn her!" Révis commanded his servant. "Round, round, round!"

The squat man quickly, eagerly, obeyed, letting his hands run along Betty's body as he did so. His thick, large lips spread open, his small dark eyes twinkled as his fingers pressed greedily at her chest.

"Stop that, Tommy! I'm a cultured man, I won't put up with that kind of thing in my presence. After all, the lady's already frightened to death!" Révis screamed insanely, gripping the arms of the chair with both hands, half raising from the seat. "Do you hear me!"

"Yes, Master," Tommy said in a sad, disappointed voice. "I'm sorry—it's just been so long!"

Révis made an irritated action of his hands that meant the subject was closed.

"She's not too good...huh?" he asked, indicating the woman's figure with a nervous flick of his fingers.

"No, Master, *very* good!" Tommy toyed with the front of her blouse, grinning widely again.

"Stop that!" Révis ordered in a high screech that bounced around the room like some invisible alien life form.

Betty was trembling, and tears began running down her face.

"All I want is some food," she whimpered in such a low, shaking voice that it was hard to understand her words. There was a sad resigned hardness in her eyes that implied she'd do anything he wanted just for a meal.

That made him grin. "Sure, my child. Food it is!"

"What do you think, Master?" Tommy asked, his eyes now glistening with eagerness. He rubbed his palms nerv-

114

ously together. "Sexy little dish—no?"

Révis laughed at that. His whole face contorted into humor wrinkles, his lips trembled against the force of the laughter.

"Sexy little dish?" he repeated, drying his eyes with the cuff of his laced shirt.

Betty was looking from one man to the other in open bewilderment, as if she thought this was a madhouse.

"I only want food and water—I thought…" Her eyes searched the room, as if attempting to find help. There wasn't any. Her lips muttered sounds, half sobs. "I…you might—you can…do anything you like with me," she managed in a trembling voice. Then her eyes shifted to his. It was obvious that the idea of intimacy with his shriveled body was less than appealing—in fact horrifying. But probably not much more than some of the men she'd already submitted to. She sucked in a deep breath, and for just a moment there was a resigned recognition as to her fate. Her eyes welled with just the suggestion warmth, as if she were attempting to look seductive. "Anything, of course…"

"Betty, only speak when spoken to!" Révis snapped.

The woman's body leaned back, as if physically struck. Those words seemed to have crushed something inside, maybe beyond repair. She trembled only slightly, but enough show her horror.

She half whimpered in despair. The woman was, obviously, not quite right in the head; no doubt crazed by the last years of living death. She was clinging to false hope, desperately seeking a little more time; another day; hour; minute.

We are were all like that, Révis silently admitted to himself. Every living thing wanted to stay alive.

He smiled, motioned with his hand, said kindly: "Come over here!"

Tommy pushed her forward.

The fear remained in her eyes. But she did not move away from Révis. She stood there, waiting, lips set hard, as if holding back a scream of horror.

He reached out and felt her fingers. They were bony, thin.

"You certainly could use a little fattening up, I must

115

say," he observed, almost gently.

She smiled slightly, quickly reacting to his kinder sounding words.

"Please, lady, forgive me...but I must do this!" He placed trembling fingers on her chest, feeling the hard muscular swells there. Then he reached down and felt the firmness in her legs. They were sinewy, thin, coarse.

She winced at his touch, but did not move away.

"Take off your clothing," Révis finally demanded in a tired voice.

Betty's body stiffened as if it had been jolted by an electric shock. She started to step backwards, but Tommy grabbed her from behind, his fingers squeezing hard into those thin arms.

"Please, you're hurting me!"

"Now, Betty, I'm not going to hurt you. I just want to see your figure. After all, you can't deny an old man such a simple pleasure in return for what you are asking!"

She stood there, frozen for a moment, then slowly her hands moved up to the top of her dress.

It had been a long time since he had seen a *live* woman's body. Oddly enough he was almost trembling with excitement.

Her skin was coarse and muscular, hard. Her breasts were tight knots, unattractive and disappointing.

One look at her small, narrow, bony hips, thin starved looking legs, and Révis sighed, turning his eyes away from the sight.

Very disappointing, he thought. But what else could he have expected. Right from the start she'd been unpromising. Yet hope was eternal, even for a cultured man. In fact, even more so with a cultured man like Révis. Wise though his mind might be, the more basic hungers of the flesh made the imagination want to distort some realities by simply coloring over the ugly details.

In this case, though, even his mind magic was being stretched to it ultimate limits to make her look desirable.

"Not my type, but she'll do, Tommy. Take her out and fix her up—and be sure to scrub her good. I can't stand a dirty girl!"

116

"The usual?" Tommy grinned, smiling anxiously.

Révis simply nodded; he had already lost all of his eagerness. But one had to be realistic. She would certainly be better than nothing!

Tommy moved closer to Révis and leaned over, whispering in his ear. "I have a little fun, first, Master?"

Révis motioned the man out with a shrug of his shoulders, which meant he didn't care what Tommy did.

"Oh, thank you, sir," Betty cried, gathering up her clothing and following Tommy out of the room. Her step was lively and firm, her movement that of a woman who has been given hope, or who has escaped a terrible fate.

Those mood swings revealed a lot; not logical at all; not sane.

But it really didn't matter to him.

Révis smiled as Betty slipped out of his sight, then he pressed the chair button that automatically closed the door, dimmed the lighting and turned up the volume of the music.

It was some minutes before Révis heard Betty's first scream from the room above.

He turned up the volume of the music, hoping that would drown out the sound of the woman.

But her screams cut through the blasting blare of the stereo music. The screams sounded again and again, first in terror and then finally in agony.

Révis shuddered inwardly. *Tommy just wasn't a cultured man! He never had been.*

The screaming faded some, but continued for a long time before stopping. By then he was mentally focused on the beautiful sounds Stan Kenton's jazz band playing its theme song.

Révis sighed out his relief, and then took another sip of wine, savoring its full bodied taste. His ears followed the musical lines of the jazz soloist as they fingered through complicated runs and arpeggios.

An hour later there was a knock on the door.

"Master, dinner is ready!"

Révis pressed the button at the side of his chair, which opened the door, so that his servant could enter. Tommy came in and placed a large tray filled with dishes on the table before his master.

"Sexy girl! Real wow! Crazy dish!" Tommy smiled as he left the room.

Révis looked over the large serving of broiled meat with very little interest. This was going to be another one of those yucky meals.

His mouth was really watering for chicken or steak, but he realized that such luxuries had to be doled out carefully, otherwise they would disappear in a very short time.

He shrugged and forced himself to start eating. After all, there was only one way to fill out the food supplies!

Each bite was sickening to him.

Well, anyway, it was at least fresh food.

And he'd have to admit she tasted one hell of a lot better than she'd looked!

As a change of pace, so to speak, with a quick tour of a very distant place somewhere across the galaxy, we meet a nervous guy about to do his best to be impressive and successful in his new job in the travel business! This was his First Tour as a guide and he was determined to make a good impression. And he had a whole bag of tricks ready to make it a really successful...

⊸GUIDED TOUR⊷

In the year of our Lord 8564 on the world of *Senourousis,* there lived a young man and a young woman. One year after their first mating Mrs. Ee gave birth to a son, which they called *Flatter,* because his head was "flatter than a pancake."

Flatter grew up to be a large and strong son, and, like his father, learned the *arts of* magic. But by the time he was old enough to begin to work, magic was an unpopular art. So with heavy heart he went to the next best thing:

His job was Guiding tourists through the jungles of *Planoutious,* the sister of his own world and the only other planet in the solar system.

Planoutious was a Virgin World and all the gay posters advertising it made the most of this fact. People from all over the galaxy came by the billions to visit this tropical paradise; sometimes called The Virgin World.

So, to be a guide on such a popular planet was really something to make one proud. He was given the position because his gray-haired father still had political pull; though it was believed the old wizard had cast a spell in order to get the job for his son. But thus was the magic of rumors.

Anyway, as it turned out: it was a horrible mistake.

All through his life Flatter Ee had always been in some kind of trouble or another, mostly because he had the bad habit of always doing things wrong. Even in his magic spells it was just as likely that if he wanted to conjure up a beauti-

119

ful girl it would turn out to be an ugly old man.

Well, to make a short story even shorter, a terrible thing happened on his very *first*—and it might be added, last—guided tour.

No sooner had he jetted his extremely intelligent looking client and wife into the tropical reaches of the southern tip of the Virgin World than things started developing. Or was it under-developing. That was the problem with Flatter; he could never get those details quite right. Too many times doing things all backwards, rather than forwards.

Most confusing.

Not only to his embarrassment so many times in the past, but also now to mark his final doom! Of course he couldn't know that until it was too late!

First the man and his wife wanted to go down and look at this red-feathered beast, then at that fur-covered bird. They couldn't get enough "looking" at the strange and wonderful jungle creatures, taking dimensional color pictures of each and every one to "show the folks back home".

Within a matter of hours, of course, the horrible thing happened.

Just as they were about to return home, too! Can you imagine?

They found themselves trapped with a *Zaiter,* the most dangerous man-eating creature on the Virgin World. It stood, fangs exposed, claws extended, between them and the air-jet.

Suddenly magic was demanded.

"What will we do?" the man cried in open terror, even forgetting to take a picture of this savage beast.

"Help us, *please!"* the woman screamed, clutching to her husband, but staring at their guide.

Great Magic, with a Cap GM, was definitely demanded! And our hero was more than anxious to show off his magnificently magical talents in such a moment of need.

"Never fear, Flatter Ee shall save the day!" was the promised, confident statement of the young man.

Pulling the small black pocket *magic-spell-maker,* which he always carried around with him—a gift from his father some fifteen years before—he quickly made an invisible circle around the three of them by pointing the V-shaped

120

device in the air. Then carefully placing his finger on the little red button he said: "Go...go away to nothingness!"

His finger crushed the button.

Blackness slammed down like the falling of an ink-blanket, surrounding them.

Flatter Ee felt a horrid grind at the pit of his stomach. Frantically, he released the red button. But it was too late.

He'd done it backwards...again!

"What happened?" the man's voice demanded.

"Yes, where are we?" the woman pleaded from the blackness.

He should have made the circle around the *Zaiter!* How could he have forgotten such a simple rule?

He explained, ending with: "You see, I've cast a spell that can't be broken. I meant to send the *Zaiter* into nowhere—but instead I sent us—"

There was a momentary silence and then he heard the man groan in a rather dull, humorless voice:

"Which just proves, damn it, that Flatter Ee will get you nowhere!"

Well, okay, back to reality, of sorts. Criminals and rapists are not just a problem of past and present societies, but could very easily be just as dangerous in the far distant future when the galaxy is being explored. Now you take this fella and consider his chances of finding a heavenly reward on the...

◄PLANET OF THE LOVE FEAST►

As the small spacecraft entered the atmosphere the very winds seemed to offer up a deep sign welcoming pleasure, anticipation. It had been a long time...much too long...

The planet around them was alien; the star-charts claimed it was Earth-type G, but semi-desert. The crash landing had been unfortunate. But the planet had seemed beautiful and inviting from space, even though they had landed in a desert, bordered by distant mountains. It would be an easy matter to get to more pleasant surroundings and begin a life on this virgin world.

Darkness had fallen a few hours earlier and Jon Crayford built a campfire from the wood sections of the small space car that had brought them there.

He looked at his lone companion, letting his eyes rove over the woman's lovely figure. He couldn't have made a better choice. She would surely be an inviting companion in the coming weeks, months and probably years. Lean and intelligent looking, full bodied, full lipped and so wonderfully young; she was in the prime of life. At the time, though, there had been only one thought in mind: get a hostage. The escape from the Penal-Ship, which was taking him to Penalton Planet, had been impulsive, sparked by the unexpected trouble among the Ship's officers. He'd grabbed the first Citizen near him, threatening her with the small "shiv" he'd made from a short piece of metal in the Shop where they had been keeping him working during the trip.

122

Now, he edged closer to the woman.

"You're really very attractive," he announced, huskily. "And we're going to be together for some time."

Her eyes widened with quick alarm. "Don't get ideas. Rescue will be coming soon enough."

Jon laughed mockingly and touched her arm. It was silken soft. He ignored the slight cringing and pulling back from contact with him. That would change; quick enough. She was the first female he'd been with since his conviction for rape and murder several months before; and what a beautiful companion with whom to be marooned on an alien world.

"Don't fool yourself. We're trapped on this planet for the rest of our lives. We might as well make the most of it."

"Leave me alone! Just please be—"

"Don't give me no trouble!" He grabbed at her, as she pulled back. "I just want to make us one…loving unit of joy and passion and desire. You will soon learn to enjoy every moment in my arms. Believe me!"

Tears welled in the woman's eyes; her lips trembled in open terror. "Oh, God—what have I done to—"

Jon reached for her, folding his large arms around her body. He was beyond even trying to pretend to be a gentleman. He had always considered women lovely toys to enjoy and this one was prime for his taking.

"Don't…" she screamed into the deaf night air.

"Forget the past," he muttered, voice husky with desire. "There's only *now!*"

"Please!" she screamed, recoiling from his touch. "*Please!*"

She pushed away, frantically attempting to free herself.

"All I want is for us to enjoy—"

Then she suddenly twisted, her knee slammed upwards, smashing brutally between his legs.

Pain erupted through him like sharp sparks of blazing fire. He crumpled backwards, air choking his throat.

"You bitch," he groaned, rolling over, avoiding the swift kick she swung at his face.

Leaping to his feet, he slammed a large fist into her soft stomach, and then pushed her down onto the sand. Red anger

123

clouded over his vision, anger that bubbled away sanity. When awareness returned, the woman was lying under him, her eyes staring blankly into the night sky.

He didn't have to take a second look to know she was dead. The same scene had been enacted months before when he'd attacked his girl after she told him about her engagement to another man. Insanity had overcome him then, as it had now.

"You stupid bitch!" he screamed. "Stupid, stupid!"

In seconds, the full implications flooded over him. He was now alone on a strange planet, about which even the star-charts revealed little.

"Oh, God, not *alone*!"

A soft murmur flowed through his mind: *Not alone!*

The wind touched his face, bringing with it the sound of cold, chilling laughter. *Not totally alone!* He thought it was his own laughter, and panic suddenly burst through him.

We promise you…not totally alone any more!

Jon wasn't aware of running, stumbling insanely across the night desert. It wasn't until morning that he became conscious of his surroundings.

Exhausted, thirsty and hungry, he collapsed to the blue sandy desert. For a long time he lay there, the hot sun baking his exhausted body.

"Earthling—come…come…*come,"* a voice called in his mind, jarring him awake. *"Come."*

For a moment Jon was stunned, believing he was imagining voices. A convulsive shiver ran through his large frame.

Slowly he stood up, looked around at the sandy desert and then froze.

There was a naked woman standing on a sand dune several yards away. She had long, golden hair that rippled behind her in the morning breeze.

He must be mad!

She waved a slender arm toward him, as sunlight glinted on her full breasts. His eyes followed the dip of her waist and the flare of her hips, then downward to the solid thighs and legs. Where had she come from? From a mad-driven mind? Maybe the Solar-Judge had been right about his being insane? Maybe he *should* be locked away for life.

"Earthman, I am as real as you—do not be afraid," a pleasant thought sang gently into his mind. "We do not judge you. That you are here is all that matters." It was like a caressing hand soothing into his fevered hot brain. "We are not like that silly woman you lost last night. We long for what only you can give us!"

He surely was mad! Totally insane. It was all illusion, surely, mere madness driving him to delude himself that he was not alone.

"Earthman," the woman called out, "we have been waiting for you!"

He tensed, struggling with the irresistible urge to step forward. His mind warned him to flee from this strange creature before something terrible happened. If she was real, then she could hardly be human.

But if illusion…might it not be a wonderful one to enjoy?

Now he recognized her as an alien being—something that had been bred upon this forsaken virgin planet and not in a tortured mad mind.

Alien but beautiful beyond anything he had ever seen. More desirable. More loving than his hateful mother had been!

"You can't be real!" he muttered half fevered with desire.

"I am as real as you!"

When he coiled up, frightened still, torn between wanting to believe and wanting to be rational. What horrors could such a divine creature want to vest upon him?

"Nothing will happen," she smiled, reaching out invitingly. "You are what we desire most of all. We love Earthmen."

Suddenly, against his will, he felt himself being physically lifted from the ground and carried forward.

Calmness flooded over his panic-thoughts; but part of him was still near the edge of hysteria. Then sudden soothing peace was coming from a force outside himself, not from within.

"We will bless you! Eradicate all your sins. Make you

whole and perfect!" Something was *forcing* him into a sense of well-being. *"We understand the passion that drives you."* He was set down in front of the strikingly beautiful woman. *"We have read into your very soul and seen the reflection of all your desires...which match ours! We are fully in tune with your inner being."*

She had golden eyes; they matched her silken hair. Her skin was creamy white, like the snows of earth.

"You are forgiven of all your human sins and will become one with us in our glory and power and passion."

A smile taunted him with a very human promise.

"This world upon which you have landed will give you a new beginning; washing away all that horrors of the past and opening up a new found chance of a rewarding ecstasy in our arms. Here we understand. Here we are dedicated to fulfilling your greatest desires. Here on our world you'll become one with all that we are!"

She reached for his hand and he felt a strange electricity surge through him, binding his body to hers in an ecstatic moment of intimacy. "Come to your new found beginning, a second chance at perfection!"

He hesitated, wondering how this creature could seem to read his mind. Or was she illusion?

"No. We are real. As real as you. And yes. We can see into your very soul, your mind, your inner being and know what you want, what you are, and what you can and will become as a very part of all that we are! We have waited for you," she murmured. The thin accent was strange but delightful to hear. She gazed deep and hungrily into his eyes. "The others before you—"

Those words stunned him; brought momentary sanity to the madness creeping into the very ends of every nerve.

Madness? No! Something far more wonderful!

"There were others?" his mind inquired silently. The nearness of her, the seductive perfection of her body suddenly pressed away all fears. Surely such a woman could be nothing but loving and kind and warm. His lips formed the words slowly: "Where are they?"

"You will find out soon enough, but first you must experience the Love Feast!" Her eyes lighted. "You must do as

126

all before you have. They all feasted on the altar of love—blended with us in a fiery ecstatic union. It is the ultimate act that makes it possible to become one with us...for we are hungry for Man, as hungry as Man is for Woman!"

"But..." he was unable to believe the implications of her words. If this were true, then he was surely in paradise. That woman he'd killed wasn't a loss at all, but rather where she belonged with her prudish ideas!

"She wasn't real. She was an illusion. The past does not exist any more. All that is real is what you see before you, now. *We* are real. This *world* is real. Nothing else matters. Embrace that reality and you'll be forgiven of all your sins!"

He grinned in anxious excitement at the very idea of possessing this wonderful creature who desired him so totally that she seemed to be visibly trembling with wanton need.

"Yes...yes..." he murmured, heady with ever growing desire. No. Compelling hunger beyond anything he had ever known before.

His head was spinning dizzily, as if from some intoxicating liquor.

The beat of her chanting invitation pounded through him: "Come, be embraced by my passion for you. Let me envelope myself around and through you! Be mine tonight!"

He gazed into her eyes and saw all the images of love, the flowery forms, the scented beauty, the unspoken promise of sensual perfection.

"Our consuming passion will wipe all traces of past sins, and make you pure to feast at our table of passion, to become the center for our love feast!" It was like a gentle hand caressing his body, soothing any fears, calming all possible doubts.

"Come," she murmured, leading him up the crest of the sand dune. When they reached the top, he felt the breath break from his lungs.

A shimmering city of tents, flashing in vivid reds, blues, yellows, greens, lay stretched out on the desert floor.

"This is our home," she sang out softly. "There is nothing to fear."

His doubts were eclipsed by a sudden raw animal excitement her mere words created.

She led him down the sand hill and through the alien village.

Women stepped from the tents and stared eagerly at him. They giggled to themselves; they sang soothing chants and reached out to gently caress him as he passed.

Oh, what pleasure their very touch created.

He looked for signs of the other Earthmen the woman had told him about. But there were none.

"Where are the others—the men?"

"They are here," she explained softly, leading him into a small green tent. "You will join them shortly—but I want to feast upon you first. I want to taste the joyful ecstasy that is yours alone to give."

He felt his body burn with a hunger her words promised to fulfill. He laughed inwardly, drunk with the idea of uniting with this lovely creature, blending her alien form to his. Then doubt froze his laughter.

If she was alien, how could it be possible that...?

"Be not worried," a voice reassured him. *"We have been waiting for Man. We have a deep hungry need for him!"*

The woman leaned closer and the perfume of her body made him giddy. Her lips caressed his and their softness melted all suspicion.

"Kiss me again, let me have the taste of your mouth," she breathed, pressing tightly to him.

"Let me feast on your lips let me swallow the nectar of your moist tongue!"

Their lips met and the ecstasy, which shimmered through his mind and body, made him totally weak and helpless in her embrace. She drew his tongue greedily into the depths of her mouth, as if devouring a rich, intoxicating wine, which she could never tire of drinking.

She pulled away, gazing lovingly into his eyes—she trembled visibly and her breath came in deep wracking sobs. Yet her words were a series of caressing raptures enveloping his total being.

"You're like a rich flowery *lun,* like the wine of *Gjille.* You are voluptuous food to my starved hunger, golden drink

128

to my raw thirst! Undress and let me feast upon you. Let me devour you with my lips and body—let me drink in the sweet taste of your liquid form—let me become a fiery *One* with your very soul and mind!"

He stripped eagerly. Yet wondering what he had done to enjoy such a reward. His life had not been without sin; without wanton lust for all women.

"Lust as I have for you!" she murmured. "Hurry. Let me see the full glory of you! I want my eyes to feast upon what my whole soul and body so desperately hunger for."

Those words flowed over him with such force that he was totally helpless to their commands.

She reached out and their fingers interlocked. She urged him to the far side of the tent, to a soft grassy mat, smeared with grease and rusty stains. Strangely, he didn't mind the dirt, or the mildly decayed odor that welled up as if from an open grave.

They lay down and she folded her arms around him, drawing his rough muscular body against the supple softness of hers. The silk of her flesh fused tightly to his.

"Oh, the love feast…oh, let me feast of your passion, on all that you are!" Then her warm lips found his very inner being; gliding along his flesh, tongue licking fiery over every nerve, creating tremors of utter joy beyond imagination wherever it caressed.

This time the pleasure was so intense that he hardly noticed the voluptuous power of those strong lips as they frantically suckled on him as if attempting to drain all his blood, all his moisture into her body.

And as the kiss lingered, the pleasure mounted to such intensity that it became overpowering. It was at the very edge of terrible agony. Overwhelming.

Every muscle struggled against the pleasure-pain, fighting to somehow escape this all-enveloping power the woman now possessed over him.

Her arms locked tightly around him, pinning his body to hers. A low growl, animal and alien, broke from her as those silken lips slid greedily down to his shoulder.

That hungry mouth clamped softly, caressingly to his flesh.

129

He found himself melting into a dark funnel of pleasure, ecstasy, helpless being driven at such powerful pulses of energy that all he could do was totally submit.

Then the tingling pleasure of her teeth tenderly nibble electric waves of ecstatic joy into the meat of his muscles as her jaws crunched tight with intense need.

It was then that ecstasy soared upwards and burst into a sharp awareness of intense pain. He felt the horrible voluptuous anguish of sharp teeth shred deep into his naked shoulder, clamping tightly together until the jaws closed.

He screamed. His lungs burst raw in fiery agony.

A moan of deep satisfaction broke from the woman as she drew away a bloody mouthful of flesh from his shoulder. Her lips were crimson-smeared as they greedily chewed; her golden eyes rolled upwards in their deep sockets. She convulsed in ecstasy, body writhed in spasms, arms breaking away and falling to her side, flapping like tendrils. The skin drew tight across her suddenly more angular bones, stretching in a blur of movement as she shuddered in the grip of uncontrolled convulsions.

Horrified, Crayford struggled to his feet. The pain in his shoulder, which was torn raw to the bone, wasn't half as bad as the fantastic nightmare form the woman had now assumed.

He was looking down upon a greenish-tinted humanoid, its flesh stretched gaunt and pulsing over thick bones. Large beady eyes stared upwards, blindly.

He screamed and rushed out of the entrance, sickeningly aware of what had happened to the other spacemen who had come to the planet.

A crowd of beautifully formed women danced before him, seductively offering themselves with eagerly outstretched arms, their beautiful lips inviting, their breasts pumping rhythmically with the hungry panting of their lungs. Their eyes were golden bright, blazing into his.

"No!" he screamed, raising an arm to blot out the sensual panorama.

Then the writhing women reached for Jon, touching his body, waving the electrifying pleasure over him, weakening all efforts to escape. With his eyes covered it was almost

130

possible to battle away the images of all those voluptuous vixens from paradise. But hands grabbed at him, powerful fingers rapped around his arm and forced it away from his eyes. Once again the images flushed away all resistance. He hungered overwhelmingly to be totally taken by these incredible creatures.

All their forms seemed to stretch together and then contract into a vast surge of undulating female flesh, smothering him, drawing him into their very depths.

"Earthling!" they all said as one in his mind, *"we have waited so long—waited hungrily for you! Be not afraid—we only want to become one with you—to blend spirit and soul!"*

And their words had real meaning—he now realized the horrible truth of their alluring cry.

Then they closed around him, caressing, kissing, and clawing in wild passion, hungry to feast on his body.

And with every caress came that wonderful flood of ecstasy. The wild fiery pleasure became stronger and stronger until its intensity burst into pain—and he was screaming, screaming, screaming, until the sun fell on the planet, and the chill of night blanketed the desert floor. His screams went on for a time, then slowly became softer, until the breeze drowned them out completely.

The next morning all that was left on the blue sands was the newly stripped skeleton of the Earthman. The soft breeze whispered among the bones like lonely voices.

The moaning wind sighed sadly, and seemed to gather in on itself. It was always a long time between visits from other worlds.

The planet of the love feast quietly awaited its next meal!

Every author has a story they enjoyed writing and even re-reading at times. This is one that I enjoyed. That doesn't mean the reader will agree with me, but it has a publishing history that includes being in the pocket book collections IF THIS GOES ON (1965, Book Company of America) and IMAGES OF TOMORROW (1969, Powell Sci-Fi). And also translated into Spanish in the sci-fi collection LOS MEJORES RELATOS DE ANTICIPACIÓN (1969, Bruguera Libro Amigo), and APRÈS in French (1970, Marabout). Well, that's as much as I know about. It, like many stories, may have appeared elsewhere in unauthorized editions. But not necessarily in exactly the same way twice. And its title has changed, too, for a while being "The Groovy Homo Sap" which I decided to drop in this latest version. It has now been given its last "update" to bring it into the twenty-first century. But it continues to be...

⟨THE HOMO SAP⟩

Somebody pushed the panic button!
And that is where the story began.
It didn't matter what caused the final conflict, it just happened!
The world exploded, rumbled, shook; great destructive ripples bloomed into existence over every civilized center of Man. Monstrous tidal waves reached out like hungry, gigantic arms, flooding the continental coastlines, as if attempting to devour the land. Then came the waves of viral sickness to wipe out those who had survived the first wave of death.
The human race gave one last fluttering moan, and died. Humankind had had its glowing moment and now it was over; darkness had fallen on its grand design. Mankind had fumbled the ball beginning with the mistake of Eve and Adam listening to the seductive voice of the snake and then continuing to feed upon the forbidden Tree of Knowledge throughout the ages.

132

The problems of this species didn't exist any more. Didn't count. All the egocentric biased wisdoms and super-charged belief systems had crumbled against one another in that final conflict. By the middle of the twenty-first century the *homo sap* had fooled around with the wrong "apple" and been computerized right out of existence. The human hard drive had been washed clean off the face of the planet!

Still all was not lost.

As the good Gods will allow, intelligence isn't, and never was, really limited to just one creature. And lucky it was, too.

Since Homo sapiens came from a common stock with the monkeys, there was every reason to expect another homo-intellect would spring forth from that same tree of evolution.

And so it came about, much sooner than any human would have been willing to imagine, that a *homo-monk* of rather shrewd perception stepped from the ruins of Mankind's crumbling cities and looked at the world around him, sadly shaking his head from side to side.

If the truth were to be known, this homo-monk was outstanding because of several scientific experiments that it had been put through, both physically and mentally. Or maybe it was the other way around. Maybe the scientists had picked him for genetic experimentation because of his unusual intelligence. Either way it doesn't make much difference. The long and the short of it all (and he *was* rather tiny, at that) is that this homo-monk had an entirely different outlook on life than any of his fellow monks. And strangely enough, considering what the final destruction had done to the human race, there were plenty of monks running around—most of them far larger than himself. That would have been somewhat terrorizing to a less intelligent monk.

So in the words of a wise Man: *a small child shall lead them!*

Yet, with all his special ability, this little monk was rather unhappy. After all, his only playmates were just a bunch of apes. Or at least a bunch of dumb "little" apes.

Regardless of what one would call them, they didn't have the final stamp of personality that was his mark of superiority.

And, quite frankly, a super intelligence always gained control over the vulgar masses. It wasn't smarts nor magnificent strength, but merely a matter of charm that won the day against all who might confront him or attempt to challenge is leadership. After all, great leaders are born and are automatically followed by all their admirers. And he had many monks who openly admired his superior ways.

Admiration from such minor monks was hardly much of an ego-boost to our friend.

Well, anyway, being a rather far-seeing little guy, he figured there had to be at least one above average female monk, somewhere. Maybe even a superior girl homo-monk like himself! Thus he dedicated his life to finding her, so he could give birth to a lot of little monks, and thus repopulate the world with beautiful copies of his own genetic line.

As you can see, he was a very ambitious fellow. And he wasn't having much luck in finding the girl-monk of his dreams. But he didn't let this deter him in his ultimate plans. He came across many attractive members of the opposite sex to ravish, and, even though they were rather stupid, he enjoyed such momentary pleasures. Though, sometimes he simply had to force himself to do the right thing, presenting them with future children that could be gifted with the finer genetic brand of true intelligence. Thus he was planting the seeds of a possible future evolution of homo-monks, just in case he was not lucky in finding a suitable mate.

These unions, at best, were always rather somewhat degrading to his moral sense, being only "animal" attractions. Heck, he wanted something a bit more romantic and mind expanding.

Our fella needed to find his soul-mate!

Humans had decided animals didn't have souls. But what the heck did they know? They'd wiped themselves out of the equation and their ideas and convictions didn't matter anymore. Of course they had been responsible for his super-minded existence and might be considered a kind of god-like creature. Certainly his personal divine creator—of sorts, anyway! But that didn't mean our friend was a soulless beast. Hardly that!

134

At times, he would find it difficult to avoid offering silent salutes—prayers?—in memory of Mankind. After all, he didn't want to create a new religious icon for Monkdom to worship. Dedication to false idols had brought about human's horrid demise.

That was something to avoid! And at times, when pausing in the ruins of the lost civilization turned almost to dust, he would wonder, and worry a bit. But not for long!

Our monk simply shook off such doubts and continued his dedicated search for female with enough soul to match his own.

Yet, as the years progressed and he populated the world with hundreds of seedlings for a future generation of superior-type personalities much like his own, he began to actually doubt that there was a super lady-monk.

Years passed, and white streaks peppered his finely combed fur.

He became downhearted, but didn't give up.

She had to be out there…somewhere!

That was the mantra that powered his search.

Then one day, when he was just about to give up all hope, he heard soft murmurings. Just a suggestion. But the mutterings sent him off in a new direction.

It was rumored that way up in the north there was a rather standoffish little female monk, who had superior ways. She wouldn't let the local boys touch her, and had a reputation of being snooty in her relations with all members of her species.

Hmmmmm, he thought, *was she something special or simply a stupid little snob?*

It was also hinted that this lady was very beautiful and desirable. Monks from all around would go to her in hopes of attaining intimate favors; but she bluntly turned them all down, cold!

Well, he reasoned, jumping over a jagged and broken light post, *no girl-monk had said no to him…yet!* And his own homo pride forced him onwards, even though he fully doubted the rumbling that she really *was* different.

The closer he got to where she was living, the more talk he heard about her. And finally, when he arrived in her area, the general attitude was that this girl-monk definitely was something special.

"She can even write her own name..." one male monk told him with awed surprise. "In *Human* lettering, too!"

That did say something for her, he thought with pleasure.

"But she'll turn you down like she has turned all of us down!" another male announced.

"Well, we'll see about that!" he laughed, all confidence.

They laughed back, too, just as assured of his failure. "You must come back and tell us all about it!"

"Sure, of course," he lied; then added a warning: "But don't wait up all night—I will be very busy. In fact, maybe many nights...if you get my drift!"

It was then they cheerfully gave him directions to where she lived.

Perhaps she'd be a challenge of sorts, he tried to convince himself. Maybe. Hopefully.

Ah, but he doubted that. No female hesitated to take him on; no strings, no demands. Even this lady would surely be a disappointing rehash of all the others. *But maybe...* he thought, almost prayed, *oh, Mighty Creator of the Universe...make her my match, my soul mate!*

Of course he'd used that chant all too many times in the past to no effect.

Oh, how he hungered for a real challenge! Something to sink his wisdom teeth into!

Of course, he realized, this wouldn't be much different from past experiences.

The years were littered with endless worshipping female monks who had all too willingly submitted to his momentary needs for carnal pleasures. He had left them in a divine state of ecstasy, for he was surely a master of the erotic arts—and they were somewhat crude in their mating rituals.

And over the years he had developed a rather enlarged ego awareness of his Mighty Powers. He realized that many cults had formed in his name! Their flocks surely prayed for his quick return! Alas, they would wait forever! He had better things to do than merely returning for repeat performance! Once had been good enough!

136

So he was determined, like some pre-historic ancient god, to make this new, uppity female a true worshipper of his unlimited male charms! After all, he was as close to a god-monk as one could get in this strange new world. And she would simply bow to his will like all true believers always did before their master.

His ego demanded her seduction to his will!

After making sure he was spruced up, with neatly combed fur, cleanly bathed and looking his best, he approached her living quarters.

She lived in large home of a once rich, human family, that had somehow survived the ruin of universal war. Best of all it had a huge courtyard in which to enjoy the good life. It was a beautiful place, grown thick with trees, flowers of every color, low soft grass—a paradise for a weary traveler like our friend.

The moment he saw her he fairly flipped with joy. How beautiful she looked. Her fur was carefully combed, her teeth gleaming, yellow, the fangs so dainty and attractive. Such tiny, delicate hands. And her figure! She was the most!

He was mad about her from the first instant. Soul mate; holy mate!

After all, he was almost human, and you can't blame him for being knocked cold by a beautiful and attractive female! Even Humans were famous for their weakness for the opposite sex.

This lady-monk was real up there; far beyond anything he had ever seen. Beauty was one thing, and she had that. What impressed him most, at first glance, was how she totally ignored him. Instead of looking up, turning around and automatically taking a mating stance, she seemed completely oblivious of his approach.

She was drawing pictures on the ground with a stick.

His first glance at her artwork didn't really impress him very much, but, after all, one couldn't expect a female to be artistic.

"My dear lady," he said in homo-monk language.

She looked up with a cold expression in her eyes.

It was as if she were waking from a dream. She tapped the ground at her feet with the stick, apparently annoyed by this rude interruption of her work.

Then her eyes focused on him, taking in every detail as they swept over his form. And the moment her eyes met his they widened with surprise. Admiration flowed like an explosive fire!

All at once she wildly jumped up and down, then did a quick rolling back flip.

It was love at first sight.

The very air surged with electric waves that enveloped the whole garden in its hot fury.

He had found his equal at last! There was no doubt in that fact. The conviction was so total that he felt weak, helpless, without any will of his own. The connection between the two of them was so intense that his body shivered helplessly.

And there was no doubt that she felt the same way about him.

If birds of a feather flock together, then obviously two super homo-monks would immediately recognize one another at first glance!

They hugged each other in wild happiness, and in an ecstasy of overwhelming joy ran and jumped and swung into the trees, leaping from branch to branch. They fairly flew from one end of the garden to the other in their openly ecstatic happiness.

But, as the old saying goes, if homo-sap had been made a monkey of by a beautiful female of ITS kind, then a monkey surely was able to be made a "monkey of"—or at best a homo-sap by a girl-monk.

Suddenly she stopped in her mad flight through the lush garden. She scampered to a large tree.

"We gotta do this right by the book!" she murmured in a soft, low voice, hardly heard by our hero-monk.

Doubt teased his mind: marry her?

Well, maybe...

He came out of the bushes after her, and then stopped short, surprised as she turned, an inviting smile on those deliciously lovely lips.

Shock showed on his features. All at once it was too clear; *and* too late!

In alarmed horror his hand slapped up at his face.

"Oh, my gosh!" he screeched, looking at what this female temptress was holding out toward him. *"Not again?"*

The object in her hand was, of course, red and round and juicy-looking.

He hesitated for only a moment and then, helplessly shrugging his narrow shoulders, stepped forward and took the tempting gift.

Somewhere in the tree above, naturally, he heard a rattling and soft hissing, but tried to ignore it.

What the hell! he thought, taking a bite from the apple. So it was a repeat performance!

Thus it was that the race of *homo-saps* was born again!

Now it is time to get serious! The original publication in magazine form had this caption over the story: Any similarity between these events and reality may be strictly intentional! To which I add, right on! This is a nasty little political satire which fits into today's wars on terrorism and hard-line presidents just as it did back when it was originally written in the mid-1960s. A bit frightening how little things change in government! Even in the far distant future some interplanetary president might go a bit whacky like present-day leaders seem to be doing. Hard-lining can be good under the right circumstances, as is, perhaps, pointed out in this revelation about...

⊸THE NOVA INCIDENT⊷

BEING A SERIES OF DISPATCHES ON THE DEVELOPMENT OF THE PEACE TALKS

22 June 2101, Danton, (IWN): The President of the United Federation of Planets arrived at the Danton Capital early this morning. All questions on the war were immediately countered with one of John J. Jenning's famous smiles and a "no comment!" When asked if he expected a settlement soon with the aliens, he did offer this:

"We are willing, at great expense to our Federation and the Solar System, to continue the war as long as necessary in order to be in the best bargaining position. The opposition is well aware of this from the last offensive they made on Kartion III. Our positions, hard held, will continue to be held at all cost! It is our opinion that talks will begin in a very short time, We are, after all, winning!"

A reporter inquired why he felt we were winning, since the aliens had in two months taken several Federation planets. He merely said: "Your President has classified information that reveals a different picture on the real situation."

This statement was made one hour before the unexpected and total defeat of the Federation forces at Kartion III.

A General—to be nameless—said, after the announced defeat:

"While I can't claim we are winning, I feel that JJJ must have knowledge unknown to the military—at least this officer. That would explain his unyielding hard-line."

* * * * * * *

23 June 2101, Pluto (IWN): In an interview with the press at Martsville, Professor David Sherman Chan, well-known expert on alien culture, was asked: "What is the basic problem facing the President in regard to the aliens?"

The white-haired professor fondled his pointed graybeard, stared through thick glasses and said in his slow drawl: "One has to understand the alien culture in order to know why they must have their demands honored in public. Pride.

"The remarkable fact is that for some eighty years we have lived side by side, exchanging scientific and cultural knowledge, building a mutually satisfactory import and export exchange.

"It was probably lucky that the aliens are physically not so different as to be repulsive. They are bipeds, bi-sexual, with a face organized much along the same lines, with only color and lack of hair being any real basic or dramatic difference. While the green and blue shadings of their races seem strange, they are hardly repellant—obvious from the fad that followed the first years of contact when our women covered their skins with make-up to match the coloring of the aliens.

"What is not so well-known is that the aliens, culturally and psychologically, are very much like humans in the matter of pride, very possibly even more so.

"We are dealing here, in fact, with the first confrontation of cultural pride. They have a very simple logic in such matters and it is to be expected that they would react as violently as they have.

"It is my opinion that if our president would bend to their demands in the proper way, all else might fall into place.

"I have told the President that if he were able to find a middle road, where their pride would be satisfied, without weakening our position of apparent or real power, he would probably find it easy to bring about a rapid settlement.

"In other words, to conclude, gentlemen, the middle road of strength is not easy. A means must, in the end, be found to satisfy their pride without hurting our own. I hope that makes it quite clear."

* * * * * * *

24 June 2101, Danton, (IWN): JJJ called an emergency meeting of his staff here on the Danton system. They remained in conference for over an hour, then his press secretary Gordon G. Gordon made the following statement.

"The President received an official message this morning stating that if we were willing to make certain public admissions—statements that would be outright lies—peace talks might follow. The President has sent the following to their Chief Head:

"'We find your statements about the act of the ship *Nova,* and so-called aggressive acts against your people, as totally at odds with our own information.

"'While it is our wish to end this ruthless killing before it becomes a total conflict, it is out of the question until your government realizes that the only way to peace is a mutual gathering of our heads of state and a serious attempt to understand one another's problems. We feel compelled to say that while the action of the pirate ship *Nova* was unsound, it was not an official representative of our government, and we are doing everything possible to bring those responsible to justice. But the militant action by your government was an aggressive act against our own people in the attack and capture of a planet of our Federation, and the murder of military personnel and confining of all civilians. Such acts were against the people of our Federation, a political and cultural move of aggression that must be considered an act of war.

"'Our sole purpose of coming some ten light-years to the planet Danton, whose system has been since invaded by your forces, was to begin peace talks. We demand immediate withdrawal of your forces from this system as a sign of your willingness to seek a peaceful solution to the situation both our governments now face."

* * * * * * *

24 June 2101, Earth, (IWN): Reactions to the President's exchange with the alien government this day were, as expected, diverse, here at Capital City.

Senator Channing, well-known for his opposition to JJJ's last election, said: "I must admit to some surprise at his continued hard stand. He doesn't seem in a position to make demands, considering the fact that Danton is surrounded by alien forces. Yet, alien psychology is a wonder to behold, to say nothing of our president's. Though I am morally required to say this: It is obvious that the President has some surprises up his rocket tubes. What they might be, we at Capital City are not privy to."

Donsisky, Senator from the Eastern Complex, was a little more direct: "I believe he has no way of knowing the total power of the aliens, as is apparent from the series of defeats we have experienced under his leadership. It would have been far more effective if he had, at the beginning, launched a massive cobalt attack on their home planet and system. Of course, it is too late to make this kind of move with any real great effect. But I must admit that the President's hard stand is admirable."

But the surprising statement came from one of his own party leaders, Senator Fredericks of the Republic of South and North America. "Having known John for some 50 years, and being in close contact with his political growth I find it typical for him to believe that a strong, firm, unyielding stand is the only way to victory. Some have called him ruthless. In his ten years in the office of the Presidency it has been his continued habit to never back down, no matter what the odds against him might be. Nonetheless, there are times when we must admit the reality of a situation. To be quite frank, I can't imagine what secret weapon gives him the courage to hold fast to a tough, no-bending line. If there is some secret lever, he is playing a good game of stellar poker.

If, on the other hand, he is at his old game of bluffing against losing odds, he's a very bad Judge of the opposition and a terrible poker player—and God help us!"

* * * * * * *

25 June 2101, Danton, (IWN): The official statement of the alien government to the President's demands reported here last night is as follows:

"As long as your government continues to show such a lack of honest willingness to cooperate in developing a mutually satisfactory situation that might offer solid grounds for setting up realistic considerations for peace talks, we will now discontinue all efforts in this direction."

The President appeared before the press this evening to say: "I find their attitude puzzling. But as far as this government is concerned, we feel justified in our demands and will stand firm. We will continue our defensive and continue to hold our position."

It was made immediately before our defeat in space at the battle of the Three Suns. Nobody here knows for sure if the President was at the time aware of the coming defeat.

* * * * * * *

25 June 2101, Earth, (IWN): The following incomplete message was received from our presidential correspondent.

"The unexpected attack on Danton by the alien space fleet has left the planet and its population in a state of shock since its beginnings a few hours ago. As we stand here recording this report, the sound of distant battle is loud in our ears. We have heard that the President and his staff are already making plans for the immediate lift-off to an unnamed planet."

The message was broken off at this point and we, at Interplanetary World News, are at a loss to know what happened to interrupt it so suddenly and without any explanation. We have received reports that the planet Danton was taken in one bold stroke by the aliens, within a few hours of their attack.

144

* * * * * * *

27 June 2101, Unknown, (IWN): My last report was cut short by the announced alien break-through into the capital city of Danton and the immediate offer of withdrawal on the President's ship for all news correspondents. Until now we have been isolated from all communication outlets. We are deep within the surface of an unnamed planet, which is atmosphere free, well protected from any outer attack by very powerful laser screens. The President remained isolated with his staff until early this morning when he ordered a gathering of those reporters who came with him. The following is his statement.

"The attack on Danton and our necessary retreat here have not in any way changed the position of our government. We are quite able to defeat the aliens in an all-out conflict. There is no reason to back down one word of our original statements to their government.

"However, I have received a message from the alien government, which says in part:

"'It is our wish to end this conflict. Admit to aggressions against our people in the unwarranted attack of your spy ship *Nova* upon one of our freighters. Refusal on your part is considered a sign of your unwillingness to find peaceful alternatives.

"I sent the following answer: 'Your unprovoked attack on Danton and the implied attempt to capture or kill the President of the Federation is deplorable. Unless you stop this fighting, return our planets, we will take them back by force.'

"We are not fighting this war over the issue of the *Nova*," he continued to tell us, "but over the total concept that *no* government, human or alien, has the right to attack and capture a planet by force.

"On Earth we learned this lesson after bitter years of Cold War conflict. Since then the World Government expanded to Solar government, then with the united knowledge and efforts of *all* Mankind we were able to create a star drive.

"Man has in the last hundred years learned not only to live in peace with himself, but to accept the concept that there are other intelligent creatures in the Universe and we have room in our hearts to embrace all forms of intelligent life and live side-by-side with them. But as equals—on terms that will profit both sides equally.

"We have attempted to restrain ourselves. I, as your President, have not been blinded to the realities of the problem now facing us. I am aware there are many, our Vice President for one, who would have attacked immediately in force. Instead, I've tried to learn from the lessons of the past and restrain my hand.

"It would have easy to say we were in the wrong, but such an admission would not be taking into account that the enemy, without warning, struck at our Federation with military might. We cannot allow this to go unchallenged. It is necessary to show the alien authorities that if they have a complaint they should come to us, sitting down like intelligent, rational beings, and seeking a logical, intelligent and rational solution. It is a two-way street.

"Friendship, but with the solid understanding that it is given freely, not demanded. Co-existence, side by side, as mutually equal partners, with mutual respect.

"I have avoided attacking any populated planet of theirs on the principle that it is immoral. But since they continue aggression, we must follow their example. We are now in the process of revealing at what cost they have taken Federation planets.

"Our forces are at this very moment attacking their capital system of Mjio, an order that I reluctantly was forced to make."

* * * * * * *

28 June 2101, Unknown, (IWN): The President, when he arrived at a press conference this morning, called unexpectedly at 0605, looked haggard.

Gordon G. Gordon made the following announcement before the President spoke: "We have received notice that our attack on Mjio was repelled and defeated. All our ships were either destroyed upon landing or taken captive. The alien government immediately sent this message:

"'We find it necessary to now make one simple demand: Surrender or an immediate counter-attack will take place on your home system.'

"Now the President."

President Jennings stepped forward, said: "We have obviously reached an impasse. Where the conflict up until now, has been a political and military game of chess, we are now facing all-out war. Our military advisors assure me that any attack on our solar system would be repelled, and would never be launched. It has also been reported that our defeat on Mjio was a miscalculation. We had used no more than the element of surprise and minor, planetary weapons. I can assure you that there is nothing to fear from the enemy. I have sent the following a few hours ago to their government:

"'While we have regretted the action of the ship *Nora* against your freighter, and admit it was uncalled for, and that the action on your part might have been, in part, justified, we still feel it would have been far better if you had notified this government, which would have taken action on its own—and in fact has—against the ship *Nova.* Your actions of aggression have been unprovoked attacks against our people.

"'We demand your surrender or we will make an all-out offensive attack which will bring total war to your home planets. It is obvious that you are not interested in...

At this point the President was interrupted by an aide who whispered rapidly in his ear.

JJJ turned and said in a tired voice: "Gentlemen, something has come up that calls for our immediate attention."

With that he left the room, followed by his staff. All attempts to learn what took place have been fruitless.

* * * * * * *

28 June 2101, Earth, (IWN): A sudden and swift attack on our system has made us captive of the alien government. While all personal and private enterprise has been, in effect, left alone, the government itself and all its functions have been temporarily taken over by the alien military. What was

left of our military space force took immediate flight, once defeat was certain. The following alien statement was sent to all news services.

"This last move on our part was taken in reluctance. We have sent an ultimatum to your president as follows:

"'A statement of apology concerning the *Nova* incident is demanded. This demonstration of our total power has been forced upon us. We will keep those planets taken in battle, other than your solar system, for a period of twenty of your years, in order to educate those colonies as to the true nature of our society and civilization. We wish peace talks. The decision is up to you.'

No human government official is at liberty to make public statements, being confined under alien military guard.

* * * * * * *

29 June 2101, Unknown, (IWN): The President appeared before the press and stated briefly: "We can either make our stand here and now, with the united military forces at our command or bend to the wishes of the enemy. Since they hold the trump rocket, and in order to avoid any further deaths on either side, I have sent this message:

"'All requests on your part will be met, under the following conditions: 1): A return of the Solar System be made immediate; 2): A withdrawal of your troops from that system; 3): Peace talks to be immediately brought into effect in order to arrange the withdrawal of all your forces from the planets taken since the beginning of the conflict. 4): That it is agreed at this time that no occupation will be forced upon such planets as suggested by your communication to us of 28 June'."

* * * * * * *

30 June 2101, Unknown, (IWN): The President was smiling when he appeared before the press this morning. He waved several pieces of paper in front of him as if holding a victory banner. His eyes twinkled in good humor as he said: "The following communication, I am certain, will please you. We

148

received this message early this morning:

"'Conditions for peace talks as stated in your communication to our government are agreeable, except for the following points: We are willing to return those planets taken, once a fair price for the conflict has been leveled against your government. Before peace talks can begin, however, your remaining forces must disband. It must be agreed that some of the planets captured during this conflict will remain under our control. You will agree to all our demands without argument.'

"I answered in this way: 'I find it necessary to demand the following before peace talks can be entered into: 1): You will return total function to our military; 2): That a fair payment to you for war expenses will be settled only when peace talks are in progress."

"Their answer was simply: 'Agree to terms.'"

It is enough to say that everybody in the room cheered our President. Some had tears in their eyes In the end it would seem that the President's lifelong habit of a hard-line paid off in seeming victory in the face of total defeat.

* * * * * * *

23 July 2101, Danton, (IWN): The President came out of the first day of conference with the aliens, his face drawn in hard, tired lines. It was obvious that things hadn't gone well. He did, however, make this statement to the press:

"While the aliens have some advantage, considering their unexpected surprise attack on the solar system, and their turning the screw to force public announcements in favor to their unyielding point-of-view, I find it amazing how incredible their demands at this conference have become. While I can't state in public what these demands entail, I can say this: It is not the policy of this government—and *never* will be—to buckle under to the opposition; and while we did take a slight set-back last month before the peace talks, it will have no effect upon our present stand. If necessary, we'll use all the force possible to hold every inch of soil that our science and exploration has colonized."

One reporter asked if he could tell us exactly how far he

was willing to go.

Flashing one of his famous victory smiles, JJJ said: "With things returned fairly much to the state of affairs as they were at the beginning of last month—plus the very satisfying fact that all the government officials of the Federation have now sworn total support to any move I might make—I can honestly say we are certainly in an even better position to make any kind of demand we wish. The Federation has never so totally supported any political leader. After all, we have not lost a war and if I know the human race, it won't buckle under.

"As our honorable and powerful political opposition, in the voice of Senator Channing, stated after our diplomatic victory that brought about these hard won peace talks: 'The President is a hard man to do business with, but his present stand has certainly justified his position, as did his past record.' Coming from such a learned and respected voice, I find it highly satisfactory endorsement of a continuation of hard-lining it to the very bitter end."

Three hours later a public statement was made by a spokesman for the alien government.

"After long deliberation with your president, we have made it clear that in order to keep peace between our people we have only one of two choices: Reconquer in total and govern the human civilization, or retreat to the original borders that existed before the *Nova* incident. To avoid this, you have only to meet our demands. While we do not wish to conquer, we will not allow any doubt to be entertained that we are afraid of your Federation. The decision we left up to your President before closing the conference this afternoon.

"We are awaiting his official answer, sent through diplomatic channels, before taking any action of a military nature."

Knowing the President, and considering his statements to the press, the reporters are in agreement about one thing:

Considering his past record, and the total support he has suddenly gained from both government and public alike, it is hard to imagine that he will buckle under to the demands as presented today. Yet he seems to have no other choice.

We can't help wondering if it is possible that he will

really hold firm as he has done in the past.

And is it possible that if he does so, the aliens will follow through with their threats?

The long silence from President Jennings and his staff has caused a great sense of concern here.

It **is** the serious hope of everybody in the official Presidential press that the middle road, one that will not make it necessary for the President to either admit to total defeat or force a total conquest by the aliens, will be found.

Like the aliens he has two choices. What we are waiting to learn is which one he will make.

From political satire we jump into another one of those wonders in less than 1000 words (in fact: 674). Maybe if we'd have this guy around in the previous story things might not have been so drastically mishandled. It is always nice to have a local missionary to save the day on a savage planet of aliens. Well, under any circumstances we all need somebody like...

⊷THE GOOD DOCTOR⊷

When the Commander and his space crew of eight landed on the planet *Maa-Geek,* they were immediately confronted by a wild army of aliens who quickly set out to war with them. Just as the Commander was about to order the super-atomic ray gun on the savages, after a terrible and losing battle on his side, the last of his crew fell over dead. Quickly he turned to the ray gun and was beginning to squeeze it when a loud voice called to the savages surrounding him.

The aliens stopped their battle.

All but *one* who was already in the process of swinging an ax at the man's head.

The Commander fell with the rest of his crew. The primitive aliens of Maa-Geek had won the day! Joy be to the Maa-Geek!

They were about the pound their chests with hairy fists in proud celebration of their well-earned victory, when out of the jungle stepped a regal looking humanoid, who had long gray hair and carried a small black bag. The victory celebration was thereby frozen to stunned silence as he sternly scolded the savage aliens surrounding him.

"You shouldn't do such things!" But to himself he sighed helplessly: *What good...savages will be savages... that's the trouble with missionary work...I should be with my own people across the ocean...*

He looked at the Earthmen, examining each in turn. All

were dead except the Commander. The ax had fallen on his head, making an ugly gash.

"Well, maybe the damage isn't so bad after all. Oh, my children, you must learn civilized manners!" he said to the cringing alien savages, now almost bowed double in confusion and shame.

Happily he opened his black bag and started cleaning the wound.

Ah, he thought, taking out a needle and thread, *he would be able to save this one, and maybe these creatures from another world would forgive and forget... One could never tell, because anything might happen on the world of Maa-Geek! Then he could direct this being to his own people on the other side of the world, and their planet could learn the secrets of space travel...ah, what a grand possibility.*

He grinned, looking at the huge rocket ship so close to him.

Carefully he inserted the needle into the gashed head of the Commander. Then he pulled it

Through the flesh, making a perfect stitch.

And a masterly stitch it truly was! he exclaimed silently to himself. He prided himself in his artistic workmanship.

No Sooner had he finished that first stitch than the Earthmen jumped up, perfectly mended, and alive. All of them. As if by magic! And magic it certainly had to be!

He couldn't believe it.

Neither could any of the Earthmen.

They looked at themselves and each other with shocked surprise.

"You were killed..." one would say looking at some other member of the crew.

"You're supposed to be dead," another cried.

The alien missionary doctor looked around in a dazed and bewildered fashion. "But...but how? Are you immortal creatures?..."

The Commander looked at the doctor. "Hardly! My men were all dead! I saw them fall! I...I don't know what you did...but you saved all of us from death." He extended his hand toward the alien doctor, smiling.

"I owe my life to you, sir!" he announced. Then he introduced himself. "I'm Commander Fah Tym of the..."

He didn't get a chance to continue, because the "doctor" suddenly doubled over with laughter. Finally, after a while he gained control of himself and looked knowingly at the nine Earthmen.

"I know how I did it! I know I know I know!" he yelled over.

"What do you know!" everybody cried. Even the alien savages chirped out their shocked surprise.

"I know how I saved you all..." the Good Doctor announced, proudly.

Then very seriously he told them:

"You see, on this planet of Maa-Geek, a stitch in Tym saves nine!"

This story came out of a question: Is blindly conforming better than rebelling against authority? Being a bell-ringing "beller," it is obvious that I'd favor ring-a-ding dinging this one again and again! Forrest J Ackerman, in his Introduction to my collection Images of Tomorrow *(1969), announced this was* "a satire on regimentation in offices and factories and everywhere else in life where there are Rules Rules Rules to which human being are required to mechanically conform. One thinks, perhaps, of Dr. Keller's 'White Collars,' Francis Flagg's 'The Metanicals'." *Universal Utopia can be a damnation into hell for some people. And my character Carl Johns, as revealed below, was willing to risk sanity in order to escape...*

⊶THE WORLD THE WOMB MADE⊷

He was aware of screaming but no sound came from his lips. The electronic straps held him securely to the cold hard table as the distant voice of WOMB purred softly in the darkness.

Where was he? Who?

He tried to remember as another fiery bolt of anguish tore his nerves back with crushing pressure. As the pain subsided, memory ebbed into existence.

First came remembrance of a book. But why was that important?

Something invisible and cold probed his mind like icy electric fingers, touching nerve centers, sending waves of fire through the passages of his dimly awakening memory. And suddenly he knew:

This was Reconditioning Center.

His name: Carl Johns.

Pain erupted, then subsided as nerves and muscles tensed against the raw fire.

The visual picture of Gordon Gordon James III focused in his mind. It was a harsh, stone-like image of icy eyes that

155

tried to appear friendly and protective as they narrowed coldly in grim contempt.

Sudden hate swelled up like a ball inside Carl Johns' body, so intense that the next slashing electro-probe of torture was numbed almost out of existence.

Consciousness spun like an insane top. All awareness compressed into the last hour he had spent in Gordon Gordon James' office.

* * * * * * *

"Mr. Johns, as you know, your work in our company has been pretty good up until now!" the fat little man had said over a thick cigar. "It's been so good that I find it necessary to at least ask the reasons for your actions during the past few days—before recommending Corrective Detailing."

Carl Johns had leaned forward on the small, uncomfortable chair, nervously working his hands together. He knew the seriousness of the situation, but didn't know quite how to really handle it. Certainly there must be some way to convince this hard man of the Truth. If only he could make this other man realize how wrong things were.

"Sir. I don't know where to start. It began some time ago but I guess you know that, sir."

Gordon James III nodded, tapped a small metal card that contained the totality of Carl John's living experience, from birth to this very instant, even now itemizing more details to be endlessly monitored by the mechanical master of the world. "Yes, WOMB has noted that, of course. A rather hazardous change in routine, I might add. You refused to take WOMB's suggestions. You rebel against the happy direction of your life that WOMB so generously offers in Its All-Knowing Wisdom."

"Yes, yes. It is true. I know that. I understand all that!"

"At least, you are being honest. That's a good indication."

"Why should I be anything else?"

"Yes, of course; lies wouldn't do you any good at this point, would they?"

"No. After all, we are totally under the loving, mechanical guidance of WOMB from birth to death, aren't we?" Johns stated in a slightly sarcastic voice. The bitterness welled up in him, coloring every word, and now flooded into the last ones with full fury: "Our ever-loving mother WOMB!"

"Yes. But why do you resent this?" his employer inquired, leaning forward across the clean desk, his face taking on a mockingly fake fatherly expression. "I want to help you, son."

Carl Johns nodded, nervously fingered his moustache and forced himself to lean back in the chair. He had to somehow control the emotions churning inside his mind. His very existence surely was being dearly threatened. The Corrective Detailing Center would change him back into something he never wanted to be ever again!

He looked around him, at the uncaring man and the office that contained nothing but two chairs and a small desk—and, of course, the two of them.

The room was cold with bare, white walls. There was nothing fatherly about this man. Like the world they lived in, he was mechanical, uncaring, going through the necessary required actions with automatic perfection. He was playing out his role of the "fatherly" boss. And not too good at being convincing—nor seeming to even attempt to hold back his true feelings.

"You will now tell me what happened to change your life pattern, Johns," Gordon Gordon James III stated in a very kindly sounding voice. It was a command, and the answer would mean life or a living death.

He frantically tried to convince himself there might be some hope; there had to be a way to convince this SOB.

"Well, I came across an old book—a friend of mine is a collector of old books—WOMB allowed this because my friend is the type of person who can take such intellectual stimulation without being adversely affected. What puzzles me, sir, is that WOMB allowed me to come in contact with him and most of all let me read the books. If it was wrong why was I not stopped immediately?"

"WOMB is not God, it can only direct, inform, and suggest. WOMB is nothing more than a marvelous mechanical

Brain. As its total name suggests, *World Operational Mechanical Brain*, it is nothing more than an instrument made to serve man. After all, quite frankly, we here in Central Control know these truths, for they are self-evident! Of course many people worship WOMB as a mighty force, almost a Religious Deity; but it isn't anything like that. Wise, informed, fully programmed. Sure. It knows all about all of us, from birth to death. The success of WOMB is that it has always been right. Never wrong!"

"*Never*, Heaven forbid!" Carl Johns exploded.

The man sighed, shrugged, said: "As you realize, Johns, WOMB knows everything about us from childhood on. It almost knows what we think. It can suggest the right meal, the right clothing, the right entertainment at the right time. Just think! All you have to do is ask WOMB and it will give you the complete routine for the day. You don't have to worry about making the wrong decision. No responsibility is left in your hands. Mother WOMB takes care of all her children."

Gordon Gordon James III was quoting right from the *Book of WOMB*, and Carl Johns didn't dare interrupt.

"And if you merely follow WOMB's advice, direction, you will be a Very Happy Man. How can you fail? WOMB never fails!

"Do you know that WOMB has cut down mental cases to almost zero during the last two generations? People are Happy! There has been no war, no problems either internationally or internally.

"Utopia is for everybody, tailored to each person's ideal of their personal utopia!"

He verbally leaped at that point: "That's just it, sir."

"What?" The man's face turned hard.

"WOMB is *not* perfect! It has not succeeded in *every* case. Look what its done to me! It cannot make everybody totally happy."

Gordon Gordon James III started to say something, but Carl Johns was abruptly warming up to his subject and now leaned forward, spreading his hands wide in front of him.

"That's just it, sir. You gotta believe me. You see I read this book and discovered what it was like in the twentieth century. That's when it all began, you know, sir, with the beginning of computers and mechanical brains. At first it seemed a wonderful thing. Computers could be used in business for billing and for just about every menial activity that people had been forced to do up until then. A computer could predict elections within a few hours of the closing of several key polls. People became numbers. Rather than a name. Then the day arrived when giant computers were being used in projecting just about anything. Larger and larger computers were developed. Finally schools, hospitals, businesses, governments were using computers for just about everything imaginable. Then the greatest event in history took place: rich people could have private outlets to Master Computers, then the middle income person could have them and finally everybody in every home was connected to a world wide Internet! They had been used in space travel for decades, and by the twenty-first century it was universal.

"At first it had been DOS that changed to WINDOWS, and finally XP, SUPER P, and ECSTASY! It was international, world-wise. Very wise. Too wise! And it could run anything connected to these private links to Universal Happiness! You're homes were connected and ran themselves, turning lights and heaters, and you name it, on and off at happily selected times. What a Wonderful World life had become! This was an Internet of connecting super brains that could run all the governments of the world while at the same time paying full attention to your personalized territorial domain. Why it could be programmed to satisfy your every whim! Fantastic. A marvel to Mankind's inventive mind— such wonders had never been imagined even in the Good Books of Old, those ancient religious tomes that had been such a dominating factor before modern times wiped their influence almost out of existence!"

"I know all that," the cold face before him said with an irritated nod. "WOMB replaced all that. Wiped out the endless quibbling over whose God was the Real God and whose the most powerful, and which God would rule the world at large. The Religious Wars were finally resolved into dusty memories! WOMB saw to that and saved Mankind from its foolishly blind belief systems! You need not give *me* a history lesson!"

"Stay with me, sir. Please. For I have much more to re-veal! I promise you!"

"Well, if you must! I want to be fair about this. Offer you a full chance to realized you've been given a totally open hearing before final judgment decides your fate."

"If you wanted to go to a restaurant but couldn't make up your mind what kind or just didn't know which ones were nearby all you had to do was feed the information into your computer outlet and several top-rate suggestions would be offered, programmed on what you required. Like say you wanted to go to a French restaurant, but didn't know much about the ones located in your town. You requested and got the information and the best of recommendations.

"Come. Come. I know all this. You waste my...our time! Do you have to continue to lecture me on details quite obvious to all of us? Must you continue to babble like this? Say something reasonable—something that'll help you, not sink you deeper into the pit you've so foolishly created for yourself."

"Please. Sir.

"You requested and got the information and the best of recommendations." Johns repeated as if he'd rehearsed this speech over and over again; which he had. "Finally the event of having a file on everyone's likes and dislikes came into being. Now a person could say, in effect, to the computer: Considering my personal tastes, what are the possible things that might interest me, tonight? The computer would offer suggestions. The next step was logical enough: a total file detailing all things about a person from childhood on. The computer could project what each of us might like or desire to do; it could *anticipate* the human. After that came Total Prediction, and what we know as WOMB."

"Yes, yes. You rattle and prattle and...say the obvious!" The man stood, tapped the small card almost hiding in the palm of his hand. "This contains all that you are. I know, I know! WOMB, like a loving mother, holds our lives in its embrace, feeding into us everything and anything we might need to be a happy addition to this Universal Peace, this Utopia where the fury and plague of wars have been mas-

160

tered out of existence. WOMB monitors all that we are and all that we do in such a lovingly skilled fashioned that we don't have to be concerned about any foolish decisions! The perfection of WOMB's guidance is beyond question. We not only get what we want, automatically, but what we deserve! We are fed night and day with the perfection that this world can now offer each and every once of us! WOMB is our perfect guide—well, better than all those religious cults and orders and, you name it—all those false systems that threatened our very existence in their determination to be universal converters to their...well, you know how it was and how it is!"

"Yes. How things are, here and now. Quite frankly, things have just gotten out of hand."

Johns sighed, as if exhausted.

"Johns, that's dangerous talk. I must warn you. Very dangerous."

"But it is so. Quit obviously so."

"You are damning yourself to the hell of Corrective Detailing Central! Be warned! Every word you speak deepens your grave future!"

Johns was beyond being reasonable. "WOMB is out of control. Our world has gone beyond Utopia to a new kind of hell! I've telling you," his voice lifted even more fanatically louder: "We're out of control!"

"Things haven't gotten out of control, but *into* control, and you accept that...fully! Or else!"

"Sir. You did instruct me to tell you the truth, the *full* story. I'm just trying to tell you how it all happened."

"Yes, yes, of course, you're right. I only want to help. If I can help you won't have to suffer automatic correction—but considering your crime, it's very unlikely there is a way to keep you from being sent for Reconditioning, for your own good."

Johns shuddered and looked down at his hands. He didn't want to be changed back; he wanted to stay the way he was. He wanted to remain a *total* Man.

He looked up at his boss, considered the offer this man was making. It would be possible to bend, to claim he saw where he'd been wrong. The temptation was great as fear ate deep inside his mind and guts. But another urge choked at his throat and finally forced itself out.

"Sir," Johns said after some moments of silence, "Did you ever wonder what it would be like to go through a day *without* following the suggestions of WOMB?"

The other man yanked the cigar from between thick lips, cried: "That's insane. That's insanity. Why in hell would you want to do that?"

"Well, consider. We are led from childhood on by WOMB—the perfect guide through life. We are told what activities will make us happy. We are even told who to marry."

"Well, of course! It would be insanity to find a lifetime mate without WOMB advising who is best for us. After all, WOMB knows everybody and knows which two people will fit best, who will balance one another emotionally, mentally and physically. It would be insanity to do it otherwise!"

"Man used to pick freely years ago, you know, sir. Then came the computers and it was a marriage game—even played out on international television shows—in the beginning. The computer would select the best possible mate and sometimes it *would* be right. Two people would thus meet, fall immediately in love and marry. But where was the challenge in that?"

Gordon Gordon James III glared at Johns, his heavy eyebrows netting together in thought.

"Challenge?" He stumbled over the word as if it were meaningless. "Challenge?"

"*Challenge!* A tiny thing. But in the past centuries before WOMB, everything was a challenge. Survival was a challenge. A child grew up not knowing what kind of person it was, its parents just as ignorant of the real direction of its life. Parents might have the dream of their child of being a doctor, but it would want to be an actor or work in industry. The challenge was, many times, for the child to make up its mind what it would be: either what its parents told it to be or what it wanted to be. Then the following challenge would be to struggle hard and either succeed or fail. If you turned out to be a hard worker, had any talent and determination, you might succeed. And even then you might fail. If you suc-

162

ceeded, though, there was the glory!"

"What if you failed? What then?" Gordon Gordon James III pointed out triumphantly.

"It would be hellish, I would imagine," Johns admitted with a weak smile.

"Thank God we don't have this kind of problem today. With WOMB nobody is a failure!"

"But wouldn't it be nice to fail just once?"

"Well, you're coming very close to doing just that! Failing!"

"That's not what I meant, and you know it!"

"I don't get you. It is not nice to fail—period! Success is the only way to total happiness. It's been that way since the dawn of time—it will always be that way. The difference is that we all succeed, now, because of WOMB."

"Sure. But when that success is your own, isn't it just that much more sweet?"

Gordon Gordon James III tapped the desk with thick fingers. "Boy, boy. The more you talk the more convicted you become. You need Recentering, Readaption, Revision, Reliability, Redirection, and re-re-re! Total Reconditioning, Johns. Your words not only ask for it, but demand it. You doom yourself, my friend! Failing! How foolish can you get? That's more than Madness!"

"Sir, just think about it for but a moment," Johns cried, desperately. He was sure nobody could miss the logic of his next points. "In the past a man would take up the sword and stand alone against another man. He would say, in effect, I wish to fight you and see if I'm a better man than you are. If I'm wrong, you will kill me; if I'm right I will kill you. Think of the challenge!"

Gordon James shuddered convulsively, his fat features seeming to vibrate against the bones. "Insanity!"

"Nobody wants to die, sir, but think of the glory if one could win! Just once to put your head on the line and see if you are right or wrong, on your own! On your own ideas and your own thoughts and your own nerves. This book I read was about the history of the past, from the twenty-first century and back to the very beginnings of history. Until WOMB, man either won or lost on his own nerves, mind and

163

muscles. He stood up and said, I am a Man, I will fight and I will either win with glory or die in the effort. He was responsible for his own mistakes and was willing to pay the price."

"Mr. Johns, surely you can see the insanity of such mad ideas. I'm not a total fool. I've read about the past. But I see agony, pain, suffering, war and hate, struggle and defeat. In our world of today we have nothing but perfection, happiness, a promise that we will not fail, that we will not be bored at any one time. WOMB knows how to vary our entertainment, different for each person, without error. WOMB selects our daily activities in such a way that there is never any boredom, never any moment when we must be unhappy, lying back in some room, drunk with the evil effects of liquor or drugs—as it was in the twentieth century and before. There is no boredom to drive men to desperate actions in order to seek happiness—or escape from failure. We don't have to worry about our jobs or about taking undue responsibilities that will create guilt feelings or cause unnecessary emotional strains. We don't have to worry about our jobs, because we might make some foolish mistake of judgment. We don't have to be concerned about being a blind believer in the wrong God—worshipping the wrong religious order.

"All these ugly problems are simply flushed away! No fear of the wrath of some unforgiving God to mar our existence! No guilt to be forced upon us by false dogmas and outdated Laws. We are now protected from such perverse dictates; totally secure! We can get up in the morning with a happy smile on our faces, because it is just a joy to live and there will be no problem that can't be solved. We will do our jobs, without frustration, because it is the kind of job suited perfectly to us. We know that the evening will be a glory of entertainment: maybe it's a meal in some Mexican restaurant or a concert in the local Music Center or just watching WallVision—that doesn't matter. The thing is, WOMB will tell us *in advance* what will make us Happy—and it is *always* right! There is no question about total happiness, every moment of our lives—we have it from birth to death. It's just that simple!"

"*I'm* not happy in that kind of limited world, sir. I was *very* unhappy."

164

"Yes, so the report states. Do you want to hear what WOMB has recorded about you?"

Johns shrugged, for it didn't matter to him what WOMB said.

"I'll read the meat of it to you. Thus states WOMB: 'He must be readjusted to the Norm because he has moved from the center of his happiness pattern. He has broken this pattern and anybody who breaks the pattern will find unhappiness. He has convinced himself that happiness has something to do with being a man, but he is a man. He believes that by making his own decisions, and his own choices of entertainment, he will find greater happiness in the uncertainty of the results. He is not afraid to fail, only afraid that he will not be allowed to fail. Such attitudes are totally unbalanced.' I agree, Johns. And I might add, your ideas touch the edge of madness. They are not rational. Not for an adult."

"Sir, in all due respect, I read something in one of the books which hit me as very strong and I'd like to tell you about it."

"If it can help you in any way, my son," his boss offered silky generous, in his most fatherly manner. "Please say something that can be used to save you!"

"I can't remember the author, but it ran something like this: *'There are basically two types of people. One is the person who wants to grab life with both hands and struggle to the top, without help from others, without being pulled down by rules and regulations; and this type of person will either become a great success or frustrated and unhappy; if the latter, he must either bend to the rules of society or will become a criminal. Two: the person who wants to have a job where he is told what to do, where the rules and regulations will release him from personal responsibilities—he will go to work, religiously follow the rule book in blind devotion! He will be quite happy and content, secure in the fact that if he adheres to the* Book of Laws *he will surely succeed. This latter person is actually happy in such a situation because it is like living in a mother's womb. The former person wishes to cut away from the womb and wants to prove himself a man. He is able to think for himself, and as a fully mature adult willing to take the results of failure'."*

165

Johns leaned forward, staring into those still cold eyes, and said: "I would put it another way, sir: One of these two can be replaced by a robot; the other is called a Man!"

Gordon Gordon James III sadly shook his head, lighted another cigar, and then said: "And you truly believe this? Religiously believe?"

"It's because of this that I started thinking about *what* I was," Carl Johns stated, not realizing how ineffective his statement was. "Which of the two was I? All my life I've done what I was told, found a form of happiness that I accept totally and without question because of the society in which I was born. Then I began to wonder what had happened to the person who cried out, 'Let me be a Man, not a robot, not a thing that a machine can replace!' I began to wonder about myself and what it would be like to just once, *one* day in my life, discover if there really was any difference.

"Then one morning I woke up and decided to do just one thing different from what WOMB told me to. After phasing WOMB for breakfast, I waited in the small dining area of our little single apartment, actually shaking with excitement. When the two meals came out, fried eggs, softly grilled with crisp pieces of bacon for me, and one very soft-boiled egg on toast for my wife, I quickly grabbed her plate. I told her I wanted to try *her* meal."

"Wasn't that a little childish? What did your wife *do*?" Gordon Gordon James III inquired, puffing so that his face was clouded, the expression hidden behind a screen of smoke.

"Believe me, she looked surprised, but said nothing. She seldom says anything, you know!"

"I would imagine!" the voice muttered, disgusted sounding. "What a horrid experience for her! How could you want to do such a thing to somebody you loved?"

"Well, sir. It was just about the greatest adventure in my life. As for the wife, she tossed the plate sent for me out the slot, ordered another meal for herself. We ate in silence."

"You mean you *liked* the meal—the one offered your wife?" Gordon James III demanded, stabbing the air with the thick cigar. "I doubt it!"

Carl Johns shrugged. "It was a simple thing. But you'd

166

be surprised at the satisfaction I experienced because of it."

"You didn't answer the question."

"No. Okay. I didn't really enjoy the food itself as much as I would have savored the eggs and bacon offered as my breakfast. But I received a wonderful sense of power, knowing that once in my life I had done something on my own; failed, sure, but succeeded in learning the thrill of making my own decision."

"Well, so you see, WOMB *knows* what's best, after all. That should have been the end of it for you. And would have been merely considered a quirk. Everybody does something silly and childish like that one time or another in their life." The man seemed satisfied. "What did your wife think?"

"Nora was shocked, you could see that from the sidelong glances she gave me. But she said nothing. After all, she was a perfect wife in every way and loved me. If she reported the event, I'd have been in trouble. If she had said anything about it, it would have automatically gone on our records. She's very careful about that, sir, you can understand."

"A wise woman...though...I mean—I can understand her concern and desire to not want to get you into trouble. As it surely would have! But look at the trouble you're in now. If it had only been stopped at that point, things might have been far easier to correct."

"Nora is a perfect wife, sir, as all wives are perfect for all husbands, because WOMB selects the right wife for the right man. We simply said nothing about this event."

"You do love your wife, then?"

"*Of course I love* her very much, sir."

"You would never have known her if it had not been for WOMB. I notice she came from a small island in the Pacific."

"I probably would have met somebody I could have loved just as much. Who knows? In any case I wouldn't have known the difference, would I?"

Gordon Gordon James III shook his head again, but white billowy cigar smoke covered the expression on his face.

"That night, before pressing the evening program for the

two of us, I took out some writing materials, and then wrote down what sounded good to me. There was a play dealing with the colony on Mars—you know, 'Love Under Two Moons'. I had been interested in seeing it, but knew that WOMB would pick the best time for that event. I wrote that down. When I pressed the WOMB button we were advised there were two tickets in our name for the new Mars play. Immediately my mind began struggling to think of something else I might like to do—anything other than seeing the Mars play."

"That's—just crazy!"

"Maybe, sir. Maybe. But you miss the point."

"I'm quite sure any sane man would."

"Let me continue. I went with Nora to the International Playhouse, then at the entrance claimed I wasn't feeling well. She merely asked: 'But, didn't WOMB know that?' I shrugged that away and convinced her to go on in, that I'd meet her at home when it was over. After she disappeared into the theater, I started aimlessly walking, trying to think of something to do. I went into a cocktail lounge, had a couple of drinks to help me decide. Suddenly the mood of adventure became sharp. I realized that it didn't really matter *what* it was I did—just so I did it. I decided to move on impulse, let my subconscious mind make the decisions.

"I continued to walk along the street, after leaving the bar, and several times almost went into one of the many feelie films—but passed them by. I wanted something totally living—totally alive. I breathed the air as if it were the cleanest smog-free air in the world. Everything seemed brighter. Sounds, laughter, lights became flashing, dancing sensations that brought almost physical thrills to my body.

"Then I paused in front of one of the LOVE-MATE HOUSES and on impulse went in, selected a charming, dark haired ersatz, went into her private chamber, shaking with excitement."

"I thought you loved your wife. From your personality file, since marriage," Gordon Gordon James III announced, touching a button on top of his desk in a very casual manner, "you've been totally committed to her, and her alone."

Carl Johns nodded. "I hadn't come there to use this

168

Love-Mate's more obvious services. Naturally she was beautiful. Where my wife is lovely in a willowy way, I'd picked a Love-Mate who was more voluptuous, large eyed, full lipped.

"But I told her I merely wanted to talk. It was the adventure of it all. The fact that I could, if I wanted to, experience anything at all with this ersatz-lover was enough for me to know. I merely wanted to talk to somebody—but no *real* person who has well, to be honest, been brain-washed."

"Does that sound like a reasonable thing to want? Does a reasonable man go to a Love-Mate for…conversation? That's not only silly, it is madness. Talking to a machine! It proves you are quite—"

"Nobody ever said there wasn't another use for these creatures. And they aren't machines; they're something else! Well, anyway, I wanted conversation but unlimited, broad, open, not programmed. As you know, sir, the only thing WOMB records at the LOVE-MATE Palaces are the fact that somebody went in—nothing else. Here I could say anything I wanted to say. I could be myself, to some extent with this synthetic ersatz woman. It was like talking to yourself, but having a reasonable pre-conditioned answer fed back to you.

"I realized that someday I might have to face someone like you…this thing we're going through now. I…impulsively began telling her everything I've told you today."

"And?"

"We talked about history and she laughingly fed me the normal line WOMB offers. Instinctively, perhaps, knowing I'd also laugh it off. It was like a grand satire, played out by the two of us, each knowing it was all a kind of crude, ugly joke. Her words were mockingly presented…and…well… you know…the standards about how wonderful things are now that WOMB is here to lead us to total happiness. It made both of us laugh hysterically. She automatically picked up my mood and mirrored it exactly. To listen to that chatter, well, one would think that WOMB believes *it* made the world, rather than God."

Gordon Gordon James III shook his head sadly. "You miss the point. Man made WOMB. WOMB serves us."

Carl Johns was almost blinded to everything around him by now and merely said: "I found it a *very* wonderful experience. A little later I left and went home feeling better than I had ever felt in my whole life. When I got home I dialed a cocktail and after finishing it, dialed another. By the time Nora returned home, I'd passed out from the effects of the liquor, but had felt wonderful. This is something new, a wonderful sensation—I was doing things on my own, doing what I wanted to do, without the help of WOMB—and though it wasn't all heavenly entertainment, it was far more thrilling. My nerves were alive, aware of everything around me. The next day is when I stayed home from work."

"Yes...that's in your record. And then you refused to go to Medical Center—you refused all help...you refused to come to work for *five* days. You had to be picked up—and forcefully brought here. And that's why we *are* here now, you know. You realize that all this information has been fed into WOMB—you realize that all I can do is in some way attempt to lead you back onto—the right path—that's what I've been hoping for. But now...well I wonder!"

Johns started to say something, but his boss stopped him with a little jerk of his cigar. "Let me tell *you* something, son, and I want you to understand the full implications of it.

"When *I* was a *child* I did something very much like what you have done. Having intelligent parents, I was handled in such a way that I never forgot the lesson. But for them, I might have...well—never mind that.

"Instead of going to the playground, like WOMB had instructed, I just walked around the city and was late returning home. When my parents discovered the truth, they spanked me and said: 'Only an immature child tries to prove themselves wiser than their betters. Only a child who has not experienced what life is all about will attempt to argue the wisdom of WOMB.' They went on to say that maturity is knowing where you belong, accepting yourself totally and accepting your place in society, without questioning the wisdom of WOMB. WOMB was built to make Happiness for Everybody, to take the insecurity out of life, to make it possible for people to function totally, in a perfection of Happiness, taking away all frustrations, all doubts, all worries

170

about the future. There is no war, no unhappiness. You know from birth that every action, every instant will be filled with total perfection and happiness, programmed upon your own personality and desires. If those desires are bad, WOMB will generously fix your outlook to fit the sanity of our world.

"You are not the only one who has rebelled, my silly little friend. There are other people who start to question society, who wonder if maybe there is a better way, who have attempted to go out on their own—though there obviously isn't or it would have been found. You can't have everybody going off in different directions. You have to have some order—some pattern. Otherwise it would be impossible. It's insane to consider any other world than that which WOMB has made possible. These people who rebel learn through reprogramming that they were wrong. They are taught how foolish it is to attempt to be childish and immature.

"A man, my friend, is the person who buckles under and accepts society and accepts the total logic of WOMB. Maturity is total acceptance of reality. In our century we have found Utopia for *everybody*. That is, everybody who is adult enough to understand it. Reset Operations are nothing worse than mental and physical spanking for being a bad boy. WOMB does nothing more than prove to you that it is better to be a good man, rather than a bad boy. And from what you have said, I can see no way to avoid just punishment. It is obvious that you are still immature. You don't even know the true meaning of manhood. But you will learn, for MOTHER-WOMB will teach you what being a man really is—and believe me, you will thank me when we meet again. You will want to embrace me for having forced you to accept your responsibilities in this world. There is no place for the immature, emotional child who wishes to do things his own way, against the logic and loving guidance of WOMB."

As Gordon Gordon James III pressed another button on his desk Carl Johns stood up, cried:

"For Heaven's sake, don't you understand? Can't you see the truth? We aren't men, we're slaves to a machine. We are mindless things that go about our daily business without question. Only a dumb machine accepts without question. A Man questions, stands for what he believes is right and is willing to pay the price for being wrong."

But at that point guards came in and wiped an electro-tape over Johns' trembling lips.

Mr. Gordon Gordon James III said, as Johns was being taken out: "If you are a man, you will not be frightened to take the harsh results of being wrong."

Only then did Johns realize the total meaning of being a man and proudly stopped his struggles as the two guards led him out of the office. He must be responsible for his decisions, good or bad! In this world that WOMB made the Laws did not have to be reasonable to a real man like himself—and they weren't!

Again the blasting pain ripped down his memory passages, screaming with lightning, pulling at the nerves of his brain, ripping at them until he screamed again. It seemed he had been screaming all his life.

It was wrong to be punished for being right, his brain yelled at the darkness around him, curled at the electronic probes of torture that electrified his every thought in one last resounding drive of power.

He felt his consciousness twisting in upon itself as if folding inwards, again and again until a tight little ball of flickering nerves, muscles that had been ideas, crushed inwards against the infinite power of WOMB. Then as he believed it would be impossible to take the anguish any longer, awareness unfolded outwards in a wave of light, a gentle, soothing surge of total physical and mental release, lovingly opening up, thrusting joy throughout his whole being. Love, so total, so complete, so wonderful, flooded him that it was impossible to ignore the complete and infinite affectation MOTHER-WOMB smothered upon his consciousness.

For one flickering instant, which brought on a surge of jarring pain, he remembered, and he mentally repulsed this wave of surrender to WOMB.

PAIN so intense that it choked out all reality all thought all remembrance enveloped him. The blinding light flooded all vision. He tried to scream, but couldn't even remember why. All he wanted was to end this eternal anguish. He would do anything to simply escape...

172

Then like a desperate, terrified man, he struggled to embrace the light, the almost orgasmic pleasure WOMB offered with such loving gentleness. He swam upwards through the mental blanket that had smothered around him like a terrible burning vice. Maybe it had lasted for a year, maybe only an instant. He had no reference points to know. The pain continued only for a while longer, as he clawed for consciousness.

Now he screamed one last time, but in—a sheer desperate plea of acceptance, a verbalized oath to his private universe:, "Oh, God, Mother, take me, I'll be good. I accept I accept your perfection...let me accept!"

The release from the crushing hell was slow, then final. It was as if he'd been gulped down into a black hole and spat out like an exploding, expanding universe.

The nightmare was gone.

Only his words resounded against the walls and vibrated his eardrums as if to make them burst.

"I'm free..." his total being admitted in welcoming surrender.

And there was no small voice to give argument, no insanity to distort the truth of the loving acceptance of The World That WOMB made.

Oh, the wonderful alien bird was destined to be a fav delight to earthling taste buds. Natch. Of course. But there's always a catch! Beware of what you buy!

⇥HUNGER PANGS⇤

Rama Lorto hadn't had anything to eat for days, and when he landed on the planet Kaymo, he made it a point to tell the inhabitants, which the Space manual said were friendly to Earthmen, that he was hungry. They were quick to nod happily, and soon a feast was in the process of being prepared.

As he waited, his mouth kept watering because there is nothing tastier to Earthmen than the bird of Kaymo called *Kaykah.* And this was what the hosts were preparing for him.

The more he waited the stronger his hunger pangs became. He tried to tell them that anything would do, but they just nodded happily and told him to wait just a little longer.

Time continued to move onwards.

But finally the food was ready and he ate like a madman. Never had he tasted anything so good. Never had he tasted a *Kaykah* bird before. He fell in love with this new food, and before he left the planet of Kaymo he made it a point to buy as many *Kaykah* birds as he could get them to sell.

Which, naturally, was only one.

"But why?"

"It is custom! Only one to a Customer! Sorry!" they smiled.

When he offered to pay they just shook their heads and said: "No! We give!"

But according to galactic law it was impossible for any human to take anything from a planet within the Federation without paying for it. He explained, and they sadly accepted the money.

When he returned to his home planet he went to his pri-

174

vate chef and presented the man with the *Kaykah* bird.

"Fix this for me to eat!" he demanded.

When the *Kaykah* was served to him, his mouth watered as he looked at it. He felt wild hunger pangs. Quickly he sliced a piece of the meat off and raised it to his mouth.

It stopped short.

He couldn't force the fork into his mouth.

It was impossible.

Try as he would, he couldn't get any bite of *Kaykah* into his mouth. There was some invisible barrier stopping him.

He tried raising the fork itself, empty of the delicious meat, and it went easily into his mouth.

"What the hell!" he cried in anger.

Why in the universe couldn't he eat the *Kaykah* bird? It was his, damn it all! He had a right to it.

In desperation he called an old friend who worked in the Interstellar Imports and Exports Division dealing with alien foods.

Upon mention of the *Kaykah* bird his friend just laughed and said: "You shouldn't have bought the bird. If you had taken it as a gift it would be theirs legally, not *yours*."

"What the blazing rockets does that have to do with it?" he wanted to know.

"Simple," his friend explained, with dry humor,

"For some unknown reason, you can't have *your* Kaykah and eat it too!"

Everybody has their own idea of what we are all about. Religions of the world are full of their conclusive beliefs. The scientists of today would suggest one thing and their counter parts of the past another, while the future might offer up any of endless solutions to the question: What are we all about? I won't claim that the following story is offering any profound conclusions of the kind suggested in the above paragraph. I simply stated that because I wanted to make a point. What that might be is somewhat vague even to me as the story might be to some readers. The editor who published this in magazine form especially like it, and went out of his way to say so. Which is always nice to hear. I'm certain some people have had their own take on the story. Hopefully readers will agree with the editor who liked my idea of...

—THE IMAGES OF MAN—

And, lo, and they came from the skies to invade the land, splitting the male from the female.

And, lo, they took the women from their homes and split the young from the old!

And they took the most desirable, the most beautiful and the most virgin and went into the skies once more, never to return.

And these were the Gods, these were Images of Man, and that was their divine right!

This was the legend that was part of the folklore of Noloon's tribe, and in a way, one might even say it was a religious teaching of his people. And like all legends and folklore, the young laughed and mocked the truth of what it claimed. For how could one come from the sky? Even a God. For nobody had seen a God, for God was that which surrounded all, which created all, which had made the stars, the sun, the universe.

And Noloon, like many of the other young people of the

176

tribe, laughed and did not believe. Until the day when thunder crashed in the heavens, when there was no Thunder God, and the air crackled like snapping twigs when the lightning God was sleeping, and the world shook, trembled in terror when the Earth God was resting quiet.

He was walking in the woods, up in the hills, with Tanja, the One-Who-Is-Mine. And as all lovers will, they held hands and talked about the time when they would go to the mountain of love, where Birth made them One together.

And as all lovers will, they held each other close, and kissed and felt the moment when Oneness is near.

"I love you, Noloon. I breathe for the day when you take me to the Mountains."

"It'll be soon when the winter crops are cut—my Father needs hands to help bring in the harvest—then we'll go we'll be One and return with a grandson for my Father."

It was then that the world around them seemed to shudder, as if falling apart, a trembling which roared through the air as if the Wind God had rumbled across the lush purple forest lands, the thunder groaned like a screaming animal who had been mortally wounded.

They both looked up into the skies and then into each other's eyes.

"There's no storm!" Tanja cried, hugging close to her man.

Noloon took her hand and they ran through the forest, down the hills, into the meadowlands of his tribe, where his people had lived for as long as the oldest Elder could remember.

They ran to his Father's hut, where the old man was standing, staring into the sky.

The aged farmer was mumbling softly to himself: *"And they came from the skies to invade the land, splitting the male from the female. And they—"*

"It cannot be that," Noloon whispered, wanting to laugh at the old man, but suddenly not able to.

And the village waited in a stunned silence, as if some Magic God had cast a spell upon them and would not let them move. A creeping terror shivered up Noloon's spine and his mouth grew dry as if the desert lands of the east had rammed between his teeth.

They waited, looking into the heavens. Waited for the Gods to come; who could not come, because there were no such Gods.

A black cylinder broke from the clouds, slowly slipped downwards on a flaming pillar of red fire, screaming out as if in agony, roaring around their ears in deafening thunder. Slowly it came closer, until great gulps of wind were shipping Noloon's long black hair into his eyes and face.

The huge cylinder attacked the hill above the village, its hot mouth eating into the dirt until it gulped its last breath of life and died. But the cylinder remained.

The silence settled over the frozen world as if all sound had been stopped, as if some God of silence had squeezed its hand tight against all sound. Then slowly the God-like hand opened and the world murmured back to normal.

Noloon felt Tanja's fingers tense against his and he turned to look into her large brown eyes. It was then that he knew what must be done.

* * * * * * *

Noloon's little band of twelve young men waited in the dark shadows outside their village, like silent guards against the terrors of the unknown. They were armed with crossbows and long swords, silently watching the huge Cylinder that stood quiet as death on the hilltop.

Nothing had moved up there for many hours and they had waited almost fearfully for something dramatic to happen. The Unknown, the legend of the *Images of Man,* the dread of Gods, raced superstitious fear through their minds. It was only Noloon who felt something other than terror.

"We cannot fight Gods," one voice shivered in the darkness behind him.

Noloon's hard muscles tensed, undulating like flexible steel. "Be they Gods or men or something other than men, they will feel death when my sword cuts deep into their flesh. They will not take Tanja from me. *Our women or our lives!"*

"But the Elders said it was wrong to—"

178

"Then it is wrong. I know nothing of right or wrong except my feelings for the woman I love. I only desire to be left alone. They will not take Tanja. I would rather face the wrath of the Gods—the all mighty God of Creation, rather than lose the woman I love. Death would be a sweeter end than life without Tanja!"

There was an uncertain murmur of agreement to his words. For now the world was overcast with harsh clouds that seemed to silently whisper stark warnings to turn back. Fear ate so powerfully at them that even Noloon could feel it pulse through his very nerves.

They waited. The night breeze chilled over their half naked bodies. Hours passed.

Then sound came on the wind, a sound that was not of the night world. It reached out, clutched their full attention to the dark Cylinder.

Noloon's fingers gripped tightly on the long sword, the blade thrust out in front of him, gleaming as moonlight reached down and touched its naked point. He stepped forward and the fear moved with his steps.

Suddenly there was an opening in the Cylinder and a more terrible blackness showed beyond it.

His steps were like night shadows, fluttering without sound across the thick foliage. Sweat oiled his tan hardened flesh as he slowly moved up the hill; fascinated by the gaping hole in the Cylinder. His breath clutched tight in his throat.

Something moved in the darkness.

He heard a terrified moan from behind him.

A form stepped from the Cylinder and stood on the hilltop, looking down upon the village behind Noloon. It was shaped like a man, but covered strangely with something alien, something that terrified the very core of Noloon's mind.

The strange clothing that covered the man-shape was like the Cloak of Shame that sinners wore, hiding all physical details. It had grossly bloated arms and legs and head. For a moment it stood there, unmoving, and then one arm made a gesture and two other "men" joined him. They stood, looking across the valley, and then after a few moments started moving in Noloon's direction. He blended into the dark shadows surrounding the path.

The three figures came closer, slowly moving toward him, until finally he could hear the sound of their footsteps against the ground, until at last he heard the strange murmur of their voices floating in the night silence.

Noloon choked his fingers around the hilt of the sword.

His eyes examined their clothing, their faces, and he wondered about these strangers, for they were much like men of his tribe. Surely they could not be Gods.

The clothing that covered their bodies was silvery bright in the moonlight, gleaming like stardust spotting the skies at night.

Noloon leaped out, sword rose.

"Go in peace or die!" he warned.

Three pairs of steel eyes angrily examined his body. Then the nearest "man" laughed, making a quick motion to the others.

"Put down your weapon Native—no harm will come to you!"

Noloon was suddenly aware of being alone in his bold attack, yet no fear entered his mind. He could not blame his fellow tribesmen for running, for they did not have a woman as lovely, as wonderful as Tanja. He had more reason to fight. His sword swiftly swung in an arc, the point reaching for the nearest "man's" throat. It came to a stop a few inches from the desired target, as if held back by some invisible wall.

Noloon raised his weapon again, higher over his head, holding it in both hands, and then with all the strength of his muscles he swept the sword down toward the "man" in front of him.

The blade whistled against the air, slammed into that invisible protective wall.

His arm rebounded with the sword. Every muscle charged with white fire, which shivered over every nerve like lightning had struck. His throat dried; the air swirled before his blinded eyes. Frantically, he fought back the blackness, attempted to attack again, but his arms wouldn't move, his muscles seemed paralyzed in hot fire. Every nerve

180

burned as if encased in molten metal. Then all at once the blackness squeezed away awareness.

He was aware of light, and then sound. The dryness was still alive in his throat, but the pain had ebbed away.

Slowly, Noloon forced his muscles into action and he stood, looked around him. Everything seemed perversely normal. He turned, stared at the Cylinder on the hill. It was silent, waiting.

With an anguished cry, Noloon rushed toward the village.

When he burst into the clearing, which was the outer fields of the tribe's farmland, he saw two lines of people standing in the village square. The three aliens were walking along the line of females, touching those women who were youngest and most beautiful. His eyes desperately searched for Tanja, spotted her in a small group to one side of the clearing, near two huts.

Weaponless, with only the strength of his naked arms to give resistance, Noloon slipped forward, keeping the huts between himself and the aliens. Then he moved between the two huts nearest Tanja.

He whispered her name, just loud enough so only those in the small group could hear.

Tanja turned frightened eyes in his direction. He motioned her to come to him. Slowly, timidly, she moved, stepping backwards, her eyes fastened on the three aliens who were busy picking more beautiful maidens to take away with them.

"What happened to you?" she whispered, once at his side.

Noloon said nothing, merely took hold of Tanja's hand and motioned her to silence.

"Follow me," he whispered. "We must run."

She hesitated and then did as told.

* * * * * * *

Half running, but silent, they rushed away from the village. Once beyond the fields, just within the forest, Tanja stopped, her eyes wide, frightened. "We can't run. The Elder

181

said there's no way to escape...that what you had done was a sin—"

"They are no Gods. For Gods would never look upon a woman as they do. Did you see their eyes? They are mortal 'men'—and they can die!" he assured her, holding down the doubt that his short battle experience had created about these creatures. But men or Gods, they would not have Tanja without a hard fight.

"They will follow," she said, trembling against him. "We cannot run."

"They can follow only one at a time on the path to the Cave-Where-Two-Become-One." he pointed out.

"But—"

"There I will make my stand," Noloon announced, a plan now forming in his mind.

As he led the way through the virgin forest, Noloon tried to convince himself that there was some advantage on his side. He knew the country and would have a head start. The Strangers, be they Gods or men or supermen, could only follow on foot to where he would go. And there, high upon the narrow ledge that led to the Cave-Where-Two-Become-One, he would have his only chance, there he would make a bold stand. They could follow only one at a time, and once there he would discover if They were Gods or—men, for surely They could not survive a thousand foot drop over jagged rocks if They were anything less than Gods.

* * * * * * *

The forest was silent around Noloon and Tanja as if all the creatures of the woods guessed the sin the two of them were making. The hot sun baked down over the tropic world and slowly began to slide toward the horizon, yet still they had not reached the mountains. It was a long, difficult journey. But this was the road to Oneness that all took to become One with their mates, and thus became a test of conviction— a test of love.

They rested, slept, when the sun slipped into its Den of Sleep. The next morning they continued, until the forest thinned out to high rocky country.

182

No sign of pursuit had been in evidence as yet, but he couldn't help believing that the Strangers would soon discover what had happened. Then they would surely follow.

The two of them continued until night rested over the land. Sleep soothed their exhausted muscles once more. In the morning he was awakened by distant voices. Noloon jerked up, grabbed Tanja, pulled her after him.

The high land blended into mountains, which were a jagged high barrier before them. Noloon hurriedly looked for the pathway that would lead up the face of the mountain to the cave. Both were exhausted from their long journey, the sleep had done little to give strength, the meager food they had picked from the ripe purple jaal-trees had refreshed, not filled their hunger.

Noloon spotted the narrow pathway and pushed Tanja before him. The sun burned down on their bodies as they climbed upwards. Tanja stumbled several times, but he caught her, urging the young woman forward.

"I can't keep on," she kept pleading, tears of desperation running down her lovely cheeks.

Noloon would look back, seeing the three Strangers making their way up the path behind them, and then he pushed Tanja onward. "You must keep going. To the Cave. There we'll fight."

It seemed a terrible nightmare, each step taking them higher and higher; but never seeming to get them any closer to the top. The canyon below dropped deeper away, into a toothy mass of jagged rocks below.

Still they climbed.

They had gained some, because the Strangers didn't seem used to the long climb. But it was only a matter of minutes before Noloon would have to face them for the last time, since his pathway led to the heavenly blind alley, where Two-Became-One. *The Cave.* There he would push the large stone into place sealing Tanja into the cave, safe from danger as he made a last stand against these Strangers who would take her from him.

Finally the cave came into sight. Tanja stumbled and fell, exhausted, unable to go further. He quickly lifted her into his arms, easily ran the rest of the way, setting her down inside the gloomy darkness of the Cave.

"They'll kill you," Tanja sobbed, eyes cloudy with tears.

"No." he promised, holding her close for possibly the last time. "No—they will not have you..."

He heard footsteps on the path behind him, turned. Stepping out of the cave, Noloon pushed the large stone into place, then faced the three Strangers as they rounded the last bend and came to a stop before him.

The leading one said: "Where's the girl?"

"You can't have her," Noloon scowled.

The wind answered him, brushing against the canyon wall, whipping past the three Strangers and waving his long black hair in ripples behind him. The silence was seemingly endless as he waited for the wrath of these so-called Gods.

"We must have her," the leader announced in a firm voice.

"She is mine. You can't take my woman away from me. We are on the Mountain of Oneness—where Two-Become-One."

The leader turned and stared at the other two men, then returned his attention to Noloon. "You are unarmed—alone. You cannot stop us from taking her. Be reasonable!"

Noloon forced a laugh, fighting back the raw fear gnawing at the pit of his stomach. "You are as unarmed as I. And can come only one at a time. If you be Gods, you surely will survive the long fall to the canyon floor below."

There was hesitation before any of the Strangers spoke, and when they did, it was the leader who addressed Noloon.

"As you know, we are Gods. And what the Gods wish, it is their divine right to have. You must accept this—as all your other people have."

"I do not accept! I do not accept anything on blind faith. I would rather die than have life without my Tanja. If you are Gods, as you claim, then prove it and be done with this. If you are as human as I—or something other than human— then make your stand, for you will not have Tanja without killing me."

They stared at one another, amazement in their eyes.

"It's a stand-off. We can't let him get away with it," the leader whispered softly, but the wind carried his words to

Noloon.

The second "man" nodded. "If one gets away with defying us, the others will, too. Then what will we do for women?"

"I told you we should have come armed," the third cursed. "These Natives don't know..."

"I'll tell him," the leader announced. "He'll understand then. It's the only way." As if to point out the logic of his words, he looked down at the gaping canyon a thousand feet below with its jagged rocks like gigantic teeth waiting to shred the life away from anything that might fall into its hungry mouth.

The leader stared at Noloon for a long time and then slowly began to speak. "I don't know what you think of us— it doesn't matter. But maybe a little story will let you understand." He took a deep breath and then continued:

"A long time ago hundreds of women and men came to this planet. Some disease plagued our civilization many generations ago. Most of the planets on which our vast Federation lived became sterile—only a few were untouched— those on such virgin planets as yours survived and continued to breed. Our Fathers said to leave you alone and take from you only those who were young and strong—bring them into our worlds to breed a new strain, an immune strain. Take only those necessary to keep our populations alive. These women that we gather from a thousand worlds like yours live in the middle of luxury, they feast on riches, they live like Goddesses. Their lives are made happier than you could ever understand. We worship such women—we offer them all that our vast civilization can give. For these are the Women of Life—they are making our race strong and beautiful."

Noloon listened, understanding little of what was being said, except the fact that the Stranger's words proved but one fact: they were men, humans, not Gods. But finally a general thread and pattern of what was being said began to form in his mind. And doubt as to the truthfulness of the man's words.

When he had finished, Noloon stood silently for a while and then slowly shook his head.

"The woman is mine—and if you try to take her from

me, I'll fight."

"Surely you know that's impossible. You could not touch us with your sword—how do you expect to touch us with your hands?"

"I can try."

The second man cursed. "Enough talk—let's be done with it."

"He's only one and after what you've told him, he must die, anyway!" the third added.

Hesitation and fear showed in the leader's eyes, and then he stepped forward.

Noloon leaped, not waiting for them to reach him. Every muscle went into his attack. His fists, locked together, swung at the first man's body, aiming so the blow would knock him off the ledge.

His fists connected against the man's left side and Noloon was surprised to feel the body flinging off balance, hanging momentarily on the edge of the pathway and then slowly falling sideways. A scream pierced the air as the man went down the side of the canyon. His body bounced several times before distance dwindled his form into a tiny dot that came to rest at the bottom of the canyon.

The other two stared in shock and then the first said:

"You fool. Nothing but cattle. What right? What right do you have to dare to oppose your Master!"

The violence of the outburst caused Noloon to silently listen.

"Cattle—that's all you are!" The features seemed to blur, suggest something more horrible than he could allow his mind to accept. They were shriveled; loose purple skinned, the eyes deep-set, close together. He closed the ugly image out of his mind, refusing to see it.

"We've *let* you live on this virgin planet—and only demanded a few women for our Great Leader's feasting table. What right? What right?"

Noloon leaped, throwing the man over the side of the cliff.

The third glared at him and then sighed. "Just listen to me, Native," the man said. "You are but wasting your effort. It matters not what you do—you are just a research project—

186

no more. Killing me...that does nothing."

Noloon looked at the man, grinned.

"Some *more* lies to get my woman?" he demanded.

"No, no more lies. You are not even real, not human! Just creations...you are—"

Noloon merely stepped forward, lifted the man in his arms, high over his head, and threw him over the cliff.

Then slowly turning, Noloon pushed the boulder aside and swept Tanja into his arms, smothering her lips with kisses. He had already forgotten the lies that had been spoken to him.

Nothing that had been said made sense; nor was it of any real importance. All that mattered was that Tanja was his, and he was hers, and they would never be separated by those horrid Images of Man!

They made love, as lovers will on their wedding night. And slept. Somewhere in the cave a murmuring sound whispered in the night chill, followed by a soft purring. Then footsteps, soft little footsteps came closer and closer to the unconscious lovers, and then stopped.

Noloon woke, suddenly. Startled. Then he smiled as his eyes admiringly feasted on the young boy who now stood next to Tanja. He reached out his arms, said: "Come, son."

"Father," the small boy sighed, rushing into Noloon's arms.

A little later, Noloon, Tanja, and Noja—their son—stepped out of the Cave where Two-Become-One and moved down the mountain path and later, out of the mountains, returning to their village.

Well, back to the pun is fun in the sun routine. A bit of wisdom, I suppose, considering the title this one holds with great pride. If they had only known the truth! The warning signs were all around them. But they were far too excited by this newly found alien world!

─◄WORD TO THE WISE►─

Willington Weaver was the second in command of the *Starship V.* That made him flunky. Why you might ask! Well that's because the only other member of the exploration team was Captain Smart, who was first in command.

But he didn't let that bother him much, because, after all, *every dog has his day,* he would think.

When the *Starship V* discovered the new world, called Famos by its inhabitants, Smart landed the rocket in the very center of the largest city they could find. That was the Smart way to make First Contact with the biggest, most powerful center of civilization the planet seemed to offer!

Taking out their translator they left the ship.

No sooner had they touched the alien soil than they were surrounded by hundreds of "aliens."

"My, what cute little creatures," Captain Smart exclaimed. "They look just like animated pitchers."

And *surely* they did.

Willington wildly shook his head up and down in excitement. "It just goes to show: you can't tell what you'll find on the other side of the hill!"

Smart nodded to his ship's first, and only mate. "Turn on the translator," he demanded in his most grand manner.

Of course Willington did so, as ordered, quite proud of himself in this grand historical moment.

Smart took the mike from the other's hand and spoke into it. His words went into the translator and came out in the language of the milling aliens that looked so much like pitchers. He tried hard not to indicate in his voice or manner

188

this mental picture of them, which could, naturally, seem somewhat belittling and smug.

"I came from Earth, the center of the Galactic Empire, and we have come to offer you membership in our organization..."

He continued on with the stock speech which he had learned in Spaceman's School well over twenty years before. And it was a grand and long-winded speech which was being delivered by him for the very first time. After all, the discovery of a new world of intelligent aliens wasn't an everyday event. Well, at least, not for Smart!

The *pitchers* looked questioningly at the two Earthmen, and then seemed to strain their small ears toward the speaker of the translator.

One of them stepped up and said: "I'm sorry, but will you please talk louder? We can't hear...we're hard of hearing, you see..." It made a contortion of its face, and pointed to its infinitesimal ears.

"Turn up the volume!" Smart ordered.

Willington did as ordered.

The speech was repeated, and after that, a regal looking member of the crowd around them stepped up and said: "We welcome you, Earthmen, and I'll take you to our leader."

They followed him, quite excited and proud. After all, they were making First Contact! They'd go down in history.

Finally they were led into a building and taken to a small room, where several small "pitchers" came out and stared at them.

"These are the leader's children," the large alien guide explained. "I shall return."

Once left alone with the children the two Earthmen started talking in soft whispers.

"This is going to be a cinch!" Smart announce.

"You said it, dad! They'll just jump at the chance to be conquered. And what a world...did you see the way they looked at us?"

There was little doubt that this world would be willing to do anything the Earthmen told them to do, and before they knew it they would by conquered people, slaves for the Empire.

189

A moment later several aliens entered the room.

No sooner had they done so than one of the children cried in alarm to its elder: "They're planning to conquer us!"

Willington looked at Smart. Smart at Willington.

They couldn't believe it! After all, how could the little creatures have heard their whispered exchange?

Or were they telepaths?

Just before the firing squad shot them, Willington stepped forward with raised hands. "Please wait! At least tell us how the children knew?' How did they hear us?"

The commander in charge of the firing squad smiled as he said:

"Didn't you Earthmen notice that *little* pitchers have *big* ears?"

This story has a history. Enough to offer just the following: It was published the same month that man stepped on the moon for the first time. And I received my copy from my agent Forrest J Ackerman one month after my father's death in an envelope which had written on it: "A Day For Living!" Well, the story appeared in Worlds of If Science Fiction *and then later in Isaac Asimov's* The Science Fictional Olympics, *in which was written that the story features a special kind of gladiatorial contest, one which we would not want to participate in! I could not agree more with those words for only one could survive the Games! And now it is offered up to a twenty-first century audience as...*

⊸A DAY FOR DYING⊢

Realizing that it was probably the last time I would ever see them, I watched the tall, endless buildings rush past the police ground-car. They were glassy structures, colored in rainbow brightness, slipping by one after another. The people walked the night-streets and moved into neon-lit clubs happily, as on every night of their lives, unaware of the hard fact that they could be snapped away to the Tele-Games, without even a moment to say good-by to their loved ones.

I, Charles David Travers, a peace-loving Citizen of the twenty-second century, had been arrested for some unnamed crime, to appear in the Tele-Games of March 8th, 2134. And yet the world around me continued as usual.

Finally we arrived at the Tele-Games Court, a large white building that reached upward to disappear into the night sky. The officer who had presented me with the official papers now ushered me out of the car, up the steps into the building.

The walk through the Courthouse was a flashing series of dark impressions that disappeared almost immediately. I was pushed into a small courtroom, invisible death hanging from its clean white walls.

The gray-faced judge stared down at me as if made of cold steel.

"Charles David Travers, for Judgment sir," my escort announced like a robot. "Case 2-99 63567489, of Los Angeles Major, California."

The judge looked at me. He said, "You are brought before the High Court for treason against the State. How do you plead?"

Every muscle knotted in disbelief. "I've done nothing. This is a farce. You have the wrong man."

The judge asked, "You *are* Charles David Travers, son of David Jay Travers and Joan Marianne Travers? You have a mistress by the name of Julie Thorson? You work at the International Message Service as a file clerk, Code-SB? You are a collector of old books, adventure novels, and are in the habit of spending hours in libraries and in your one-room bachelor apartment reading? You are the Charles David Travers, who wrote an article in college defending the concept of the Tele-Games as a logical means of controlling the world population and relieving our civilization of criminals, of giving the Citizens the kind of violent entertainment they so highly desire? An article which had its tongue-in-cheek subtle double-meaning obvious, now in light of what we have learned about your true activities."

"Yes, but—"

"There is no mistake," the judge announced with finality. "You have been the companion of Julie Thorson for the last six months, working with her in an attempt to overthrow the government. You are guilty of first-degree treason. Miss Thorson has confessed."

"It's a lie!" I shouted.

"Silence! You will appear before the National Tele-Games of March 8th as a Man-at-Arms to do battle to the death. In the event you should be the sole survivor, you will be freed, never again to be sentenced to the Tele-Games. So is the fair judgment of the State's Justice."

Dazed, I followed the guard out of the courtroom and down a series of corridors. He stopped before two large iron doors and presented an identification card to the guard there, who allowed him to lead me into the inner chambers of the

Central Los Angeles prison.

I was led to a narrow door marked 71134. The guard ordered me into the cell with a wave of his arm. The door closed behind me like the clanging of some morbid trap.

"Charlie!" came from behind me. It was a voice that cut into my agony. It was filled with a mixture of surprise and pained horror.

All the emotions rushed up in a flood, choking all senses like invisible fingers blotting out sanity. Whipping around, I saw the tall woman who had been my mistress these last months. But I couldn't equate this beautiful creature with the lover I'd shared silent walks through building-top parks or companionable evenings in my apartment or simply dancing gracefully in the dim night-clubs, chatting happily over a dinner and cocktails. This couldn't be that same woman!

Madness clutched at my brain.

There stood the creature that had placed me here. Through the emotion of wild fury I looked at her voluptuous body, draped in a green glowing cloth that wound around her slim waist and angular hips above firm thighs, dropping like silken waves about every beautiful and loving curve of her body. She didn't seem real, standing there in the drab coldness of the cell, her arms stretched out in offering.

Sanity snapped like a thread.

"You lying tramp!" I yelled, leaping. My hands gripped her silken white throat; my fingers squeezed the air back into her lungs, trapping it there.

Maybe it was the look of surprised horror in her large brown eyes that jolted sanity back into my shocked brain. my hands lowered as I slowly stepped hack.

"Those lies...I've never done anything against the State."

She clutched at her throat, gasping for air, and finally said, "Charles...believe me—I didn't tell them *anything!* So help me God!"

"Then why?" I managed, confusion defeating all hatred.

"Why do they have the Games? Why is a person sent to his death for voicing objection against the State? Or getting drunk in public, or being late paying his bills? There doesn't have to be any logical reason!" she blurted.

"But they had to have *some* reason!"

"You were my companion. Oh, Charlie, believe me, I'd do anything to get you out of this!" Her eyes pleaded with me to forgive her. They blurred with moisture and then closed, tears running down her creamy cheeks.

How could I hate her? She had been created for love. And I knew she returned my love. Looking at her I felt a flood of overwhelming emotion.

Helplessly I folded an arm about her waist, gently raised her chin until our eyes met. And as I looked at her, reality slipped away to become a fantasy of love.

"Oh, Charlie, thank God!" she breathed. "I was afraid you wouldn't understand! Or forgive."

After that the insanity of need overwhelmed all other considerations. There was only my sensations and Julie's form.

Some time later I was aware of Julie moving from me. I sat up and asked, "How'd they pick you up? Why?"

She shook her head. "They brought me to the Games Judge and announced that I was guilty of treasons against the State, sentenced me to the Arena and brought me here. The next thing I knew you were in the cell. That's the whole truth, Charlie." She shrugged "We're living in the most terrible Police State mankind ever devised. In our grandparents' day it was different."

I merely nodded, aware she spoke the truth. Yesterday I would have refused to believe.

My own grandfather had told me that in his youth there were television shows of violence, but they were plays written by fiction writers, performed by professional actors; violence was the keynote. Then sporting events became more popular than drama, because of the real violence. Reality shows became the real money makers. After that, well it was a logical step to take hardened criminals, already condemned to die, and let them fight to the death for the home audience. Freeing the winner always promised a more exciting battle. With universal peace, an overcrowded world, unemployment and depression, the development of the Tele-Games became a natural evolution. Now it was an international institution that fed the greedy public with the blood-violence it so craved. People were killed, but they were other people—not you! That made the difference.

It might have been only a couple of hours or a day before two uniformed guards stepped into the cell and ordered me out. I was taken into a small room where several rows of chairs were facing a blank wall. As I sat, the guards flanking me, the door opened and five grim-looking officers stepped in; four seated themselves directly behind us and the fifth, a Major Reginald, stood in front of me.

"You, Charles Travers, have one way to lower the sentence against you. Placing you with Miss Thorson was a waste of time; therefore, we will show you part of the recording of her interview." He then sat.

The room darkened and the wall glowed into shimmering blue life. To all appearances, it disappeared to reveal another room beyond; in reality, of course, it was one of those huge Tri-D screens.

The major was standing in front of Julie on the screen. "You've been seeing Travers for months. What is his connection with the underground movement?"

"I can't tell you."

"Miss Thorson, you don't seem to realize your position."

"I'm fully aware," she spat out. "We don't give information about our activities."

The Major nodded to one of his companions who held a small steel box. "This will give the information we want."

Julie's eyes flashed toward the box and then jerked back to the officer. Her shoulders sagged as she announced in a cold voice:

"Charles Travers is my contact. He got me into this. I don't know anything else."

The screen went dead and the lights snapped on. The real major stepped in front of me. "The rest of the information's classified. We used the Brain-box to check it out. There's no reason for you to deny connection with the Underground Nationalist Movement."

Sweat broke out over my body. No matter what I claimed, they wouldn't believe me.

The Major said, "Just tell us who your contacts are."

I shook my head. "I don't know what you're talking

about. She was lying."

The Major nodded and one of his assistants stepped forward with a Brain-box.

I looked at the mental probe and then shrugged, remaining silent.

One of the men clamped a small band on my forehead. The man holding the box pressed a button and reality blacked out.... Then the room snapped back into place.

I blinked and looked at the major. It seemed as if a great, terrible pressure had been lifted.

The Major frowned, grimacing in puzzlement. "It would seem Miss Thorson lied or one of you has been conditioned."

A gnawing cut at my stomach. "How could I afford conditioning? Only the Government has the machinery for that!" I stood, rage tensing every muscle.

"There are ways. If you are a member of the underground, there would he ways." The Major laughed. "But it makes no difference. You have been sentenced—even if wrongly—and it will be carried out."

Violence snapped sanity as he turned. I leaped, grabbing his flabby throat. A great feeling of power came over me as I gazed into his reddening features; his eyes were popping out and his tongue was convulsively struggling for air. Then I felt the other men clawing at my arms and body. Something hit the back of my head, but I didn't release the Major's neck until another hard object slammed once more at the base of my skull.

I had awakened in the blackness of a cell hours before, unable to see anything. It was a small place with little room for my six feet to stretch out. There wasn't any bed or covers, just hard steal to sleep on. Time passed slowly; then guards came to take me to a huge chamber packed with over a thousand people, locked behind large barred doors.

I was standing there for some time before a gentle hand touched my shoulder. I turned to see Julie. Her face was white and drawn, her lips thin, pale trembling lines.

"I...had to lie," she stammered. "The cell was tapped."

I tried to feel the hate that should be inside me, but it wouldn't return. No emotion at all effected me. "There's nothing we can do about it."

196

"I have to make you understand what you're dying for." She hesitated, then pulled me aside, away from the guards. "I was arrested trying to make contact with a man I had to lie to save him. He's very important."

"What's his name?"

She shook her head said. "I can't tell you. You might use the name to save yourself."

I started to argue the point, then shrugged. No matter what, I'd be sent into the Arena—to my death. The chances of survival were reduced to zero. Yet there was still hope as long as I lived.

I found myself reviewing all the major combats I'd witnessed in the National Events. They were bloody battles between inexperienced citizens armed with clubs, rapiers, broadswords and spears. No modern-day weapons were allowed for fear they might be used against the guards or the cameramen who were lodged just above the fighting area. The Arena was surrounded by an army of Games Police with weapons that could cut down every occupant of the Arena at a moment's notice. I'd seen, in viewing countless Games, that many people stood frozen in fear, letting themselves be killed. Others, more realistic, would keep outside the range of the battle until it narrowed down to two combatants. This I hoped to do. After that, if I survived, I'd try to join the underground movement. But it was useless to tell Julie that; she wouldn't believe me.

The two of us stood together, holding hands. Finally we were ordered out through a corridor in single file, to another larger room lined with armed Games Police. There we were handed primitive weapons for the Event.

I was given a small short sword, like the ones the Romans had used in battle. It was light and made of strong steel—unlike Roman weapons.

It was the thought of personal survival on which I focused as we were herded like a mass of dumb animals into the confines of the Arena.

At that point something unexpected happened to me, like a cutting off of all sensation. It was a sharp mental shifting, a release from fear, like a switch had been pulled, disconnecting emotion.

I looked at Julie, letting my eyes run along her flesh, but felt nothing. It was as if I had suddenly become a zombie, without any desire other than the want to kill.

I automatically swung the short sword in the air in front of me. My huge arms flexed as I stood there in the middle of the Arena, surrounded by fellow citizens, awaiting the command to kill.

Then it came. A loud blast of horns.

My sword swung into the skull of a man standing next to me. I didn't wait to let others defend themselves. The short sword moved, cutting into arms, chests, heads, and necks, creating a bloody passage of death until a mass of bodies were cluttering my passage. Then I was facing a tall man carrying a huge broadsword.

He swung the weapon right at my head. Ducking to one side, I whipped the point of my blade toward his chest; it cut lightly into the flesh, drawing a thin line of red. He swung again, a slicing blow at my stomach. With speed and skill I shouldn't have possessed, I leaped in close and rammed the short sword deep into his gut, twisting with sadistic delight. Withdrawing my sword, I turned and dropped the edge of the bloody blade into a woman's skull. The weapon wrenched from my hand locked in the bony tissue of her head.

Turning, I picked up the broadsword from my fallen male antagonist of a moment before and swung it in a circle through the neck of one man and across the chest of a woman whose body sliced open, the insides bursting out like a bloody fountain.

I made a path of dead bodies before me, like cutting wheat in the fields; then I spotted Julie holding a Scottish broadsword and making a path of death much like my own, without any emotion on her face. There wasn't time to marvel at Julie's unnatural skill; she should have died in the first moments.

It's amazing how fast a couple of thousand people will die when all are enemies of each other. It seemed but minutes before less than a dozen people still lived and I found myself without an opponent. My eyes searched the Arena. I spotted Julie still alive, cutting down a tall muscular man with one swing of her blade. She looked savagely magnificent standing there, the broadsword clutched in her hands, long hair hanging loose and flying as she turned to make another kill. But now there was none other than myself.

It seemed strangely ironic, even fantastic, that it should have ended this way.

She rushed at me calmly, a primitive, mindless killer. Her blade swung at my right arm, but merely cut the outer layer of flesh. It was enough to make me accept real danger. Her light sword, built for fast movement, might easily prove superior to my heavy weapon.

Instinct snapped my broadsword toward her head. It would be over quickly. At least she would die without much pain, I told myself.

But her sword met my blade with superhuman strength. Then the point jerked out and flicked at my chest, just missing. Our eyes met at that moment, but there was only a black expression on her face.

In the next minutes we exchanged blow which must have given the Tele-Games' viewers the greatest excitement in their lives.

We weren't two amateurs battling to the death; we were expert fighters. Where either of us had learned our skill was impossible even to guess. How could I have known the truth?

I moved with all the sweeping speed in my muscles, attempting to put a quick end to the duel. It was as if some Fate had made us almost perfectly matched. Each was skilled to perfection; each was seeking the death of a former lover.

Then she suddenly leaped forward, the point of her sword reaching for my chest. I sidestepped, using every muscle in my body. At the same time my sword moved in an arc toward Julie's middle.

She had been caught off balance, unable to check the forward movement. My blade sliced cleanly across her midsection.

Oddly I felt nothing but relief. It was over. I'd survived.

Then I noticed something so alarming that I couldn't believe it at first. Where Julie's body was cut open appeared an odd, twisted mass of wires, circuits and plastic flesh.

Without thinking, without wanting to guess what this

implied, I collapsed over her form as if exhausted. My hands turned her body so that the gaping hole was hidden from view. How much this explained!

I stood and walked to the Freedom Door, the cameras following my every action. As I stepped from the Arena, I was surrounded by international reporters, eager with questions that I answered until a small dark man stepped up. He said, "Come, follow me."

His attitude was so much that of an Official of the Games that I followed automatically. He carried a pass that let us through the guarded corridors and out into the streets of Los Angeles. He indicated a car parked in front of the building and we got in.

As we pulled away from the curb and sped hurriedly down the street, I demanded in alarm, "Where are you taking me?"

"I'm Julie Thorson's contact," was his answer. "All will he explained shortly."

"But Julie was—"

"An android?" He smiled in a strange, almost sad manner. "Everything will be explained." We drove in silence through the streets for half an hour before stopping at a small building in the outskirts of the city. He escorted m into the house and I found myself in a living room filled with people.

All stood and turned, looking at me.

What I saw then scared me far more than anything I'd experienced in the last days. There, standing before me, was Julie Thorson, quite alive and beautiful! I started to take a step forward when a man beside her turned and began to speak. I stood there, stunned.

"You see, Charlie," he said, "we secretly developed perfect androids; we gave them truthful memory backgrounds up to a point and then added a fictional background to hide information that we couldn't let the authorities know about. We had to find out how perfectly they had been made, to see if it were possible to fool the Government Officials. Of course nobody, outside of those in this room, knows about our discovery. And nobody would even imagine such a thing if the evidence were put before their eyes."

He paused, smiling sadly, then continued, "You see how

200

valuable this will be in our efforts to overthrow the now existing governments and end the Tele-Games. Agents who have inhuman strength and ability, programmed to know nothing other than the 'instinctive' missions given them. The Brain-boxes will reveal nothing. We even had to give our androids sexual drives and a sense of synthetic excitement; the absence of such small things might prove a give-away. That explains why you were able to enjoy a seemingly normal sensual relation with...*your* Julie Thorson. The experiment worked out perfectly. We couldn't have wished for more."

I stood there dazed, shocked into believing what I saw and heard. It all fit perfectly together.

"What about me, now?" was my only question.

"After you have taped a full report you will be reprogrammed," said the real Charles David Travers.

DIMENSIONS, BY CHARLES NUETZEL

PART FOUR
NEW DIMENSIONS

⸺◂PREFACE▸⸺

And now we come to a rather exciting place in this collection. From the old is born the new, could be a trite offering. But I'll avoid saying that. Heaven forbid that I might end up being too trite!

The following stories are published here for the first time. I want to give full credit to a woman who has proven to be an outstanding friend and editor who is too shy to take many bows for her help: Heidi Garrett. The fact that she liked these stories makes it possible to feel quite comfortable offering them up to the reader as the concluding section of this book. I liked every one of them. But, of course, I had to be fired up enough at the time of writing in order to have suffered through the act of giving them birth.

For many very down to earth, non-artistic reasons stories simply don't find a market at the time of their writing and end up in a file, being lost, so to speak. Sometimes it is possible to take a look at them and wonder why they didn't find their place where they could be seen by readers. In fact, sometimes those unpublished works are far better than those which actually end up in print.

A hard secret of publishing is that many factors other than quality or art enter into the decision of what is bought and is tossed. Sometimes it is space, sometimes it is lack of space, sometimes it is indigestion (of the editor, of course), and sometimes it is simply a matter of "we have one too much like it" or "it doesn't fit our immediate needs" or you name it. I've had stories chopped and cropped, books brutally shortened because of space! On the other hand, I've had things published because the editor needed something, anything, to fill in some blank pages. Shocking, perhaps, but true. I've even had a story bought and then not published because of policy change, the editor changing, or the publisher going out of business for one reason or another. There are endless reasons.

In the case of the following stories, I hope the readers will see why they found a place here, and will enjoy their pulse and action. Some are pure fun, others are nightmares.

This story came from the simple idea that children many times become the masters, and the parents the slaves. Children can become monsters, especially in their teenage years, when they are exploring adulthood and discovering that ol' sexual reality which will be so much a part of the rest of their lives. But, even at the terrible age of two they can be little demons exploring their homes with destructive force. I wondered just how far this can go, how powerful a child gets when trying to control their home. And they do continual battle for dominance! Do they rule; or are they ruled? Perhaps a silly idea, but there are far too many parents around who in their pride, love, and devotion tend to not just spoil the child, but to literally allow them such freedom that one might wonder just who is actually...

‣MASTER OF THE HOUSE‣

In reconstructing what took place during the last three months of Carol s life, I have used the evidence of her written notes.

Carol rented a safe deposit box in which she had, daily, placed a new page of scribbled writing. In effect she kept a daily report on her discoveries concerning Johnny. At first she simply listed books he read—at a rate of four to ten a day—then continued by reporting what he did away from home. The evidence piled up so quickly that it was obvious why she never confided in me. A lawyer was co-signer of the safe deposit box, and had instructions to give its contents to me if anything happened to her.

Maybe I should start at the beginning.

It started some eleven years ago, and when I think back to that time, remembering the joy Carol and I had experienced, I find it difficult to relate the past to the present horror. The beginning and ending blended so gradually that it is hard to define when love turned to suspicion and then to fear. The hate came only in the last few days.

206

The first evidence that Johnny Junior was different came early; but every parent is overjoyed to discover their child is special even if this is in the form of strange—almost totally frightening—intelligence for his age.

When it was discovered I couldn't have children the solution was obvious: adopt.

Johnny was what is called a foundling. The story of his being discovered outside the State Adoption Agency is not necessary to detail here, only that fact is important to note. Because of this the Agency couldn't know about his parentage. Johnny was two weeks old. He had dark hair, deep, almost black eyes that seemed remarkably intelligent. He seemed to plead for our love and acceptance. We couldn't refuse.

As with all children, once he became a part of our home he took over. They say that parents are the teachers but it is always a two-way street.

Though dependent like all children, he seldom cried but when he did, his message was *communicative*, letting us know what he wanted: food, change of diapers, affection.

By the time he started to walk he had learned to control his bowl movements and knew to use the bathroom. He walked almost before his muscles should have been strong enough to make it possible: three months after we adopted him. Speaking began almost with walking. Carol's mother—Mrs. Hendricks—exclaimed, "It's almost as if he's learning a *new* language, rather than learning to understand the *idea* of speaking!" Mother Hendricks was a heavy woman, but with a sporty manner. Carol was almost her opposite, blonde-haired, quiet—though, like her mother, determined and strong-willed—a delicate, doe-eyed female who had captured my love almost at first sight.

If it hadn't been for my mother-in-law, we might not have noticed Johnny's fast advancement as being so outstanding—at least not for some time. Parental pride will accept any outstanding traits a child has without question.

By six months he was able to say, "MO-her" and "FA-her." Instead of taking a year to fashion words into requests it was only a matter of weeks after this. Where most children will take up to two years to begin constructing simple sentences, Johnny developed the intense need to do so within a month after beginning speech. The efforts were intense.

His tiny face would contract in deep frowns, as if concentrating in an intelligent, knowledgeable way.

He listened to our conversations. His face revealed the hard effort it took to comprehend the meaning of our word-sounds and relate them to actions and objects.

He never played with the normal baby toys, having rejected a rattle in less than a month. He was little over four months when he started observing and handling small items about the house, studying them as if making a mental photograph. We thought it cute; not strange. We accepted his growth and actions as natural for *him* rather than natural for a child his age. His kind of play was the observation-game; the learning-to-speak-game. It was a deep study of his immediate surroundings, as if sucking facts into a computer mind.

By eight months he was asking what things were and wanted to know their purpose.

I never had to repeat more than once the name of objects—and the repeating was more because of his difficulty remembering the *exact* pronunciation rather than his attempt to remember the word or understand its meaning. He never had to be taught how to turn on and off a light switch. But his early interest in books was the first really startling revelation as to his advanced intelligence. He asked what they were. I'd hardly had time to say that books have words on their pages than he immediately wanted to know the printed words for mother and father and chair—and all the basic objects about the house.

What seems fantastic now is my casual acceptance of the implication of his quick understanding. He was not even a year old. Almost shaking with excitement, I thumbed through a book and found some of the words he asked about. He caught on immediately. He wanted to learn to read.

On his first birthday I presented him with two simple "ABC" type children's books. Mother Hendricks' face blanched. "You must be joking!" she cried in a high-pitched voice.

Johnny glanced thoughtfully at her, said: "I want to know how to read."

208

Mother Hendricks took a deep breath and said: "Why, of course. Why shouldn't you?"

Johnny jumped from the table, clutching the books like some rattle or toy doll to his tiny chest. "I want to go to bedroom...read."

Nobody objected.

Once Johnny left, Mother Hendricks was white-faced as she looked at us. It was some time before we could speak. She hadn't visited us for months, having been in New York with one of her sons.

The look on the older woman's face said so much, and held shock, fear, pride, confusion. Nobody was saying anything for some time. I guess both Carol and I were being faced with a hard reality we had merely wondered about but never before let ourselves actually come to terms with. Carol broke the silence. "After all, he's not some kind of monster..."

Her mother retorted just as defensively: "He's *not*! Of course not, dear. But...wanting to read at...oh, my God! Do you understand what he is?"

Angrily, I snarled: "Christ! We're acting like there's something *wrong* with Johnny. Sure...maybe he's gifted for his age. That's all. A little advanced, but..."

Mother Hendricks laughed, a bit too nervously: "He's more than advanced." She then advised us to take him to a special school.

Carol violently, unreasonably, rejected the idea, face tensing, mouth tightly constricted on her words. "I don't want him to be one of *those* children people point out as freaks. Not *my* son!"

It was useless to argue with Carol. I didn't even want to. For the first time I wondered about Johnny's real parents. Who were they? Why did they reject him? This was to plague me in coming years. Carol, no doubt, was tormented by this same line of questioning but we never brought it out into the open. Johnny was ours. We'd had him since he was only two weeks old—and that fact makes parents more than mere biological acts.

Up to this time, Johnny didn't have the chance to really be exposed to other children. We had kept him away from anybody who might recognize his remarkable ability. Since we were, by nature, the type of couple who keeps to ourselves, it wasn't difficult. Nor did it seem strange in any way. Though, when we did have guests, Johnny willingly went to bed and stayed there. We accepted his own ability to take care of himself alone, at home when we went to visit friends.

Looking back, I now find it amazing how we never questioned our actions. After that first birthday party Mother Hendricks made only a few phone calls. Any invitation to visit was always put off. A few months later she suddenly died.

A marked change came, though, after some friends unexpectedly visited us. They had a two-year-old girl. I immediately warned Johnny, as if joking, "just lie there and be quiet." The humor in this command didn't hide the true warning. He lay on the floor observing, watching the little girl who acted like any normal two-year-old; which is to say, like a retarded ape compared to him.

The next day he wanted to know what was wrong with the girl. Carol quickly pointed out that some children weren't as bright as others.

Johnny was thoughtful all day, sitting in his crib. From then on he seldom talked except when necessary or when requesting more advanced books. By then he was reading simple children's books—he was fascinated by stories about young children and didn't want to read anything else. He struggled for sure, at first, but finally asked fewer questions. Sometimes we would peek into his room and find him in bed, a book held in small hands, kept open by his arms.

The more he read the more "retarded" his actions became until there was a point where he seemed to *stop* advancing, staying at the level he'd been at the age of fourteen months. In fact, his frozen-state was almost as unnerving as what had preceded it.

He was becoming more like a normal child and at two years seemed little more advanced than any boy that age. The only difference was his reading.

A few months before his second birthday, though, I had another jolt. Upon entering the study, where I had quite a collection of books, I found him hiding a book he'd been looking at. I demanded to see the book. It was on child psychology, telling how to handle children during their first few years. This was the first evidence that Johnny was learning how to be a "normal" child.

I was too unsettled to tell Carol.

The next six to twelve months seemed so normal it was difficult to equate the Johnny of one year with the Johnny of two and three who now lived in our house. He was, if anything, too normal.

Now he would go outside and play with other children, most of them older than himself, but managed to appear merely a little bright for his age. He was three then.

Two more years passed and Johnny became so completely "normal" acting, other than that ability to read—now done in total privacy in his room—that we were able to function as a fairly normal family unit. At least it certainly seemed normal to us.

Johnny never asked how high is up, as children will. But he did ask, in his fifth year, a question reserved for far older children. I was reading a book when he asked:

"What is sex, Father?"

Under the best of circumstances such a moment is a bit frightening to parents—so I've been told. Usually a father has some warning, at least a normal run of years until teen-age has come. Given that much time I might have handled things different.

He hadn't even bothered to form the question into a "Where do we come from?"

Before I could respond, Johnny, having sensed my shocked hesitation, said: "I know children are born from a mother's body. I don't understanding the *meaning* of sex. The dictionary says it's the difference between male and female. But a book I read said it was the action that causes children to be created. It's something men and women do together, isn't it?"

I sat there unnerved by the implications of his question. He *knew* what the word implied, but didn't understand what acts were involved.

211

I stared into his intense features, so child-like, with the frowning black eyes and the upswept tiny nose, the pouty small lips, the rounded, full pink cheeks. This was the face of a five year old but stamped with the expression of a mind struggling for maturity. Johnny wasn't going to drop the subject. I might put him off by a command to stop but it would not last long. I promised to get a book on the subject for him to read. This satisfied him only when I promised to do so the first chance I got.

The next day I went to the public library requesting a book on sex aimed at young teenagers. All the way home I fought a mental battle about giving Johnny a book slanted for children more than twice his age. When I got home I merely handed the book to him. Two hours later he returned and asked: "Why do people do things like that? What *makes* them *want* to?"

He now wanted to know the driving motive that caused people to enjoy and desire sexual contact. At this point, he hadn't discovered hard-core porn, yet. The idea of telling him the answers to his question terrified me.

Furious with frustration I shouted: "I don't want to talk about it! You're too young, got me?"

No matter how intelligent the child, when a parent takes a strong, unyielding stand, there's little that can be done to get around it. Johnny accepted this with visible effort, frowning up at me, dark eyes blinking.

It was never brought up again.

By six Johnny entered school where he showed remarkably *average* results, though only after having startled his teacher by asking questions far beyond his age-level. (These "mistakes" could only have happened because of his lack of actual experience in such situations—he was highly intelligent, but lacked experience/sophistication.) Twice his elderly teacher contacted us. The first time she explained: "He wanted to know why I didn't teach mathematics and science—and why the books were so crudely childish. I thank God he asked this after class. I don't know what the effect would have been on the other children." She said he was an outstandingly intelligent child and wanted to give

212

him some special tests. I argued against it, but her insistence was so firm that there wasn't any way around it.

I talked to Johnny about what his teacher had said and he answered: "I was wrong in asking?"

I pointed out it was best to just go along with the class, no matter how slow the others seemed. His answer revealed why he'd made such a mistake in the first place.

"But I thought school was for learning." I explained that some children learned faster than others. He accepted this with a thoughtful nod. I said that anything he wanted to know he could ask me. Then I told him about the coming IQ test. "She believes," I added, "that you should probably go to a special school."

He made no comment, but turned and went into his room, where he remained for the rest of the evening.

Two days later his teacher came to our house, with the results of the tests. She was quite upset. "I'm sure he purposely flunked. But he couldn't have. These are highly sophisticated. Panels of bright, intelligent, experts...well, you don't get past them and...well, to be truthful...I just don't understand! But here. Look!"

The results had been so average as to seem sub-normal. When she had left, Johnny shrugged, grinning. "It wasn't difficult. I read the school books we have and figured what would be expected of a child who was learning from them. It was really easy to trick the test."

It is enough to say most intelligent adults would find it quite impossible to fool an IQ test, even with an outstanding knowledge of its psychological workings.

Strangely enough his teacher was transferred to another school and a new one took her place. She seemed to please Johnny far more than the other lady.

One doesn't suddenly hate any child; especially your own. Even the idea of fearing your own son comes hard. I believe the first real fears began when I realized how casually he had beaten a highly sophisticated intelligent test. I wasn't at all surprised to learn that his report-card reflected a perfect C average. Some subjects went as high as A—in sports—and as low as D in math. His new teacher commented that reading could improve. She had also claimed he didn't pay any attention in class.

I asked Johnny about this last comment and he snapped, "I don't have anything to learn from that woman. Why should I pay attention to nothing?"

The contempt in that remark chilled me more than I wanted to admit.

But the next few years settled down to such an appearance of normalcy that I was almost able to forget the past with all its strange and highly frightening revelations. It wasn't until he had turned eight that another shock reminded us of the truth.

One afternoon Carol called me at the office. Her voice was so hysterical that I couldn't ignore her plea for me to come home right away. I arrived home ten minutes later to find Johnny covered with Band-Aids, a black eye and swollen lip. He explained his teacher had said that of all the stars in the sky the sun was the only one to have planets and he'd challenged her on this. After school three boys had ganged up on him, using this argument with the teacher as an excuse to be sadistically brutal. Then he said in such a cold determined voice that I felt chilled: "But I'll get them. You'll see. I just might kill those boys."

I forced a smile: "Its better to avoid getting into fights, son. Don't look for them. There is always somebody bigger and better than you. If you want to, I'll teach you how to defend yourself—but that's all." He smiled winningly and threw small arms about my neck, promising never to start a fight if I'd only teach him how to defend himself.

During the next weeks I taught him what little I knew about boxing. When that was quickly exhausted, he begged to be taken to a boxing instructor. For several weeks following that he went twice a week, spending hours at the YMCA gym. One day his instructor told me: "He's an outstanding student. He's almost frighteningly strong for his age. He's so intense, determined."

About three weeks later Johnny came home late from school, his face cut slightly, knuckles skinned, but a wide grin on his face. Carol asked what had happened and he'd said:. "I showed them." He refused to say more.

214

Shortly before I got home, Carol received a call from the parents of one of Johnny's fellow students. They were threatening police action. By the time I arrived, the school principal was on the phone. Carol, who was shaking, tears running down her delicate face, simply handed me the phone. I learned the following: Three boys had started a fight with Johnny. Witnesses had told the school authorities that Johnny tried to avoid the fight, but when he turned away, the biggest boy had grabbed his shoulder, swung him around, hit Johnny on the right cheek. After that, none of the other two had even touched him. According to those who saw the fight, Johnny had very coldly gone about striking down all three boys, hitting them time and again, even when they wanted to stop. The end result was that one child was beaten almost unconscious, another's nose had been broken and the third had lost several teeth. It was the brutal and scientific manner in which Johnny had beaten them that was so frightening. When two ran, he continued hitting the remaining boy until friends managed to pull him off.

I never learned what started the fight; I've always believed that Johnny had been responsible for provoking it; but I was scared to even question him about this. I did, however, warn him that the next time anything like that happened he had better stop the instant he saw the others were finished. He merely laughed, almost sadistically. "I'm not worried, Father. There isn't a boy in school who would dare fight me. Not now."

How right he was.

The fight made him part hero and part villain. The older boys admired him; others were simply scared.

Carol's attitude changed from that moment. At first it was simply in small, tiny things. If he wanted something— like staying up a little later to see a television show, or another ice cream—she immediately gave in when he said: "But, Mother, I *want* it." Somehow he managed to make that sound not *quite* like a threat. Yet, Carol backed down every time.

I believe that by then I, too, accepted my own sense or fear. It was more like an inner awareness that it was not a good idea to cross Johnny.

215

He had just about exhausted my personal library of books. It wasn't until he started bringing library books home that I realized this. Instead of children's classics he studied basic science, including simple books on Relativity. He showed interest in anthropology and then went on to history and philosophy. By the time he was ten he'd completely devoured a total understanding of *advanced* theories of Relativity and all related scientific learning of that level. He never revealed this knowledge but he silently observed the books. He seemed to visually gobble them down into his computer-like mind. Carol commented on it only once, a little jokingly: "At this rate he's going to know everything any university could teach."

How prophetic that statement was.

I don't know when the real change came over Carol. Maybe it started with the light statement about his reading habits, a year ago. She became more introspective; spoke little when Johnny was around; never mentioned him in anything but the most general terms when he was gone.

I was involved with my work for the local newspaper and managed to keep my own mind lost in the events of the world, rather than the events of my household; a reaction motivated by a personal need to ignore the truth that we were now both scared.

Johnny came and went as he pleased. We never questioned his activities and seldom saw him beyond meals, except when he went through a phase of compulsively watching television, almost every waking hour. It wasn't necessary to question Carol about allowing this; for we had, by then, reluctantly become "guests" in our own home. Johnny didn't rule; it wasn't necessary. He simply did what he wanted without obstruction.

Of course, this is a standard reaction many parents will have concerning their teenage children. They all go through those stages of being totally challenging and demanding as they mature and discover their way in the real outside world. Maybe that excuses our down right blind refusal to look at the facts and come to an obvious conclusion. Instead we tried to avoid the whole issue.

216

For one year we watched a ten-year-old child build up his knowledge about the workings of mankind and human society through books and television. During this time, he even became interested in some contemporary fiction which included such literary works as *Fanny Hill*, *Candy*, and other acceptable "adult" writings. Such was our non-involvement in restricting him that he had total freedom insofar as what he was actually exposed to. One wonders what restrictions would have worked in the first place. What he wanted, he got! He was studying the human side of man: what made society tick, what motivated it, what were the cultural and social trends. We observed without understanding, while he filled his mind with a total knowledge of history, past and present, culturally and socially, politically and morally. He was, in effect, feeding the highly sophisticated computer of his greedy damned mind with information concerning the human race.

Then, a month ago, it happened.

And now I sit here knowing what will come and yet unable to stop it. I await what must take place.

Helpless.

Up until this very last month, Carol had not been inactive. Outwardly she was withdrawn, moody, almost like a person who was slowly going into a catatonic state. Yet her madness was more like that of a woman possessed by fearful convictions that demanded facts to support them before her mind and emotions could totally accept what seemed true.

One month ago I came home to discover Carol's head stuck in the gas oven; all the windows closed, the rank sweet smell of gas chokingly thick in every room. There had been no note left but the police, following agonizing investigations, assured me it was, unquestionably, suicide.

I don't wish to go into the horrid details of that discovery. The shock and pain and the agony immediately followed. Such information hardly belongs in this kind of report. The cold facts say enough.

I was never to be given enough time to recover before even more shocking information jarred me further into a pit of pain and most of all, angry terror.

Carol had planned well. Her death was something she had expected; prepared for with evidence that sent me explosively out of the numbed shock of personal sorrow, grief and depression to even greater hate and fear.

The police report was followed so quickly by the funeral that it all became a blur of hours, days. Both Johnny and I went through all the emotions of a grief-stricken father and son. He was quite convincing and I found myself drawn close to him for a brief time. The funeral was hellish. The aftermath swept over me with a long depression that left me drained, walking around the house like something half-alive; for, beyond Johnny, Carol was my whole life. The paper had given me several weeks leave. The vacation-time was due, in any case. And how easy it would have been to go mad, at that time, but Johnny was a great help those first few weeks. His dear little form would hug me, small arms flung around my neck in tender understanding—and thus we seemed like two anguished people comforting one another through a harsh period of personal loss.

Three days ago all this changed. I was contacted by an attorney named Carl McDavis. At his office he handed me a huge stack of paper, held together by a rubber band and string.

I won't go into the total details of this packet of stunning information. It was a kind of daily record. It covered three months, starting with the statement, in Carol's handwriting:

"I do this to keep my sanity."

Day by day the notations became more frightening; almost as if her mind were being stripped of reason. The fact that we had, for so long, accepted things blindly is the only excuse I can give for my not having noticed any marked change, even in Carol.

In reconstructing what took place during the last three months of Carol's life, I have used the evidence from her written notes.

An early entry read: *"Because of my growing fears, I'm certain Johnny is up to something. I've decided to follow him tomorrow, learn what he does away from home."*

At no point up to this time had Carol indicated what her fears concerned.

218

During the next days she followed Johnny. For three days he merely wandered about the city, ending up at a public library, coming out with books. The change of pattern came on the first Friday, when she wrote: *"Right from the beginning he moved with determination. His destination was an old boarding house on the lower east end of town. He went in with the books he'd taken from our house, stayed there for some hours before coming out with three other children who looked about his own age, their eyes so dark like his...or did I imagine this?"*

Each week he returned to the house. It was in the second week that Carol reported: *"Johnny was met by a young girl—and this time I was close enough—using field glasses. She was his age, with the same black, intelligent eyes. I didn't imagine it. They didn't say anything, but went into the building together."*

The next Friday Johnny was met by a young boy, whom Carol claimed looked like Johnny, as if he were a brother, *"maybe even a twin—brother."*

It was on the Thursday before her death that Carol wrote: *"I must be crazy. Or what I've learned of these meetings...the children who look too much like him...what does it mean? How can I even think he might be—more than human? What madness? Other than human? Oh, where is my sense of sanity? My mother love? Yet he isn't a child of my flesh. But he is—our son. Why should I fear him so? He's always loved us. He's been a good, dear boy. Why then this...an illusion of my mind or woman's intuition?—that he might and would quickly remove me as I would any annoying fly? Why fear? I must confront him. Tomorrow, at the house—there he'll be forced to confide his secret. He can trust his mother—sanity can't hold out long without truth— Oh, God, give me strength. If only I could talk to John— but...can't expose him...not yet...if I'm wrong, how terrible to say such things to the man who has been his father. Maybe I am mad."*

Then it ended with a last statement directly speaking to me. *"Forgive me, my love. If I'm right...you must act with speed, before it's too late. Is it possible that a father could kill his own son?"*

When I'd read the final entry I was convinced that Carol must have been mad. Yet, all she recorded had a perverse sanity about it, if it could be connected to all of what I already knew.

It was three days ago that I neatly folded the pages of her reports, tucked them into my suit pocket and then, like some man *walking* through a fantastic nightmare, went up to Johnny's room. He was, like so many times in the past, lying on his bed reading a book. He looked up and his childishly innocent features flooded with tender love as he said: "Hello, Father."

I stood there in the doorway, torn by the unbelievable statements Carol had made; trying to convince myself that it had been a madness that had led to her self-destruction. I looked at the appealing little eleven-year-old boy and fought the natural impulse to rush to his side, pull his dear form close, feeling his insistent need for my love. I choked down the idea that instead of embracing, I should kill.

I simply said: "I'm stepping out, son. Be back later."

He nodded and returned all attention to the book.

I drove to where Carol had said the rooming house was. The place had a look of crumbling decay; old, weathered. At one time it had been the home for a rich family, maybe fifty years before. Now it was part of the gray, sooty slums.

Several drunks were staggering along the street that was dark with night, broken only by dim lights from shaded windows. Getting out of the car, I hurried across the street to the tall, two story house, up worn steps. A small paper note on the mailbox told that the landlord was in room One. An old, weathered, unshaven face answered my knock and demanded what I wanted.

"Every Friday a young boy of eleven comes here—with other children——who do they visit?" I inquired.

The man's thin lips snapped: "No snot-nosed kids here. Look at the place. You think kids come here? Its for old men."

I pushed on the door to stop it from being closed. "I tell you there's a boy that comes here every Friday," I insisted, following with a detailed description of Johnny. But he stubbornly shook his head.

220

Pulling out my wallet, I exposed a twenty dollar bill. This brightened his weary dull eyes. I smelled the stale wine on his hot breath as he slid close; his eyes greedy on the bill.

Taunting him with the money, I demanded information about the tenants.

He insisted: "Ain't no kids. You police?"

After denying that, I impulsively asked: "Are there any *strange* tenants?"

"They're all strange. Beg for money—buy wine. Don't wanna pay rent. Only Mr. Johnson pays every month, on the dot. Don't drink, neither. Fact is...hardly see him."

Ice chilled me. I repeated the name as if it were something alien. Surely Johnny should have been more original, I thought. "What's he look like?"

"'Bout my age, I guess. Clean-shaven, though. Come to think—has black eyes. Strange friends, too. They come...you said on Friday? Strange. Every Friday, they come. Only time I see him, come to think of it. Lots of friends; same age. Some women, too. Don't question my people...live, let live, you know. Every Friday they come. Go up and—don't hear nothin'. Not a peep. Never speak. Walls like paper you know...buildin' is old, cracked with age. Can hear everythin'—can tell when a woman's up in a man's room—hear that thump, thump, thump. Dirty. Nasty sounds. Moans. That kind of thing." A high crackling sounded from his line lips.

I gave him the twenty, pulled out another. "For a look in the room."

His eyes were beady as he crackled: "Ain't police?"

"No. I just want to look inside. This...Mr. Johnson might be an old relative of mine."

"Ain't sayin' I believe you, ain't sayin' I don't. All the same with me. Ain't no key for the room. Can go up, if you want, look in. Don't touch nothin'. Don't wanna have no trouble with Mr. Johnson. No way! Never! Don't want that with Mr. Johnson."

On impulse I asked if a young blonde-haired woman had been asking questions a few weeks ago. He shook his head violently.

Without a word I moved up the dark steps, found the door indicated. It opened almost to my touch. I don't know what I expected to find. Hardly anything very commonplace.

The light hung from the ceiling like a small, naked sun on a long string, flooding dimness into the tiny room when I flicked the wall switch.

There was a bed, covers neatly in place. Five chairs ringed it. Where the headboard leaned tiredly against the grease-smeared wall a large blackboard rested. Chalk marks had been arranged on the board, but in a strangely organized pattern that blatantly suggested mathematics but of a form I'd never seen before—symbols of flowing design, but unearthly is the only description I can offer. It wasn't high math or the new math—there was no meeting between that and what I saw.

Something, at this point, snapped inside my mind—caused by what I saw and a combination of the grief and a sudden raging fear. It was an emotional surge ripping from the base of my spine and feeding its way out and upwards like a creeping wild thing until it clutched the back of my head. Seething hot fingers clawed around my brain, crushing. Invisible nails probing as if fire—hot knives were slashing at tissue. My vision blurred and even as the brain cells seemed to drain of their life-giving oxygen, I flung my body at the blackboard, hands slashed across the dark surface; rubbing, striking blindly now at the chalk marks as if they were phantom shadows of my son's innocent face.

Consciously I was aware of making this attack while at the same time convinced its motives went deeper than mere sudden, momentary madness. It was almost like being drunk. What I didn't know at that immediate instant was the frantic mental struggle going on between me and the...

I can't find a label, name or verbal tag to put on that horror! My mind was aware of another being—thing...mental presence—before any visual image presented itself.

My hands were frantically rubbing at the chalk marks, my brain was in some kind of drunken—doped?—frenzy; vision blurred. It is surprising that I became aware of anything at all other than what I was doing.

The invisible pressure—probing power—seething around, even through, my brain, constricted without warning, and my every nerve fiber seemed to curl, recoiling from something quite alien and ugly beyond human understanding. It was as if the cells of my whole body were aware of some other presence before my conscious mind realized the truth. The mass of chemical material that makes up the human body, the countless independent cells, living microscopic beings without thoughts of their own, instantly knew and reacted to the alien thing attempting to take control of their functions. Each one seemed to scream in an effort to reject the slimy, clammy alien object, as the body will attempt to reject any foreign substance that tries to invade its structure.

My first unconditional realization of what was happening was when I found myself balanced on one foot, hands clutched outwards in mid-air, frozen, unable to move a fraction—stopped in mid-flight towards the blackboard. I was unable to even use the focusing muscles of my irises.

One never realizes how little the human eye actually sees in sharp focus—only a pinpoint in the center of their visual field—until they find it impossible to move. The eye normally flints from point to point so rapidly that the mind is able to piece together a larger picture of the object appearing on the brain's visual screen in total and in sharp focus. All I was able to see was a fine pinpoint of a smudged chalk mark, with everything else blurring out of focus around it. I believe this was as frightening—if not more so—than being frozen.

Off to my right, there was something totally unnatural...

Approaching me was a thing; a lump of substance; a swirling mass of activity; threatening; alien—no! How could such a thing even be from our own physical universe?

Then from where?

Under normal circumstances I'm convinced the human mind would have stopped functioning sanely. It would retreat into the safety of total madness. I could see the thing only as a blurred shape out of the corner of my eye. Under normal circumstances, too, one would have glanced at that horror and then certainly complete insanity would have followed. Not being able to move, and at the same time bio-

223

chemically keyed-up, along with that mind-force holding me helpless captive, I had but an instant to react to the threat. I was barely able to realize that any chance of survival had to come through sane, *controlled* mental power.

All of this analysis probably took no longer to conclude than a minute—from the time I attacked the blackboard until being aware of an alien thing—which couldn't possibly exist.

The mind, in moments of personal danger, seems to speed up infinitely. Time stands still, freezing, while the thinking process frantically races.

I realized something was attempting to take control of my mind and body. The physical sense of cold sweat was very real; emotional fear climbed down my spine, nerve by nerve.

The only possible weapon I had was the releasing of raw violent mental hatred; physical force was out of the question.

Like a computer, my brain concluded this obvious fact. Then it automatically released all the primitive, naked emotion the human animal is able to expel.

It was motivated by naked fear but charged by the human instinct for survival. When trapped, a creature will strike out blindly.

Exactly how or what this actually triggered, I can't imagine. The result was a sudden sense of power—and freedom from that thing invading my brain.

My arms slammed down on the blackboard with such brutal force—continuing their uninterrupted move—until it was dented.

Immediately I twisted around, staring directly at the thing in this room with me. I could only guess that it must have been under the bed when I entered. It was now recoiling physically from my mental unleashing of such violent emotional fury.

That sight—I'll never forget it as long as I live—ate my brain cells like a branding iron might char flesh.

To attempt to verbally picture it will merely needle the imagination and certainly not be faithful to reality—if that is what it truly was—but I'll try.

224

Jelly-like or swirling mass? Both might be correct. The thing wasn't bigger than one foot high and two feet around. It seemed to be enclosed by an energy mass, twinkling with diamonds, or sparks; a foggy swirl radiating from the lumpy colorless, slimy form that was massed with folds or wrinkles. This inner core seemed to continue changing its surface features in an undulating way, like the surface of the ocean that is never the same from instant to instant. The suggestion of winking "eyes"—or some kind of hungry gasping "mouths"—waved in and out of existence. The whole mass pulsated with a rhythm that had no set meter. A crackling, static kind of noise uttered from it.

Gagging in horror and sick at this sight, I frantically grabbed one of the chairs, my only thought being to kill, if possible, before it was too late.

I was raising the chair high over my head when a dizzy, light-headed feeling assailed me.

"Daddy, don't!" a voice pleaded, "It's only a child." I was looking at what appeared to be Johnny standing where the thing had been. My stomach knotted sick, twisting up inside like a spiked ball.

"What are you—?" was as far as I got. The image of Johnny was at least a foot too small, one leg longer than the other. This adjusted itself instantly as I recognized this flaw. Then I realized that this "Johnny" was how our boy had appeared at the age of seven. No sooner did I note this than the image adjusted itself again, growing, aging, the muscles filling out.

"Please, don't hurt me," *this* Johnny pleaded in a high-pitched crackling voice totally different from my son's. "I'm theirs—one of them...their children..."

I still thought of Johnny with a parental sense of love and found it difficult to keep from emotionally responding. Nothing can completely wash away those years of conditioning.

As I stood there, hesitating for that instant, the nerve endings in my body started curling as the beginning threat of alien "fingers" started to clutch my mind.

Immediately I sent out a wave of fury and hate, and at the same time flung the chair as hard as possible to where the creature still had to be. Right at "Johnny."

The mental probe lifted and I heard what could be nothing less than the actual scream of a creature in mortal pain—but it was soundless; a cry floating through the mental ether.

I grabbed another chair; rushed forward; struck it at the now quivery jelly-like substance. The energy "bubble" around it seem to be swirling more rapidly; the spark-like stars flickering like exploding suns. I struck again, and in return felt such a driving, invisible mental spear of force strike out at me that I was knocked backwards across the room.

I don't know if that was a last dying gasp from the monstrous thing or not. The fact that I was able to insanely rush from the room at full run without being stopped certainly indicates that I'd at least won some kind of battle. It doesn't matter now, though.

I ran and didn't stop for a long time. It seemed as if this scene and the next clear reality merely blended together. Maybe I'd lived and relived that insanity while moving physically away from the apartment, driving to the bar, ordering drinks. I only remember being suddenly aware of sitting on a barstool, loud electronic music blaring, my head groggy from liquor, an empty martini glass clutched in my hands.

All was too normal. It would have been easy to believe none of this had happened; that it was a part of my imagination.

The rest is self-evident.

Returning home meant I must try to kill Johnny. That creature had obviously attempted to use my love for Johnny as a means of protecting itself. But Johnny would surely be stronger and more powerful than his—its—"children"... baby?

God, the very idea sends cold sweat through me. Call me insane. Call Carol insane. Maybe we both were driven mad. Maybe this is all an illusion. Yet with all these fears comes terrible conviction.

226

Johnny learned that Carol knew about the room and his friends, and he surely must have killed her. Once he knows I've learned the truth he'll be forced to get rid of me. That simple.

That he could appear as an old man to strangers—that he could, with children his age—as Carol reported—go up to that strange, shoddy room for silent meetings, drawing strange equations on a blackboard—create (or board?) that crawling horror—in a room without a lock...being *that* contemptuous of discovery? That he could kill the woman who had been his mother for eleven years, in such a manner as to make it look like suicide? All this staggers and overwhelms the mind. Yet there is no other conclusion or theory I can think of; the evidence points directly to Johnny.

Thursday night I learned the truth, leaving the evidence of my passage in that room. My disappearance would reveal the obvious to even a sub-normal person. Friday, Johnny would have known what happened. I know he must be looking for me and because of that I've been running, attempting to survive in a society he knows more about than any human. He and those...what? Foundlings? All left by some unknown "parent" from...where?

What conclusions can any man make? Maybe its madness that offers the obvious answer:

Aliens, left to take over the world after learning about the human race from foster parents. Is it my own madness or sane realization, brought to focus for the first time? While living with Johnny for eleven years, him taunting us with his exceptional mental ability, did we naively and willingly kept secret from the outside world? Had it been our love for him that made us hide his exceptional mental talents—or some strange power he possessed that controlled us to take such action?

But who would believe me?

I was witness; a daily observer of a child too advanced for his age. He, a foundling who became first a son and then master under my own roof. If but for the other children, of which Carol wrote, I might pass Johnny off as merely a very intelligent, bright child—maybe a step upwards in the human

227

evolution toward super humans—perverted by his advanced brain; easy to do away with.

All that's left now is this warning to the world. If this tape gets in the right hands, and God willing, somebody believes, maybe the human race has a chance. By that time, I'm certain, all evidence will have been wiped away, other than this recording—as my own life will surely have been coldly stomped out by a being who surely thinks of us humans as man considers the insect. And who would believe such a story?

If I have failed, hopefully someone, somewhere will believe this warning and find some way to fight back—before it is too late.

This offering is something a little different, maybe a little more fun. And certainly long: some 12,000 plus words. It takes us to a distant world, across the galaxy, once again, and into a place where people fight hard to survive and live in closed tribal-like societies. They have their territories and their power-structures and rules. And some are more powerful than others. Now, what if it became necessary to rescue some very important people who were captured by one group that was totally unfriendly to all others. And, most importantly, how could anyone possibly succeed in this kind of situation in bringing about a....

—◄MISSION OF MERCY►—

CHAPTER ONE

"And, lo, on the island of banishment, the planet of violent death, you shall struggle, sweat upon the surface dirt, feeding upon one another like beasts of prey. Honor will come only with the joining of hands, with the higher purpose of mercy for your enemy; so go forth on a mission of mercy and face death with honor, for there lies total salvation."
—From the Voices of the Torshi

I saw the girl immediately upon cresting the low hill. The tall purple grass swayed against the soft breeze of the Torshi plains, whipping the trembling legs of my mount. The talio I'd been riding was exhausted from the long, unbroken days of riding. It was the fastest stallion in my father's stables. High—pitched scream of hopeless terror brought on my instant burst of speed as I had directed the mount up the grassy hill. Even in enemy territory a man of Hamton will honor a female's cry for help.

There was no time to consider the mission, the Spacers or my people—who now shifted to second moon. The scene before me was of horrid beauty: a startling and vivid statement of hopeless bravery.

Striking the huge pointed head of the talio, I felt the wind god breathe down my body as we shot toward the now prostrate form of the girl, desperately attempting to fend off the hungry beak of a giant Haki-bird, using only a thin needle sword. Those huge monstrous devils of the sky have the habit of diving from so high up that it would seem they drop from the heavens. They are a dreadful challenge for the strongest and most skilled warrior. One will hear the whistling of wind fluttering through their multi-colored feathers just moments before an attack.

The slender girl couldn't have been under the Haki-bird for more than a few moments, and it was as certain as the fact Qui travels around our world seven times a day that she couldn't last much longer. That I hadn't seen the bird's drop was caused by my mental pre-occupation upon the mission that had brought me this far.

The talio loped awkwardly down the hill like a leaping boulder falling off the side of a cliff. I jerked the long thick broad sword from its scabbard, pressing the activating stud on its hilt of gold, aiming my first electronic bolt at the huge, gnarled flapping wings of the Haki-bird.

A jagged crackling fire-beam of blue electra-arc slashed out like lightning across the air, sputtered low, close to the scrawny body of the feathery monster, sparks fountaining like a spray of volcanic blue lava around the helpless girl.

A high-pitched scream, a crackling thunder insane laughter, cut the eerie silence that had surrounded the deathly battle scene. The Haki's narrow blue beak slashed madly at the gaping black cavity of charred feathers and flesh in its side.

In the moment of hesitation, as the effect of my unexpected interference froze the death battle, my throat shouted the Hamton battle cry and my knees frantically directed the tired talio into close quarters. I had time to release but one more blast of crippling blue fire. There was only one remaining charge left in the blade's battery cell, and this I saved for the right moment, for otherwise it would do nothing but irritate this huge creature of the Five Moons—as the Jolli natives call it—that stands three times taller than a big man.

Swinging the huge blade, I aimed at the bird's long leathery yellow neck, but cut empty air as the beast snapped upwards with a great flap of its wings, sounding like drum beats against the hot, heavy air.

The long wrinkled neck slinked down jabbing its beak only inches from my face was stopped short by the heavy flat of my sword's blade.

The battle had become mine. Death breathed from the creature's huge beak with the sickening smell of rotting flesh. Nausea choked my throat constricting my insides into tortured knots.

For a moment the two of us stared at one another, each filled with the same animal hatred that comes to all creatures as death breaths hot. There was no way to know if the Haki-bird was brainless or had some strange kind of perverted intelligence so totally at odds with human beings to be impossible to recognize a mutual brain power; yet, in that split second of time—freeze, it seemed as if there was a hot flicker of probing intelligent hatred in the bird's large saucer brown eyes, not unlike that felt in man towards a human enemy.

Then my blade moved, made a whipping circular parry under the beak, shot upwards and lunged into the pulsing neck. My index finger released the last electro-charge. With an explosion of blue sparks the bird's neck popped and spilled into a flood of horrid smelling yellow blood. A convulsive shudder snapped through its headless body and then it collapsed to the ground like a fallen lump of mud-soaked jungle foliage.

Turning, I spotted the girl sitting on the ground, supported on one elbow, looking at me as if I were some evil demon of the Mountains of Kass or some Wizard of the Via Swamps.

"Are you all right?" I inquired, swinging from the golden saddle on the Talio's broad back.

"Where are you from, warrior?" she demanded coldly, carefully standing, ignoring my question, blade held forward as if to cut down a hated enemy.

"From the south; several day's ride." I sheathed my own weapon to reassure her.

"Don't you know you're in the Dalli country, the Plains of Torshi?" she demanded, raising the point of her sword—a long, thin-bladed weapon. Her face was white, drawn tight with deep strain. For a moment it seemed she swayed, as if dizzy. "If you are from the South—death rides your back in our lands."

I started to take a step towards her, for she seemed quite weak, but the sword thrust forward, touching my naked chest, above the harness strap and the belted leather garments about my middle. Why are you here?"

"Is this the gratitude offered by the people of Dalli? The honor of the Torshi?" I countered, more amused than miffed by her formal, threatening attitude.

For a moment she stood there, staring almost blankly at me. Her frail form once again seemed to bend against some invisible, unfelt wind. The delicate features of her tense face relaxed. The sword point lowered briefly and then jerked up again, as if with effort.

"Answer my question! Why are you here, warrior? Speak or die!"

How dare she threaten me! For a moment I had to swallow down the automatic, instinctive urge to enter battle with this ungrateful creature. Assuming I could avoid being run through by that naked, sharp blade threatening my chest.

Women, I thought, in disgust!

If it hadn't been for a woman, even an unknown hated Spacer female, I might have been happily plowing my father's fields.

Or I'd be hunting in the beautiful gold of Hamton's grassy plains for the Tonia, that squat, muscular beast who, once baked over a roaring fire, charred an inch into its soft flank, offers a delightful mouth-watering meat. It is much in demand for the Feast of the Five Moons; the beginning of our growing season.

232

I might even have found the soft pleasures of a young woman as a mate during the feasting days.

Instead I had traveled across the lands of Hamton, up through the barren, dry yellow Desert of Hellus to the territory of the mysterious and hated Torshi. These are our long-time enemies—those of the First Coming. They have perfected the Powers to a mystic level of sometimes-frightening proportions.

This mission, which I had been forced to accept, had brought me to the immediate moment. And this beautiful, arrogant female! How dare she challenge me?

Women could be monsters! Yet we men of Hamton prided ourselves on quick, almost mindless response to a woman's need. (In fact it was the unknown fate of a Spacer female that had been partly responsible for my father's decision to help the Spacers.)

I continued to fight the fury bursting up through my gut.

I stood there simply watching her for some long silent moments, trying to decide the proper response to her demand.

She was quite beautiful, with long blonde hair, golden eyes, flecked with sky blue, firm, full lips. She wore the long blue cloak of the Dalli, under the folds of which a one-piece white toga—so common to her people—folded about sweeping curves of that delicately proportioned body. The silver band around her forehead, though, immediately announced that she was a member of the mystic cult of Torshi. This, plus her controlled attitude, warned me to play out the game on her level.

"I saved your life," I pointed out, spreading my hands wide. "What do you fear?"

"That blade—it's of the Hamton people. You have lied to me or are a thief. Which?" she challenged, not once moving the point of her weapon from my chest.

"Probably both, but if you kill me you won't get the truth—nor would it be of the highest standing of the Torshi." I had come to see her people, but on a mission of great danger to myself, for they were warlike and long-time enemies of the Hamtons. "Is this the way the Torshi welcome guests?"

She compressed her lips, then lowered the blade. "You *are* right, of course. Under the circumstances it's not the way of my people, nor my own way. You have saved my life. I guess I can assume you meant no harm."

"If I'd meant you harm, I'd have let the Haki kill you," I pointed out. "Let me tend to your wounds."

She suddenly looked at the short rip in her cloak, which exposed a bleeding shoulder. But that was enough to have poisoned her body. First came the look of utter alarm and then out-right terror as realization set in.

Then without warning she slumped to the ground, un-conscious.

CHAPTER TWO

"And, lo, I say to you, that a man who moves where his heart is served, will serve his people well. The servant of Honor will find service from that honor. You who would strike your enemy down, without mercy, are without honor. You who will use honor to gain your own end shall be struck down; you who would force a debt of honor for the gain of many shall be blessed."

—From the Voices of the Torshi

It was late evening, the stars like a blanket of light stretched across the black heavens, and two of our small moons were swinging through the sky from north to south. The small fire I had built was the only light or warmth, flick-ing against the black chilly night. The girl was still uncon-scious, but her fever had broken.

I had sat over her for hours, washing her face with drinking water, caring for the wound with certain compounds we received from the Spacers. I was eating some of the warmed dried Unnes meat when a moan came from her di-rection.

I moved to the woman's side as she opened her eyes.

"Feeling better?" I inquired.

She squinted, and then reached to her side, where the needle sword had been buckled in its golden casing.

"I thought it might be uncomfortable," I explained, though there had been far better reasons for taking the weapon away.

She sat up, glared at the firelight. "What do you intend to do with me?"

There was just an edge of fear in her voice. Obviously her Torshi-mind had suffered from the poisons of the Haki-wounds. I'd heard about the Torshi rites and knew something about their beliefs and mental controls. Enemy though she was, my own feelings softened. Regardless, she was a very beautiful woman. Even if her people never allowed for this difference in sex, the people of Hamton are trained to worship women.

Even annoying, challenging warrior-women like this one had proven to be.

"There's nothing to fear from me. What do they call you?"

"Vemsa."

"I'm called Han-Ja. I'm a warrior of Hamton. If you understand any of the customs of our people, you'll know that we consider it honorable to protect women."

"A mistake, Han-Ja—one that could cause your death. I owe you a debt, and my people value the payment of such a debt as honorable—no matter what the cause, no matter with whom it might be. I am in your service." She stood, giving a very stiff bow. Her attitude had become formal, cool.

"Then you will take me to the Torshi, in the morning," I announced.

Pulling her cloak about narrow shoulders, she nodded. "But it will mean your death."

"Not if you use the Powers to defend me," I observed.

Her features squeezed tight, almost ugly. "The Powers are used against our enemies—we don't invoke them against our own people. It would mean banishment or worse."

Again the fear was in her voice, but those golden eyes remained calm, level, directly fixed to mine.

235

"It is important that I speak with your leaders—and since I've heard they are honorable men, they will certainly listen to me.

"They will listen and then kill you—for that is custom," she announced with finality.

"Not if you invoke the Powers."

"I can't bring a shield against the full powers of the learned Ones of the Torshi. Even if I wanted to."

"You owe me a debt," I said, sick at reminding her, sick at finding it necessary to force her help. "But possibly you won't have to do anything, considering the importance of my mission."

"What could be so important, coming from a Hamton warrior, that my people would listen and allow their enemy to pass from their retreat, alive?'

"A mission of mercy."

"What kind of mercy?" she inquired, her face tightening into a puzzled frown.

"All I can say now is that it might be as important to your people as it is to mine—important to the whole world. And it is said that the Torshi are honorable people."

"What is important to those of Hamton is not—could not—be important to my people!" She stared with contempt at my leathered warrior's garment, which fell to the knees and rose about my middle, belted by the metal of my weapons harness; a functional, but hardly beautiful dress.

"We have battled bitterly for generations. Maybe the time has come to stop warring," I offered calmly, in a reasonable voice.

"Since the first Coming," she snapped, as if quoting from a holy book, "the people of Jolli have struggled for mere existence against the elements and against the natives of this world. Those who followed attempted to take from us what we have scraped from the very dirt of this world. War is the very nature of Man on Jolli."

"War is not the nature of man, it is the nature of the beast of prey. Survival causes war. There have been many Comings. The lands we are allowed are poor for the growing of human food; the animal life, for the most part, is deadly, when taken into our stomachs. Possibly more people will be

236

coming in the next few years. A civilized man knows honor and fears not the stranger; he feeds those he can. But hard survival can make beasts of honorable men," I countered, stating the true feelings of our people.

She shook her head. "Honor will not save you. Intelligent fear would send you back to your people—for surely you will die; and there will be little in my power to even help you."

"It is a risk I'll take," I assured her.

"Then it's a risk I'm honor-bound to assume, since you are not willing to unbind me from this debt." Contempt showed like burning fires in her large eyes.

"I asked your help, only."

She started to say something then seemed to have changed her mind. "The ride is long and you'll need rest. I'll keep watch—if you'll return my blade."

I hesitated only for a moment and then went to the fire, where I'd placed her sword. As I handed the weapon to her, she began to raise its point; then, with an angry intake of breath, sheathed the weapon. "A debt is a debt. I will honor it."

Relieved, I decided to get rest, and after giving her some food, I curled up in a cloak, which had been hung over the back of my saddle, and closed my eyes, safe in the knowledge that this woman of another tribe, my mortal enemy, would stand faithful guard. But I couldn't help but wonder how different her attitude might be if she knew my mission concerned the mutually hated Spacers.

It was hours later when out of my dreams came the sense of impending danger. It was as if some finger had touched my brain, then a voice whispered. A cold chill seemed to close over my body as consciousness leaped into being. I attempted to stand, only to find myself paralyzed. It was impossible to even move an eye-lid. Panic set in swiftly. Cold-sweat poured from every part of my body. I strained to move a muscle, but every nerve was held in some fantastic outer control.

"Struggle not, warrior, for you have not the power to do battle against us of Torshi," stabbed a voice in the very center of my mind. *"Resistance against our Powers will bring*

237

death. You will go into a deep sleep, passive, restful...deep slumber, moving at the direction of our voice, acting at our command, totally submissive to our will."

It was the last thing I remembered until awaking in a dimly-lit chamber, chained against a cold, damp wall of stone.

CHAPTER THREE

"Lo, I say to you, those who would hold their honor high will suffer pain, no matter how great that pain might be, to keep their honor. But only a fool will let honor stand in the way of survival, unless there is more at stake than pure pride."
—From the Voices of the Torshi

I don't know if it was by plan or accident that consciousness returned at the same moment the door in front of me opened. I was confined in what looked like a cave cut by human hands into solid rock. Only the flicker of torchlight, held in the hand of a hooded figure, laminated the surrounding cell.

Two hooded figures stepped forward. The tallest raised his hand and pointed at the metal rings that clamped my right wrist. As he directed his hand toward my other wrist, without making contact, I felt the clamps break away.

"You will come with us," my liberator announced in a deep, rumbling voice.

I'm not a man to be easily frightened, but I had heard much about the Inner Circle of the Torshi, spoken of in hushed whispers, and about those who wore purple capes and hoods.

They are known to possess such powers of the inner mind that they can control all matter. Certainly this little demonstration had been conclusive. Call it science or magic, it doesn't matter. Even if it is smart illusion; it is effective. Few people of our world would call it pure science. My people, who are bred along more rigid lines, believe there is a logical explanation to all things, no matter how fantastic. Our

238

original leader, a very learned man of science, who had made the mistake of giving into temptation, was responsible for this attitude. So I found it difficult to believe what my eyes had seen.

Then, of course, the town of Hamton was settled several centuries after that of Dalli, where the secret cult of the Torshi developed and now thrives. Nonetheless, the unhooking of the clamps about my wrists, without even touching them, was enough to give the most scientific mind great doubts as to its sanity.

I followed the two hooded men along the stone corridor, with a sense of restraint. (Memory of childhood stories about the Torshi haunted me, holding back any plan I might have formed of attacking these two men whose backs contemptuously faced me. I merely followed like a meek, mindless beast.)

The gloomy corridor made several sharp turns, and then ended abruptly, opening into a huge cavern some hundred feet high and twice that in length and width. The walls were cut smooth and detailed gold outlined pictures were colorfully drawn upon the plastered surfaces depicting robed figures actively praying or writing in large leather bound books. Immediately I guessed that I was in the Caves of Torshi. It was rumored that the Inner Circle of the Torshi lived below ground or deep in the side of a mountain.

There was a sense of the supernatural about the ultra detailed gigantic pictures of the Torshi rites that decorated the high walls like some demigods of another world. They dwarfed the human creatures that numbered close to a hundred, crowded in scattered groups upon the floor of the chamber. Like these artistic drawings, the hooded men and women seemed mysteriously silent even while softly whispering in hushed voices to one another. Beyond the darkened folds of the purple hoods, they were tall, handsome people, but grim in their serious intent. There was a golden altar at the end of the chamber. I was escorted in that direction.

An elderly man with a small white beard stood on the raised oblong dais, in front of the altar. His eyes were like golden pools of liquid rock as he glared down at me with deep, probing consideration. It was as if he were attempting

239

to read the very depths of my inner thoughts. I felt mentally naked, stripped of clothing, of skin, bone, and left innocently bare of all but the invisible structure of my mind. This weird illusion pressed in like phantom fingers of darkness and left me emotionally shaken.

"Han-Ja," the ancient face said, lips like thin lines of wine barely moving, "warrior of Hamton, you have a Voice who speaks for you. Vemsa, may she be forgiven, my grandniece four times removed, says you have saved her life from the Haki-bird. For this we are thankful, though puzzled. Nonetheless, she also states that you are here on a mission of mercy, but could not tell her what that might be."

As I started to speak, he raised his hands in front of him, as if to ward off any comment. "It has been decided by the High Council that before you speak certain judgments must be made in order to prove the worth of your words. Vemsa has stood before you, like a metal shield, using her Powers to cause a protection that makes it impossible to take your life without taking hers, too. Such action among the Torshi is treason. The death sentence is automatic for anybody who uses the Powers against the wishes of the Inner Circle. We do not use the Powers against our own people. But, of course, Vemsa explained this to you."

He paused long enough to take a deep breath, his hallow, lined features seemed to squeeze tighter into a mass of wrinkles. Then he raised his arms high above his head. "If your mission is worthy of our ears, you will be permitted to attempt to defeat one of our Chosen in combat. If you do this as an honorable warrior, we will listen to your words; if you die in combat, your voice will be silenced automatically by defeat in death. If your words are worthy, you may pass from our lands, after we have listened."

I started to say something, but his right hand thrust forward, palm before my face.

"Speak not, for one word will bring instant death. So it is Spoken." He turned left, said: "Bring forth his combat mate."

I turned to find Vemsa standing to my right, cloak stripped away from her body, with only the brief toga and sword harness about her narrow waist.

240

"Honor among men who honor themselves must be proven by their acts. As you saved this woman's life, as she saved your life, your lives are now intertwined, intermingled and thus you must face death together. For either to speak will bring death to both. For either to do less than their best to engage one another in combat will bring about the same result. Arm Han-Ja and let the duel begin." The aged Torshi stepped back, hands at his side, face without expression.

I looked at Vemsa, unable to believe what was happening. It was against the custom of my people to engage a woman in combat.

I started to object, and then remembered the Torshi's warning. Any word would bring instant death to both of us.

I was handed a long, thin-bladed weapon of perfect balance, whose hilt was made of pure gold, inlaid with several colorful stones. Its weight was much less than the swords I was used to.

Facing Vemsa, who had drawn her weapon, I considered the possibility of letting her kill me, then again remembered the old Torshi's warning that less than our best effort would bring instant death upon each of us. That, plus the importance of my mission, left me no choice but to fight to kill.

Vemsa moved gracefully forward, swinging her sword in a downward arc, which I easily parried. Seeing an opening, I thrust at her chest. A moment of hesitation held the total follow-through, but even then it would have been impossible to connect with the lunge. I felt my blade flung to one side and then experienced a tingle of surprise as the point of her sword just broke the skin of my left shoulder. That wound convinced me that hesitation would be fatal.

Immediately I leaped back, parried two quick, deathly slashes of Vemsa's blade that whistled through the air. Automatically my own weapon returned the blows, which were skillfully blocked short at both sides of her beautiful head.

Each of us, having now discovered the ability and the determination of the other, slowly circled one another. We lightly tapped blades as if testing for an opening. Now we knew the duel was deadly serious. For myself, I realized that a sword does not care who holds it—in a child or female

241

hand it can be just as deadly. I had no choice but to accept the challenge of the blade. Even if it was held by a very pretty and desirable young woman I would hardly wish to kill.

The weapons were beautifully balanced and light in weight. In those few moments of circling one another, we exchanged a short series of quick thrusts. Our attacks were like the snapping of whips and twice as fast, difficult for the eye to follow.

In any kind of swordplay, where both duelists are skilled, defense and offense become automatic. The fingers and wrist whip the sword in attack and parry or block, without any conscious commands of the mind. Put a sword in the hands of a truly skilled artist and it becomes an extension of the subconscious mind that takes in, through all the senses, every piece of information necessary to respond to your opponent's moves. Each of us was quickly discovering the highly toned skill of the other. It was a lesson to myself, bringing home a hard point that one does battle with sword against sword; not necessarily against the person holding a weapon. The mental control behind the weapon becomes the object which must be stopped, outwitted, out-fought, out thought; and thus: killed.

Still, having never fought against a woman, I found my situation highly frustrating for the very mission that had brought me here was at stake. While my mind demanded that I make every effort to get the advantage, my emotions fought for control over the logic of necessity. Most importantly, Vemsa was a skilled fighter, used to the lighter weapon, while I had been used to the heavy, thick blade of my electro-sword. Nonetheless neither of us were gaining any real points, other than driving each closer to the point where mere physical strength or endurance would balance the scale one way or the other. In a truly outstanding duel it is a question of how long you can continue to carry the strain, both physically and mentally. Endurance will always decide the outcome of such a duel.

For me there was the added factor of while attempting to keep Vemsa from killing me to find some means to bring the battle to an end without harming her. Yet I would kill this woman rather than allow death to end my own mission, even before it had a real chance to get under way.

As the weapon's weight become more natural to my sword arm, through mere experience, I developed a few tricks of my own, and devised a plan that seemed to hold promise as a means out of the duel—without actually killing her. Things had, before, developed so quickly that there had been no chance to reason or plan. Now I had to take a chance on a move that might, in the end, prove useless. But it was my only hope. With all the skill I could muster I began working Vemsa backwards, aggressively swinging a brutal series of cuts at her head and body. After an exhaustive effort, I finally allowed her to take the offensive, as if now I was physically tired from the prolonged burst of speed.

With a yell, Vemsa charged, swinging her sword sideways, then it leaped forward into a perfectly timed lunge that might have run me through if I had not actually been waiting for just this kind of attack. My sword point licked in, the blade moved with lightning speed, twisting as its tip touched the cross-bar of her weapon. One mighty snap of my wrist and the sword tore from her small hand, clattering across the chamber.

I lowered my sword's point, turned to the head Torshi, who had ordered the duel, and bowed.

For a moment there was a murmuring, which resounded throughout the chamber. Then the High Torshi stepped forward, looking down at me with beady eyes.

"You have not killed her," he announced.

"I have won," I countered, sure that now there was no danger in speaking. I also saw something in the old man's golden eyes that glimmered with odd relief.

"But you have not killed her," the High Torshi pointed out again.

"It is not necessary to kill in order to defeat. The fact that I might have killed her is enough, would you not agree? The fact that I would rather let her live than commit murder—for it would be such to kill an unarmed opponent—should be considered honorable." I stuck the sword into the ground in front of me. "I wish to now communicate my request to the Torshi. With your permission, of course, I will do so—for you have promised that if I defeated her in battle I could speak and you would listen."

The High Torshi nodded and then raised his arms above his head. "Listen Torshi—the warrior from Hamton has boldly proven himself in a test of honor. He is worthy of our ears." Then turning his eyes toward me, he commanded: "Speak."

CHAPTER FOUR

"Lo, and is there a man of honor who would turn his hand away from even an enemy in need? For all men are those of the God of the universe, breathing the light of life in their lungs, dreaming the dreams of all Mankind. Honor turns it's blessing upon all men. Go forth and be honorable to all men in need, if they prove themselves worthy of such justice."
—From the Voices of the Torshi

I turned to face those in the Chambers of the Torshi, taking my time before speaking the first words of my father.

"Men of Dalli, Men of the Holy Torshi, I speak in my father's name, and the name of all his people, those of Hamton. My voice comes at a moment of great need for there are those among us who plead for help, and are we to turn away our head and our hands, though they might be enemies? I have heard that the Torshi are honorable men—and though they have been lifetime enemies of my people, I say that our wars are wars of personal matters, that in time must pass from our world. War is a means for survival. On our world there is little laughter between men and women who must claw out an existence upon an alien soil, plagued by creatures not of Mother Earth, but of such alien shape that there can be no inter-seeding of species, either through the means of the body or the Soul or mind. The natives of this world, though small in number, have plagued us for generations—holding to the swamps and the mountains, leaving the dry grassy plains for the invaders of their world. They have no wish for us, we have no desire for their world, but have we a

244

choice? None. We have made the best of it. They have fought to slowly destroy us.

"The history of this planet, since the First Coming of Man, has been that of struggle, survival and war. Each group founded their own "tribe", their own form of government, for that was as the Spacers who brought us here planned it. You of the Torshi, who have survived longer than most, have a recorded history on Jolli for many long generations, have rejected what we know as science for the Powers. You have stayed netted together, resisting all strangers who come along or among you. As for the rules of the planet, each must make their own way; without quarter given. It was the way of the First Coming and it will be the way of the last coming, for those who are sentenced to Jolli have committed their own sins and must find their own avenue of escape, either through death or survival.

"But I tell you this: Man is a social creature. Man must join hands and seek answers if we are to be strong. Each tribe being another finger upon the hand, another cell among the body, another hair upon a full head of hair, each important in its own way. Continued fighting among ourselves will destroy us all. We must prove ourselves greater than our Masters."

"And what is your message for the Torshi?" Their leader demanded. "For you have told us nothing new."

"Only that we know, too, and realize the necessity of recognizing this Truth." I bowed in his direction, then towards Vemsa. "I could have killed her—but I chose to do otherwise."

"Thus was the test. If you had killed her, you would have been killed," the High Torshi informed me in a cold voice. "For your lives are one."

Though the announcement was surprising, I merely nodded. One learned to accept strangeness when dealing with the mighty Torshi.

"The Spacers have brought us in groups and left us here to survive or die. They come at times and leave scientific supplies and food and books. Once a year we receive such contact with them. Each trip is to a different tribe. This year it was for our people they made their landing."

"Yes, we are aware of this." The High Torshi jerked his head in the air, as if chopping aside my remark.

"In simple terms, we all know from where we come. What we make of ourselves here is something else. We are descendants of criminals. But that does not make us criminals. Many planets like this exist. Penal Planets. Worlds where murderers and thieves are dropped to die or survive, but isolated from the Galactic society as unfit to be known as Citizens. Some of us are newly arrived, some several generations removed from those originally condemned. We have adapted, have survived and are building a world which someday may enter the Federation—but only when the Spacers see hard evidence of our true worth. It is enough to know this."

"The point?"

"Obvious though my words are, their meaning must be recognized here between us. You of the Torshi have existed since the First Coming. Thus it is only right that you be among those who would act in mercy towards our masters, the Spacers."

A murmur uttered throughout the chamber, for we all hated the Spacers, even while they brought scientific and medical help. These were, in reality, our true, common, most hated, enemy. They blocked us from Space, they isolated our original worlds. They made us suffer for the crimes of others, fathers, grandfathers, distant relatives of the past who had been brought here to live and die. They were the greatest common enemy we of Jolli knew.

I continued: "We recognize them as enemies, but something has happened that needs our attention. A Spacer ship landed a short time ago and it was attacked by the Jolli, who took several prisoners. As you know, the Jolli will not make gifts to their Gods until all their gods are in the heavens; the day of the Five Moons.

"We have but a short time to act. The Spacer Mate, second in command, came to my father and requested our help. The Spacers know little about our planet. As we all know, each ship that arrives is commanded by a different crew. We were told that Spacer ships will make their drops only when they are in route to some destination that takes them passed

246

our planet. On this Spacer ship was an important Federation official and his daughter. Many Spacers, including the captain and these two—father and daughter—were taken prisoners. It has been requested that we offer our help in rescuing these people from the Jolli natives. My father's first reaction was such as yours might be—totally reject such a request. Then he considered rescuing the prisoners and demanding acceptance into the Federation for their return. But that was rejected, too. Finally my father offered his help on the condition that the Torshi would join with him—for, as we all well know, it would be totally impossible to leave the lands of Jolli without use of your Powers and your personal help. But he has stated that we will not allow the Spacers to interfere. The agreement was thus made.

"I have come to request your help on this mission of mercy. Our hatred for the Masters, those who have isolated us on this world, cut us off from the Federation, caused us to suffer for the crimes of our fathers, must be tempered with mercy, understanding and recognition that they are fellow human beings. As all of us are fellow humans. It goes without saying that such an act would automatically help our own people, considering the importance of this man they call Gardon, Secretary of Peace in the Council of the Federation Government. His gratitude surely would not be without its rewards."

The High Torshi nodded to my last statement. "We will consider the suggestion. You will be given quarters with your servant, Vemsa, for now she is yours to do with as you wish, that is our Law. You have saved her life, a debt for which she was honor-bound to repay; and also defeated her in honest battle, which makes you master and her the slave. Thus I have spoken."

CHAPTER FIVE

"And, lo, the slave of honor will be his own master, and the master of honor will become slave of that honor. Slave and master, master and slave are one and the same when honor

is their code. And the master and slave with honor will know
mercy; and to know mercy is to be a giant of men, a master
of all men and thus their slave."
—*From the Voices of the Torshi*

The sun baked hot, the air was dry, the plains sweltered
without wind. Vemsa and I rode side by side on our two talio
mounts. The words of the High Torshi still burned at me.
"Go forth, and if your cause be just and it is right that we of
Jolli help the Spacers, then you will succeed, if it is wrong,
you will fail. Thus it is Spoken, and thus it will be."

As we looked down the slope of the hill, the hot air of
the murky swamps seemed to choke out like some sickening
disease of rotted flesh, decaying vegetation. Before us stood
the lands of the Jolli, a tangled mass of sick gray forest,
gloomy lands of slimy moisture, dripping vines, like a net-
work of webs draped down from the lacy twisted branches of
gnarled trees.

I turned to look at the woman whose life I had saved
twice in so many days. "Your Powers, Vemsa—how great
are they?"

"Untested against the Jolli. We know so little about
them. I have had short experience using the Powers without
the help of others," she stated in a dull, level voice that con-
veyed far better than anything else the total hopelessness she
felt. Ever since we'd left the chamber of the Torshi, she'd
been cold, detached, resenting the set of circumstances that
had brought about this bitter slavery to a strange warrior.

"But you know more than we of Hamton, since you
have lived on the Jolli's borders for generations. We only
know their hairy purple shapes, their wide slit mouths—that
they look much like humans, but are totally different. We
know they will band together and strike our villages, but fall
back with quick determination when shown a strong, united
resistance. We know the mood and color of their attacks, we
know how to repel them—with a stronger and more united
front. We know little about their culture, though, and little
about what moves them. We know little about their natural
intelligence. Like most humans on this world, we have restricted our efforts towards personal survival. We have cen-

248

tered our dreams and work for the day—today living, battling the elements and whatever else the Gods level at us. Only your people know much about the Jolli; and you of the cult of Torshi surely must have information as to what we are up against."

She remained silently thoughtful and I found myself nervously continuing with: "We know that the Spacers would have defeated them immediately without any trouble, if they had only known how to handle the Jolli natives. The Mate said that his captain had instructed them to welcome the aliens in friendship. This was their defeat."

"The Jolli," Vemsa told me, as if speaking to a child, "are small in number, living in what they call 'family clans'—that's the closest translation. Twice a year they band together and attack—their weapons are primitive, but they have strange abilities that we of Torshi only guess at. In each tribe there is a Holy Person, who has mental abilities—much like our Powers, but not quite the same. He is able to direct his warriors as one body—as if but fingers of his hand. Our Powers can at times block this ability. That is as much as we know. They have never attempted an attack on our people since we developed the Powers. The High Torshi sensed the honor of your words, and believed in the honesty of your mission. He believes that through combat all great Truths are recognized by the High Power that created the Universe. If it is right, at this time, for us to accomplish our purpose, it will be enough to have one Torshi with you. If it is wrong—all the Torshi would not be able to help you."

"What is right is won by force and knowledge and ability—not destined by some God," I told her, touching the hilt of my sword. "I regret your High Torshi's decision."

"All the Torshi decided. His was only the Voice through which my people spoke. If it is right, so it will be; if it is wrong, all the powers of the universe cannot make it otherwise. If there is a Cause to create an Effect, then we will bring into motion this Cause to create the Effect of rescue. Force of arms will not necessarily reward you with victory. With the Jolli it is sometimes simpler, sometimes more complicated. But brute force alone will not win *all* causes into the desired effect. If it is not to be, then we will fail. We believe this!" She spoke as if reading from a very Holy book.

And such is Fate, I thought. Yet such blind belief in ancient text or mythical legend, or mere Teachings, could bring total disaster upon civilization. For it was such blind acceptance of mystical rules that always ruined the very people who believed without challenge. It was through challenge that change and understanding brought growth and wisdom.

But belief in some mystical power would not bring success on the battlefield.

I felt the blaze of anger that no army had backed me. Force was the only possible sure way to rescue the Spacers. My arc-sword would surely serve as a powerful force against the primitive minds of the Jolli and Vemsa's Powers would neutralize their Holy Person.

Touching the sides of the Talio's head, I urged it down toward the swamps below. Vemsa knew where the Holy Place of the Gods was located. We were not more than half an hour's ride. As we entered the swamp, I lifted the arc-sword an inch from its sheath, making sure it would swing free upon instant command. Several charges were clipped to my belt, and a fresh one was already pressed into the sword's hilt.

As we entered the mysterious swamp, the smell pressed hotly about us, the silence of frightened creatures seemed loud as we passed along a well-worn trail. I felt as if eyes were watching from the large fern-like leaves surrounding us.

By the time we were deep within the swamp the sun seemed to be already working hard to drop below the horizon. The swamp itself was pressed with shadows that refused the full strength of the sun. I realized how easy it would be for the Jolli to spring a surprise attack and hoped that the reports about their cultural habits would prove true. If so, they would be gathered for the rites of their worshipping the Five Moons. Since they wouldn't be expecting humans to enter their territory we had a hope of having the element of surprise on our side. What I was supposed to do then I didn't have the least idea.

250

As night pressed dangerously close about us, Vemsa drew her mount to a stop. "We should be entering the lands of the Five Moons. Rumor says that it is on solid ground, open to the sky."

I started to say something, but she raised her hand to silence me. Her eyes closed and I watched as each muscle in her lovely face seemed to relax. After a moment she nodded.

"We aren't far. I can feel the presence of their Holy Person, not far from here."

I started to ask how she knew this, but decided it was best not to question a Torshi about the secrets of their mysterious Powers. Not until this journey had I been personally exposed to the Torshi Powers. Now I respected them so totally that I felt almost more faith in Vemsa's Powers than I did the ability of my sword arm or the effect of the arc-sword.

We moved our mounts forward and communicated mostly by hand motions. When we'd traveled along the narrow trail for some minutes, she stopped, motioning me to dismount. We tied the talios to one of the gnarled swamp trees and then went forward on foot. Vemsa told me we were not far from the Place of the Five Moons.

I became aware of strange alien chirping sounds which sent automatic shivers down my spine. I'd heard them before, many times outside our village of Hamton just before an alien attack. How could the Torshi expect just one woman and one man to succeed against a tribal gathering of the Jolli? My people had expected the Torshi to offer a force of warriors to help me. It had been a mistake not to take men of my own village; a decision made on the belief that the Torshi would be far better in combating the Jolli natives. I felt totally helpless.

As the chirping grew in volume, I gripped the hilt of my arc-sword, wishing we had a band of warriors behind us. I remembered what Vemsa had told me about the alien's Holy Person. If she were able to control him and he was the actual controlling factor of his forces, it might be possible to make good our mission.

If...

In the distance a flickering light filtered through the undergrowth—campfires.

We moved off the trail and kept under cover of the twisted purple swamp brush. Several times we were unable to see the lights because of intervening brush and trees. The swamp had become a muddy nightmare, sloshing around our ankles; black with looming shadows. I drew my sword, trying to convince myself that the aliens, being on a low level of evolution, knew little about hand-to-hand combat. But all arguments seemed unconvincing in the darkness of the shallow swamp.

We were nearing what appeared to be a clearing ahead when a rustling in the brush around us commanded our attention.

I heard Vemsa whip her sword from its sheath. It was the only warning. Suddenly aliens—huge, ugly spears in their hands, surrounded us. I swung back and forth, turning, keeping Vemsa to my back. The two of us moved almost jointly, each protecting the other from being struck from behind. Now I blessed the fact that the Dalli taught their women the art of fighting; for having faced Vemsa in combat, I knew her to be an expert with the sword.

We were hopelessly outnumbered; and even though our weapons were far more sophisticated than those of the Jolli, mere numbers would soon overpower us.

I made a desperate play by touching the stud of my arc-sword, sending a full charge in a half-circle about us. The air crackled and the swamp lighted eerily for a split moment as the blue electro-charge swung like a water spray, flashing bright fire upon the purple faces of the squat aliens surging around us.

Their gaping leathery mouths, wet with saliva, sprinkled about a double row of jagged yellowed fangs. Their large oversize, staring red eyes, peering blankly at us, sent a cold shiver of sick revulsion through my body. There were at least thirty such creatures fairly dancing about us.

Just before the electro-charge flashed away, I saw the few aliens who were struck by its burning flame jerk back in sudden anguish, doubling over, their bodies charred black.

I pressed the stud again, spraying the aliens. At least five more fell, burned almost in half. Then, as I sent the last charge at them, something hard struck me dully from behind. A black fuzz gulped around me as all consciousness ebbed away.

CHAPTER SIX

"And I say that defeat to an honorable man is not surrender; only the loss of one battle. He who is honorable and strong will fight to turn defeat into victory."
—From the Voices of the Torshi

There is a certain terror to darkness; even when in natural sleep; but a far greater sense of looming horror heavily presses in upon the conscious mind when that total black comes with wakefulness. I became aware of being alive, realized my eyes were open, but blindness continued.

Lying on hard ground, cold and black, I felt a deep throbbing stab of panic. It was not enough to know the pain at the base of my skull, indicating that I surely lived and hadn't been thrust into some unknown afterlife world. I had never considered what it must be like to be blind until that moment, and the mental images of such sharp knowledge convinced me that it was far better to be dead than to be without sight, for a man is helpless without use of his eyes.

Such was the immediate impression upon my return to conscious awareness.

The next impression was knowledge that I wasn't alone. You feel life, absorb it from your pores, hear it breath, know its nearness by smell. You can almost taste it.

Maybe that's what comes with total blindness, a sharper awareness of the other senses.

My nerves were alert and at full attention to my black surroundings, aware of others near, yet unable to reach out to them. I felt psychologically paralyzed, though realized it was still possible to move.

I was lying there, gathering impressions of the non-world about me.

Then I heard a whispered voice, but the words were meaningless. If the sound had not come first, I might have whimpered in fear. But it was the announcement of life followed by the touch of a hand upon my chest.

Immediately I started to sit up.

"Who are you?" asked a voice thick with accent, which I recognized as being that of a Spacer.

I tried to see about me, but there was only darkness. "Who are you?"

"Commander Looms, Captain of the Spacer ship."

"Is Gardon and his daughter here?" I quickly sat up, touching the man in front of me.

"Yes," sounded another voice to my right. "We are here."

"I've come to rescue you," I announced, as if this would give them hope.

A light, feminine laugh mocked me.

"Quiet, Gaal," snapped the voice of Gardon.

The Commander said: "I'm afraid you have failed, my friend, but tell me about it."

After I had done so, I was introduced to the different voices about me. The mocking laughter was that of Gardon.

"What happened to the girl? The one with me?" I inquired.

"She is here, but still unconscious. We've done what we could for the two of you," Commander Looms told me.

"How long have we been here?"

"About two hours, I'd say," Gardon announced.

"We don't have much time to plan an escape. Revive the girl, if you can," I instructed, taking immediate command.

In the darkness the voice of Commander Looms was offered with his hand, which touched mine. He led me to where Vemsa was lying unconscious on the cold dirt floor.

"Does she seem injured?" I inquired, worried.

"Nothing but a lump on the head," Gardon told me. "We checked the two of you out as carefully as possible in such darkness."

I touched Vemsa, finding her face and forehead in the darkness. "Isn't there anything we can do?"

Commander Looms said: "Only wait. As we did with you. But what can we possibly do to escape this hole?"

"We're in the chamber under the surface," Gardon explained. "There's an opening about twenty feet up—that leads to the surface. It's the only exit."

I checked my harness and discovered that the arc-charges were still clamped in place.

"I believe there's a way to get out of here, but we have to get Vemsa revived first," I told them.

I didn't reveal how slim our chances were. I wouldn't even know without consulting Vemsa. We had very little time before the Rites of the Five Moons.

Little was said while we waited for Vemsa to revive. Time seemed to stand still and there was no way of guessing how much time passed. I'm sure I slept for a few moments. The Spacers talked among themselves in the Federation language, which was different enough from my own to make it impossible to follow.

I kept feeling Vemsa's forehead, which was cold then hot, then cold. I had almost completely lost hope when a soft murmur sounded from her.

Commander Looms said at my side: "Easy with her." I felt his arms reach forward, across me. It was some moments before Vemsa's voice fluttered weakly.

The moment I was assured that she was totally conscious I quickly explained our situation.

Vemsa said when I was finished: "The pits. They will take us out in mass when the sun reaches its high point."

"Can you feel the Holy Person here?" I asked. "What can you do? Is there any way to communicate with him?"

Silence answered me.

"Well?"

"Quiet!" Vemsa retorted.

The only sound was the breathing of those within the chamber, some twelve men and two women captured by the thick darkness.

"Only that they are puzzled by your sword. They say it has great magic," Vemsa said. "There's hope!"

"Yes, but is there anyone of them you can either communicate with or take control of?"

"I can impress upon him some command, but can't be sure he'll respond. Once in his presence, he will communicate with me. That's all."

A plan had formed vaguely in my mind. I turned to where the commander had last been. "What is the situation with your men? How well can they fight without weapons?"

"They are trained in hand-to-hand combat. But the numbers are too great against us. Those creatures work like one unit—as if controlled by a single mind."

Vemsa said: "In a way, that is exactly how it is."

"Vemsa can take care of that—if your men can fight. Then we have a chance."

"They'll die fighting if I give the word."

"Well, tell them to follow my lead," I instructed.

There was hesitation, then Commander Looms said: "If you have a plan."

"I've been told that Gardon and his daughter are very important. My father has promised to help all he can to return them to your ship. I have the only hope." I explained about the electro-charges and what I could do with them.

"If you give us a chance," Commander Looms announced, "we can follow and fight to our deaths...if necessary. Just get the two of them out of here safely and you can expect high rewards."

I carefully selected my words. "It is the hope of our people that the successful rescue will bring great credit to our world and possibly prove us worth of recognition."

Gardon told me in a careful voice: "I can promise nothing other than my personal thanks and my dedicated efforts to make such a recommendation. There is little else one lone man can do. I can promise to do everything possible to make you and your people qualify, if circumstances permit. How long it might take is another matter."

"In either case I would help, naturally," I assured him. There was something about the man's voice that convinced me he was highly honorable. Hope is far better than no hope at all; maybe in my time we would see Jolli recognized as a planet of the Federation. Assuming we could escape from our present circumstances.

I turned my attention to Vemsa. "Attempt to impress upon the Holy Person that the man they just captured is a man of great magic and that he wishes to demonstrate this. Impress upon him that it is to his people's benefit to question me. Can you do that?"

"That and more, once I am in his presence," Vemsa promised. "I'm not sure if I can now. I'll try. Now, quiet!"

Again we were plunged into dark silence. It might have taken but a few moments or half a day—time can distort under pressure. Suddenly a grating sounded from above and light shafted its way into the chamber. I saw that we were in nothing more than a huge hole clawed out of the ground. Above us a circle of blue sky showed, ringed by aliens.

Vemsa spoke in a halting, flat voice: "You with such great magic come forward."

I said quickly: "Impress upon the Holy Person that I must have you with me."

After a moment of silence, Vemsa said: "It is so arranged.

We stood in the shaft of light and a long, wooden ladder was lowered towards us.

CHAPTER SEVEN

"Even unto the presence of evil in the den of the hated non-humans, honor must be recognized and worshipped. And honoring those Gods of others will bring blessings unto him who does so, for there is the means of mutual communication and understanding. Remember that all Gods are but the images of the only Creator of the entire Universe, seen through different eyes. Honor of your enemy's gods simply proves you have a closer hand in God's work and you will be pleased."

—From the Voices of the Torshi

They took us to the center of the ring of stone pillars, carved with images of their people, one for each of their Five Gods—the five moons of Jolli. Crowded about the pillars were more than a hundred purple aliens, their huge gaping mouths slit wide, cutting their heads in two, as they chirped weird chants to the blue heavens and their five gods. It was a primitive picture from some hellish nightmare, yet they seemed, in many ways, not much different from primitive humans, about to worship their gods.

Seeing these aliens for the first time in their own natural surroundings, I realized how foolish our own hatred was for the Spacers. Here were alien creatures, non-human beings that we accepted as merely a part of our world, and the Spacers had been blindly hated. We had never really hated the natives; and we had never really known much about them. Survival on Jolli had been difficult enough without considerations about the natural intelligent life, which had evolved upon the world. Like the beasts, the birds, the insects, we accepted them as merely something to deal with; not to understand or feel emotional about.

The Spacers had seemed more alien to us; yet they were fellow humans.

Vemsa and I were escorted by a group of aliens to the center of the circle of pillars and then a native, clothed in rough animal hide, stepped forward, carrying a thick shaft, carved with weird designs and images, and in its other hand my arc-sword.

He stood in front of us, just beyond reach.

Vemsa whispered: "This is their Holy Person. Notice he's the only one clothed. He's studying you, puzzled."

She broke off, then said in a dead, cold voice: "What makes you different?"

I realized that she was speaking the alien's message. They were in mental contact.

"Tell him my magic makes me different—as he saw evidenced by the sword's lightning."

Immediately Vemsa answered: "How does such magic work?"

"Only I can do it!" I countered. "Give me the sword and I'll show you."

258

The alien's face gave no indication that it was aware of the conversation; it was blank of any expression, its large red eyes merely stared at me.

Vemsa said: "You who have invaded our lands coming from the sky have taken from us much territory. We have asked nothing in return, but to be left alone. Why have you come?"

"Because you have taken some of our people," I offered, as if talking directly to the alien. There was a mental bridge between this creature and Vemsa. It was a strange experience.

"I ask you why you have come to our lands—many lifetimes ago," Vemsa's lips spoke the alien's words.

"Men of great magic placed us here. We are, like yourselves, captive to the whim of this world." I was attempting to find a nearby fire. There was only one at the end of the circle of pillars, beyond the alien Holy Person. That was 20 yards away.

Silence followed my last statement. I heard the wind sighing through the swamp that surrounded us. Then Vemsa spoke again in that dry, flat voice.

"What magic can make your sword spit lightning? What magic can save you from our Five Gods?"

"Truth," I countered. "For all gods are but the images of those of us who understand something created all that is. Your gods are the same as our Gods—but I know more of my God—and thus have powers which your gods can not match!"

The alien's large eyes seemed to recede within its hard-shell face. Immediately I felt the presence of some sharp invisible force flow through me. My will seemed to flutter away and I stood there, helpless, knowing that an alien mind had probed total control over my own. At the same time I realized how this Holy Person was able to control his armies. What kind of culture did they have; what kind of beings were they? I could only guess that they must be like some insect culture, where the queen controls the colony. I was sure this alien mentally controlled its fellow creatures. The thought was sickening.

Suddenly the feeling of being mentally invaded, as if invisible fingers had probed deep into the flesh under my skull, into the very pits of my brain, assailed me.

"It is through me that the mind of the Gods direct those of my kind. I am the Flow, the Servant of the Gods—their focus, through which Plan and Order come. I am the Living Presence for our living Gods," a voice whispered within my mind.

I tried to question, but it was impossible to speak, even my thoughts seemed sluggish and frozen within the confines of some mythical wall, shimmering and invisible.

"Accept our Gods!" the voice exclaimed. "Bow to them! For they are the only Gods worthy of worship!"

If I had been able, I would have willing bowed to any image of Gods, for I recognized it was only the reflection of the God of the Universe seen through other eyes.

The alien seemed to sense or read my very thoughts, for it said: "You believe in Gods, but understand nothing. Our Gods are the only true masters of the world. They live within the Five Moons. They are more powerful than your limited concept of a god. If this were not so, I would not control you through the power of our Gods. But you will understand as your bodies are torn in the rites and your life is bled upon the ground, as your bones are picked dry by the Gods themselves."

I attempted to move forward, intent on somehow killing this creature, but its control was too great. The violence of my hatred and desperation was turned back towards me—like a mirror reflecting an image—flooding me with a sudden irritable urge to die. Slowly I felt myself slumping under the terrible pressure of the violent emotions that fed back upon me, knowing it was my own thoughts that caused the damage, but I was unable to stop them. It was as if a bursting dam were drowning me. My legs began to tremble, crumbling. Light, sound, fluttered out of being. I was in some black night, burning with hot fires. Then suddenly a thrusting third *thing* slashed at my brain with stunning force, like a bolt of lightning. My eyes became aware of light, shape, sound flooded in about me. Invisible hands ripped at the very tissues of my brain. Claws seemed to peel back the very cells, one at a time. Black enveloped me for a very long moment. Light fluttered into being. Then they were gone.

Vemsa cried out, tensely: "Get the others! I can't hold him long."

Without thought, I rushed toward the pit where the Spacers were held. I saw in one glance that the aliens were unmoving, as if turned to stone. Their chirping had stopped; their eyes were dazed.

When I reached the hole, I grabbed the ladder, thrust it into the pit.

"Quick! Out!" I cried. My right hand grabbed one of the electro-charges, as I searched for a near-by fire. But there wasn't any.

Turning, I rushed back to the ring of pillars. The situation was almost the same as I had left it, except that some of the aliens were swaying back and forth, as if attempting to break loose of some fantastic spell. Vemsa was white, her body tense, eyes large and filled with panic.

"Can't...hold," she murmured in a tortured voice.

I rushed to the alien, grabbed the arc-sword from his nerveless fingers, and started to run him through. Then Vemsa slumped to the ground and the creature before me leaped away from my thrusting blade.

The aliens ringing the pillars, jumped to their feet, the high chirping roared on the morning air.

Realizing our only chance was to cause the diversion I had promised Commander Loons, I leaped toward the fire, raising the electro-charge high over my head. When close enough, I stopped, thrust my hand forward.

The small cylinder shot directly toward the flames. As it hit the coals, sparks spurted, but nothing else happened. I grabbed another charge, slammed it into the hilt of the sword and then swung around in a circle, pressing the firing stud so that a spray of crackling light flashed about me.

The aliens crumbled back as the charge flickered out at them. I rushed to Vemsa's side, grabbing hold of her shoulder, dragging the girl to her feet. She was already reviving.

"What happened?" I cried.

"Couldn't keep control...too strong!"

"Can you stop him—try again!"

The aliens, chirping madly, surged forward. I sprayed them with another swing of the arc-sword. Several fell back, dead, but the others pushed forward, spears thrusting out. Slipping another electro-charge from my harness, I released the last bolt into the aliens, and as it played out, yanked the empty charge, replaced it with a new one. Then the aliens were upon us.

My sword swung through the air, chopping at the lunging purple bodies, splattering bluish blood. There seemed little hope of lasting more than a few seconds. I pressed the firing stud on the sword, spraying those in front of us, then turned, firing the second charge at others who had been coming from behind. As I started to fire the last electro-bolt, a loud, thundering explosion sounded from the direction of the fire, then a violent blast of static electric-charged bolts sprayed high into the sky. The electro-battery had finally burst!

All the aliens froze as if time had frozen still. I swung my sword, cutting them down, but they remained unmoving.

Vemsa cried: "Have him!" as we cut a path through the aliens.

"How long can you hold him?"

"Not...long."

I shoved my way toward their Holy Person, determined to cut the creature down without mercy, when the shouts of the Spacers came from the far end of the clearing. We had just reached the Holy Person when Vemsa cried out in pain. She gripped my arm with tense fingers.

The aliens immediately became mobile.

I raised my sword high above my head, aiming at the alien leader.

The creature raised his shaft to protect himself. A mental probe shot at my mind. I dropped the blade's point and just as it was about to slip from my numbed fingers I managed, in one last surge of mental will power, to press the firing stud.

A flash of blue light shot directly at the creature's chest, burned in a flare of sparks. It screamed, face contorting as it slumped to the ground.

Those who were pressing about us suddenly stopped moving, stood, as if dazed, then shifted aimlessly about, like mindless beings; dumb animals.

Vemsa and I moved through the milling aliens and joined forces with the Spacers.

Commander Looms turned out to be a grim-faced, muscular man with deep-set commanding dark eyes. Gardon was younger than I had expected, with just a flecking of gray hair about his temples; a very handsome tall man with a high forehead and kindly, though strong blue eyes. It was his daughter, Gaal, who was most striking. She had golden hair, green bright eyes and a willowy figure, dressed in a form-fitting garment that covered her from neck to ankles. Her features were fine and beautiful, only her eyes revealed a sense of cool aloofness.

Vemsa told me: "With their Holy Person dead, they are helpless until another arrives or contacts them. How long that will be I can't say. But they all are mere units. We would be well-advised to leave this place immediately, before it is too late."

Some time later, as we were moving out of the swamp, Gardon and his daughter riding the Talios we had picked up on our way, the Commander said: "Your world is still culturally undeveloped. But your efforts to rescue us will speak highly of your sense of honor, and moral development. I'm sure Gardon will be able to reward you highly for your cooperation. Many times such events take place on worlds like yours, and the people merely laugh at us when we request help. I'll do what I can to help you. It's the only thanks I can give for saving our lives."

Gardon, who had overheard the Commander's words, added:

"Honor in Man is the highest order of civilization. Dishonor is what brought the original settlers to such planets as this—to be confined away from moral society. With a great and compelling desire to honor one another and to honor outsiders, because it is the moral thing to do, is, in truth, civilized; more than any scientific or cultural mutation. If all your people are as honorable as yourself, Han-Ja—you can be assured of Federation recognition and all it will bring of modern civilization."

Vemsa smiled and then leaned close, whispering in my ear: "If all men were like you, Han-Ja, I would willingly be a slave to all of them."

It was the way she spoke those words and the bright glow in her eyes that seemed even more startling—or promising—to me than those words of the Commander's and Gardon's.

Strange how a man will seek greater glory for the people, chance death for future generations and finally be able to look forward to the hard won rewards of his efforts. Yet only to have them all seem almost meaninglessly empty because a woman has spoken soft and gentle words to him. I knew then, for the first time, that I loved Vemsa—a brave, delicate woman who could stand up against a man in battle. Yet follow his leadership. How strange and wonderful she seemed.

I looked up at the blue sky. The sun was at its highest point, the five small moons could be seen spread out across the heavens, and in the distance, from where we had come, flying over the swamp, were a flock of Haki-birds.

I couldn't help wondering if there was some connection between the Haki-birds and the rites of the Five Moons. Maybe someday I would find out the truth; but this day we had narrowly escaped being a fatal part of the Rites of the Five Moons; moons from which the natives of Jolli believed the Haki-birds came.

It could not be long before we would be at the small, wood-shack village of Hamton—home. It felt good to be alive and never had the future been more promising.

And here's a short which is of a somewhat different nature. I'm simply going to warn the reader that it might be a bit difficult at times, but to me it is well worth the trip. There are, of course, for all who survive, the ...

➤BENEFICIARIES◄

The only thing Management knew was that the Storage Vault Life Support Systems had been mysteriously shut down. It was Technician Gnorm's job to find out how and why—and fix things. He was leaning over the scope, intensely involved in the delicate programming of the CP, when the outside thought leaped at his mind.

WE DON'T WANT TO LIVE!

"*Stop* there, Val!" His voice echoed loudly in the tight confines of the room. "Run it back!"

"Is he conscious of us?" his assistant asked.

"If so we're in for deep shit!"

The operation area was a small table top between the two white robed men. A compact scope stood there before Gnorm.

"Sharpen the image, Val."

"Ready to run."

"Back to the beginning cue. Play it slow. Mark as I indicate. Set Destruct-Lazes."

"I can't believe he could actually harm us—"

"Whatever this fanatic did—it was with his mind." Gnorm pressed the button attached to his suitbelt, wondering if he *would* survive to dine with Bev.

He was suddenly aware of other places, other times, other *images,* as he once again was able to electronically observe their subject's thoughts...

* * * * * * *

—oblivion had come, then departed. The reality of this horror was stunning. He made no effort at self-identity; was aware of mere existence. *He had died and now he was reborn!* There was something very grave about that. The word GRAVE stood out like some sardonic symbol. He should be in a grave—or more to the point: atomized. A memory flashed unwanted across his mind:

"Joey, dear Joey, they're gonna take you—"

"I lost, then."

"We *all* lost!" The answer came from her ancient face. He tried to remember the younger, firmer lines; but the image of old flesh, sunken eyes, thin purplish lips held.

"Kate," was all he could manage. Other words choked in his throat. He tried to lift a hand to touch her thin fingers. She reached for him; her grip was weak, yet communicated understanding, caring, love, and the grim agony he felt. Joey tried to remember the sensation of her young trim body embraced in his arms. Nothing came. Too many years had passed. This old woman was all that was left of the girl he'd married.

"I'll be okay, Joey," she lied.

"For how long?"

A shrug answered him, then: "We've lost our right to die. And Management'll be our beneficiary."

"Not that we had much left after the legal expenses," he whispered to himself. Then more to Kate, he said: "You certain there's no more hope?"

"They won. That's final. There is no hope. The Law is locked in, solid!" she managed in a forced strong voice. "I was the best trial lawyer—"

"I know—"

Bony fingers stopped his words. "Now, don't you go arguing. I haven't lost my feeling for the Law, not even after all those years. Court Computes don't frighten me at all, nor the Mechiclerks, nor the fancy—oh, well—they don't bother me!" She angrily snapped fingers in his face, like she had always done when she was angry. He saw her lips thin across gleaming perfect ersatz teeth.

Funny, he mused, how Science fixed teeth, but let the skin dry up, the age-lines depress away mature beauty. By

266

sick design; no doubt. After all, populations were way too high; something had to be done. That fact made what the Law had just done even more perverse. Science and Medicine could do some fantastic things; but hadn't conquered the mystery of real aging. People lived longer; but in aged, malfunctioning bodies. Letting people have the right to die seemed a logical solution to the crushing population problem. Science had learned how to keep the Mind/Brain alive forever, in theory! Life could be sustained until cures could be found, or new bodies offered. And the Lifers believed fanatically in the idea of doing everything possible to sustain life—regardless of the personal convictions of people like us.

"What argument," he asked a bit weakly, "finally sold the Court?"

"That it was against the Law of God, of course. The Lifer's slogan hasn't changed: *Don't Abort—Support/Don't End—Extend!* Mercy killings ended; no death on request—in the name of God!"

"If only it were...that simple." He sounded bitter.

"In the name of God they pervert everything—no matter what the personal cost. Management doesn't care about Gods—profit is their motive. The rotter of keeping old people alive a bit longer, profit from their suffering—grab their pension checks—it makes me sick! First it was the hospitals and the doctors grabbing and grabbing, then the convalescent homes, then the...oh, what's the use? Those guys were small time! Science learned how to extend life with machines and found a *cheap* way to support life...and an easy way to store an infinite number of—" She broke off, gagged on her anger, then muttered: "I don't understand it all; memory bits...Brains...Minds...Consciousness...Personalities...Life...Is it as meaningless to you, too?"

He nodded so weakly that she apparently didn't notice. Her face remained impassive—

* * * * * * *

"That's at the beginning, all right!" Gnorm observed, rather absently.

Val asked, a little annoyed: "Why didn't the Right to Die people simply accept society's solution?"

"Everybody has a blind spot."

"How could he be so blind?"

"These two lived a couple of centuries ago, before the population burst beyond containable limits, before Social Balance came about—before everything was really worked out. They were from the first generation to be put into Storage." Gnorm broke off, then said: "Continue the forward run—"

* * * * * * *

—IN THE NAME OF GOD! The thought filled Joey with horror. It was terrifying to realize how powerful the very word God could be. All things fell before His Word. Only trouble was that everybody had a different idea *what* His word actually meant. Everybody read the Holy books differently—and there were countless such books, the ancient teachings of long crumbled civilizations. The Holy books of the world had created endless wars all in His name! Or Her name. Or Its name! The final mockery was when two armies prayed to the "same" God to protect them—then on the day of battle they went off to butcher each other in His name. In His name came the Witch Hunts. But civilization— in fact the whole history *and* prehistory of humankind—was filled with endless perversions in the name of one god or another. When would it all end? When would human beings realize that their concepts of a Creator had to be limited— because the mind of *Homo sapiens* was tragically *limited.* And so in the name of God—

* * * * * * *

Val asked: "What do they mean, in God's name?"

Gnorm considered, offered: "I think that's just another term for Management."

"At that time there was a lot of argument about the legal importance of human life—"

"It is important."

"Sure—we should know *how* important, too. But Earth has limited resources and—"

"The Repro-Board kept things—"

"The RB still keeps the Balance!" Gnorm broke off, then continued with: "Never mind *that*! I want to finish this Op in time for Dining in the Dome."

"With the cute Tech in Recs?"

"Bev? Yes."

"Serious?"

"For a Standard Relate—maybe longer."

"Thinking of applying at RB with her?"

"Haven't considered Baby-Making."

"Better arid soon—consider your age bracket. RB is—"

"Restrictive. It limits a single legal survivor per person. We're lucky. On Earth in our grandparents' time it was still 'half' a kid per person. It cut the World Pop down by allowing only one child per couple. They dropped the Pop to the Stable Number of two billion—the Ideal Max. A Stable Pop here is crucial for survival.

"Anyway, it isn't Repro—Time with Bev—we 're more in the Game without Pain stage." He chuckled, thinking of her deliciously firm bod. "Back to work."

He refocused all attention:

* * * * * * *

—Joey tried to let memories resurrect the delicate image of the old woman who had been his wife. They were slow in coming. He was ninety years old when he met Kate. She was tall, a slim body with long flowing blonde hair, full lips, hauntingly intelligent blue eyes. In their mid-years together Kate had filled out more voluptuously, her hair had been dyed dark brown, then red, then black, as the true color shaded gray to white. They had started life in a small single apartment, and then moved into a large house with two bedrooms. They could afford that on his salary as a Commercial Sensitive (a profession many people considered hokey-pokey fraud; but Believers clamored to him—it made life rich). The children had come along, then left, grew old and died long before his real sensitive abilities surfaced in a scientifically viable way. He was involved in research with Dr. Jamison, when the terrible accident happened. Perhaps if the doctor had survived, things would have been different. Maybe—

* * * * * * *

Val commented: "Then he apparently has true mental..."

"Of course. Such powers are uncommon—but not unheard of... Something happened here last week. Apparently Joey was responsible—such talents would be helpful—but—they're dangerous here! Let's find out what he did—"

* * * * * * *

—"TRAFFIC COMPUTER BREAKDOWN" the headlines read. Dr. Jamison was one of the casualties. He should have known, predicted the danger—if he actually was a Sensitive. Mental talents that couldn't be used to avoid life-threatening events weren't worth having—or developing. That was when he lost all interest in further experimentation. The research doctor was the first of his friends to die. The last 10 years had been a kind of social isolation for Kate and himself. Now even that was gone. And death would bring no escape from the pain, only more terrible isolation—total and endless, an infinity of black, formless consciousness. Death was a mockery. Science mixed with legal and religious garbage had let Management win—

* * * * * * *

Gnorm stated: "The man is mad!"

"What is madness?"

"Mal-adjustment! Okay, so there isn't such a thing as madness—only those who don't fit the accepted Norm. But we'll fix that—now won't we?" Gnorm's attention slipped back into Joey—

* * * * * * *

270

—He tried to turn his head; and felt the illusion of having done so. He attempted to open his eyes; but couldn't. Dark was all conscious reality. Panic set in, then slowly ebbed flat, offering him a sense of bland awareness. Consider: You were dead; they want to keep you alive in a purely legal sense—and they have! A grim mental smile formed. They wanted to keep people legally alive—legally aware—so that Management's Credit Line could be continually transfused with the Government and Company Pensions of "legally alive" patients. Even with the pension cash value reduced for the "dead" it seemed as if the system must, given enough time, break down—who was paying whom? Then what would happen? But the moral logic was perversely simple: in time Science might discover a way of reviving those "living souls"—and Man didn't have the right to take a human life. Hog—

* * * * * * *

"Leap ahead a fraction," Gnorm instructed.

"What'd he mean about the system breaking down?" Val wanted to know.

"That," Gnorm replied, "was a kind of fanatic, outdated logic! From what I've read in Social History books, if the government were paying all those pensions to Management, who was paying Government the money to pay pensions— insurance firms, banks, workers? The money had to come from *someplace* other than the Mint. The end was obvious. Business couldn't support such a system forever. The Pension System started to buckle; Management slipped in, grabbed control of more and more organizations until it had finally *become* the government. The system, in the long run, worked; that's all that counts, now—how isn't important; nor who profited at that time. We exist because Management was successful on a worldwide basis. Then it formed Stellar Worlds Inc. But that's all history, anyway. That's how the present came into being. That's how it worked. But that was all a long time ago."

"I guess you're right," Val admitted, a bit lamely.

"Of course. Anyway...slip ahead. I want the exact point he begins to openly rebel—that's where we must set our cues for Total Delete.

* * * * * * *

—*maybe* there's a way to beat these bastards! The thought plagued Joey; for how long he didn't know. Time had frozen into a meaningless experience. Days, years blended. Joey had let himself become aware of his outer mental edges—the limits of self, like he'd done in those scientific experiments. Somebody had once stated: *"The universe is contained within the confines of your skull!"* Perhaps that was true—in a very real sense! Everything was in his mind. Everything he knew and was had been constructed within the limitations of his skull. But where was his skull now? What *were* the outer boundaries of his consciousness; the extents of his mental territory? The brain was a magnificent place; a hologramic world where almost every particle of personality and memory was held in every brain cell. Any piece of tissue—

* * * * * * *

Val moaned: "Hologramic theory! Really! Take an hologram plate, shoot a laser through it and you have instant 3-D pictures."

"Right on! Even in ancient imagery!" Gnorm laughed. "Shatter the plate, pick up any bit of it and it'll reform the whole image when a laser is shot through it."

"Correct, Doctor Hologram!"

Val, taking up the mockery, continued, "Remember, students, how you can teach a rat a maze, then cut away a large part of its brain and it'll still remember how to run the maze. Thus: Obviously the brain is hologramic!"

"Right again! At least a rat's brain!" He laughed with ironic humor. "I'm amazed at your knowledge!"

"I read tapes, too. The brain is like that hologramic plate; any bit of brain can be used to recreate the total human memory/mind. Take a Micro Brain Bit, preserve it in a Life

Support System and you can destroy the rest of the person's brain and body—yet keep their mind alive to be easily replayed at will! Zap, bango! Laser lights and flashing lightning! The wonders of the twenty-eighth century reach out from the future and—"

"Don't mock it. Hologramic Theory is *not* outdated. In fact—"

"What we're involved with here is a bit more complicated!"

"But that's how we all work, remember that, and how the memory—mind system works, like a hologram—that's how Management stores memory bits—well, never mind! Slip forward—careful, we're close to where we stopped—"

* * * * * * *

—the black void seemed an endless, hellish place; a lonely, isolated existence. Joey guessed that years must have passed. Maybe centuries. He had attempted to relive his life; been somewhat successful, though felt a sense of confusion take over as if Time could be run back and forth against his will. Now, with effort, he started developing mental exercises to improve his Sensitive powers. He had tried to extend his mind—

* * * * * * *

"Easy!" Gnorm warned.

* * * * * * *

—Kate hadn't joined him. Maybe she couldn't reach him. After all she didn't have his abilities, though her mind was strong, receptive. If only he could reach her, join with her—this eternity wouldn't be quite so terrible. His mind reached out, more powerfully than ever before, focused on a mental picture of Kate...he suddenly recoiled at the sensation of something out there—

* * * * * * *

"He knows," Val moaned, "we're watching—"

"How could he?"

"He knows—you saw that—he knows—"

"But couldn't—not really!" But Gnorm set his fingers firmer against the Destruct button.

* * * * * * *

—Joey instinctively tried to project his mind, reaching out beyond his conscious limits, forcing the probe this time to be more controlled. Then as a sense of contact snapped into place, he contracted—

* * * * * * *

"Did you feel that?" Val wanted to know.

"I felt something—"

"And so did he!"

* * * * * * *

—Joey lay there in the timeless dark of his mental universe, for a long time frightened to continue his experiments. But pure boredom moved him. He reached out carefully at first, realizing that his abilities were even more powerful than before. Danger pressed in, like clawing shapeless forms. The dark nothingness became alive with something very real, something he could almost feel. Something *outside* of himself! Only with frantic control was he able to push aside the phantom forms pulsing up in his imagination. In terror he mentally contracted, attempting to become a finite point.

* * * * * * *

Gnorm instructed: "Cue this for destruct...for later—we'll come back."

* * * * * * *

274

—He remained carefully isolated, trying to understand what had happened; frightened to continue—

* * * * * * *

"Scan," Gnorm ordered.

* * * * * * *

—He'd experienced something evil—and yet something else that *was totally loving*. Something good *and* something that wanted to...kill him!—

* * * * * * *

—annoyed, he washed the feeling of raw fear away—for perhaps the thousandth time, he'd lost count—he ignored the irritating awareness of danger. Joey's mind finally swelled with furious emotion—and determination. His consciousness lifted out, very tentatively. Suddenly he merged with an embrace, a caressing awareness of

KATE!

How long have you been here?

Very long, Joey. I've been terribly lonely—What happened after—?

I don't know. I was in coma...a long time before I died.

Let me be aware of you.

How is this happening?

You know I could do things with my mind—now it is more powerful than ever before.

Dear Joey, you never give up—not like a lawyer who accepts the judgment of Law—we argue, but after that the defense rests—that's it!

I think maybe I can change things—make it work my way; for a change.

How, Joey?

I've been thinking. If there was a way to destroy these machines—with my mind....probing—

* * * * * * *

275

"Val, we're there! Mark it! Key the computer for all operative locations. I think this is it!"

"He couldn't know about us...do something to us—"

"Don't know. But if he did it the way I think, all we got to do is make key burns, first, that'll weaken him. We will delete one bit of memory after another until we've destroyed such mental powers—a damn shame, but necessary! We're dealing with something almost...*alien*. He contacted his Kate—what else might he do?"

"But he isn't alive in the conventional sense—not yet!"

"Maybe...maybe not. Who knows? Science can revive him to total life! He did *something*! Anyway, what is Life and Death? We only know legal and scientific definitions. We know how to Store Brain Bits for Management. We keep their minds intact—but what that means we really don't know—especially in a case like this. I get the feeling that Joey is very alive and could be aware of us...if we aren't careful. As he became aware of his wife.

"He somehow managed to shut down his life-support system. In effect even threaten Management. We're here to find out why, if possible, and to burn away the necessary info-bits of his memory—or simply destroy him."

"And then he wins, doesn't he? Only I don't see why all the trouble. There's plenty of them—more than we'll ever need. Why not just destruct?"

"Come on, Val, you know why. The System here on Stellar World Inc is balanced. Maybe our society is on automatic...but without the System we wouldn't be alive. We must survive—and all of them must survive—for the future. And life is, after all, considered sacred. So we save Joey; and we save Management from his power. That's all we have to know. That's all that counts. That's what we're here for.

"Are you ready to mark the areas for the computer?"

"Coded?"

"Coded. Automatic setting."

"Okay, scan forward, slow. Be ready to shut down—without delay."

"Release set. If we're endangered, our Computer contact breaks—and destruct is automatic."

276

Awareness leaped at Gnorm...

* * * * * * *

—*those* bastards *are up there.* Joey's and Kate's minds were united, totally fused. The blending of their personalities had worked. *The bastard is frightened*—

* * * * * * *

Val leaned back against the wall, sweat running down his wide forehead.

Gnorm shouted: "You broke the contact. Why?"

"They were attacking us!"

"Couldn't!" Gnorm stated, uncertain.

"Hell, they couldn't!"

"Okay. Reset, put me in Contact, direct—but you only observe—if anything seems to be going wrong, destruct—"

"Even if you're still tangled?"

"Yes!"

"That'll kill you."

Gnorm's fingers were already inserted into the instruments. Every point in Joey's Brain-Bit was cued, to this point. One command and Gnorm's fingers would clutch at the controls, automatically setting into action the Burn which would etch out all cued areas in Joey's Brain, destroying them forever—along with any mental powers he might have had.

Gnorm nodded to Val, and his mind instantly became aware...

* * * * * * *

—this time he *won't escape*, Joey stated with determination, almost instantly reaching out invisible thin, mental threads that tangled at the edge of Gnorm's consciousness.

Kate recoiled, screamed: YOU CAN'T!

DON'T LEAVE ME! Joey cried, holding to her mental strength as if it were a slender fiber trailing away into infinity. He needed her to magnify his powers. Now he knew that

277

once before he had managed to shut down their Life Support System so that they had really died. Somehow Management had turned the Systems on and brought his memory back to life. Was there no escape? Then, in the instant of touching the mind called Gnorm, he knew what he must do—

* * * * * * *

Gnorm felt himself brutally encased in an overwhelming mental force that attempted to squeeze out all of his conscious will, to take control, to become a part of him. In that instant he realized just what Joey was able to do—and how he'd shut down the Life Support Systems.

Christ! Gnorm realized in horror. *He means to overload the whole system—that'd kill them all...everything would be destroyed.*

Every nerve in his body clutched in desperate struggle to battle a force so powerful that it was actually *becoming* him! Thin needles of fire tingled spear-like through his brain, taking total control.

Consciousness was slipping, giving way, fading into a gray, horrible nothingness. Joey was winning, welling up inside Gnorm's brain to take command of his body.

Why the hell didn't Val act?

* * * * * * *

—Joey pulled inwards. *Val was programmed to burn them!* He instantly redirected his attack at that other man, the one somewhere outside Gnorm—

* * * * * * *

Gnorm squeezed down hard with his fingers, activating all the circuits in the OP System.

* * * * * * *

—pain screamed through the Joey/Kate union. Suddenly they were being torn apart. He literally felt her fading away, like a thin thread twisting wildly in some invisible wind, being sucked into a distant black hole! Management had won! There was no escaping, now. KATE, DON'T LEAVE ME! Joey cried out in lonely terror, suddenly aware that Kate had been ripped from his mental hold—his powers ebbed, faded. He tried to focus on something he had seen in Gnorm's thoughts—but that faded, too. Memories jumbled, raced backwards to form images of Kate and himself, as if he were for the very last time remembering her, how she had been when they first...

* * * * * * *

Sweat beaded Gnorm's forehead as he slowly relaxed. It had been too close. He looked at Val, a slow grin formed on his lips. He glanced at the instrument that held the micro-bit of Joey's memory. "Shame we can't tell them Management isn't an evil, profit—orientated force."

Val programmed the Brain-Bit for Storage; it was sucked away—filed. "Well, when old age makes us malfunctional we know what Stellar Worlds Inc really has in store for us—and that it will some time revive us in new, lasting young bodies."

Gnorm laughed, adding: "Our Brave New Wonderful Worlds—"

"Life Eternal!" Val saluted the air in open mockery.

"Oh, let's get the hell out of here! I have my date in the Dome with Bev."

"Dining under the stars, under the very shimmer of new planets just waiting to be colonized. Soon this Stellar Worlds Inc Starship we're in will reach its new world."

* * * * * * *

He had died and now he was reborn!

This time, though, it seemed different. It was some time before Joey realized the subtle change. It was actually a matter of light glaring in his eyes.

Stunned, he turned his head, and then looked up to see a lovely young face staring down at him. For a long moment he wondered if this were some terrible dream—some kind of taunting fantasy. This couldn't be her! Too young!

Kate said: "We're reborn, Joey."

She reached out a gentle hand and took his. Minutes later the two of them stepped across the small, hospital-like room, towards a window that showed a lush, virgin world stretched-out to the distant horizon of purplish mountains.

"They've prepared a place here for us, Joey," she stated. "Management has made us the beneficiaries of our own pensions—you might say. Since they revived me last week I've learned how Management built thousands of Stellar Worlds Inc Starships and then packed each of them with millions of Mirco Brain-Bits, and sent us all into deep space between the stars in search of new worlds. This Starship we're in has been here on this virgin world for decades. The descendants of the original crew have built a colony. We have been given new, youthful bodies, cloned from our own living cells. This new world is now ready for us to live another life—together. We're now truly reborn."

And another look at the universe of the Spacers and what else is going on in that galaxy of star systems. And another stretch into the distant future. But a very personalized experience for one man on a world that was on the...

⊶FAR SIDE OF PARADISE⊷

Darl, you fool! He was sweating, still breathing hard as he passed the two small children walking along the ruined street. His ragged face was cut deep in wrinkles, tanned dark from deep space. *You've done it again!*

"Hello, Spacer Shallen, one of the kids greeted, as he passed her.

He merely glanced at the two cherub faces hoping they couldn't see the horror and guilt on his face. They shouldn't know his name; they were babies not over seven years old. Their eyes seemed intensely interested in him.

What could they know? he wondered, frightened. *Children: They can't hurt a grown man! And at least these weren't* her *brats He'd fixed them, good!*

He pushed past another young child playing on the carved stone that had once been the cornerstone of a big house—or at least made to appear part of a ruin. This planet, many years ago, had been famous as a health spa—built to appear in a state of semi-ruin. The streets crossed at 60-degree angles, creating a stone and metal town within the graceful grip of the stark rocky mountains surrounding it on three sides. The Eternal Plain stretched to the horizon like yellow glass, coming to an end at the furious green ocean of this world. The human settlement was tiny; the planet a tired, almost deserted world on the far side of the Paradise System. The spa's time of popularity had long passed. This was a colony located at the very outer edge of the galaxy.

"A dead-hole!" he muttered, disgustedly.

"Hello, Shallen!" a nicely cultured boy's voice greeted.

Darl saw a ten-year-old with three smaller children standing on the ruins of a porch.

"Where're your parents?" He spoke without thinking. He disliked children; they were the plaque of humanity.

The boy merely asked: "Are you staying for the Festival?

She had asked the same thing!

"Aren't you staying for the Festival?" The woman's golden eyes had searched him with longing, suggestive want. They invited him; sparking a right fire that had only been controlled for those last months though daily use of the Stellar Suppliboat's Pleasure-Bods.

This was an isolated part of the Colonial System with few women willing to be nice to men like him. This Run was still better than time on a Penalworld. The Court had ordered him branded, thus marking his convicted status. There were few planets where he could be accepted: outlawed convict worlds, or non-human planets that destroyed the mind. Maybe the man who had this Tour duty before him had escaped to some crime-nest or been swallowed up by a black hole. This was a lousy area to be sentenced to, but at least he had a certain amount of freedom. And always a chance of meeting a woman like Julia.

Darl gaped at the beautiful young female as she leaned against the door of her house. The subtle arch of her slender body, hips just slightly thrust out, pleaded suggestively for him to come to her.

He was hardly fighting the erotic visions leaping fully developed in his mind. He saw no reason for anything wrong to happen. This was different. Even if the Judge had warned him: "Your crime, out where you're going, would be punished with death. Justice is without mercy." So here he was on the fringes of civilization, servicing distant start systems like Paradise. What could happen?

Them an their Virgin Births; their Sterile Families; their Cold Love!

This Julia was just what he needed!

Those large golden eyes feasted hungrily on his huge, massive form, as if she were sharing his erotic fantasy.

Few women had looked at him that way without being fully rewarded; few women were honest enough about their animal passions. The Civilized Worlds had restricted codes, especially that sector of the galaxy in which he'd been born. Even most of the colonist out here considered him part of the garbage and space junk, unfit for husband, lover or father.

"Isn't there any way I can convince you to stay for the Festival?"

The boy's voice asking that question for a second time jarred Darl's mind back the present. For a moment he was confused. Then he snarled: "Not a thing you can say or do! No snot-nosed kid would get me to stay if *she* couldn't!"

His response didn't sound at all unreasonable to him. After all, this was a strange place, a new planet for him to surrender to; a world upon which anything might happen.

He shook that thought away as pure insanity. Angrily he glared at the boy and then rushed off.

He pushed past the ruined house, turned the corner, and was startled by half a dozen kids barring his way.

"Hello, Spacer Shallen," they greeted.

"How'd you know my name?"

They giggled, stood their ground for a moment and then as he waved large arms in a half-threatening manner, the kids scattered like a flock of wild birds desperately trying to escape a demon monster clawing at their back feathers

"Damn kids...too many of them. Like insects scampering all around here in these ruins! Where're the adults?" He'd seen only one adult other than Julia. That was the old man at the spacefield outside town, who had directed Darl to the Central City. That was on his arrival to the planet.

"You'll have to go there to get your Credit Stamp. I don't have nothin' to do with that. I just watch the Computs guide you fellas in."

"Many of us come around?"

"You're the first in a year or so, I'd guess."

"How you people survive?"

"Lots of ways. There's a whole planet here—we have technology, too. The Spa always needed just a few rare, special imports."

"Yeah."

"But you got a bad run here."

"What difference? I'm just your average Penal Spacer—doing my time."

"Your term for the usual? Robbery?"

"Nothing dishonest like that," Darl admitted, a bit surprised by his willingness to be so open.

"Then something more...racy?" The old man leaned forward on the last word, eyes gleaming.

"Something such."

"Something, maybe, with a female—?" He merely nodded.

"What was your crime, then?"

"A girl screamed rape, only—it *wasn't*."

"Women can mislead a man. They imply one thing and when the man makes his move they scream another!"

"Many females around here?"

The man grinned, said: "There's Julia—she's the one you gotta see in Central city. Up there, in mid-town." The man pointed, then turned, walked across the field to its low building, standing like a squat mud hut.

Darl grunted and left for the center of the ruined city, a little less than a kilometer from the landing strip.

* * * * * * *

The walk did him good. He had time to take in the surrounding landscape, to observe the ruins of the once famous spa and to wonder what had happened here to so drastically make it into a deserted colony. The town had been built of stone and baked mud bricks supported by basic steel, all giving a comfortable ersatz ancient earthly appearance. A wall broke here, a column lifted there, arches and domes stood in their full glory or crippled in half-shapes. Towers and flat roofs remained on the top of buildings still standing strong; rubble piled high where Time seemed to have smashed furious fists down into the town. Much of this was faked; some real. There was a gardened plaza further in from the Eternal Plains, and there appeared to be a huge platform for Civil Events, with a dais neatly placed on top—an interesting and intriguing ancient touch, almost religious in its suggestive

284

form. Its artistic effect here at the ancient spa had been to lift man's spirit. Mankind needed a sense of roots; such archaic earthly places were scattered throughout the galaxy. Still, these planets on the galactic outskirts sometimes fell out of popularity; they were lost to the central culture. This whole section was like that. But this world was especially lonely, a sad place; almost alien. Buildings crumbled into the street, dust and sand propped up the sides of broken walls. Yet, throughout, there were some areas where everything was very soft and beautiful, delicately carved in bright colored patterns, golden flecked. It was difficult to tell where reality ended and fake ruins began.

Like the woman with the golden eyes and the golden hair and the golden body, who had called to him, saying: "I think you are looking for me."

It was difficult to believe her beauty, or her implied invitation.

She stood before a neatly cut doorway. Her golden gaze seduced him. Her golden tanned beauty was embraced in a yellow, lightly woven cloth that draped tightly about her seductive body. Everything about her was a silently spoken promise, an intimate offering from deep within her probing eyes.

"Spacer Shallen, you aren't goin' to leave us, are you?" the small child's voice now questioned him.

He was jarred out of his memory of Julia once again, and startled to discover several children were following him down the street. They were gathered closely about him, almost touching, invading his space.

"Get away. Leave me alone!" he cried, suddenly anxious that he might not have cleaned up all the evidence.

"The Festival takes place at sunset—you'd be the guest of honor," a young girl said, high pitched voice nicely matching the golden purity of innocent,

Shallen felt a shiver race down his spine.

"I don't want to be no guest or anything!" He pushed past the girl.

"*Don't!* Don't hurt me!" she screamed, running down the street.

It was what the woman had said!

285

His mind blurred over the memory of what had happened; and was happening. It seemed as if he'd been walking for a very long time; the city was still packed thickly about him, and the sky was beginning to get dark. Clouds formed above the town, distant lightning flashed, threatening thunder followed. The setting sun cast the mountain shadow closer to the buildings. Soon night would blot out this ersatz world.

Julia had been so liltingly seductive.

"You'll have to come in...here," She indicated her home; a low brick building. "I keep all my citi-records there—you know the official stuff."

"In there?" he asked, noting the darkness beyond the door. "You handle business in your home?"

"Where else but in my own home? The city is lonely...there are so many children. But...what's a woman like myself to do?"

The meaning of her words seemed vague, and totally un-business-like.

She silently motioned him to follow her into the darkened house, through the gloomy living room, across an inner courtyard and then into a tiny bedroom. It wasn't until they were in front of a massive pillow, and the only furniture he had seen, that he realized the truth.

Her shimmering yellow gown slowly slid down over her wide shoulders, revealing the upturn of soft, swelling breasts, the delightfully flat belly and the invitingly wide hips.

She stood there, an open nude offering, arms outstretched. "We're as lonely here as you must be."

He needed no other explanation; it was easy to understand her loneliness. A woman her age, with such beauty, must find it terribly difficult on such a planet.

"Where're all the men?' he asked, voice thick.

Delicate arms slipped around his neck, drawing that lush, warm body close. Velvet lips were covering his. In the heady softness of her yielding flesh he forgot all questions. Somewhere between the first embrace and the final union, time and awareness blurred. A sense of unreality settled over his mind. He was remembering the woman who had teased him with her supple, warm body and then tried to scream

286

rape when they were almost discovered. Darl had clamped his hands over her mouth, until she fell silent—and still.

And now, suddenly, he became aware of Julia's form grow tensely rigid, a gasp came from her throat.

"What's wrong?" he asked.

A child's voice shrilled from behind him. "Look what they're doing."

Darl Shallen froze, turned, saw two children standing at the foot of the bedlike pillow. They just stared coldly.

Something snapped, a fury mixed with terror raged up. All the confusion of disjointed time merged. Then he heard screams. Striking out, he knocked the children away. He never knew who had attacked whom. Maybe the two kids leaped at him. But before the haze cleared, he saw their bloodied faces, black golden eyes gazing at the ceiling.

He stood, disgusted.

The woman screamed: *"Don't hurt me!"*

He leaped at her, grabbing her throat. His fingers squeezed tightly about her lovely flesh. He watched in a state of fascination as her eyes slowly bulged, as her tongue protruded beyond bloated red lips. Her arms and legs finally stopped flailing and her body relaxed its convulsive jerking. She was now very silent.

In sudden terror he'd released the lifeless form, stunned that things had gone so blindly out of control. Somehow he washed up, and then ran from the house, into the ragged street.

"Spacer Shallen," three voices now called from across the street. *"Spacer Shallen...we know you're evil. We know what you've done to her!"*

"I've done nothing" he protested, terrified.

"We know. We know. We know all about you now, Spacer Darl Shallen!"

"You couldn't!"

He started for them. They ran down the dimly lit street. He followed, unheeding of the patter of running feet behind him, or those coming in from the side. Suddenly he came into a brightly lit, huge plaza surrounded by tall ruined structures that crumbled into neatly cleared streets. The plaza was kept trim, a garden of flowers and blue grass, of tall purple and red trees that lifted into the sky. It was the only growing thing left in the town—perhaps on the whole planet. And in the center of the plaza was a lovely carved platform, an area of block stone with steps on three sides.

A clamor of running feet and the welling scream of cheering voices and the clapping of hundreds of hands enveloped him,

Darl Shallen, Spacer, convicted rapist, murderer of her and her children, stopped at the bottom of the staircase suddenly aware of the hundreds of threatening tiny figures clawing the air, pressing closer. He turned to flee the nightmare; but he was totally surrounded, engulfed by a mass of small children. Then from somewhere above, a deep rumbling voice sounded; it was the old man from the spacefield.

"I see you've joined us for the Festival—I figured you'd be guest of honor."

"Help me!" he desperately cried. "Help me.."

"Why're you frightened?" The old man reached out a hand to take his. "Come to the top—you'll be okay up there."

The old man was dressed in a flowing golden robe that draped about his slender frame. His hand was cold as it touched Darl's. "Come, the Festival's about to begin."

"The Festival?"

"Of course—I'm certain you've enjoyed your...Rites of Passion with the lovely Julia. She was the last, you know.

"Last...what?"

"Illusion of the last woman."

"Illusion—?" The question was left hanging as Darl watched a terrifying transformation take place. The old man's eyes turned from golden yellow to deep red, the features around them began to slowly flush, fill, the gray wrinkles lifted away, the cheeks puffed bright pink, like bloated peaches. Darl was suddenly looking into the over-ripe face of a perversely huge child. The old-man body had bulged thickly under the robe.

"What are——you?"

"I," he was answered by the hooded creature, "am the Voice for us all. We come from across the black void. We are the Pure Ones. We have come to reveal to your galaxy the Words of the Cosmic Voice. We are the True Missionaries. And we have breathed life into the illusions of your evil mind. We have come to your universe to offer the Judgment of the True and Divine Creator of all things."

"Judge?" His voice was choked, dazed. He was being helplessly led up to the top of the platform to where a carved stone altar stood.

* * * * * * *

Darl pushed away from the robed figure, but found himself suddenly encased within an invisible force. A cold flame burst in the air around him; and he screamed in terror as a shimmering white light ate across his clothes, totally consuming them.

"Only the Pure survive!" the Voice screamed.

It was the last thing that Spacer Darl Shallen ever heard. Frantically he slashed at the air around him, once again able to move. His fists crashed into beaked faces and undulating feathered stomachs, he tore at glittering, slimy green flesh. But this desperate attack was futile. The enraged tiny creatures swarmed over his huge frame like insects, fluttering, clutching, to totally bury him. He felt the terrible pressure of their tiny bodies and talons, pushing, shoving; then the pain of teeth nibbled, and ripped into his naked flesh, tearing it away from the bones. Blood flowed as the small, clawing, biting monsters fluttered convulsively over him.

The tall, hooded figure standing above, screamed to the darkened sky, and lightning flashed to reveal a hideous green-skinned, shriveled head. The skin gripped tightly around ridges of bone. The face was cut down the middle by a gaping mouth of purple; rows of teeth dripped yellow slime.

When the tiny creatures, transformed into miniature versions of their giant leader, were finished with their feast, they reached out now gentle eight-clawed hands and lifted the bloody bones and placed them on the alter. The one who called itself the Voice lifted a rod and raised it high above the grisly remains. The creature's lips peeled back, sounds, low and raspy, came forth, merging with the sudden swell of wind that raged through the plaza. The shattering of a thousand screams now rose around the platform. The Voice lowered the rod, touching the stained bones, which instantly powered into golden dust to be furiously blown on the wind, lifted high above the gardened plaza and rushed towards the nearby hills. There the ashes of the hundreds of other humans had peppered the lands during the last few days.

In the name of the Holy Order of the Divine Cosmic Voice, they had stripped their own galaxy of all living matter. They were the Devout Missionaries of the Pure, and would now spread Its Final Judgment throughout this new galaxy: *For the Un-Pure must die!*

Well, strange as it might seem, this is a story with a positive note, a resounding musical chant that rings out across the Cosmos with a resonant ring of hope. Well, I do like to be positive about such matters. After all, this is the last time I have, in this Dimension, to hold the reader's attention to the last word. I could offer, at this time, a long essay about Gods and Creations, myths and legends, masterful paragraph after paragraph of totally dull, uninteresting, and down-right self-indulging personalized statements of what I believe to be important and not so very important.

I could also comment on the dangers of being so dedicated to a cause or belief system, that it can be a danger to all the human race, to say nothing about all the other creatures of the planet...and beyond. But, of course, I've said much of that previously in this book. So maybe just a little comment about what follows and finally ends this collection. This is a kinda mix, this story is; and in a flavor somewhat different from some of the other offerings above. A touch of the romantic and a touch of the violent. My, how those themes tend to reach into many a tale, from time to time. But this one, even in its title suggests that we are never alone, that there are, always, up there, somewhere...

⊷THOSE WHO WATCH⊶

It started much like all the other days of summer, during his eighty Seasons. The sun rose hot on their village, where it nestled beside the James River, a broad expanse of water that moved snake-like through the lush forest of Normerica. The setting was considered so desirable that his clan had made camp two Seasons before and planned on staying at least until the birth of the new children this Fall.

Nattan heard from inside his mud hut, a latticework structure, the morning Chant of the Gods:

Open your Love to us,
Oh, Mighty Gods of Morning.
Reach out and embrace,
Yes, embrace your Children.
For we wash in the Pool of Life,
We hunt in the Lands of Paradise.
Open your Love to us.
Oh, Mighty Gods of Morning,
Breathe the power of your Might,
The strength of your Magic,
The will of your Hearth,
Into all that lives and communes
Within our happy legions.

It was the voice of Undalle, son of the Voices of Legions, who had earned the right to sing the morning Chant only a Season before, when his voice turned from the high pitch of youth to the low, richness of Manhood.

Undalle had been a good friend of Nattan when they were children. Now it was only the song he now sang, that touched his life each morning—for this young man had to learn the Legends of their people, and was not a hunter like himself. Nattan felt a mixture of envy and pity for Undalle. During the Rites of Manhood they had both engaged in the Ritual of Love, experienced the true first knowledge of woman. It was the last time Undalle had known a female of the tribe of Teeua, their sister clan. Any male or female chosen to sing the glory-songs of the Gods was, sadly, restricted to the joys of love only on the Night of Love Rituals that came but four times a year. But in return they could truly learn the meaning of the Legends, study the Forbidden Books, discover the Secrets of Paradise. It was a high price for knowledge.

Nattan turned slightly in his hut, feeling the eager warm body of Reena lying naked under the thick, warm fur bedding she had fashioned from the animals he killed. Reena was prized for her ability to change the toughest hide into soft sleeping furs, and many warriors and hunters came with their kills to have her turn furs into warm blankets to keep them safe from the night cold. Many hunters and Elders within the clan had offered him rich rewards for Reena. Other men might have sold her; even Nattan's father had called him a love-sick fool to prize a mere female so highly. Perhaps everybody was right. Nattan really didn't care what others thought. They had known one another for as long as he could remember, and ever since she had grown to young womanhood, Nattan knew this maturing child had to be his. She was only eight Seasons younger than Nattan. He had known no other female, for they had mated on his first Rites of Manhood. He would never sell Reena, even for Rights of Clan Leadership.

Leaning over Reena, to see if she were awake, he said: "We are going to the High Hill today."

A shiver rushed through her tiny frame and she slipped closer to him. Gently, silently, they made love, soft moans of pleasure mingling only during the last moments.

Sometime later Reena sat up, said: "I must join the others in preparing the morning meal."

"You don't have to," Nattan countered.

"I want you to think of me when you—"

"I'll think of you—always!"

She moved his hands away from her, stood, and gathered a fur blanket about her body, like a shy Virgin on the Night of the Rites of Manhood. But it was only the morning chill that kept the fur about her tanned body. As she slipped into the soft leather garment that folded about her silken flesh, he caught sight of those small, well-formed breasts, a naked rounded hip. He wanted her again, but there was no time. They had already delayed too long. The men might jokingly tease him, but that was expected. For another three Seasons they were still newly mated and expected to bend the rules.

Slowly he got up, reached for the heavy, softly formed, leather pants that Reena had made for him. He strapped on his wide-bladed steel knife, whose razor sharpness was encased in the sheath his father had given him,

Reena said nothing as she moved to the entrance of their private hut, though her large expressive eyes studied him, as if wanting to memorize his form. He returned her gaze. Then she was gone through the flap that hung over the entrance.

293

Nattan quickly got up as she walked rapidly towards the campfires in the middle of the clan's community area The sun was barely creeping over the Eastern horizon and the sky dimly lit; he could see very little, but knew this place quite well.

"The young lover", a gruff voice sounded from behind him as a heavy hand slapped his shoulder. "Ready to experience your first real battle?"

Nattan turned, saw his brother Galut standing there, very tall, muscular. The man was thicker boned, like their mutual father. Nattan had never seen Galut's mother, though had heard she was a strong, powerful female, one of Sanz's early women. Nattan's mother had been small, even more delicate than Reena.

"I'm ready," Nattan stated, turning and following his older brother. They moved in the opposite direction Reena had taken.

"Be careful, today. This is not like boldly facing a beast, nor like fighting a friend in our own clan. Hunting rules were devised to save lives on the Hunt. The Rules of Argument restrict methods of battle when one is confronting a fellow clan member. What you will see today defies *all* rules for there are no rules in war, only the Law to kill and survive. So be careful

"And win no honor in battle?"

"Brother Nattan, I can tell you this only once, for a million times will not make it different: The only honor you can earn is returning to Reena alive. You are young and have much to learn in the coming Seasons. What you will see today will perhaps sicken your mind. If you become sick, the enemy warrior will not hesitate to cut your guts open just to see them spill on the ground, or more quickly slick a sharp knife across your neck. There is only one rule: Kill without mercy. Don't play for an audience, but for the quick, no-holds-barred kill. Strike from behind, if need be. Remember that every man you kill will be one less that can kill you or your fellow warriors. Most of all remember that even if you do not fight this way, the enemy will. I know—I have seen much more than you." Galut lead the way along the neatly

treaded path, then towards the huge Community of Warriors'
Hut. "Remember what I've told you."

Nattan followed the other into the huge hut that could
house a hundred fully armed warriors. The place was already
half filled.

All the men were dressed alike and he saw Sanz with the
Elder Warriors, those who would lead the direct attack. The
Leading Elders would hold back, staying behind to observe.
New warriors, like himself would stay behind the actual
fighting forces. It was cowardly to direct men into combat if
you were not actually freely exposed, personally involved.
Only when age slowed the power of a man's arm, legs,
dulled his skill, could he take a place behind the battle; an
honored position earned by hard survival in many fights. A
young man like Nattan's brother was leader of a clan-bloc,
directly under their father. Galut had proven himself a violently intelligent killer of men, admired by others for his raw
courage in the two major war Meetings at the High Hill that
had taken place since he first became a warrior. He honored
his father, family, mate and children.

Nattan remembered Galut's words of advice, but their
warning was not supposed to turn his courage into the fear of
a trembling child. He was expected, instead, to follow
Galut's example. He would join the fighting, if possible. He
would become the most violent, savage and ruthless young
warrior on the Hill. If he got the chance. He would be sta-
tioned just behind his brother's clan-bloc, in a position to
leap forward with quick determination, and thus claim his
right to combat. The battle, though, might come to him, if the
enemy warriors managed to break through and attack the
Leading Elders. Once the Elders were killed, it was over.
Then the slaughter would really begin. The winning clan
then killed the old or ugly women, men and children. The
beautiful, like Reena, would be taken as slave-mates, until
such time as some warrior claimed one as his own woman,
thus giving her status. Reena's mother had been a captured
slave-mate, as had Nattan's.

It was like it had always been. Warriors went to battle to
win treasures, rewards, and women, all in the name of their
local God. And each side had their image of the Holy Pow-

ers, the Master of the Universe, and their ideas of why it was necessary to convert or kill. The rule was either join us or die brutally.

Of course those were Ancient mythos, legends, and they had become the background of their culture and very being. One didn't even question any of that, for it was simply the natural order of things. Questioning was evil, a sin, and brought horrors on one's soul and family and tribe. One did as instructed by culture and tradition. One fought when told, died when told, lived and loved when told. And if a warrior lost his life in battle his woman was taken as a slave to be used and possibly abused by the winners. That, alone, was enough to motivate even a coward into violent fury. And he was far from a coward!

He must fight to win glory and to protect the tribe and clan and his woman.

So the Rules of war were quietly structured; the High Hill gave an excellent view for the Godcopters, who watched with their mysterious eyes and reported what took place to Those Who Watched.

To dare offend the Watchers was to offend the Gods.

None of it made much sense to anybody he knew. It was enough to simply follow the rules without question. There were, somewhere, surely, Mighty Minds that understood. But it was beyond any of those he knew to truly do more than simply obey.

As he was destined to do with glory and honor on this Battlefield.

Those Who Watched would mark down on his chart up there, somewhere, all the valid points in his favor and black x's for his flaws and mistake. He had to impress them! And he wanted to serve his people, family and clan.

The voice of Undalle sounded over the murmuring of morning chatter, singing the Battle Legend Song of Warriors:

Oh, Mighty Gods, Watchers from above
Give grace and power to our brave men.
Let their weapons protect our Elders,
Let their skill bring victory to our Clan.

The warriors joined in, a rough, roaring sing-song bellow, half spoken in off-key tones:

Oh, Mighty Gods, Watches from above.
Give grace and power to our brave men,
Let their weapons protect our Elders,
Let their skill bring victory to our Clan.

It was repeated ten times, each time louder than before, until their chant rang into the morning air, strong, commanding, a thrilling swell from husky, powerful throats, blending together like some mystical force, causing the blood to race faster through Nattan's body, until he felt the War Fever bursting through him.

He wondered what song and to what false God-power the enemy sang. It didn't, of course matter; their god's were fake, lies, evil make-believe without any real power. Then let them chant themselves to exhaustion.

That's what he continued to tell himself.

Slowly the voices faded, the last word of the chant died out and then the members of his clan started leaving the huge hut to join the women for the morning meal before leaving for the High Hill. Reena had come to him, her body soft, supple, lingering close in greeting. The tribal fire warmed the clearing in the middle of the village and the warriors and their women settled before its flames and took up their earthen bowls, which contained the highly spiced stewed meat. All ate in silence. Reena and Nattan silently communicated with their eyes, and the concern on her face touched him. Then the warriors were called to gather. The long walk through the beautifully gardened forest, down across the narrow stream, up towards the hills in the distance, was a study of brooding silence. Every warrior was caught up in his own thoughts. Nattan felt both excitement and a sense of dread that he might never see Reena again. That worried, frightened expression in her eyes had said so much. As if she knew something he couldn't even guess at. That was his imagination, of course. He would not fail to return; he would not shame her.

The High Hill, a large flat area, reached by narrow steps that lifted upwards at a frightening angle, loomed distantly when they approached its foot. By the time they reached the top, he was breathing heavily, his strong, young body responding to the long strain of climbing a hundred stone steps.

He followed behind his brother's warrior-bloc, in the first rank in front of the honored Elders. A long, narrow wall faced them, from which the special battle weapons were taken, Only the heavy hilts were sticking out from the golden wall that circled the High Hill. As he stepped forward picking a sword from its slot, he was surprised at the lightness of the weapon. The metal was hair-thin, not wider than the tip of his little fingers. He touched the flat edge; the blade was surprisingly rigid. Nattan had heard about such swords, but never held one in his hand. Galut said they never knew what kind of weapons might be offered for a battle, and had spoken of such swords as able to easily slide through skin, muscle and hone. Such a sharp, rigid blade could cut across a human body as if flying through empty air. The point was tapered to needle fineness. The weapon would make a good hunting tool.

As he moved through the entranceway, a huge arched opening in the wall, a voice called from the heavens.

"Warriors of the Tribes the Combat Trial is now about to begin. Be brave and win for your side, show courage, strength. Those Who Watch honor you."

Nattan saw three Godcopters circling high above the green-carpeted High Hill battle area like gigantic insects. It buzzed over the field where twenty warriors from each side began to move forward. When they met, the killing would begin.

Strangely it seemed so natural, as if he'd know such a place many times before; yet this was his first moment of battle, his first challenge as a killer-warrior.

The enemy warriors were dressed like his own people. It would be difficult to tell friend from foe.

Each side's purpose was to reach the Elders of the enemy while protecting their own Honored Ones.

There were thirty warriors some fifty meters away, across the neatly carved circle of the High Hill. They broke into two sections, twenty men taking a forward position.

Nattan placed himself in front of his tribe's Elders, just behind Galut's bloc of four. For a moment he wondered if he would fight, and, if that happened, survive to once again see Reena. Would he bring great honor to her and the tribe?

"Begin!" the loud heavenly voice commanded.

The two rows of warriors, stripped to the waist, moved toward one another

Nattan swung his own weapon easily through the air. He would eagerly rush forward into battle, if given a chance. Only through honor in combat could he afford to keep Reena for himself. The rules of war, and the rules of the hunt and their tribe demanded that a man do honor to his people.

Fear edged through him, as he watched the twenty warrior of his tribe move carefully forward. The distance between the two lines closed. It was only human to fear pain; death. Some might be crippled, and only if they fought well would the powers of Those Who Watch be used to mend them. Imperfection was the mark of a coward. Cripples were mocked; abused.

Nattan could see the faces of the enemy warriors; grim, determined.

Then the sound of metal hitting cold metal rang across the clearing as two warriors met. The others froze, watching. This first encounter could set the pattern for what might follow.

Nattan could see little from his position; warriors of his own people were standing like a human fence, blocking all view. Yet he heard the ringing clash of swords, saw from time to time the movement of bodies, the flashing swing of blades. Then very quickly a scream cut into the air. A man's body fell, a blade lifted, dripping red. Nattan could not see if it was friend or enemy. Then it was that suddenly all the warriors on the battlefield surged, mingled, screaming in fury. A sword cut the victor down before he could use his bloody weapon to defend himself. A flash of swords rang against one another; savage screams, curses, cries of pain demolishing the silence.

Nattan saw the bodies toiling; a severed arm flew several meters into the air, hand still holding the sword. Warriors crumbled, wounded bodies mutilated. A tall warrior came running in Nattan's direction, swinging a blood-dripped blade over his head. Nattan leaned forward.

The engagement lasted longer than expected. Nattan swung his own sword at the man's body, but cut only rigid metal, he swung again; then again, each time the warrior blocked his attack. Blood splattered across Nattan's body, shooting from the other's sword point. Then the man lunged. Panic touched his mind, but automatically his blade quickly parried around the other's. He returned the attack, but was blocked. Three quick chops attempted to cut off his head. He returned the savage blows, then lunged, cut, lunged so rapidly that the man could not block the last thrust. Nattan's sword slipped easily through flesh and muscle, point running out the other side of the man mid-section. He yanked the weapon from that already dead body just in time to bring it up to block a new attack.

Nattan had no time to see what was happening around him, now that the battle was raging, or see who was winning. He remembered what Galut had said about not giving anybody a chance. He slashed, lunged, hacked hardly thinking, blood-mad, cutting at anything around him that offered threat. His sword thrust through an arm, hacked deep into the nose of another, almost cutting off the man's head, then lunged into the chest of a third warrior. All this killing happened in such rapid succession that it almost seemed as if he were fighting but one warrior. Then, just as he realized what a bloody mass surrounded him, something struck from behind with such force that his knees buckled, refusing to support his frame. The world spun, his eyes saw swimming Godcopters circling around in the sky above. A terrible, agonizing burn charred up his right arm. He looked, saw his hand fall away, still clutched to the sword, and bounce on the carpet below. Then something passed through his gut, offering almost a pleasant sensation, a tickling caress deep inside him.

Oh God! Reena! He would never see her again. What would be her fate, now?

Nattan realized what was happening but was helpless to do anything other than accept the obvious fact that he was being killed—was dying!

Before consciousness started to fade, his mind was counting the men he had killed. Four had fallen before he was struck from behind, cut down like a mindless beast. It all seem so useless—and for what? He would never see Reena again. His glory at battle had ended in the pointlessness of death.

Blackness crushed consciousness away. That lingered forever. Then something strange happened. Light flickered.

The next thing he knew was the sound of voices. They were distant, as if coming far away, yet whispering—soft, talking in strange words he could not understand. Something wet touched his forehead, he tried to open his eyes. Something cool pressed his arm. The voices faded; sensation stopped. Returned. A throbbing hurt his hand. Automatically he squeezed his fingers. Then remembered. Phantom nerves, phantom fingers, phantom hand. His mouth opened, attempted to scream.

He had been wounded...killed!

His mind had no chance to continue that thought. Again the unconscious sleep clouded through him, a dreamless, endless black void.

Voices were muttering. Strange humming sounded, lifting and lowering in pitch.

Nattan continued listening, becoming more aware of his immediate surroundings. Sound was all he had. He was not even certain it was possible to move. Then the thought touched him, strange, frightening, sending panic through his nerves; maybe he was dead. This was followed by an even more terrifying concept: perhaps he was in the Place Beyond.

But he had fought bravely, killed several warriors.

Instantly he attempted to open his eyes.

The visual image that smashed at him was stunning.

It was some kind of huge cavern, but with strangely smooth walls, squared, and long. There was an opening at the far end. Along the left side were a series of small barred compartments that caged naked men and women, some to-

301

gether, most of them alone. There were bars in front of him and it took little thought to realize he was in such a small cave, too. In the middle of the room long tables lined the right wall. Strange gleaming tools and containers littered their surfaces. But more startling were those who worked at the tables. They appeared quite human, though covered with weird yellow material that clung loosely about their bodies. All these things he saw as very strange, meaningless; and terrifying.

But it was the strange, bluish human-like creatures that sent near madness through him.

Those Who Watched!

At the same instant he became aware of the fact that his hand was whole.

Legend spoke of these strange, blue creatures with horrible red eyes, knotted, horned heads, gaping mouths, bird-like noses of hard purple bone. Their hands were huge with seven fingers, two thumbs, delicately tapered. Several rushed forward as he started screaming insanely, grabbing at the bars with his hands. One of the creatures pressed a metal rod against his flesh.

The world spun, blacked out.

The next thing he knew he was lying in a bed, looking up at a gentle, kindly face. For an instant he didn't recognize his old friend.

Then the features of Undalle began to make sense.

"Don't bother with the questions, Nattan," the man said, gently, though sadly smiling. "We've been through this scene before, in many variations. There is much I can tell you...but you will not remember when we next meet. I am one of the few who always know the truth."

"The truth?' Nattan felt a sick sensation at the pit of his stomach. "What kind of place is that?"

"Heaven? The Place Beyond? The Land of the Godcopters? Does it matter? The factory? Call it what you want. But it is a place where you have been healed by advanced science—if you want to think of' your recovery as such. You've been made right, again. We are what is left of a great civilization that once spanned this planet, Earth. It was a warlike civilization that burned itself off the surface of this

302

world in one horrible savage war of mutual hate. We had even reached gentle fingers into the sky, beyond the heavens where the Moon and the Sun and other worlds float in the black void. But we proved unworthy of survival."

"I don't understand—"

"What's to understand? We are the last...representatives of the human species. Nothing but shadows—flesh and blood to be sure—merely animated dolls kept in shape to play out our primitive, warlike traits...to serve as visual dramas of what happens when a species lets their primitive drives control them. We are examples for history classrooms, we are games of chance for vacationing gamblers. We serve as lessons as to the horror of hand-to-hand combat. Visual plays, which also offer sensations of pain and fear to be experienced by the more adventuresome of the aliens. We are living creatures, only part animal, part machine, kept alive as actors for the children of the universe to watch..."

"I still don't—"

"Of course, you never do, you know. No matter how many times you come here—and you have been here many times before. The battles end differently, of course—but the warriors are brought back to be mended and then returned to the set of Paradise. We return to being the illusions created by the finely crafted science of an alien species. We are distant memories coded III DNA/RNA. The aliens, now masters of what is left of our world, solar system, expanded throughout this part of the galaxy long after man become extinct. We are plastic bio-robots, actors in games of chance and history studies, nothing more.

Undalle leaned over and pressed a tube against Nattan's arm. "Rest and awake with your Reena. For she awaits you. She will always wait for you. The softness of her arms, the caring of her love. That is the good part that you will always be able to experience. For eternity. Enjoy your moments with her. For you will awake to play out your one day of combat again and again and again. For the Godcopters. And they will continued to broadcast it in its endless variations."

* * * * * * *

It started much like all the other days of summer, during his eighty Seasons. The sun rose hot on their village, where it nestled beside the James River, a broad expanse of water that moved snake-like through the lush forest of Normerica. The setting was considered so desirable that his clan had made camp two Seasons before and planned on staying at least until the birth of the new children this Fall.

Nattan heard from inside his mud hut, a latticework structure, the morning Chant of the Gods:

Open your Love to us,
Oh, Mighty Gods of Morning.
Reach out and embrace,
Yes, embrace your Children.
For we wash in the Pool of Life,
We hunt in the Lands of Paradise.
Open your Love to us.
Oh, Mighty Gods of Morning,
Breathe the power of your Might,
The strength of your Magic,
The will of your Hearth,
Into all that lives and communes
Within our happy legions.

ad infinitum.

◄CREDITS►

"Plague of the Past" by "Fred MacDonald" was published in 1963 in *Gusto*.

"The Stand-In" by "John Davidson" was published in 1963 in *Chere*.

"The End of a Town" by "Charles Alexander" was published in 1963.

"Gardia's Mistress" by "Albert Augustus, Jr." was published in 1969.

"The Witch of Hollywood" by "Stu Rivers" was published in 1963.

"Shark Bait" by "John Davidson" was published in 1963.

"Drink Deep of Revenge" by "Alex Blake" was published in 1963.

"Vegas Last Laugh" by "George Fredrics" was published in 1963 in *Knight*.

"A Very Cultured Taste" was published in 1960 in *Jade*, and also in book form in *If This Goes On* and *Images of Tomorrow* (1969).

"Guided Tour" was published in 1965 and 1969.

"Planet of the Love Feast" was published in 1963 and 1969.

"The Homo Sap" was published in 1965 and 1969.

"The Nova Incident" was published in 1969 in *Spaceway Science Fiction*.

"The Good Doctor" was published in 1965 and 1969.

"The World the WOMB Made" was published in 1969.

"Hunger Pangs" was published in 1965 and 1969.

"The Images of Man" was published in 1963 and 1969.

"Word to the Wise" was published in 1965 and 1969.

"A Day for Dying" was published in 1969 in *Worlds of If*.

DIMENSIONS, BY CHARLES NUETZEL

The following stories are published here for the first time:

"Master of the House"
"Mission of Mercy"
"Beneficiaries"
"Far Side of Paradise"
"Those Who Watch"

⊸ABOUT THE AUTHOR⊷

Charles Nuetzel was born in San Francisco in 1934, and writes:

"As long as I can remember I wanted to be a writer. It was a dream I never thought would materialize. But with the help of Forrest J Ackerman, who became my agent, I managed to finally make it into print.

"I was lucky enough not only in selling my work to publishers but also ending up packaging books for some of them, and finally becoming a 'publisher' much like those who had bought my first novels. From there it as a simple leap to editing not only a science-fiction anthology, but also a line of SF books for Powell Sci-Fi back in the 1960s. Throughout these active professional years I had the chance to design some covers and do graphic cover layouts for pocket books & magazines."

Much of his work in covers and graphics are a result of having had a father who was a professional commercial artist, and who did a number of covers for sci-fi magazines in the 1950s and later for pocket books—even for some of Mr. Nuetzel's books.

In retirement he has become involved in swing dancing, a long time lover of Big Band jazz. But more interestingly world travels have taken him (and his wife Brigitte) across the world, to Hawaii, Caribbean, Mexico, Kenya, Egypt, Peru, having a lifelong interest in ancient civilizations. His website is full of thousands of pictures taken during these trips.

www.ingramcontent.com/pod-product-compliance
Lightning Source LLC
Chambersburg PA
CBHW021953010726
47494CB00003B/720